I0678703

BROTHERS
OF THE FANG

Also by Sharon Joss

<u>Novels:</u>

Aurum
Steam Dogs

(Hand of Fate Series)
Destiny Blues
Legacy Soul
Chaos Karma

<u>Novellas:</u>

Stars That Make Dark HEaven Light

<u>Short Story Collections:</u>

Dreams of Flesh and Blood (Horror)
Solace Amid the Planets (Science Fiction)

BROTHERS
OF THE FANG
A NOVEL OF MYTHICA

SHARON JOSS

AJA PUBLISHING
USA

BROTHERS OF THE FANG Copyright © 2013 by Sharon Joss
All rights reserved.

Published 2013 by Aja Publishing
www.ajapublishing.wordpress.com

Book and cover design Copyright © 2013, 2016 by Aja Publishing
Cover design by S. Roest / Aja Publishing
Cover art © RTimages / Fotolia, © Tomasz Zajda / Fotolia
Heraldic Griffin Design Copyright © by Buch / Dreamstime

This book is licensed for your personal enjoyment only.

All rights reserved. This is a work of fiction. All characters and events portrayed in this book are fictional, and any similarity to real persons, living or dead, or incidents or events is coincidental and not intended by the author. This book, or parts thereof, may not be reproduced, distributed, or transmitted in any form or by any means, or stored in a database or retrieval system, without prior written permission of the publisher.

Please do not participate in or encourage piracy of copyrighted materials in violation of the author's rights. Purchase only authorized editions.

PUBLISHER'S NOTE:
This is a work of fiction. Names, characters, places, and incidents either are the product of the author's imagination or are used fictitiously, and any resemblance to real people, living or dead, business establishments, events, incidents, or locales is purely coincidental.

The publisher does not have any control over and does not assume any responsibility for author or third-party Web sites or their content.

PRINTED IN THE UNITED STATES OF AMERICA

ISBN: 978-0-9897828-0-7

AUTHOR'S NOTE:

Although I have taken certain liberties with the description, the High Tor Wilderness Conservation Area is a real place, located within the beautiful Finger Lakes region of central New York state. Worm charming is a well-documented practice with a long and storied history.

OH BROTHER

JUSTIN OWSLEY STOOD in the open doorway, his eyes drawn to the cage sitting in the middle of the loft. His heart pained him as he met the glare of the dark-haired man who paced silently on the far side of the room. The cage fairly screamed that the owner was a werewolf, but this guy didn't have any of the tells. His eyes were brown, not amber, like Justin's. He appeared fit and well muscled, but lacked the massive neck and shoulders that made weres in human form so instantly identifiable. He didn't smell like wolf, either.

He glanced at his trip sheet. "You Mike Bane?" The guy looked tantalizingly familiar but the name didn't ring a bell. He proffered his card. "I'm with Brothers of the Fang Charities. You called for a pickup? Says here you're donating a leather sofa, dining room table, and some boxes of cooking utensils."

Bane nodded at the room in general as he padded toward the kitchen counter. "It all goes. Everything but the cage." Justin directed Torres and Coop to start with the sofa, while he began stacking the first three of a pile of neatly taped boxes onto the dolly. Down four flights of stairs and into the donation truck, then back up for another load.

"What do you think," Torres asked, as he threw a padded blanket over the sofa. "Is the cage for his girlfriend?"

"No way. He's a lone wolf. There's no bedroom. No bed." Justin handed the boxes up to Coop on the truck. This stop was the first scheduled pickup of the day.

They started back up the stairs for the next load. "You should say something," Torres said. "That guy is burned out. He's hurtin'."

Justin snorted. "Why me? You've been through it, too. Why do I always have to be the one to say something?"

"Cause you can't help yourself."

Justin felt the warmth of their pheromone-infused humor wash over him. "Shut up."

Two hours later, the loft was nearly empty. Bane stood at the built-in breakfast bar, checking his email, his posture rigid, his eyes glued to the screen. He hadn't said a word to them the whole time. Torres gave Justin an eyebrow jerk in Bane's direction as he and Coop left with the big screen television.

"You've donated some real nice stuff here, Mr. Bane. The guys at the center are going to love that big screen. It looks brand new."

Bane eyed him with a wary look.

Torres was right; the guy was on edge. Justin had seen enough Post Traumatic Stress Disorder and Acquired Lycanthropy Virus Syndrome to recognize a guy in trouble. Most of the donors to Brothers of the Fang were either military veterans or had ALVS, or both. He looked too young to be a vet, but weres didn't age like humans.

"Glad to hear it. I can't use this stuff anymore." He smiled, but his eyes were hard—cop eyes.

What would a cop be doing with a cage in the middle of his living room? Something clicked in Justin's memory. *Oh shit*. His face had been all over the news for weeks. "Hey, I know you. I mean, I saw your picture." The lurid headlines. "You're that werewolf cop."

Bane froze. "I am not a werewolf." A tic jumped at his right eyelid.

Justin took a step back. "That's right; were-cat. I mean, I heard all about you. You're a hero. You got a bad deal, bro. Busted for eating that drug dealer-." Justin stopped at the hunted expression on Bane's face.

"Are we about done here?"

"Um, yeah. You just have to sign here." Justin handed the clipboard to Bane. "Look pal, I didn't mean to offend you or anything, I was just surprised. You're like some kind of celebrity here in Queens. A lot of the Brothers, and me too, we think you got a raw deal. One less dope dealer in this town ought to be celebrated. I can't believe they fired you."

"I wasn't fired." Bane's dark eyes glowered back at him. "I resigned."

"Yeah, sure." Were those werecat eyes? The guy could pass for human, easy.

"If you'll excuse me, I've still got a couple things left to do."

Justin looked around at the now empty loft, and the brittle appearance of the man standing before him. He had to try. "No, wait. Look, I know it's none of my business and all, but I know what you're thinking. I know you're going through a bad time. Shit, man. You lost control of your beast in a bad situation. But that's no reason to off yourself. It can take years to develop that kind of control. We can help you. That's what Brothers of the Fang is here for. That's our purpose. Trust me brother, suicide is not the cure for ALVS."

Bane shook his head. "I don't have ALVS. And I'm not your brother."

The guy was in denial. "I don't believe you. If it was me that got caught eating the brains of that Hector Clemente guy, I'd be pretty upset too. Sometimes the appetites of the beast can get a little out of control in the beginning."

A ghost of a grin flashed across Bane's face. "It's not what you think. I've got a little place on the lake near Canandaigua. I grew up there. It's already furnished, so this stuff won't fit."

"Ah, the Finger Lakes," Justin said. "That's werewolf country." Between the curfews, restrictions, and lack of open spaces nearby, city living didn't agree with most weres. The job opportunities were a lot tougher in rural areas of the state, but the rules were looser, and the Finger Lakes region had unrestricted hunting privileges for werewolves in the High Tor Wilderness Management Area. Thirty thousand acres of backwoods paradise. You could even join a pack. In the city, everyone was a lone wolf.

Bane shoved the clipboard back at him. "Like I said before, I'm no werewolf."

Justin bit back his response and reached into his hip pocket for his wallet. He thumbed through the cards inside until he found the one he wanted. "Here. This is a good friend of mine, Dr. Sarah Powers. Everybody down there knows Dr. Sarah. She's good people. She can help you learn to control your beast." He held out the card. "In *whatever* form it may take."

He hesitated, and Justin sent up a little prayer to the First Wolf. *Take it.*

"Thanks." Bane looked at the card briefly before slipping it into his shirt pocket.

Justin nodded. "Good luck to you then, brother."

"Stop saying that. I didn't ask for any of this. If it weren't for you damn werewolves, I'd still have a job. I'm a shifter, not a were." His voice was low and tight. "I'm *nothing* like you."

The heat rose in Justin's face. "Nobody here but us carnivores, Bane."

THE JOLLEY MAN

THE TINKLE OF the bell announced a fresh customer. Tom Jolley glanced up, but it was old man McNabb. "Hey Gale," Tom greeted him. "How's it going? What can I do for you?"

"The grandson borrowed my crankbait kit for the weekend and lost it overboard."

Tom winced. "Oh jeeze." He noticed the twinkle in McNabb's eyes as he neared the counter. Tom knew from long experience that fishing and his grandson were McNabb's two favorite topics. "You bragging or complaining?"

"Well, mebbe you can't remember what it was like when you were seventeen, but I do. He took that pretty new girlfriend of his out on the lake, ifffin' you know what I mean." McNabb wiggled his bushy white eyebrows for emphasis.

Tom led the way down the aisle to the lures section. "You're lucky he didn't sink more than the tackle box."

"Oh, it was an old box. Not any of my good stuff. But I think he'd appreciate having one of his own. Nothing too fancy, but he's gonna need a couple a them crawdads and a good selection of shad and a nice chartreuse."

An hour later Tom had just finished ringing up McNabb's

purchases when Mike finally walked in, looking gaunt. "Hey, Pops," he said, softly. "Wanna buy some nightcrawlers?"

"Nah, I've got the best bait in the state right here." Tom hurried around the counter and grabbed his godson in a bear hug. He fought back tears of emotion as Mike lifted him off the ground, nearly squeezing the breath right out of him.

"Put me down, boy." He gave a quick swipe across his eyes. He couldn't stop smiling.

McNabb, other hand, looked like he was going to come unglued any minute. Coming face-to-face with the 'Were-Cop Cannibal of Queens' wasn't going over too well, even though McNabb had one of the few who'd asked him for the real story. Tom hurriedly made the introductions. "Gale, you remember my godson, don't you? This is Mike Bane."

McNabb hesitated, then jutted his chin and shook the younger man's hand. "A course I do. A course you're taller'n I remember. Tom here has been borin' me silly with the news that yer finally movin' back here from the city. A man can't hardly get a word in edgewise these days. What are your plans?"

Mike ran his hand through his hair. "Ah, nothing, yet. Just a little fishing, I guess." He flashed a grin at Tom. "If you're up to it, old man."

Tom snorted, but his heart wasn't in it. So damn good to see him. "I bag my limit every time I go out, boy." Not really a boy anymore, but the beast and the Fae blood in him kept him looking half his age. He did a quick calculation in his head. God, he must be in his mid-forties by now. He looked so much like Mia. She'd always thought Mikey favored his dad, but damn, the boy had his mother's eyes and cheekbones.

He raised an eyebrow at McNabb, and the old geezer took the hint and made a hasty exit. About time. He wondered if this would be the last time he'd see McNabb in the shop. It didn't matter all that much if it was. Mike was home and that was the important thing. He yelled out for the dog. "Farley, get in here, you mutt. Look who's back."

"He's still here?" Mike's eyes widened in disbelief.

"See for yourself." The tall, shaggy deerhound trotted around the corner and paused, his tail fanning the air, graceful as a question mark.

"Hey boy. Remember me?"

The black dog lowered his head and trotted slowly across the tile floor toward Mike. Tom's heart caught in his throat as Mike kneeled down to rub the dog's crinkled ears. Farley groaned with pleasure.

"He does remember." Mike's voice was tight.

"Stop it, you two. You're going to have me bawling like a baby in a minute. Come on, boy. Let's get you settled in." He locked the front door and led the way toward the back of the tackle shop. "The renters moved out last week, and I had Taffy's niece in to clean yesterday. Dinner's at your place. I stocked your fridge with a stringer of fresh-caught brownies and a six pack. Figured we'd have ourselves a nice fry-up."

"Oh man, I haven't had fresh trout in ages. We got any of those potatoes and onions?"

He held the back door open for Mike and the deerhound. "Wouldn't be a fry up without 'em now, would it? Let's get going, I want to have a beer in my hand as I watch the sunset from your Dad's screen porch."

Farley stood at the passenger door of Mike's truck and gave a soft woof.

Mike opened the battered door of his truck. "Is there enough for the mutt?"

The dog leapt inside without a backward glance. Figured. "Nah, the mutt gets dog food. Fish gives him gas. I got you a fresh forty-pound sack."

"I'm not sure it's a good idea for Farley to stay with me, Pops."

"I've had him long enough. He's your kin, not mine, anyway."

* * *

Later, after dinner, they sat out on the screen porch at the back of the house, drinking beer and watching the light fade from the sky. The sailor's delight of a sunset over the lake had been spectacular; like a welcome home banner. They'd both eaten too much and laughed too much, but it was good. Good for both of them. Like a snagged line, suddenly freed, Tom felt they were back on an even keel again.

"This is nice. Most nights it's just me and Farley, and Farley doesn't talk much." He wanted to ask more about the fiasco in Queens, but Mike had always been so secretive about the jaguar. Of course, the press had gotten it wrong, but he couldn't bring himself to break the mood by asking.

They watched the deerhound twitch in his sleep, woofing in that weird way that dogs do when they're dreaming. No doubt chasing rabbits out on the Tor.

"I don't want to hurt him, Pops. He can't stay here. I don't think you understand--"

Tom could feel his godson's growing anxiety itch like sand under his shirt. "Oh I know what you mean. Cats and dogs and all that." Tom slapped at a mosquito. "It'll work or it won't. This isn't the city, boy. This property sits right on the Tor boundary and there's plenty of open space for the both of you. As long as you remember the rules, your beast and the mutt will figure it out."

Mike's face tightened. "The cat stays in the cage at night. I can't take the chance of him hurting anybody." He shook his head. "Ever again."

The haunted look on the boy's face said it all. *He's a grown man,* Tom reminded himself. "Quit worrying about Farley. He can take care of himself. There's plenty of Fae creatures and wild game out there on the Tor. As long as you remain in beast form, it's the perfect place to let the cat out to hunt. All the local weres hunt there, even the Mythica pack. Just remember that the High Tor Fae won't tolerate trespassers in human form. It's beasts only." Tom gave a glance to the dog. "No exceptions."

Mike rubbed at a stain on the arm of the faded blue sofa. "I'm never going out on the Tor again."

"Don't be stupid, boy. You keep that beast of yours caged up too long he'll drive you mad. Just like what happened up there in Queens. Isn't that why you came running back here after all these years?" *Easy*. He's going to have to come to terms with this thing in his own way.

His godson's locked jaw twitched as he stared out across the dusky lake. Whatever happened to that eager, clever lad who was never afraid of anything; who was just brimming with enthusiasm for life? He'd wanted to see the world. Couldn't wait to leave this place. Well, the world pretty much chewed him up and spit him out. Now he's lost his job and his citizenship. He's all alone, living in a cage. *I'd give anything to take that monkey off his back, but I just don't know what to say to him.*

Tom sighed. Maybe Farley would help. Couldn't hurt. Taking care of the dog would give Mike something to do, at least. Even if the dog didn't need it.

"I could use a hand at the store," he lied.

"No you don't. I saw the look on McNabb's face. It took real guts for him to shake my hand. I'm sure everybody in town knows about me by now. Or thinks they do."

"You know how fast gossip spreads around here. We've grown a bit, but Canandaigua is still the same small town it used to be." And that was the bitch of it. It didn't matter that Mike was a local boy, or that he wasn't infected with ALVS, or that he didn't even look like a lycan. They'd tarred him with the same brush anyway. "We're a tourist town; lycans are bad for business. Finding a job here might be difficult."

Mike gave him a tight-lipped smile. "Thanks for the offer. I just don't think I'm cut out for waiting on customers all day. You're the one they come in to talk to. Having me around is bound to affect your business. Maybe coming here wasn't such a good idea."

"Don't say that." Tom couldn't stand the thought. "I don't care what McNabb or any of them think. You'll never see a 'No Lycans Served' sign in the window of my shop. As far as I'm concerned, lycan money is as good as anyone's, and I'm not the only one around here that thinks that way. You should stop in at Taffy's place. He'll be glad to help you out with a job."

"Take it easy, Pops." Mike put a calming hand on his arm. "I don't need a job just yet. I need a little time to figure things out, that's all."

Tom pressed his lips into a firm line. *The last thing that boy needs is time on his hands to brood.* A sudden inspiration struck him. "Hey, I got it. I had McNabb's grandson all lined up to make my bait deliveries for the summer, but he's met some girl up near Syracuse and backed out at the last minute. It's been a real pain for me. Would you do it?"

The boyish grin he remembered flashed across Mike's face.

"It's only three days a week. You'll be done by mid-morning, latest. You already know most of the route. It'll be like old times. Say yes. Make an old man happy."

"Don't give me that old man shit. You've barely aged a day since I've been gone. You've got almost as much Fae blood in you as I do."

"Come on. I've got nobody else and you've got plenty of time on your hands."

"Sure Pops; no problem." Mike popped him playfully in the shoulder.

"Good. It's settled then."

Farley heaved a contented sigh and farted.

THE HAPPY HUNTER

MIKE STALKED THE rooms of the cottage while Farley snored soundly in the middle of the king-sized bed in the larger of the two bedrooms. The house was much as he remembered, although he hadn't been back since he'd become a shifter. He'd set up the cage in the smaller bedroom; empty except for a beat-up wooden desk and chair. Thick shrubbery covered most of the front of the house, shielding it from the frontage road and keeping the room preternaturally dark.

The cage was six by six foot square and four feet high. It was actually a lion cage made with a stainless steel knotted wire rope mesh; the same mesh used for animal enclosures by zoos. He'd had the cage custom made of six panels that he could assemble with a socket wrench in about twenty minutes. A simple mechanism kept the cat safely contained; a human thumb was required to open the door. The enclosure was a hated reminder of his condition; but he'd been sleeping in the cage nearly half his life.

Mike could feel the cat's restlessness inside him. If the cat wasn't allowed to roam free for a few hours every four or five days, the tenuous truce between them started to fall apart. Tom had urged him to let the cat do a little investigation of the territory, and maybe he was right. It wouldn't hurt to let the cat out before he locked himself inside the cage for the night. In the city, the closest wilderness area took at least two hours to get to. He'd drive to Moose River or the Adirondacks whenever he could, but working undercover made it difficult to keep to a schedule that kept the cat happy. And keeping the cat happy was paramount.

He checked to make sure the back yard gate was locked; not that it mattered. The closest house was a quarter mile up the road. No six-foot fence would hold him, and the cat was an excellent swimmer. He loved the water, and the property had its own private dock.

Seated on the faded blue divan on the sun porch, where they'd hoisted beers and filled their bellies earlier, Mike stripped out of his clothes and folded them neatly beside him. He took a deep breath, closed his eyes, and *let go*.

The melting sensation flowed through him, familiar and soothing now, after all those wasted years he'd spent fighting it. Instead of the bone-breaking agony the werewolves had to endure, his cat came forth like the unfurling of a flag. Only the final sensation of fur emerging through his skin tickled, but a good shake always put him right. That was one of the few blessings that came with being a shape-shifter rather than a werewolf.

All lycanthropes were shape-shifters, but not all shape-shifters were lycanthropes. Acquired Lycanthropy Virus Syndrome was a disease that altered the genetics of the afflicted. People with ALVS lost control over their ability to maintain their inherent species form, particularly during stressful conditions such as rage or the three nights of the full moon.

In spite of the brutality of the manner in which he'd acquired his shifting abilities, Mike appreciated that he had no such tie with the cycles of the moon, and felt no physical discomfort with the change. The Nagual had come to him as two separate spirits. The jaguar was one of them. Unlike the weres, the big cat's body, mind and thoughts were separate from his own.

The cat stretched fully, and trotted out the door to one of the big pines in the back yard. With his front paws, he reached as high as he could stretch and dug his claws into the rough bark. Clots of bark and dried pitch flew out from the trunk as he drew his claws deep into the tree and scratched deep grooves into the wood. The gouge pattern mirrored the landscape of the Finger Lakes the region; the long narrow glacial lakes that that local legends said were made by the claws of the Great Bear spirit of the Senequois Fae clan.

The sharp tang of fresh evergreen stung the air, dulling the scent of fresh blood and fish scraps wafting out from the garbage can. The jaguar dropped to the ground and rolled in the grass, exorcising the pent-up stress of the day. The cat liked this place, he could tell.

Seeing the world through his beast's eyes never failed to thrill him. Unlike the weres, he retained complete memory of every moment spent in jaguar form. He didn't control the big guy's actions or thinking; it was more like riding shotgun in some armored ATV in the jungle whenever the cat went hunting. He could make general suggestions, but the cat was always in control.

The jaguar's night vision was every bit as good as human vision, although the cat's sense of color was more subdued. When the cat was in charge, his color spectrum was limited to greens, blues, purples, and greys. The cat was uncomfortable in open spaces, and would avoid them whenever possible. The concept of terrain was physical texture that only mattered where it touched him. He rubbed against rough pillars of tree trunks and slunk his way through cheek-high grasses as he sought dense shrubs for hiding under.

The cat's ability to track and scent prey never failed to amaze him, and for such a big animal, he made very little noise. The cat was careful and cautious in the new environment, but there was nothing for him to fear.

The big guy was an ambush hunter. He preferred to wait for his prey to come to him, although he'd surprised and successfully brought down deer and even a bear once. His favored prey was rabbits, turkey, opossums, and if he could find them, turtles, but he wasn't really picky. If he didn't make a kill, he went hungry, but that was a rare occurrence. After all the fish Mike had eaten at dinner, the cat wouldn't be interested in hunting tonight.

After a quick dip in the lake, the cat settled beneath a dogwood tree and began to groom himself. Mike could feel the jaguar's deep satisfaction and contentment in a way that he'd never experienced before. With the bats calling overhead as they plucked mosquitoes out of the night sky, the enchantment of the lake settled over them.

If only it could stay like this. He'd forgotten how peaceful life was on the lake. *If only it was just the cat and me. We could live a pretty good life like this. Things would be different this time.* Maybe Tehuantl would succumb to the magic of this place and settle down, too. If he could keep the cat content, there would be no way for the psychotic shaman spirit to manifest. Tehuantl, sacred priest of the ancient Jaguar-people of Central America, was unstoppable once he came out. When Tehuantl came out, people died.

Mike shivered at a phantom memory of the taste of Hector Clemente's brains. He'd been damn lucky it was a drug dealer and not somebody's mother, he thought. *I was kidding myself, thinking I could keep it a secret.* But it was too late now; everyone assumed he had ALVS.

The landmark case of Stubbs versus the State of Tennessee had changed everything. William Stubbs, a US Army veteran, had sued the state of Tennessee for wrongful termination when he was laid off from his job for excessive sick days. He'd claimed the State had discriminated against him due to his ALVS by counting his moon-days as sick days. The State counter-sued, claiming that lycanthropes weren't human, and therefore not entitled to the same benefits. They pointed to the definition of 'man' in the US Constitution, the differences in DNA, the unique blood type, and the fact that transplant organs from lycanthropes were always rejected when used on humans. The State of Tennessee won, and the appeal was upheld by the US Supreme Court. Four short years later, the 28th amendment redefined the term 'man' to exclude *homo lycanthropus*.

Lycans had had their citizenship downgraded to permanent resident status. They'd had their passports revoked, lost the right to vote, put on the no-fly list, and had to have a green card in order to get a job. They had a curfew. Discrimination was rampant; not even contact lenses could hide a 28-inch neck. Mike had been on the force when the amendment passed, and decided to keep his status as a shape-shifter to himself. Even so, the guy from Brothers of the Fang hadn't believed him when he'd told him he wasn't a werewolf. He'd hoped to lay low here for a while until things blew over. Until Tom confirmed it, he hadn't really believed the area had become such a haven for werewolves.

So be it. At least I've come to the right place. No more living undercover.

Tom was right. He'd kept the cat caged far too much. Besides, if there were that many wolves running loose down here, why shouldn't the cat be allowed the same privilege?

As long as the cat was happy, it was the two of them against Tehuantl, and that was all that really mattered. And that meant letting the jaguar out on a regular basis.

The sound of a lone wolf howl echoed across the Tor. The cat paused his grooming to listen, but it was not repeated.

I'm not like them. They can't control themselves, they're animals. I don't have a disease. I'm still human, or at least partly. Clemente had been an aberration; the disastrous result of extraordinary circumstances. *If I'd shot him, they'd have given me a medal and I'd still be a damn good cop.*

The cat yawned and stretched, then sauntered toward the house. It paused in the sun porch, and Mike mentally nudged at the cat to release him, but the feline resisted, moseying instead past the cage toward the back bedroom. It stopped in the doorway to the master bedroom as Farley whimpered in sleep in the middle of the bed. The cat's ears pricked forward at the sound.

Too late, Mike realized that this could end very badly. He pushed harder against the cat. The cat knew the drill here; it was just being stubborn. *Into the cage, pal._*

In a single leap, the jaguar cleared the distance and landed on the bed next to the curled-up canine. The deerhound cracked an eye, but didn't move. Carefully, the cat settled up against the warm dog and a rumbled purr arose from the deep inside his chest.

Relief flooded through Mike. *Well what do you know. He likes dogs.*

BEASTIES TAVERN

MIKE DROVE HIS truck north along the eastern shore of Canandaigua Lake. Of all the lakes the legendary Great Bear had clawed deep into the earth of central New York, Mike thought Canandaigua was by far the prettiest. Roughly sixteen miles long and more than a mile at its widest point, it was the fourth largest of the Finger Lakes. The area was mostly pristine wilderness; other than a few scattered cottages, beer bars, and bait shops, only the town of Canandaigua, at the north end of the lake hosted a clustered population. His father's place was located near the southern tip of the lake at the end of a private drive, on the border of the High Tor Wildlife Management Area. Tom Jolley's Outdoor Outfitters was located on the eastern shoreline some eight miles north.

Located halfway between the cottage and Tom's bait shop, Beastie's Tavern squatted like a lone troll by the side of the frontage road. From the outside, Beasties resembled an Olde English Brew Pub, but no one sober would ever mistake the place for being anything else but a dive bar.

The ripe smell of the place greeted him; an odd blend of stale beer, sawdust, corn nuts, and wet dog. Mike stood in the doorway as his eyes adjusted to the dim interior. Blood-red vinyl barstools and benches stood bolted to the floors. The padded, upholstered walls were stained and patched with layer upon layer of silver duct tape, bearing the unmistakable scars and bites of past battles and celebrations. Behind a partition of sturdy chicken wire, three pool tables lined up, awaiting the crush of rowdy patrons. A half-dozen thick-necked toughs with amber eyes watched him suspiciously over a table strewn with half-empty glasses and a fresh pitcher of beer. The old place had become a werewolf bar.

"Mikey boy. I heard you were back." His Uncle Taffy smirked and nodded to a corner where Farley lay snoozing on a worn rug.

So that's where he goes. I should have known. Mike took a seat at the bar. "Taffy, you old fire plug. You haven't aged a bit." Taped to the cash register, he recognized a couple of post cards he'd sent from his tours in Venezuela and Costa Rica. From nearly twenty years ago.

"You look like shit. Your skin's hangin' on you like an old suit." Taffy wore his long auburn hair pulled into a tail that flowed bright as brandy down his back.

Mike swallowed his reaction. The reminder of his ordeal at the hands of Hector Clemente brought acid up the back of his throat. It would be weeks yet before his clothes fit properly again. "Good to see you too, you old fart."

His uncle's hand gripped his warmly. "Watch your mouth, lad. You're not too big to spank."

Mike bared his teeth. "I'd like to see you try."

Taffy sniffed. "His nibs here has been beside himself. You must be running him ragged. What'll you have?"

A new start. "Something dark. You still brew that porter?"

"Always." Taffy opened the tap against a glass and let the thick chocolate-colored brew slowly fill the pint. "Never thought we'd see you back here again."

Here we go. The old hurts never healed. He should have said good-bye before he enlisted. He should have called. The postcards on the register told him as much. "I couldn't stand it any more. My mistake cost him everything. I had to go. The Army was my ticket out of here."

"You were his flesh and blood. He never thought twice about it."

"I couldn't stay." Everyone in town knew that Farley Bane had taken on his son's punishment for trespassing onto the Tor in human form. "I ruined his life, Taff."

"Bullshit." His uncle set the pint of beer in front of him. "When you were wounded in Veracruz, you said you were afraid you'd hurt us if you came home. Staying away hurt us more."

The blood rose in his face as he stared into Taffy's reproachful eyes. *This is why I didn't come back. Because the old wounds never heal. Because you never really leave your mistakes behind when you run away. They just wait in the hearts and minds of those you love, to wound you when you're down and least expect it.* He shifted uncomfortably on his stool. "I already ruined my father's life. If I'd come home and hurt you or Pops or somebody else, I'd never be able to live with myself."

"The dog is not the problem, lad."

Mike rubbed his jaw and looked away. Coming here was a bad idea. His uncle had twenty years of pent-up resentment waiting to be unleashed, and he had nothing but excuses for answers. Seeing the reproach in Taffy's eyes brought back all the old anguish; the weight of his own guilt. He hated it.

He leaned over the bar, his face hot. "No, the problem is that I've been outed in every tabloid imaginable as the frickin' man-eating werewolf. I'm out of a job and nobody's going to hire me. There's no place else to go, Taff. So yeah, I'm back now. You happy? If you've got anything else to say about it, you might as well get it off your chest right now."

Taffy shook his head. "No, no, I think that about covers it. Nice to see they haven't taken your balls yet." He grinned and pulled a short pint for himself and raised his glass. "Good to have you back where you belong."

Mike drank, mirroring Taffy's action, swallow for swallow. The beer was better than he remembered. He set his glass down and wiped his upper lip. "Love what you've done to the place."

Taffy's eye's gleamed with fierce pride. "It's the only were-bar in the Finger Lakes. I didn't plan it this way, but it's workin' out just fine. Got a better class of clientele."

"Any chance I can give you a hand in the kitchen or behind the bar?"

Taffy shook his head. "Not without putting your cousin Sheila out in the street. You'd be better off trying your luck at Mythica."

Mike searched his memory. "The old Van Cleve estate? I don't get it."

"They run a private club up there in the summer." Taffy's eye's drifted over to the toughs, now shooting pool. "Those boys all work over there."

Mike glanced at them over his shoulder. Something about the were-men rubbed him the wrong way. It wasn't just their stiff-legged arrogance and posturing that bothered him. There was an aura of aloofness about them that appeared almost tribal in nature; like a clan or a clique. He considered going over to talk to them, but his uncle forestalled him.

"Don't bother; they're just grunts. Stick around. Rafe will be in later, I'll introduce you."

In the corner, Farley woke up and stretched. His jaws widened into a smile when he saw Mike, and he ambled over to curl up at the foot of his barstool.

* * *

Several hours later, the bar was packed; the lively beat of an old Stray Cats tune harmonized well with the sounds of pinball machines and the crack of billiards. The patrons were mostly were-men, but a there were more than a few non-weres, as well. Hard-looking women laughed loudly as they vied for attention. Wolf-girls, they were called; werewolf groupies attracted to the allure of the ultimate bad-boy. At the bar, three or four old-timers, loyal locals from the old days, hunched gloomily over their beers.

Taffy sent Sheila over with a huge bowl of steaming beef stew with carrots and peas and barley and a hunk of homemade soda bread. He ate it like a starving man, even wiping the bowl clean with the heel of bread.

"Damn, I never thought Taffy was much of a cook."

Mike glanced at the guy standing next to him at the bar. "He's not. I've just been eating a lot of fish lately, that all." The guy was idly walking an old silver coin back and forth across his knuckles. Pretty good at it too. Very smooth.

"You must be here on vacation." A second coin appeared from nowhere and followed the first across the tops of his knuckles. Just as smooth, but with more speed now. "Let me guess. I'd guess upstate somewhere. The Bronx?"

The guy wore a pinky ring with a diamond too big to be real. The coins raced back and forth across the guy's fingers at lightning speed. His hands showed no trace of calluses; his bare forearms held no blemishes, freckles or scars. "How long did it take you to learn that?" Mike asked.

The coins disappeared. "Honestly, I don't remember."

Mike frowned. The guy didn't belong here. He wasn't a werewolf, and he was no aging alcoholic. His impossibly black hair was an obvious dye job, right down to the mutton-chop sideburns and spray-on tan. Black eyeliner wreathed his eyes. It was hard to tell in this light, but it looked like he was wearing contacts, too. He was dressed casually in yellow cowboy boots and skinny black jeans that made his legs look like toothpicks. He wore gold chains, too heavy to be real, draped in layers around his neck; his shirt was unbuttoned to his belt. This guy was a total phony.

"You some kind of magician?"

When the guy smiled, the hairs on the back of Mike's arms stood up. His canine teeth were pointed.

"You a cop?"

Mike shook his head. This was not a line of questioning he wanted to pursue, but he was curious. Surreptitiously, he sniffed the air, but all he got, above the surrounding smells of beer, urine, and sweaty beasts, was hairspray, cologne, and the chemical smell of hair coloring.

"Ah, the mysterious stranger wants to play twenty questions. Let's see. Here we are in Beasties, yet you are clearly not of the brethren clans. I seriously doubt that Taffy would bestir himself to cook for anyone but a very old friend indeed, so I must conclude you are a friend of the family?" He closed his eyes and inhaled deeply. "One of the Fae, certainly. Are you perhaps fair Sheila's brother?"

"Not bad."

"Oh fer yikessakes," Taffy interrupted. "This is my nephew Mike Bane. He's the son of that black Tor Hound sleeping over there in the corner." He turned to Mike. "Rafe is Ambrose Van Cleve's business partner. He runs the amusement park over at the Mythica estate."

Mike froze as he met Rafe's gaze and the knowledge dawned on him. *Oh crap.* "You're a vampire." From the dark depths of his soul, Mike felt Tehuantl stir. Frantically, he forced the curious shaman back into the depths.

Rafe nodded to him. "You're the shape-shifter. Welcome back."

Mike glared at his uncle. *Why the hell would Taffy be friends with a vampire?* The beef stew rolled uncomfortably in his stomach. He could feel Tehuantl's curiosity about the vampire pushing at him. "Taffy, you bucketmouth. What else have you told him?"

Taffy ignored him and headed off to the kitchen, leaving him alone with Rafe.

The vampire grinned at him. "Taffy and I have been acquainted for decades. We have no secrets."

But before he could consider that thought, a gorgeous, dark-haired were-woman stepped between them and murmured something into Rafe's ear.

Every were-man in the place stopped what they were doing to watch her. Tension thickened the atmosphere to a stifling level.

The smell of her perfume wafted over the close, gamey air with the heady scent of gardenia. Something about her triggered a memory that Mike couldn't quite place. He stared as Rafe and the were-woman shared an intimate moment that left a trace of pink lipstick on the vampire's cheek.

Mike rubbed his mouth, unable to look away, but embarrassed somehow. He'd seen only a few were-women in his life. Tough, independent, and more than a little scary; a lot of them were muscle-bound and aggressive. They might have been a different species. None of them looked this good. She carried her wolf like some exotic warrior queen.

Rafe excused himself. "I apologize for leaving this conversation so abruptly. Lovely Yolanda here tells me my presence is required elsewhere. Please tell Taffy I'm afraid our business will have to wait until tomorrow evening. Nice meeting you, Mike. I always wondered about that dog." He wrapped Yolanda's tanned arm in his own, and they left.

Almost immediately, all the pressure and tension in the room dissipated. After a momentary lull, the volume and activity levels returned to normal. Several of the patrons changed seats to keep an eye on the door. Mike understood the sentiment. Even from the rear, lovely Yolanda looked good enough to eat.

THE SMELL OF BLOOD

THE DREAM ALWAYS started the same way: machete in hand, hacking and sweating his way through the rainforest; soaked to the skin, he was alone, but part of an invisible unit, creeping up on the compound belonging to one of the big money men. They thought they'd hit the jackpot; a magnificent residence surrounded by several outbuildings. The guy even had a private zoo. But they'd arrived too late, and the place was deserted. Abandoned. The animals were all dead or starving. They opened the cages of the still living and let them go. The black jaguar was nothing more than a ratty pile of skin and bones huddled in the far corner of a huge cage. The guys in his unit wanted to kill it; put it out of its misery, but he wouldn't hear of it. After they finished searching the grounds, he sent everyone on ahead for safety, and opened the door.

The poor thing hadn't twitched a muscle in all the time they'd been there. Maybe the guys were right; the cat was too far gone. To this day, he didn't know why he didn't just leave the cage door open like the others. An overwhelming compulsion came to him; to see if it was alive. He never figured it had enough strength to turn on him. Never imagined it could move so fast. He never had a chance. If one of his buddies hadn't come back to check on him and shot the creature as it was ripping him apart he would have died at twenty.

Three weeks later, while on medical leave in Vera Cruz, he'd awoken in the jungle with no memory of how he'd gotten there. He'd been covered in blood, the broken corpse of a man lay beneath him. The young man's skull had been crushed and his heart ripped brutally from his chest. As Mike vomited up the bloody pulp in his stomach, Tehuantl made himself known for the first time.

A week later, the local newspapers quoted several members of a doomed hunting party. Each man claimed they'd been following the track of a big black El Tigre. Their pack of mongrel dogs had cornered it against a cliff face. As the men closed in for the kill, the big cat transformed into the spirit of a Nagual; one of the ancient jaguar-men of Olmec legends. The hunters fled in fear as the creature grabbed their leader; the only one among them with a gun. His body was never found.

A week later, the remains of Fabienne Martinez, one of the local cantina girls, was found dead in her room above the bar. Her heart and internal organs were missing. The headlines were lurid, the locals terrified. As one of the patrons of the bar where she'd worked, he'd been questioned, but the authorities found no reason to hold him. Two days later he was on a flight back to the states. As far as he knew, they'd never identified her killer.

It became a pattern for him. Since he had no memory of Tehuantl's actions, he'd had to go by what was written in the press. Every time the papers reported a murder victim with similar wounds, he assumed it was Tehuantl and moved on. He told himself that the deaths had nothing to do with Tehuantl, but deep inside, he didn't really believe it. He moved a lot in those early days. It wasn't until he figured out how to keep the cat happy that he'd finally figured out how to control the shaman.

Mike opened his eyes as cat's lithe form retreated smoothly back to wherever it went when it left him. Scent was a powerful trigger.

That was why he'd had that dream again. Yolanda's perfume brought back sweet memories of Fabienne.

* * *

Tom teased him about the new shirt at dinner, but he'd shrugged it off. By eight o'clock, he was back on a barstool at Beasties. The rowdies from the previous evening were seated at one of the tables, watching the NBA playoffs.

Mike pestered Taffy for answers, but the barkeep wasn't talking. Yes, Yolanda came in occasionally, but usually just to get Rafe. No, he didn't know why a she-were might be dating a vampire. In fact, he wasn't very forthcoming about vampires in general.

"I've known him more years than I care to count, but we don't talk about that. Vamps tend to keep their personal lives private."

"But don't you wonder about it?" Tehuantl's reaction to the vampire had worried him, but Mike wasn't certain that his own curiosity was entirely separate from Tehuantl's. From what he'd surmised and read about the Nagual, the warrior priest's lust for blood was unnatural. Was it possible that Tehuantl was some kind of vampire? "You've never asked him how he was made? I mean, is it like the blood exchange they show in the movies?"

Taffy busied himself, wiping clean glasses, avoiding his eyes. "I don't know that it's the kind of thing you can come right out and ask, directly. It's too personal."

"Oh sure. It's fine to blab about my personal life to a vampire, but you won't give me the same quid pro quo. What kind of business do you have going on with Rafe, anyway?"

Taffy grinned. "Ask him yourself, lad."

A hand clapped Mike on the back. "Ask me what?"

Mike's stomach dropped as he turned to see the vampire Rafe and a black were-man.

Embarrassed, he shook his head. "Nothing." Out of the corner of his eye, he caught the gleam of laughter in Taffy's eyes as he pulled a fresh pint for the newcomer.

"Silas here is one of our security officers out at Mythica," Rafe said. "I thought you might appreciate some company while Taffy and I take care of business. I'll be back in a bit."

Silas took a seat on the stool next to him and closed his eyes as he took his first sip of Taffy's foam-topped porter. "That's nice." He wiped the white foam off his upper lip with his forefinger.

The guy had a very relaxed, loose demeanor. Against the darkness of the big man's skin, his yellow eyes positively popped. The were-man turned around on his barstool to face the room, and gave a solemn nod to the toughs.

"Friends of yours?" Mike asked.

"Pack."

"Don't you have to go over and sniff their butts or something?"

The were-man did a double-take, then grinned. "Nah. They're still pups in training. I'm the only big dog in here tonight." He took a long swallow of porter. "You got a problem with that?"

"No."

The silence between them stretched. It seemed less and less likely that Yolanda would be stopping by. Mike finished his beer and stood to leave, when Silas asked him a question.

"Excuse me?"

"Rafe brought me here to meet Farley's son. Said you might be looking for a job."

"Oh right. Yeah."

"Is the dog really your dad?"

Mike waved him off. "Yeah, but it's a long story. I don't like to talk about it."

"Is he a shape-shifter or a were?"

"Neither. He's Fae. They turned him into a dog when I was five."

"But you're shape-shifter, right?"

"Not according to NYPD."

Silas took a long slow swallow of beer. "You're lucky then."

Mike pressed his lips together. This guy knew nothing about what it had been like for him, or what it was like to be responsible for destroying his father's entire life. He didn't have a clue what it was like being faced with his father's sacrifice every single day, and people telling him he'd ruined a good man. Because Farley Bane had been a very good man.

He let it pass. It wasn't worth it. "How's that make me lucky?"

Silas nodded to Farley, dozing at their feet. "Your father loves you."

Something about the sound of Silas' voice caught Mike's attention. "Well, I'm sure your father loves you too," he answered lightly.

Silas grimaced, his face a mask of pain. "My dad infected me intentionally on my twenty-first birthday. I thought maybe the same thing had happened to you."

Struck speechless, Mike could only stare. The ALVS virus had been developed as a biological weapon to use against troops stationed in the Middle East. Those who survived beyond the first few months onset of the disease generally learned to control their beasts. With reasonable precautions, accidental infection rarely occurred. His father must have been human when Silas was conceived. Mixed human and lycan marriages were not unheard of, but conception between the two species wasn't possible. The idea that a father would intentionally infect his own son; he couldn't even imagine such a thing.

He didn't know what to say. Silas must have thought they shared a common tragedy. Instead he'd bared what had to be the most painful experience of his life. "Oh man. That sucks." It sounded so lame, but he couldn't think of anything else.

Sheila came over and set two fresh pints in front of them.

"Drink to your daddy?" Silas raised his glass.

Still speechless, Mike could only nod and drain his glass.

"So. You High Tor Fae or what?"

Mike choked on his beer. "You always this nosy?"

"The reason I'm asking is that you obviously don't know much about vampires. If you're going spend time around guys like Rafe, you need to know that vampires prefer the taste of Fae blood to human. Like whipping cream to skim milk. Get it?"

Great. "Got it."

"But the High Tor Fae have a blood treaty with Ambrose Van Cleve that goes back more than three centuries. No fighting, no biting. The Van Cleves can't touch the blood of High Tor Fae. They are restricted to volunteer donors or their own little spit-heads."

"Spit-heads?"

"Blood stewards are addicted to the unique saliva of the vampire who feeds off them. So what'll it be?" He grinned. "You High Tor Fae or buffet?"

He'd pronounced the word like *buff-fae.* Fun-nee.

"Now that you mention it, my father was mostly High Tor Fae; my mother, only half. I guess that makes me mostly High Tor Fae too."

"There. See how easy that was?"

"Okay, thanks for the tip." The door to the bar swung open, and Mike glanced up expectantly, but it wasn't Yolanda.

"You expecting someone?"

Silas didn't miss much. "Not really. There was this were-woman who came in here last night looking for Rafe--"

Silas laughed; a booming, joyful sound. "Oh get in line, pal. Everybody's fond a' Yolanda." Silas glanced over his shoulder at the toughs watching the playoffs. "Guys like you and me don't have a chance. She's alpha bitch material; the only thing she's interested in is finding the right pack and the right wolf. Right now, that big guy over there is running neck and neck with our pack Alpha, Vince."

Mike glanced over at the group of were-men across the room. The largest of them returned his stare with hostile interest. Mike looked away. "The galoot?"

"Yeah, he's Alpha material. Or so he thinks. We've lost several senior pack members over the last couple months. Him and all the rest of those guys over there are all new recruits. Trick wants to be Beta, but Rafe won't have him."

"What happened to the old guys?"

Silas made a face. "Silver bullet, probably. Self-inflicted, no doubt. Or that's what the sheriff thinks. Local law enforcement doesn't spend much time looking for lost dogs; even you should know that."

Yeah. Without human DNA, lycans were out of luck where justice was concerned. "Why would what Rafe thinks have anything to do with a wolf pack? Isn't that the Alpha's job?"

"Hey Vince is a good Alpha. Things are run a little differently at Mythica. Everybody likes Rafe, so we make sure he likes the wolves who work closest to him, that's all."

"So why was that fine-looking were-woman kissing on him last night? Rafe is no wolf."

"Yeah well, that's just Rafe. The guy's a frickin' babe magnet. He's like catnip to women."

"He's a complete phony." It made no sense at all that a beautiful woman like that would be throwing herself at a dead guy. Although he had to admit, Rafe seemed like a decent enough guy. For a vampire. It wasn't right. "He dyes his hair."

"Yeah," Silas nodded. "She smells good, too."

"Tell me about it."

THE EARLY BIRD

MIKE DROVE INTO the parking lot of Fat Frank's Bait and Tackle in the pre-dawn darkness, but the only vacant space available had a water-filled pothole deep enough to fish in. He paused, as the dim words of his father echoed in his ears.

"Potholes are portals to the land of the Fae, son. Ordinary people don't have to worry; they can just drive right over them. But people like us; people with more than a little Fae blood running through our veins have got to be careful, or we'll get sucked right in."

So while other kids had grown up with stupid superstitions like breaking their mother's backs, he'd grown up worried about potholes and the High Tor Fae.

Farley whined on the seat beside him as he maneuvered the Chevy to straddle the depression. To the right of them, a shiny-new black Silverado was parked with a BassCat outboard trailered behind. The boat had a custom paint job of a yellow and green striped bass rising to take a fly. The New York State license plate read WERE117. Damn nice rig for a werewolf.

The smell of fresh-brewed coffee greeted them as he opened the glass door to the tackle shop, and Farley trotted inside like he owned the place. The deerhound seemed unbothered by the morning crowd of men loading up coolers of beer and bean dip for the big Finger Lakes fishing tournament on Canandaigua Lake. The place was packed. Tournaments were always good for business.

The big black dog moved behind the counter to greet the owner, and Mike saluted to him as he walked past. He edged his way through the cluster of fishermen gathered around the four-pot coffee station, past the glass-fronted refrigerators full of beer, soda, and sandwiches toward the back of the store.

"Hey there, boy, how's it goin'? I got it right here," he heard Frank cooing to the mutt. Mike grinned as he heard the top of the jerky barrel twist off; a ritual repeated at nearly every bait shop on their morning route. "There you go, Farley. Good boy."

A genial aura of quiet humor pervaded the store. The sound of chuckles faded away as he halted in front of the Minnow Master bait refrigerator. Mike restocked the supply of night crawlers from the portable Styrofoam cooler of fresh inventory he'd brought with him. After checking the sales tally posted on the door, he recorded the numbers with a stubby pencil in his spiral notepad. Tom was right; business was booming. He strode back to the front, called to Farley and they headed out the door.

As he neared the truck, a voice called out from behind him. "Hey, Mikey. Mike Bane. Is that you?"

He turned and did a double take. The amber eyes were a dead giveaway for ALVS. Not to mention the guy had a neck like a water buffalo. The guy was a were; there was no doubt. In fact, they were both wearing the same Velcro-seamed shirt.

Mike searched his memory, but didn't recall meeting any other werewolves besides Silas. "Do I know you?"

Buffalo-neck grinned and punched him square in the chest. "David Stripe, man. Remember me?"

Recognition slammed home, as he coughed and rubbed his sternum. He grinned ear to ear and punched back. The guy was as solid as a bag of cement.

"Striper Dave, as I live and breathe. How the hell are you?" Farley danced around them, his tail wagging gracefully. The mutt remembered, too.

"I never thought to see you back here again." Dave rubbed Farley's ear and the hound moaned with pleasure.

They'd practically been joined at the hip when they were kids. Enlisted on the same day. Dave didn't look a day over twenty-five. Obviously he'd been a were for a good many years. A lot of military veterans came home from serving in the Middle East with ALVS. He'd probably gotten it in the service. "I can't believe it's you."

"You livin' in your dad's old place?"

"My place now. I moved in a few weeks ago."

"I heard you were NYPD."

Dave knew, then. Hell the whole town must know. He shrugged. "Not any more. I'm back for while, at least. Queens is no place for man nor beast; if you know what I mean."

Dave made a face. "Yeah. Well, a lot of weres end up here." He gave Mike a puzzled look. "Funny, you don't look were." He took a deep breath and grinned. "Don't smell were either."

Mike met his golden gaze. "I'm not a were."

Dave grinned and shook his head. "Take it easy, Mikey. I know that." He wrinkled his nose. "What is that smell?"

Mike hooked his thumb toward the truck. "Night crawlers."

Dave looked askance at the battered truck and grinned as he shook his head. "You haven't changed a bit, you old worm charmer. You used to start up that damn worm farm every summer, remember? I can't believe you're still doing this shit."

"Doing what?" Another guy with ALVS came up to Dave with a twelve-pack under one arm and a box of Tom's night crawlers in his other hand. "Let's go," he told Dave, and got in the passenger side of Dave's truck.

"Oh hey. Mikey, this is Steve-o. We work security together over at Mythica."

Mike nodded to the new guy, who answered with a stony stare.

Yeah, well, same to you pal. "Is this your rig?"

"Yeah," Dave slid his hand along the dent-free door panel. "Jealous?" He opened the door of the black truck and reached inside. "Check this out." He pulled out a box of filled with ornately carved fishing rod handles and offered him one. "I made these myself."

Mike examined the beautifully crafted pieces. Even as a kid, Dave had been crazy about fishing. They'd been shop partners in junior high, but these were a work of art. He flexed his wrist, simulating casting action. "Nice. You making custom rods now?"

"Yep. That one is Gabon Ebony. This one here is Red Heart, from Mexico. I use all kinds of exotic wood." He pulled out a cardboard box from of the back seat and pulled out several two-by-two-by-twelve-inch blocks of wood. "This is the raw material stock. Everybody wants custom gear these days," he explained. "It's just a hobby, mostly."

Mike gave the handle back and grinned. "I can't picture you as a security guard. They must pay pretty good."

"Yeah, but they make you earn every penny." Both were-men laughed, as if at some private werewolf joke. "Hey, we're heading out to the tournament." Striper Dave ran a proprietary hand across the smooth finish of the BassCat's fiberglass hull. "Wanna come along?"

Mike was tempted, but Dave was a werewolf now. It was going to take some time to get used to that idea. And his old buddy had a new vibe; an aggressive kind of energy that didn't feel right. "Thanks, but I've got deliveries to make. Maybe some other time."

The two men drove north out of the parking lot. Mike headed south, still in shock at the sight of his childhood friend's amber eyes. Striper Dave in the flesh. Werewolf flesh. No shit. This place was crawling with them.

* * *

Fifteen minutes later, he rounded the bend and turned into the nearly deserted parking lot of Jolley's Outdoor Outfitters. He pulled the Chevy to a stop in front of the store and waited for the billowing dust to settle. The sun hadn't risen yet, but the horizon was light with the coming dawn. *Where are all the cars?*

In the big plate glass window, all the neon beer signs were lit, but the sign on the door indicated the place was closed. With the tournament starting today, the place should be hopping, just like Fat Frank's, but the only other car in the lot was a white van. Something wasn't right. Years of undercover work had taught him to listen to his instincts. He got out of his truck and cautiously approached the store entrance.

Beside him, the mutt whined, his attention riveted toward the corner of the building, his ears pricked forward. A second later, a pair of wolves came trotting around the corner, followed by a third were, in human form.

Adrenaline flooded through him at the sight of the three weres. The guy, dressed in Velcro-seamed leather, held a tranquilizer dart gun in one hand and a pair of silver handcuffs tucked into his belt. The two wolves spread out in a clear attempt to circle around behind him and Farley.

He backed closer to the building. "Hey pal, what's the deal here?"

"You Mike Bane?" The leader's feral expression leaked through his eyes as he neared; the two wolves with him held their position, about a dozen feet away.

It wasn't really a question. The guy already knew. Even with his limited werewolf experience, he knew it was hard for them to maintain human form in the company of other wolves. Werewolves emitted pheromones when they changed that made it nearly impossible for other nearby lycanthropes to remain in human form. If this guy lost his control, he wouldn't be able to hold onto that weapon. The guy must be pretty confident, given all the leather he was wearing.

"Sorry. Don't know him." He kept his eyes focused on the were-man's face, in spite of his concern for the dart gun aimed in his direction.

"Name's Randall. There's a guy in Queens looking for you."

At the mention of Queens, the jaguar inside his head screamed. He sent the cat soothing thoughts and tried to remain calm. *Clemente is dead. He can't hurt us anymore.* Queens was the past. There was no way anyone could have traced him here. Not so soon. He never should have said anything to that damn mover.

"You remember Hector Clemente, doncha? Seems ol' Hector has a brother who is mucho special to the Pomp."

Randall had a hard face. One of the side effects of ALVS was a slowdown in the aging process, but this guy looked like a forty-year-old escapee from a chain gang; all hard muscle and weather roughened skin. He had to be pushing ninety or more. Most guys couldn't take it that long.

"You've got the wrong guy, pal. I don't know what you're talking about. Don't know anyone named Clemente or Pomp." Farley growled. The sun would be up any minute. He wondered where Tom was, and his stomach lurched. He should have had the place open for business by now. *Oh god.*

"You know, the Pomp. *The Pomp of Queens?* The head Vampire of the borough. Hector's brother Diego is the Pomp's new Number One. And Diego would very much like to chat with officer Mike Bane about Hector's unfortunate demise." Randall opened the sliding door of the van, revealing a four-by-four-foot steel cage.

The first rays of the sun pierced the horizon; the glare hit him like a slap in the face. Only a few cars had gone by. *Stall for time.* "You don't sound like you're from Queens, Randall."

"Nah, my people are Texan." He nodded at the battered truck with the bright new decal on the side. The logo had been Tom's idea. "Night Crawlers, eh? Well, Diego's put out an open contract on you.

Guess I'm the early bird, worm boy."

"Hey you're funny." He prayed that Tom was okay.

"What'll it be, Bane? Ketamine or the cage?"

This can't be happening. Maybe someone driving by would see something and call the sheriff and this whole thing could disappear before somebody got hurt. *If it wasn't already too late.* He pulled his shirt off over his head in a single motion and threw it to the ground. "You didn't bring enough muscle, cowboy."

The wolves edged closer, and Randall adjusted his stance. "Easy Bane. There's no reason to get so het up about this. Clemente is going to get you one way or another. Says he's got a pair of pliers and a truck battery with your name on it. I'm giving you an opportunity to come along quiet and maybe give him your side of the story."

The cat screamed again. "What can I do to persuade you I'm not your guy? What's this Diego guy paying you, anyway?"

Randall clicked the safety off the pistol.

Damn. "You pull that trigger, you'll never live to collect that bounty."

Randall didn't even blink. "Maybe you can talk your way out of it."

Not likely. "We both know that's not going to happen, asshole." The velcro-seamed shorts tore off in a single motion, and before they hit the ground, he reached for the cat. The melting sensation flowed through him; as fluid as a swallow of cold beer on a dusty day.

Both wolves leapt forward, and Randall shouted at them to stay out of his shot. The big cat batted the first wolf through the plate glass window of Jolley's Outdoor Outfitters like a ball of yarn, setting off the alarm. The second wolf was smacked straight back at Randall, and took the dart meant for the jaguar. The wolf's body hit Randall square in the chest, and their momentum slammed them both back into the van. The metal door buckled on impact. The first wolf staggered out from Jolley's and went for Farley. The dog took off with the werewolf in hot pursuit. The number two wolf was out cold, and Randall, his control gone, began to shift. The jaguar pounced. He grabbed the bounty hunter by the skull just as three sheriff cars raced into the parking lot.

A uniformed officer raced up, weapon drawn, and assumed firing position just beyond the cat's reach.

"Freeze," he shouted. "You're under arrest, kitty-cat. I've got silver-tipped ammo here. Now let go of that werewolf or I swear I will shoot you in the head. What'll it be?"

BAD COP, BAD COP

BARE-ASSED, MIKE crouched on the cement floor of an end kennel. The arresting officer told him their clothes and shoes had been confiscated for their own safety, as people with ALVS didn't do well in captivity. *No shit.*

He gripped the steel mesh with his fingers and rocked back and forth. The image of Tom's bloody body flashed before him every time he closed his eyes. It looked as if Tom's throat had been completely torn out. He'd never seen anything so horrible. He'd begged to be allowed to accompany Tom to the hospital, but the officers had refused, assuming he was one of Tom's attackers. They were right in principle, if not in fact. The assault on Tom had been all his fault.

He wanted to kill Randall, but they had him locked up at the far end of the row. Across the aisle, the ketamine-drugged wolf lay in a puddle of drool. In fourteen police precincts covering all of Queens, there were only three holding kennels for people with Acquired Lycanthropy Virus Syndrome; the Kennel Room at the Ontario County Sheriff's Office held eight.

Hours later he was given his clothes and led to a beige cubicle to face a still-bristling Criminal Investigation Officer, Lieutenant Bill Dixon. Mike struggled to maintain a calm demeanor, but all he wanted was to get to the hospital.

"How is Tom?" He asked.

"I'm asking the questions here, Bane. The sooner you cooperate, the sooner we'll get this mess straightened out."

"Hey, I didn't ask to be attacked. I'm a victim too."

"Can it, Bane. There's nothing you can say that will convince me this wasn't your fault. I don't care what you animals do to each other, but Tom Jolley is a citizen."

Mike closed his eyes and took a deep breath. *I am not a frickin' werewolf.* Losing his temper wouldn't get him out of here any sooner. Dixon wanted answers. "Okay, I get it. Let's get this over with."

"Every town in the region depends on tourist dollars in the summer months to carry them through the winter. The human citizens are in an uproar over this. We've got an assault on a local businessman and attempted kidnapping in broad daylight. I've taken a dozen calls from the local lycans, many of whom I know and trust, disavowing you as an outsider. They're terrified of the backlash against weres. They say you're a menace. What the hell are you doing here?"

Mike felt the heat rise in his face. "I live here. Tom Jolley is my godfather. *Is he still alive?*"

Dixon ignored the question. "You live here? Why aren't you registered as a resident? Lycanthropes are required to register their current address, just like the sexual predators."

Mike's forced himself to unclench his fists. "I already told you. I don't have Lycanthropy. I'm not ALVS positive. Legally, I don't have to register." He held up his hand to forestall the interruption. "Okay, okay. My legal status is hazy at the moment; it's working its way through the courts. Until there's a final ruling, I don't have to have a green card. I was planning to stop in and introduce myself, but I hadn't gotten around to it yet. My bad."

"Failure to register your address with local law enforcement is a misdemeanor."

The tension in his shoulders eased. If Dixon was threatening him with a misdemeanor, he sure as hell wasn't going to arrest him for assault. "You know I didn't attack Tom Jolley. I don't know if he's alive or dead. Please. Tell me what happened to him."

"We found him in a dumpster behind the bait shop. The EMTs told me his throat was crushed. They had to do an emergency tracheotomy. He made it to the hospital and was taken directly into surgery. I called twice, but there's no news yet. That's all I know."

He swallowed a moan. "Look, I need to get over there. Are we done here or are you really planning to arrest me?"

Dixon's irritated look turned to one of concern. "When we searched the van, we found a large quantity of Ketamine and a nine millimeter Ruger loaded with illegal silver ammo. Gabe Randall's wolf buddy is wanted in three states. Why did they come after you?"

Mike debated how much to tell him. He didn't want to talk about any of it, but the detective would have little trouble finding out the truth on his own, anyway.

"A few months ago I was working undercover on a narcotics case in Queens. Ecstasy, ketamine, narcotics, you name it. The ass-wipe we were looking at was a middleweight dealer in the Magos biker gang. The case went south; the dealer didn't survive the arrest. Randall told me the dealer's brother has a contract out on me." The cat screamed silently at the memory, still as fresh as if it had happened yesterday. *Easy boy.*

Dixon smirked and closed the file folder. "Yeah, I heard about that. Got a buddy worked narcotics with you a few years ago. Said you were a good man to have in a tight spot, but you lost it."

"I didn't lose it." Dixon was just yanking his chain, and they both knew it. The urge to get to the hospital was nearly overwhelming. "Are we done here?"

"You shifted on duty, man. The way I heard it, your beast took out Clemente and was about to help himself to some of Hector's brain puddin' when your partner shot you. Twice. You don't call that a melt down?"

Mike struggled to keep the expression off his face. Only the fresh scent of his own blood had finally conquered the ketamine-induced stupor the cat had been kept in for two weeks. "You can't believe anything you read in the newspapers about that case, Lieutenant. Clemente trapped me in beast form and was in the process of skinning me alive with a silver-edged blade. Internal Affairs exonerated me. The DA called it justifiable."

"So why walk away? What made you move down here?" A sneer crept into Dixon's voice.

Because when the big cat is unhappy, everybody's unhappy. And when the cat is threatened, Tuhuantl takes over and people die. In a moment of clarity, he realized he'd spent most of his life running away from one problem or another. "You already know the answer. I was forced out on a technicality. I don't have ALVS, but it didn't matter. My cover was blown." This conversation wasn't going anywhere. "I had a chance to start over here, and I took it. If people think I'm lycan, fine. I'll live with the wolves. And this part of New York is the frickin' garden of Eden for werewolves, isn't it?" His voice cracked. The sight of Tom's broken, bloodied form flashed before him. "What's not to like?"

"The wolves don't want you here, for one thing. And neither do I." Dixon's expression hardened. "Other hunters are going to come sniffing around here looking for you, and I can't have that. We have a sizable population of lycanthropes living in this county. Most of them keep a low profile. But every time a werewolf causes a problem, it reinforces the stereotype for everyone with ALVS."

Surprise, surprise. Dixon had a soft spot for weres. Maybe a brother or buddy. For all the cement and bars, the kennels had been immaculate. Cleaner than the holding cell at the 104. "Message received. Can I go now?"

"Let me clarify a couple of things for you, Bane. Whenever a citizen is attacked by a werewolf, it's bad news. When people hear about werewolf problems in this part of the state, it's bad for the tourist business, which means it's bad for the fine citizens who live here. Incidentally, it's also bad for the law-abiding lycans who have enough problems already. This county, in fact the entire region, has more than its fair share of families affected by ALVS. We don't need the kind of outside attention and violence you're bringing into this community. Nobody wants you here. I think you should find yourself another place to live."

"I was minding my own business. That is not a crime. Would you be saying this to me if I worked at Mythica?"

Dixon frowned. "Mythica is a private estate in another county owned by the Van Cleve family. They are well-respected members of the community, and one of the original founding families in the region." Dixon rubbed his fingers together in the universal 'they got lotsa bucks' sign. "They're not my concern."

"They're vampires."

Dixon's jaw twitched. "Old news, kitty-cat. They negotiated the first territorial boundaries with the High Tor Fae and established the first vineyard in the region. They're the largest single employer of werewolves in the state, they pay their taxes, and I've never heard even a whisper of a problem happening out there. Their private amusement park is only open four days a week, but visitors bring a ton of out-of-town money into this area every summer. On the other hand, the only thing you've brought is trouble."

"From what I hear, they have a lot of lycans go missing out there."

Dixon's face colored. "Vince Dazak is the Security Chief for the estate, and an Alpha wolf to boot. His Beta lived here in Ontario County, and when the officer went missing, Vince brought me the surveillance records himself, without being asked. Everything checked out. Mythica microchips their employees, and has just about every square inch of the premises covered with surveillance cameras."

"Look Bane, Mythica is one of the few places in the state that actively recruits people with ALVS. They even offer medical benefits. Vince told me his Beta's attitude had changed recently. He'd become alienated from the pack. The Van Cleves became so concerned, they even hired a therapist to talk to him."

Mike shifted uncomfortably in his seat. Must've hit a nerve.

Dixon counted off his actions on his fingers. "I checked phone records, credit cards, bank transactions. Even fishing charters and boat rentals to see if he might have gone fishing out on the lake and capsized. We got nothing."

"Why are you telling me this?" *We're wasting time.*

Dixon paused, his face a mask. "He had a gun registered in his name, and we couldn't find it or his cell phone. Wherever he is, he's off the grid. He's a grown man with no family or support system, afflicted with an incurable, isolating disease. I don't know about the others, but we won't be finding this guy. That's how most of 'em go, you know."

"I thought wolves in packs fared better than lone wolves."

"Lycanthropy isn't about wolves, Bane. I would think you, of all people, would understand that."

He pressed his lips into a thin line. *I'm not like them.* "I need to get to the hospital."

Dixon sighed. "Listen, we try to treat the local weres just like anybody else around here, and that's a damn sight better than they can expect from law enforcement up in the city. I know you're worried about your godfather, but you have to understand my position. We've got a one strike tolerance for werewolves in this town. Your continued presence represents a real threat to the citizens I am sworn to protect. What happened to Tom is your fault."

Dixon jerked his head in the direction of the Kennel Room. "I'll have the writ of execution for your two buddies in there by the end of the day. They'll be out of their misery by midnight. This is the only warning I'm going to give you, Bane. Get out of town."

BITE INSURANCE

IT WAS PAST nightfall when the doctors came out of surgery to talk to him.

"His wounds are extensive, Mr. Bane. Your godfather is stable, but not out of danger yet. There was severe crushing damage to the throat and right carotid artery, but we've been able to partially repair the damage. There may be some nerve damage as well, but we won't know for quite some time. He won't be conscious until sometime tomorrow." The surgeon's nametag said Dr. Jalil Singh.

The doctor's gown bore traces of blood spatter. Tom's blood. Mike was no wimp, but looking at it made him nauseous. "Is he going to make it?"

"He was bleeding out when he was brought in, but the infection from the wolf bite is just as worrisome as the wound itself. He's very sick."

Every word the doctor said felt like a physical blow. Mike fought to maintain a neutral expression.

"The likelihood of lycanthropy transmission in a case like this is extremely high, but not guaranteed. We have had some small successes in early intervention by diluting the patient's blood with transfusions."

"Does Mr. Jolley have any other family?" The woman's nametag indicated she was a doctor, too. Sarah Powers.

The name rang a bell. "I'm all he's got. I'm responsible for him. This is all my fault." Lieutenant Dixon's condemnation still rang in his ears. *In more ways than one.* "Is he going to live?"

"I'm sorry to put this so bluntly," Dr. Singh said, "but the only way to be sure is to perform surgery. Typically, the lycanthropy virus heals the body with no further treatment. However, if he has not contracted the virus, he will certainly die without extensive surgical intervention and reconstruction. The costs associated with this kind of specialized surgery are quite substantial and not covered by ordinary health insurance. Do you have access to the kind financial resources required to cover the costs of his care?"

Mike felt the blood drain from his face. "What do you mean, they're not covered?"

"Lycanthrope-caused injuries of this nature are specifically excluded from standard policies. The mere presence of a lycanthrope contaminant in this hospital represents a substantial threat. In order to limit financial exposure and risk in cases like this, the hospital has implemented a policy of requiring evidence of ability to pay prior to further treatment."

"Are you saying you don't treat lycans?" The bitter words stuck in his throat. *This is my responsibility.* His mind raced as he estimated how much money he could come up with. Nowhere near enough. A heavy weight settled on his shoulders.

Dr. Singh shook his head. "You don't understand. The arguably miraculous benefit of the lycanthropy virus is that the patient's altered DNA allows the body to heal itself from even the most devastating injuries. Even severed limbs can be re-grown. ALVS sufferers never require medical care unless the wounds are contaminated with silver."

"I get it. So is he infected or not?"

"Unfortunately, Mr. Jolley's exposure to the virus occurred at the same time as his injuries. The antibodies, if they are present in his bloodstream, take time to build up in his system. Our tests cannot detect the presence of the disease until after the onset of the first event."

"You mean the full moon."

Both physicians nodded.

He raked his hand through his scalp. *This is a frickin' nighmare.* "But that's weeks away."

"Precisely my point," agreed Dr. Singh. "If Mr. Jolley has been infected, he will heal on his own, even though we cannot detect the presence of the disease. If he has not been infected, he will die without the surgery."

"Do the surgery."

Both doctors looked relieved. "We'll need you to sign the necessary papers before we can proceed. The finance office is on the first floor, there is always someone on duty."

I'll bet there is. He wondered how much the operation would cost. It didn't matter; not really. Whatever it took, whatever the cost, he'd make it right for Pops. He'd put the cottage up for collateral. He'd figure something out. He *had* to. Tom's future depended on it. He'd already ruined Farley's life. He couldn't wait for virus to *maybe* kick in, and he sure as hell wasn't going to walk away. Not again. "How soon can you operate?"

"Let's wait and see how he makes it through the night. If he does well over the next few hours, I can rearrange the OR schedule."

He released a long breath. "Thanks, Doc."

Dr. Sigh excused himself, leaving him alone with Dr. Powers.

"I can see this comes as a shock for you, Mr. Bane. But your godfather is quite fortunate he was brought here to Thompson Hospital. Most emergency rooms won't accept ALVS patients; they're referred to local veterinarians."

"I can't accept that." Not my Pops. Selling the cottage was a no-brainer. He'd move in with Tom and take care of him and run the shop while he recovered. He'd leave as soon as Tom was back on his feet—

"Mr. Bane? Are you all right?" Dr. Powers touched his arm.

"Yeah, sorry. Could you repeat what you said?"

"I said the initial onset of lycanthropy does not need to be traumatic. Our understanding of transmorphic physiology and modern hypnotherapy techniques have given those burdened with ALVS a much higher quality of life than in the recent past. It's no longer quite the burden it once was."

She was just a tiny thing, really. Couldn't have been a stitch over five foot nothing. Her most arresting feature, aside from the thick mop of blond hair, was her expressive, aquamarine-colored eyes.

"Science is just beginning to recognize ALVS as a possible genetic schism rather than a disease. We are seeing newly-afflicted lycanthropes demonstrate acquisition of a common telepathic ability and cultural knowledge of previously undocumented legends. There is even growing evidence to support that lycan pack members acquire a shared consciousness and belief system."

"Could you repeat that in English?"

"Try not to worry." She took his hand. "I don't often get a chance to work with patients from the first day of infection. I plan to retrain his subconscious to accept the inevitable changes at the genetic level before the onset of his symptoms. It will reduce the trauma to his psyche and give him better coping tools."

"If he does have it." Mike paused, unable to continue.

"I'm one of the few certified ALVS therapists in the country, Mr. Bane. We've pioneered techniques here that are now used worldwide. He'll be fine." She smiled encouragingly.

But not even her kind words could lift the weight of guilt off his shoulders. "I wish to god I had never come back. I'll never forgive myself for this."

"That kind of talk has never helped anyone." She tilted her head, as if to study him. "Can I ask you a personal question?"

She didn't wait for his answer.

"The news reports said you were a were-cat. I've never met a were-cat before, but I confess you don't feel anything like a lycanthrope. What are you?"

He jerked his hand away, angrily. Canandaigua was a small town. He'd never considered that his encounter with Randall would end up in the local news, but of course it would. This was the Queens catastrophe all over again.

"I'm sorry if I've made you uncomfortable, but I have a sixth sense about these things. It's one of the reasons I made working with lycanthropes my life's work. I can feel your beast, Mr. Bane, but it's nothing like anything I've ever felt before."

Mike stepped back. "I better go. I've gotta get down to the finance office and fill out that paperwork."

"I feel your pain, Mike. You're at war with your inner beast. I'd like to help you."

Nobody can help me. And right now, she was the least of his problems. "Save it, Doc. Save it for Tom." A defenseless little thing like her wouldn't last two minutes in Tehuantl's hands. "It was nice to meet you. I appreciate anything you can do for him." He edged toward the stairwell.

She followed him. "I mean it. Fighting only makes things worse. Believe me, I know what you're going through."

"No you don't." *You have absolutely no idea, lady.* It didn't matter how attractive she was. "Good night, Doctor."

TEHUANTL AWAKE

SHE IS VERY attractive, no? Tehuant's voice echoed in his head. He stumbled and nearly tripped as he trotted down the stairs.

Panic shot through him. *Shut up. She's not for us. I mean, you. Ever.*

And perceptive. She's smart, that one.

Don't even think about it. I am not letting that woman anywhere near us. No doctors. Especially no head doctors.

You disappoint me yet again. How long has it been since you've known the flesh of a woman? Do you even remember? I do. I remember it very well.

His heart pounded. *I said shut up.* Oh god, he would give anything to get rid of Tehuantl's voice inside his head. The sound of the smarmy sadist's voice grated inaudibly in his brain.

You do realize I can hear your thoughts.

Not all of them. Not when you're asleep.

I'm not sleeping now. Besides, the First Jaguar tells me everything I wish to know.

Mike paused on the stairs, hunched over the railing, and clenched his mind against the intruder. Go back to sleep Tehuantl. The shaman's eerie laugh echoed in his mind. Mike reached out tentatively, but the spirit was gone. *Good*. He'd discovered that if he used Tehuantl's name as part of a command, the priest usually obeyed. As long as there was nothing else of any interest going on.

He drew a shaky breath and blew it out slowly. He knew the cat and the priest communicated directly, but he had no access to their conversations. His own communications with the cat were completely nonverbal. He could send it soothing thoughts, or try to pressure it in one direction or another, but the jaguar made its own choices and never acknowledged Mike's presence directly.

Tehuantl, on the other hand, after years of relative quiet had become a much stronger presence lately. Ever since the episode with Hector Clemente. Every time Tehuantl popped up with one of his little comments, it was like a waking nightmare. Tehuantl seemed to relish making him uncomfortable.

Mike felt like he was losing control over the whole situation. Coming home had been a huge mistake. If it weren't for Pops, he'd have left town as soon as Dixon released him, but running away was not an option.

Tehuantl's attraction to Dr. Powers was a pattern he'd come to recognize. No good could come of it. He'd have steer clear of her, but that might be difficult. He shook his head in frustration.

Not only that, but the cat was starting to resist him. Tom had been right. Trying to keep the cat stuffed with fish wasn't going to satisfy him much longer. Sooner or later, the cat would decide to head out to the Tor and bring down some real meat. Better to keep the cat happy than risk losing control over Tehuantl. The cat had already decided he preferred to sleep with the dog on the big king-sized bed. He wouldn't even go near the cage any more. That cat was no fool.

SON OF A BITCH

"WHAT'S THE NEWS," Taffy asked him. He had the local paper spread open on the bar in front of him. Mike could see a photo of himself sitting in the back seat of the sheriff's car, although he didn't recall seeing anyone on the scene with a camera.

"He's alive. Unconscious still." Mike settled onto a stool. "They don't know. The doctors think he's been infected, but can't be absolutely certain. They had to give him a lot of blood, which could dilute the risk of virus transfer, but there's no way to know until the full moon. If he's not infected, he'll die without major surgery. I told them to go ahead with the operation. I won't take that chance. They'll do it tomorrow."

"Who's the surgeon?"

"Dr. Singh."

Taffy nodded. "Good man,"

"Hope so." He hunched over his beer. "You should go visit him."

"You'll never see me inside a hospital again." Taffy tapped the newspaper in front of him. "Says here you ripped the head off one of 'em."

"You can't believe any of that shit. They were legally executed about an hour ago." He glanced into the corner, but the dog's rug was empty. His heart skipped a beat. "Where's Farley?"

"Haven't seen him all day. I figured he was with you."

A heavy sense of foreboding washed over him. "No, he took off running with the third wolf after him." His jaw clenched rhythmically. *Not Farley too.* He pushed the beer away and stood to leave. "Maybe he's at home."

"Paper says only two were arrested." Taffy's eyes narrowed as he focused his attention behind Mike's shoulder. The jukebox had gone silent.

Mike felt the soft slap of a rolled-up newspaper across the back of his head and the heavy pressure in the air around him increased.

It was one of the toughs from Silas' pack. "Bad kitty. This is a wolf bar, not a litter box. You don't belong here."

The guy was big. Behind him, four of his pals watched expectantly.

"This is neutral ground, Trick," Taffy warned. "Take a step back and turn down the heat, lad."

The pressure around Mike increased to a stifling level; the urge to kneel was nearly overwhelming. He'd heard of lycan pheromones of course, but never experienced anything like this. His skin itched with it. Silas was right. Alphas were different. In his head, the cat laid its ears back.

"Take chill pill, Taff. I'm talking to the pussy cat." The only sound in the bar was that of the newspaper slapping against the side of Trick's massive leg. "Scram, pussy."

There was a flicker of motion to his right, and Mike caught a glimpse of Rafe and Silas in the doorway. Both of them stared at him with shocked expressions. The pressure to kneel increased. Instinctively, he knew that walking away was not an option. He clenched his fists. *I'm not backing down to a goddam wolf pup.*

Impulsively, he grabbed the bigger man by the neck, just under the jaw. He stepped into Trick, squeezing upward on the pressure points of the were's massive neck. The lycan grabbed him by the wrist, and he squeezed harder. The helpless were-man froze and the pressure around them evaporated.

He could feel Trick's panicked pulse beneath his fingers. He kept his voice low. "The thumb is an amazing appendage, isn't it? In the right situation, sometimes a little thumb pressure in the right place is all that's needed. Wouldn't you agree?"

Trick's throat convulsed with a soundless swallow.

With minimal pressure, he pulled the taller man's head down to whisper into his ear. "I'll bet you feel pretty stupid right now. You've pissed off a guy who's had a really bad fucking day, and I reacted without thinking. And now we have a situation where neither one of us can reasonably back down. Entirely my fault. I can tell you didn't mean it, am I right? Blink twice for yes, once for no."

Trick blinked several times in frantic succession.

"So in order for both of us save face here, I'll tell you what I'm going to do. I'm going to laugh and let you go, and you're going to laugh even louder, like I just said the funniest thing you ever heard. Then you're going to go back to your table, and I'm going to finish my beer and leave." He snatched the rolled up newspaper out of the other man's hand. "And before you answer, consider this. I've already ripped the head off of one werewolf today; one more isn't going to matter to me one way or another. Do we have an understanding?"

Two careful blinks.

Mike could feel the cat's humor bubbling up inside him. He threw his head back and laughed as he released his grip on Trick.

The other man gasped for breath, then tagged him with a semi-serious thump to the chest before swaggering over to join his buddies at the table. Angry red welts striped his neck where Mike had grabbed him.

Sore loser. Mike wanted to rub his chest, but thought better of it. It hurt, but the last thing he was going to do was give that bottom-feeder the satisfaction. Somebody dropped a token into the jukebox, and the moment passed. He took a seat at the bar next to Silas. Taffy came over and put a fresh pint in front of each of them, then wordlessly followed Rafe through the kitchen door into the back.

"Nice job." Silas jerked his head toward Trick and his pals. "That Trick is too powerful for his own good. One of these days that hot temper of his is going to land him in real trouble."

Mike bit his lips shut. The pressure of the day was getting to him. He wanted to hit something. He stared at the empty rug one last time, then downed half the pint in front of him in a single long swallow.

"You ought to come work for us. We could use a cool head like yours."

His eyes strayed to the vacant rug in corner. Maybe Farley was at home. If he left now, he'd have to concede the bar to Trick and his pals. Five more minutes. "How the hell can you stand to let those vampires feed on you?"

Silas shook his head. "Man you don't know anything. They don't feed on us. They can't. Vamps can't digest ALVS-infected blood properly. That's what blood stewards are for. It's one of the reasons weres and vamps work well together. We look out for each other."

The realization hit him hard. His lip curled in disgust. "That's why Rafe comes here, isn't it. Taffy's just another blood meal to him. Fae blood is like shark chum for vampires, right?"

Silas frowned. "It's not like that. Rafe doesn't use blood stewards. He doesn't have to. He's just doing this as favor to help Taffy."

"A favor!" Heat rushed into his face. This was too much. It was time to go. Not trusting himself to speak, he pushed himself away from the bar. A soothing coolness flowed over him, stopping him cold.

Silas put a placating hand on his shoulder. "Hold on a minute, would you?"

Standing there in a werewolf dive bar suddenly felt like the most Zen-like place on the planet. How the hell did werewolves do that?

"Let me tell you a couple things about blood stewards. They all have their own reasons for wanting to be bound to a vampire, and by law, blood stewards have to volunteer and sign a contract. If you have a problem with Taffy, take it up with Taffy. As vampires go, the ones at Mythica aren't much different than we are."

Mike gave him a look. "They're dead."

"They pay me to protect them," Silas countered. "Good money."

"Nobody in their right mind would work for a vampire." It came out harsher than he intended, but Silas didn't seem to take offense.

"Hey, Rafe is a good guy. I don't have to tell you this, you know it. Everybody does."

He had to admit it. There was something sort of likable about Rafe's obvious phoniness. It worked for him. He had utter confidence that he was this really cool guy, and in a way, he sort of was. He wondered what Rafe had been like when he was alive. He shrugged reluctantly, his anger evaporated. "He's an Elvis man. It goes without saying."

Silas nodded at the paper lying on the bar. "I heard what happened."

He drained his beer. "Everybody did, apparently."

"You alright?"

Mike bit back a retort. Silas hadn't done anything to deserve it. Any other night, he might have been tempted to stay and hoist a few; something he never would have considered in Queens. "I'll live. Now if you'll excuse me, I need to go look for my dog."

AMBROSE

AMBROSE VAN CLEVE sat at a card table in the warming room and considered the puzzle piece in his hand for a moment. He smiled has he placed it correctly into its proper position. The puzzle was a new one; a two thousand piece landscape of the tulips and windmills of his homeland.

The warming room was the place they gathered after waking every evening. The furniture was worn but comfortable, and there was a microwave in the kitchenette for warming up the bags of donor blood. After the initial feed of the evening, Ambrose usually lingered, taking his ease in this snug room before heading upstairs to the demands of the noisy hubbub of the park.

Tonight, however the tension in this room distracted him from the puzzle. Cobb and Vince were at odds again. Ambrose hated to go against his Alpha werewolf, Vince, but Cobb was his first-made son. Family interests had to come first.

"You already agreed we need more pack members, Vince." Cobb waved the front page of the newspaper in front of Vince's face. "What's wrong with this guy?"

Vince smirked and slapped it away. "The guy's a were-cat. You can't bring a cat into a pack of wolves. It's all wrong."

"I don't see the problem," Ambrose said.

"At the heart of any functional pack is group of hunters working cooperatively for a common goal; ultimately the good of the pack and the protection of the territory. Cats don't think like wolves, they don't hunt like wolves. I won't have it."

"A were is a were, Vince." Cobb smoothed the newspaper across the coffee table. "Don't be so quick to turn your nose up at this guy. He'd be a great addition to your little team."

Ambrose pressed his lips together. As often as he had warned Cobb against it, his eldest enjoyed baiting Vince. He gazed at Cobb over the top of his reading glasses. "Cobb, I daresay our Alpha wolf knows more about running a wolf pack than we do."

"Thank you, Ambrose," Vince said. "For werewolves, hunting is what drives us. Hunting as a pack builds the bonds of interdependence and trust between us. Cats don't do that. We hunt cooperatively by trailing our prey to the point of fatigue. Cats can't do that. Our physiology allows us to keep pace with our intended victim over long distances. We can keep it up for days. Cats won't do that. Pack membership is cemented through the ritual of the hunt. The pack will never accept any member who cannot hunt with the pack. Cats are loners. The pack bond is communal; it's everything."

"Okay, so make him a lone wolf," Cobb countered. "Loners don't hunt with the pack."

A look of annoyance flashed across Vince's normally impassive face. "Lone wolf status is a reserved courtesy for friends and family. We don't know anything about this guy. Let me do my job, Ambrose. You put me in charge of security for a reason. I can't let a guy like this onto the estate."

"You didn't even read this," Cobb argued. "Says right here he was Army Special Forces. Two tours of duty in the drug wars in South America. Decorated twice for valor. He's an ex-cop. Hell, you should love this guy."

Ambrose interrupted before Vince could explode. "That's enough Cobb. Calm down, Vince. He's right. I had Felix check out our Mr. Bane. He's got everything you always look for in an officer, and he's discreet. As an undercover narcotics officer, he kept his condition hidden from NYPD for years."

"You're always yammering about control, Vince." Cobb tapped the paper in front of him. "This guy has it in spades."

"Cobb." Ambrose regretted the irritation in his voice. That vamp could try the patience of a saint. "The point is, Vince, we're still a little short of wolves around here, and Rafe isn't happy with Trick. What about the female?"

Vince shook his head. "Absolutely not. Yolanda is hasn't decided to join the pack yet. I'll raise Silas to Beta status. He and Rafe get along great, and Silas has the maturity and experience to merit the Beta position. It'll be good for the pack."

An icy chill washed over Ambrose. *Over my dead body.* No matter how much Vince favored him, he could never allow the Mythica pack to be led by a blackie. Not as an Alpha, not as a Beta. He pushed himself away from the puzzle and took off his glasses.

"You know how I feel about that one. We've been through this before; I am not going to change my mind. The topic is not open for discussion." After living with slaves for three hundred years, one didn't change one's opinions of them after a few decades of emancipation. "Trick will be named as Beta."

Vince held himself rigidly. "We've been over this already, Ambrose. Trick lacks experience. He's still too much of a hothead."

"Give Trick to me," Cobb said. "Tryffin doesn't need a personal bodyguard anyway."

"Shut it, Cobb. I won't say it again." Ambrose sighed. "I grow tired of your protests, Vince. The summit is coming up in a few weeks and we're running out of time. We need the pack at double capacity if we're going to make the case for Cobb to get his own territory. We do not have the luxury of turning our collective noses up at such an obvious asset."

"It's my pack. My decision."

Yes, but Mythica belongs to me, my pet. "Of course it is. I know you don't like me interfering, but I'm just trying to help. It's settled then. Mr. Bane will come onboard as a lone wolf for Rafe."

Vince stood stiffly. "As you say. Just for the record, I don't think this is a good idea. The pack will never accept him. Rafe is your partner, Ambrose. He's never had anything less than a Beta for his bodyguard. He'll never accept a low-ranking loner like Bane."

Ambrose smiled and placed another puzzle piece into position. "He already has.

TO BE OR NOT TO BE

THE WARM TOUCH of a woman's hand on his arm brought Mike back from a light doze. Dr. Sarah Power's face hovered uncomfortably close, her extraordinary blue-green eyes inches from his own. The bones in her hand seemed as fragile as a bird's. Embarrassed, he pulled away, relieved to see he was still in human form.

He'd let the cat out last night, hoping the feline's superior senses could find the mutt, or at least figure out where he'd gone. But the jaguar hadn't gotten the message, and had been delighted at the prospect of being out on the Tor. In spite of his entreaties to search for Farley, the jaguar spent half the night scent-marking new territory. Then he'd found a vantage point near a deer trail where he'd settled and refused to budge. After two hours of waiting, he finally ambushed an unwary boar raccoon, which he devoured with all the gusto of a gourmand for French cuisine.

After another lengthy grooming session during which Mike's anxiety reached a fever pitch, the cat had finally sauntered home near dawn. The cat was miffed at Farley's absence, but they were both exhausted and fell asleep quickly. The alarm clock went off an hour later. He'd stayed awake in the visitor room through the surgery, but must have dropped off.

"I told the nurse I'd come get you," Dr. Powers said. "Tom is awake. He's asking for you."

"Thanks, um." Mike scrambled to his feet. She'd dropped by the waiting room several times throughout the day, and had been there when Dr. Singh had come out after the operation to say that the surgery had gone well. Mike had tried to brush off her attempts at chattiness, but she seemed determined to offer moral support, despite his protestations that he didn't need any company. She even brought him a sandwich from the cafeteria, which made him feel guilty for being rude. But her nearness bothered him more.

"Please call me Sarah," she'd told him. "We're going to become very good friends, I'm certain."

But he couldn't do it. Sarah was far too tender a name to say out loud. He realized he was comparing her to prey, and was appalled.

The Intensive Care nurse told him Dr. Singh would be stopping by to talk to him, and cautioned Mike not to stay too long or over-stimulate the patient. She told him Tom would not be able to speak, but could communicate by writing on a notepad.

He swallowed an involuntary moan when he saw Tom's bruised and purpled face. Both eyes were blackened and Frankenstein stitches stretched across his nose. His throat and one shoulder were swathed in bandages, and a breathing tube was in place. An intravenous drip was attached to one arm.

"Hey Pops." He pulled the nearby chair closer, so that Tom needn't try to turn his head. "They said you're doing fine. I'm so sorry." He lowered his head and kissed the older man's too-cool hand. He smelled faded and weak. That scared him more than anything. "Are you in pain? Can I get you anything?"

Tom's eyes smiled back at him, and he motioned to the pencil and pad on the nightstand. Mike handed it to him and Tom scribbled a short question. "AM I WOLF?"

Oh jeeze. "They aren't sure yet. It's too soon to tell. Try not to worry."

Tom scratched out another question. "SHOP?"

"Locked up tight. The front window was broken, but I got the glazier to come right away. There's a brand-new front window there now." He gave Tom a brief rundown of everything that happened, telling him not to believe anything written in the papers. He didn't want him to worry.

"FARLEY?"

He rubbed his jaw uncomfortably. "Oh, he's fine," he answered, with a confidence he didn't feel. "He's probably out on the Tor right now. I expect him back tonight." Tom shrugged, as if to indicate it wasn't the first time the mutt hadn't come home.

"NO INSRNCE!" Tom stabbed at the notepad, breaking the pencil point.

Mike sighed. "It'll be okay. I put up the cottage as collateral. I'll take care of everything. The only thing you need to do is rest and get better."

Tom shook his head and struggled to sit up.

"No, wait. Relax! What is it? Here. Write it here." He held the notepad at a better angle for Tom. This time the message was longer.

"CAN'T SELL - TOR LAND - BLNGS 2 FAE!!!"

Tom's face reddened; his eyes looked bright with worry.

Oh, right. The land was a special easement within the Tor; granted as a wedding gift to his parents. He was making a complete mess of everything. It broke his heart to see the man who'd raised him so upset. "I'm so sorry, Pops. Try not to worry." He remembered the offer from Silas. "I might have a line on a job over at Mythica."

Tom slapped him with the notepad, making his disapproval clear. The nurse came in, and seeing her patient's distress, told Mike to get out. He protested, but she wouldn't hear it.

Feeling as if his head was about to explode, he ran into Dr. Singh at the nurse's station. The surgeon informed him that the operation had gone smoothly, and that Tom was doing better than expected.

"So does the have the virus or not?"

Singh made a face and shook his head. "He's done very well, but not beyond the capabilities of what can be explained by a normal healing process. He still has a slight fever, which indicates that infection is still present. It's still too early to say."

"Well, when can he come home?"

"Not for another four or five days, at least. Of course, it all depends on him. We won't keep him any longer than necessary."

"For his sake, I hope he doesn't heal too fast."

"Nor do I, Mr. Bane."

* * *

Mike arrived at Beasties a little after midnight, and updated Taffy on Tom's condition. The bar was nearly empty, and Taffy had sent Sheila home for the night, so he helped his uncle clean the place.

"Silas offered me a job at Mythica." He watched Taffy for his reaction, but the barman merely nodded. The silence stretched between them.

There was no polite way to say it. "I know you're Rafe's blood steward."

Taffy glared at him. "He tell you that?"

"No, I figured it out on my own."

Taffy attacked one of the tables with a wet bar towel, rubbing the surface with a lot more vigor than it needed. "You always were a clever lad. No doubt you want to offer your condolences. Well don't bother. I don't want your sympathy."

"Sympathy? How could you let him do that to you? Doesn't it bother you that he's feeding off you like some leech?"

"You don't know what you're talking about. He didn't want to do it."

Mike frowned. "He's a vampire, Taff. Of course he wanted to do it."

"No. He didn't. I blackmailed him into it. We'd been friends for years. When I got the diagnosis, I was ready to call it quits. Rafe figured out what I was planning. He made me promise not to kill myself. Found me a specialist up in Rochester and ran the bar on the nights I was too sick from the damned chemo."

Mike put his hand to his mouth.

Taffy's eyes met his. "So I guess the detective didn't know the story, after all." He looked away. "I was clean for three years, but it came back. Rafe takes a little blood from me every week. It's the least amount he can take that keeps the cancer away. So yes. I'm his blood steward."

His uncle concentrated on re-folding the bar towel. "Vampire saliva is the only thing that beats cancer. Rafe doesn't like using blood stewards. He doesn't want the responsibility; but when I asked, he didn't bat an eye. I suppose I could have gone to someone else and become one of those fang bangers, but I would have lost the bar. Rafe is my friend, Mike. Without him, I'd have been dead years ago."

AN OFFER NOT TO REFUSE

WHEN HE PULLED into his driveway, the bright sliver of a waxing moon had risen high enough in the sky so that it illuminated a lone figure seated in the old rocking chair on the front porch. Mike's heart thumped uncomfortably as he got out of the truck; the hairs on the back of his neck and arms stood on end.

The man uncrossed his legs, but made no other move. "I apologize if I startled you, Mr. Bane. I mean you no harm. May I call you Mike?"

"Where's the mutt?"

"Beg your pardon?"

"Where's the dog?"

"I assure you, I have seen no dog on this property all evening. I would speak with you on another matter."

"Who are you?"

"I read about your little encounter in the newspaper. I have it on good authority that you handled yourself most respectably. Am I to conclude that the authorities are not pressing criminal charges against you?"

Criminently. Not another damn bounty hunter. He ripped off his shirt. "You really think you can take me?"

"Excuse me?"

The man's confusion seemed authentic. *Who the hell is this guy?* "Didn't Clemente send you?"

"Ah, I apologize for the confusion. I seem to have forgotten my manners. I'm Ambrose Van Cleve. I believe you have already met my business associate, Rafe Fontaigne. We own and operate Mythica, the world's only supernatural amusement park. You are familiar with my estate, are you not?"

Another vampire. "I don't mean to be rude, but I'm kinda busy right now. What do you want?"

The vampire stepped to the edge of the porch, but approached no closer. He was short. Short as a woman; the scuffed work boots he wore added a bit to his height, but not much.

"I have a business proposition for you to consider."

Oh this is just perfect. "Sorry, pal; I'm all tapped out."

Van Cleve continued as if he hadn't spoken at all. "Every ten years, the Globus of New York calls a gathering of all the Pomps for a summit. We convene for three days to renew treaties and alliances, discuss issues, and as is often the case, realign territorial boundaries."

"Why are you telling me this?"

"This year the summit will be held in my territory; at Mythica. It's the first time in a century that we've met in such a rural location. It is a great honor for me and mine, but there is also great risk for the hosting nest as well. Any misstep on the host's part can result in a loss of face, or even territory."

A sense of dread washed over him. If the Pomps were coming here, no doubt Hector Clemente's brother would be accompanying the Pomp of Queens. *Shit.*

Van Cleve stepped off the porch. His light-colored eyes reflected silver in the pale moonlight. *Other than the Fae, I'm the largest single landowner in the Finger Lakes region. I'm a farmer, Mike. I work my land; it is everything to me. The land is eternal, like me.*" He smiled, but no emotion reached his eyes. "My land and my territory are what

I value above all else. I see that comes as a surprise to you."

"A little." This guy was nothing like Rafe. Power rolled of him in waves. Not like the wolves; this was something different. He smelled like...different. A hint of blood and disinfectant soap and dust. Mike wondered if the vampire could smell his blood.

"I pay taxes, I run a legitimate business. I have expenses. I pay my employees. My land and territory support my home and family."

Mike slapped at a mosquito on his arm. The silver eyes of the vamp flicked to the smear of blood streaked black across his forearm in the moonlight. *Oh that was smart. Bleeding in front of a vampire probably wasn't a good idea.* "I don't see what any of this has to do with me."

"The summit will begin on the first night of new moon in September. Up for grabs this year is a new territory. One of the Pomps upstate was killed a few years ago. His territory will be officially reapportioned at this year's summit. Disputed territory is almost always awarded to the strongest nest. I mean to secure that territory for my firstborn, Cobb. My enemies will be looking for any weakness or slight that would put me in a bad light."

The vampire stepped off the porch.

Mike held his ground.

"The Mythica wolf pack has lost several members. Our pack is no longer at optimal strength. We are actively recruiting experienced personnel, such as yourself."

Was this an interview? "I'm listening."

"I have been extremely selective as I've feathered my nest over the centuries. My family and friends have each and every one of them been cultivated for their unique skills and abilities. Similarly, your particular talents have attracted my attention."

Mike stiffened with alarm as he felt Tehuantl awaken. He didn't know what would happen if Tehuantl went up against a vampire, but he sure as hell didn't want to find out.

Van Cleve stepped closer. "I sense that you are a man who appreciates the direct approach. May I be blunt?"

Tehuantl pushed harder. Mike pushed back. He hoped Ambrose would get to the point. Soon. "Please."

"I need to remove the current Alpha wolf of the Mythica pack."

Mike stared at the vampire, dumbfounded. "Say what?"

"It's time for a change. After so much time at the helm, he has become excessively overbearing. We've lost a few pack members recently; I fear the wolves departed due to his increasingly bombastic personality. It's time for him to step down. I want to replace him with someone younger, more in tune with modern times and I need to do it before the summit."

"Why don't you just fire him?"

Van Cleve shook his head. "It's a delicate situation, one that I must insist be kept between us. As my chief of security, he holds the keys to the kingdom, so to speak. Vince isn't willing to retire, and the young wolf I'd like to install as Alpha may never be strong enough to defeat him. I read about how well you took care of those bounty hunters. I'm impressed. I think you might be just the person we're looking for."

"You can't believe everything you read."

"Don't be so modest. You come highly recommended."

"I'm looking for a job, but I have no desire to be Alpha."

The vampire steepled his hands. "That suits my needs perfectly. This is why you are so perfect for the contract. You join the pack, challenge him for pack leadership, and then surrender the title to my candidate."

He frowned. "You're talking about a fixed fight."

"Not at all. Your challenge for the Alpha position will be a fair fight, I assure you. But let's face it, no wolf pack will ever accept an were-cat as their Alpha. My pet wolf will challenge you immediately after you win, and you will surrender to him, thus allowing everyone to save face. The old Alpha will have lost his position in a fair fight, witnessed by his entire pack. He will honor his obligations by departing with his dignity intact; a mere changing of the guard. A new wolf will take his place. There will be no question that the pack will accept and follow the new Alpha. And you will walk away with a good deal of my money in your pocket."

Clearly, Van Cleve wasn't looking for him to stick around. Honoring an old soldier's sensibilities like that certainly appeared reasonable. He could use the money toward Tom's medical expenses. "Seems like a lot of effort to replace your Alpha."

"Alpha wolves continue to grow in strength and power for as long as they lead their pack. Vince Dazak has been the Alpha wolf at Mythica for nearly a century. The longer he remains alpha, the more difficult it becomes to make ah, necessary changes."

"I'm no expert, but don't you have to be a member of the pack to challenge the Alpha for pack leadership? Any Alpha that powerful would never let a guy like me into his pack in the first place."

Van Cleve shrugged. "Perhaps. But he would accept you as a lone wolf security consultant for the summit. You're perfect for the job."

It sounded good, but Tom had to come first. "I've got to be honest with you. I've got a family situation that's my top priority right now."

"You will of course be compensated for your services. I understand your godfather was injured recently and may have acquired the wolf virus. As a Mythica employee, you and your godfather will be covered with a lycanthropy insurance rider. I will have Felix backdate the date of employment to make sure all of his medical expenses are covered, regardless of whether or not he becomes afflicted."

A sense of relief flooded through him. This sounded too good to be true.

"Who is Felix?"

"Felix is my Number One blood servant. He is the CEO of Mythica Enterprises and my right hand man, if you will. It was his suggestion to hire you to carry out our little secret mission."

It was a good offer. Tremendous. Ironic; since he'd lost his job because of the false accusation that he was a lycan. A little payback seemed fair. "If you read the paper, you know there's a bounty out on me. But what's not in the paper is that the guy who issued the contract is the right hand man for the Pomp of Queens. I can't guarantee they won't try again. I don't want anyone else to get hurt."

The vampire's expression didn't change. "Unfortunate. Ivey can be difficult under the best circumstances. Yet another reason why you are perfect for the job. The enemy of my enemy is my friend. Very well, you will stay at the estate. I am confident I can guarantee your safety through the end of the summit."

"No can do. I've got my own place. And my godfather is going to need my help for a while."

The vampire looked around, obviously unimpressed. "Very well. I'll make you my blood steward. If you are my Number Three in actuality, neither Ivey nor any of her people can touch you."

Inside his head, the cat screamed, and his stomach tightened in revulsion. It took everything he had not to turn and run. *Of course there had to be a catch.*

"Thanks for the offer, but I'm not on the menu. Ever."

Van Cleve crossed the distance between them and had him by the throat before he could react. *Oh, right. Don't piss off the vampire.* It took real effort not to struggle; Van Cleve's hands felt like stone. The pulse in Mike's throat beat unhappily against the grip of Van Cleve's iron hand.

"You'll be dead in less time than it takes you to take your next breath if I so wish it. I do not beg for favors, Bane."

In the back of his mind, the cat put its ears back, and Tuhuantl swam to the surface, just behind his eyes. He gasped and shoved the shaman down in a panic.

"There has never been any question that you would do this for me. Do not imagine that this is a choice for you to make. I will not make you my steward without your consent. If you are successful, and all goes well, you may present your grievance against Diego Clemente to the Globus himself at the Arbitration Tribunal on the last night of the Summit. I will personally advocate for the nullification of the complaint against you. If you do not agree to take the contract, I will drain you this instant and present you to the Pomp of Queens myself."

"Hey, I wasn't arguing. I'll take the job. When you put it that way, how can I refuse?

THE EARTH MAGE OF MYTHICA

WORRY LAY LIKE the weight of a dead fish across Mike's shoulders the next morning. The mutt was still missing and cat's temper had not improved. Not a good way to start the day. He called the hospital, but they wouldn't say much more than to confirm Tom Jolley was still in intensive care. At least he wouldn't need to worry about the insurance any more. Tom would have the best care available. The idea that Tom could develop ALVS was a grim prospect he didn't want to think about. He couldn't fathom the idea of Tom turning into a mad wolf every month for the rest of his life. *Or until he couldn't stand it any longer and took things into his own hands.* He thought about calling Sarah, but couldn't bring himself to do it. *Coward.*

Tehuantl had been curiously silent since their late night encounter with Ambrose. Maybe the shaman hadn't been as interested in vampires as he'd originally thought. Maybe Ambrose had scared the shaman. If true, it would be the first time. *Hell, he scared me. A little.*

As for fighting Vince Dazak for pack dominance, there wasn't a wolf on the planet that was a match for the cat. No worries there. And since he only needed to subdue the Alpha, the only lasting injury would be to Vince's pride. But something about Ambrose's little motivational speech made Mike question the vampire's motive for getting rid of his Alpha. Ambrose seemed awfully determined.

He snorted. *Like I care.* It didn't matter to him in the least who ran the Mythica pack. *They're just a bunch of werewolves.* Silas was alright, he admitted. But as long as Ambrose was willing to cover Tom's medical expenses, his reasons for getting rid of Vince didn't matter.

Ambrose had told him to report to the security office at nine. The morning traffic was light, and drive out to Rushville took him less than twenty minutes. Based on what Ambrose had told him, he'd need no more than a week or two to settle in and become accepted by the pack; then he could issue a legitimate challenge to Vince.

He turned off main road and onto the mile-long, private drive leading to the Mythica estate. Most of the property was obscured from the main road by a thick screen of trees and dense shrubbery. Once he passed the trees, he drove through cultivated hills covered in grapevines. He followed the signs to the employee parking lot, likewise screened from the rest of the property by a tall hedge. The lot held only a few cars. He parked the truck and followed the signs to the employees entrance.

The door looked to be made of solid steel, set into a stone wall, which was thickly screened by an evergreen yew hedge. Security cameras covered every angle of the portal. The intercom button was located inside the mouth of a carved stone gargoyle. *Cute.* He gave his name and asked for Felix Tolland.

"You're hours too early for Felix," the disembodied voice answered. "He's not a much of a morning person."

"He's expecting me."

There was a click, and the door swung open. He was greeted by a digitally-enhanced voice with a heavy Transylvanian accent. "Good Morning, Meester Bane. Velcome to Mythica."

He grinned. Nice touch. He followed the path to a white stucco building, which housed the Operations Center and introduced himself to the officer on duty, a sizable chunk of muscle named Chaney. The logo on Chaney's black polo shirt caught his attention. It was a Ferris wheel and roller coaster against a night sky, lit up by fireworks. The motto read, 'Mythica, New York: Where Even the Dead Have Fun'. Hilarious.

When he was sixteen, he'd won the teenaged equivalent of the lottery and gotten a summer job at MacDonald's. For ten glorious weeks, he was one of the cool kids; that red, white, and yellow shirt made him the most popular kid in town. He even wore it when he wasn't working. The Mythica shirt had the same sort of vibe.

Chaney gave him some employment paperwork to fill out, but told him he didn't have the authority to process him as a new employee. "When Ambrose told you to be here at nine, he meant PM, not AM. Felix works the night shift, like most everybody else."

Oh, right. "I should have realized—."

Chaney grinned. "Rookie mistake, don't worry about it. Felix lives on the estate, but take my word for it, you do not want me to page him at this hour."

Mike shrugged. "I'll come back. Any chance you could show me around while I'm here?"

"No can do. I'm on duty, and until our Alpha gives the okay, the amusement park is off limits. Gordon's around, though. He can show you the rest of the grounds and the estate if you want."

"Gordon?"

Chaney nodded. "The Mage; he's our farm manager. Been here forever. He can tell you anything you want to know about the Van Cleves and the estate."

Why not? "I never met a Mage before."

"I saw him out in the vineyard this morning. I'll show you."

Chaney led the way back to the parking lot, and directed Mike through a small archway in the hedge. "That's him. Careful though, he'll talk your ear off, it you let him."

Mike thanked him and made his way through the vineyard toward a lone figure slowly pacing the perimeter of the field. His target looked to be in his fifties, tanned and fit, wearing a pair of cut-off jeans and a Milwaukee Brewers baseball cap. He held a forked stick in his hand. As Mike approached, he looked up and greeted him.

"You must be Mike Bane."

Mike nodded. "Gordon?"

"First day, eh?"

He grinned ruefully. "Yeah. Chaney told me I'm hours too early. I guess everybody else works the night shift?"

"Oh sure." Gordon sounded dismissive. "This time of year, the park is the big thing, but it's only open May through October." He waved his hand across the field. "The real heart of Mythica is right here."

Mike nodded, taking in the view. Sloping hills of precisely-aligned trellises stretched out around them in the warm morning light. Not even the sound of a passing car out on the main road reached them. "It's quite a place. And so peaceful. I never realized there was a winery here."

"Winery is a bit high-sounding for what we do here. Mostly, we're growers. The Van Cleves sell most of the harvest to other wineries, although Ambrose has romantic notions about our estate label."

"Oh yeah? You sell it locally?"

Gordon shook his head. "It's too precious to sell. It's reserved strictly for our valued guests and donors. We hold back less than two percent of the harvest for the making of Glamour. We only use the grapes harvested from vines growing closest to the wards. The ward-infused soil imparts the grapes with unique properties and exceptional flavor."

"Wards? You mean like Fae wards?"

"I admit my birthright, but my powers have outgrown my humble origins." Gordon bowed his head modestly. "I consider myself an earth Mage, Mike. I created these wards more than three hundred years ago as a way to stabilize the boundaries between the Van Cleve estate and the lands of the High Tor Fae. Now I maintain them to ensure they remain active."

He's foresworn. Using earth magic against the Fae, the guardians of the land, was taboo. In the eyes of the Fae, Gordon was a traitor. Even he knew that.

Gordon pointed to the craggy hills beyond the estate. "When Ambrose originally purchased the land, it overlapped territory claimed by the Fae of the High Tor. At the time, the indigenous clans were extremely war-like and hostile. Given the proximity of the Tor, the extreme territoriality of the Fae, and the continuous fluidity of their boundaries, the land was considered undesirable. Ambrose and I negotiated with the Fae. We got them to agree to the establishment of permanent boundaries between us. The wards delineate the blood oath boundary. Neither party can cross the wards without breaking the agreement."

Mike frowned. The talk of blood magick made him uncomfortable. He waved his hand over the ground beneath the split-rail fence marking the property line, then squatted down and grabbed a handful of loose soil in his fist. Oddly, the soil felt warm. "You mean you can feel me doing this?" From the hoot of Tehuantl's derisive laughter in the back of his head, he felt certain that the shaman didn't think much of Gordon's abilities or the wards.

"Yes, I can." Gordon nodded. "Think of the estate as having an invisible skin that acts the same as surface tension on a bowl of water. Anything that touches the water sends out ripples. I am sensitive to the ripples, and thus alerted to any attempts to cross the wards. The wards reach high into the sky and deep into the soil. The wards are most sensitive to Fae blood, but not even birds or earthworms pass undetected."

Mike indicated the forked stick the Mage was holding. "What's that for?"

"It's a dowsing rod. I use it to test the wards. Allow me to demonstrate." Gordon walked along the inner fence line, holding the forked ends of the stick in each hand, parallel to the soil. After thirty feet or so, the stick dipped toward the earth. The Mage slipped the stick into his back pocket, and held his cupped hands palm-down over the dirt; his eyes closed in apparent concentration.

"The wards are weaker here." He took a double handful of dirt out of the plastic bucket beside him, and sprinkled the moist soil over the area, then laid his hands over the spot for a moment, his eyes shut in concentration. When he was finished, he took up the twig again, and it held it's parallel position over the dirt. "That's better."

"So the magic fades over time?"

"On the contrary. This is earth magic. The earth is a powerful, living entity. I know how to tap into that power and put it to my own use. But like any living thing, it is affected by its environment. Earthworms and grubs ingest the warded earth and distribute it into the soil, widening the borders and diluting the wards at the same time." Gordon offered him a fistful of dark soil from the plastic bucket. "Feel this."

Mike held out his hand to receive the warded soil. A buzz of electricity thrummed around his fingers as soon as he touched it. He flung the dirt away, his skepticism evaporated. "Yikes."

Gordon returned a sly smile. "You must have more than a little Fae ancestry in your family tree. I suspected as much. Most cannot detect the presence of my blood spell."

"How the hell do you sleep at night?" He rubbed his hand against his shirt, trying to relieve the itch in his fingers. As he fought not to show his growing discomfort, he wished there was water nearby to wash off the taint that still clung to his skin. He looked at his hand, but there was no mark.

"I am attuned to disruptions, rather than normal flow. Much of it, I confess is a background hum. Disruptions occur in the presence of certain ah, essential elements."

"What, like crosses and garlic?"

He laughed. "Don't believe everything you read. No, I'm talking about specific earth elements. Fae blood, for one. Silver, for another, but I can sense any dense concentration of metal passing through the wards. I continually fine-tune the sensitivity of the wards as modern technology evolves. Obviously the automobile and electronics have presented challenges over the years, and I've had to make adjustments. The outer wards are less sensitive than the inner wards around the house and the park. I like to think that my earth magic is at least as sensitive as the manufactured security capabilities on the estate."

I doubt that. Even Tehuantl's scorn came through loud and clear. "You're telling me the wolf pack and the security technology aren't as effective your wards?" Ambrose had told him the Alpha and several of the Mythica pack members had been hand-picked for their military experience with security systems and electronic protection. The surveillance system he'd seen provided twenty-four hour vigilance. "Surely you've got to sleep sometime."

Gordon stiffened. "No surveillance camera or security technology in the world can detect the presence of magic. I was fully aware, for example, when you turned your truck onto the private drive leading to the estate this morning. Conversely, the wards muffle the sounds of the park to the outside world and screen certain areas of the estate from view to casual observers."

"Oh yeah? Like what?"

"The parking lots, for one. Certainly the hedges and woodlands keep curious eyes at bay, but neither the hedges nor the trees are actually as pervasive or dense as they appear. During Prohibition, I used a stronger veil on the building that housed the estate's distillery quite effectively. Again, something no *technology* is capable of doing."

He had no answer for that. In spite of Tehuantl's distain, Gordon's use of blood magic instinctively repulsed him. The guy gave him the creeps. He decided he did not want the tour of the estate after all. He made an excuse to leave and pretended he didn't see Gordon's extended hand when he said good-bye. He didn't want the Mage to touch him.

* * *

Mike headed over to the hospital. The nurse told him Tom was sleeping, but would not say whether or not his condition had improved. He asked for directions to Dr. Sarah Powers office, but was told she was out of the office on Wednesdays, so he settled himself on the chair next to Tom's bed.

In spite of Tehuantl's contempt for the Mage's abilities, Mike had to admit that his encounter with Gordon had unnerved him. He reminded Mike of a couple of the dealers he'd known. Like Hector Clemente. They both had that same sort of superior attitude; the same wily smile. Like they knew something that you weren't ever going to be smart enough to figure it out; and some day that something would come around and bite you in the ass.

If Gordon was Fae, why would he be working for vampires? They were traditionally bitter enemies. Why side with them against his own people? And he'd been so arrogant when he'd talked about his own abilities; all the while minimizing his dark repurposing of Fae magic.

The way he talked about the wards sounded a lot like what his father had told him about the Fae portals into the Tor. The presence of earthworms helped explain why the Tor boundaries had always been so variable. Tom had lived here all his life. Maybe he knew something about it. He decided to ask him about it when he woke up.

Tom's breathing was slow and steady. He looked better today. Maybe he'd dodged the bullet. Maybe they wouldn't need the wolf doctor after all. That might not be a bad thing. He had no intention of letting that sharp intellect of hers get any further peeks inside his head. He didn't trust himself around her. Funny; Yolanda didn't make him uncomfortable at all. Why couldn't she have been the wolf doctor?

Tehuantl's voice sounded in his ears. *This is not about you. Look at him.*

With a start, he realized that all of Tom's bruises were gone. Not just faded, but completely gone. *That can't be normal.* No wonder he looked so peaceful. He closed his eyes as the guilt washed over him. *Will you ever forgive me for what I've done to you?*

RULES OF ENGAGEMENT

MIKE THOUGHT FELIX Tolland was the very last person on the planet that anyone would expect to be the right-hand man of a vampire. He looked like he'd be more at home surrounded by his stamp collection than in this leather and chrome office, surrounded by an impressive display of Japanese fighting swords mounted in plexiglass cases along the walls.

"You don't have much experience with vampires, do you?"

"Well I've never been bitten, if that's what you mean." *And I'd like to keep it that way...*

The blood steward eyed him over the lenses of a pair of half-moon glasses. "How old do I look to you, Mr. Bane?"

Felix's name suited him perfectly. He looked like a freckle-faced, pencil-necked geek. His thin hair had no color to speak of, although it could arguably be called blonde. His skin looked like he'd spent his entire life under florescent lighting.

"Twenty-eight, maybe thirty, I guess."

"I was born in 1735. Youngest son in a family of six boys. I worked as a clerk in my uncle's accounting firm. I had no prospects, no money, and was dying of consumption when I agreed to become Ambrose's first blood steward, and have remained as his Number

One to this day. In exchange for a little of my blood on a regular basis, I was returned to perfect health and have prospered beyond my wildest dreams."

Perfect health my ass. The man had teeth like a meth addict. "I hear vampire spit is more addictive than crack."

Felix's fair skin reddened. "Blood stewards receive a minute quantity of an anti-coagulant from the vampire's saliva as it feeds. The side effects include a resistance to disease and an extended life for the donor, as long as the exchange is regularly maintained. Together, Ambrose and I have built Mythica into a model nest envied by vampires the world over."

Mike shook his head. "Aren't you worried Ambrose will turn you into a vampire?"

"Not at all. We have a perfect partnership. I have all the benefits of immortality without any of the restrictions on diet or sensitivity to the sun. Besides, I am far more valuable to Ambrose in my present condition that I would be as one of his offspring. Shall we proceed?"

"Sure." He ripped open the plastic packaging of one of the company's black polo shirts, like Chaney had worn.

"You will be employed by Mythica as an independent contractor. As a security consultant, you will report to Vince Dazak, the Alpha wolf of the Mythica pack. He will have complete control over your assignments. You will be given 'lone wolf' status within the pack. This means that you will abide by pack rules, but given the length of your contract, not required to officially join. There will be a short formal acceptance ceremony, where you will kneel before the Alpha with one or more members of the pack as witnesses, and you will agree to obey the Alpha and present your neck in a simple dominance ritual. Vince will say a few words, and you'll answer affirmatively. You'll accompany the pack in a ritual hunt, and then you're in. Should you violate any pack covenant prior to the first hunt, any and all members of the pack may punish you with impunity, up to and including death.

After the hunt, you will have auxiliary pack membership, and by pack law, only Vince will mete out discipline. Do you understand?"

He nodded grimly. The reality of what he was about to do hit him harder than he'd expected. Joining a wolf pack, even as a formality, was something he'd never imagined doing.

He'd been tested for ALVS several times, but the results had always come up negative. But being a shape shifter was one thing; joining a pack was like coming out of someone else's closet. He was exchanging one lie for another. This lie, once told, couldn't be taken back. It was a dangerous step. So far, the courts had ruled it was illegal to hunt and kill werewolves without a writ of execution, but it wasn't a crime for werewolves to kill each other.

"Got it." He took off his shirt and pulled the Mythica polo over his head. "How do we do this?"

"The rules are simple but Vince is a stickler, as well he should be. Above all, shifting into beast form at any time while on duty without explicit permission is forbidden. No exceptions.   Like Michael Jackson's Neverland Ranch, Mythica is an exclusive private club. We cater to humans. We entertain as many as a thousand guests per night, four nights a week, except during the nights of the full moon."

Mike whistled in surprise. "I had no idea."

Felix nodded. "We get all kinds here, from geeks to rock gods. Many of our members have planned their vacations a year or more in advance. They come here to have a good time and mingle with monsters. They want to be scared and thrilled, not bloodied. While we do try to satisfy our guests every possible expectation and fulfill every supernatural fantasy, we cannot allow them to be harmed or threatened in any way. Vince will fill you in on the specifics, but essentially, we look to our security staff to anticipate potential problems and keep disruptions in the park to a minimum."

Mike opened the glossy brochure Felix handed him. "What kind of disruptions are we talking about here?"

"Nothing too exotic. Guests are not allowed to bring weapons into the park, but most come in costume and occasionally something is missed. We also serve alcohol, and have had the occasional problem with drug use on the premises. While we do not report the violator, the guest is escorted out of the park, and their membership is cancelled permanently. If there is nothing more, I believe we are done here."

"Ambrose mentioned that he would take care of my godfather's medical bills."

"Already taken care of it. These copies are yours to keep." Felix slid a manila folder across the desk."

Relief flooded through him. "Thanks." He stood to leave.

"I strongly suggest you make a concerted effort to be friendly to the other pack members. It will make it easier for you to issue a legitimate Alpha challenge if there are other members of the pack who will support you."

"In other words, obey the rules, don't piss off the pack." He felt certain Striper Dave could help him make friends, and he'd already met Silas. On the other hand, Trick and his cronies might cause problems. "So how do I go about issuing the challenge?"

Felix leaned forward conspiratorially. "I caution you again about revealing any of what we are about to discuss with Vince or anyone else. Vince has been part of the Mythica family for decades. Ambrose has no desire to hurt the man or deprive him of his dignity by circumventing the accepted means for replacing him as Alpha."

"Understood. When do I fight him?"

"Once you have completed the initiation hunt with the pack, you are free to issue a formal challenge at any time. This is to be a fair fight for Alpha succession. When Vince yields to your superior abilities, he will offer his bared neck for your mercy. You will release him and he will turn over his keys, badge, and access codes and be escorted out of the park. Before the pack convenes for the ritual hunt to cement your leadership, you will bare your neck in submission to Ambrose's choice for Vince's replacement."

"And who would that be? Won't I have to fight him too?"

Felix shook his head. "Vince will be naming Trick Adaire as his new Beta wolf tomorrow. As long as you yield to Trick before the pack hunt, Trick will become the new Alpha. You do understand, of course, that we would like to have this business resolved quickly; well before the upcoming summit."

Trick. Of all people, why that guy? "Not a problem. I'm not interested in stretching this thing out any longer than I have to. The sooner the better, as far as I'm concerned."

Felix seemed pleased. He led the way out of his office to the reception area, where Mike immediately spotted Yolanda seated behind the desk. "We'll get you micro-chipped after you talk to Vince. With the chip, you'll be able to access all of the public and business areas of the park. Vince will determine your duty assignment. The private grounds of the family estate and vaults are all off limits, but there is a clubhouse area reserved exclusively for pack use. It has a gym, showers, and locker area as well as access directly onto the Tor for pack hunts."

"Sounds good. I guess I'm ready to talk to Vince now. What's he like?"

Felix's eyes slid away. "He's loyal to a fault, but a stickler for detail. Don't piss him off and don't underestimate him. I suppose you could say that about Ambrose and myself as well, come to think of it."

"Where do I find him?"

"I'll take him." Yolanda came around the desk and slipped her hand though his arm. She winked at him and his heart did a happy dance. She was wearing pink lipstick. Even Tehuantl and the cat seemed to approve. Tall, dark, and voluptuous. *Just my type.*

"Come on. I'll give you the grand tour." Her hands were warm; her grip powerful.

"I'm all yours."

She sighed theatrically and tossed back her long hair. "They always are."

WHERE EVEN THE DEAD HAVE FUN

MIKE FOLLOWED YOLANDA through the hedge tunnel leading from the operations center into the park. As they emerged from the tunnel, the sensory overload stopped him in his tracks. The park echoed with a sudden cacophony of sights, sounds, and smells. As he stared, Yolanda's low laugh reached him in places where the neon ribbons of light, the scent of the food court and the screams of the crowd couldn't.

Across a broad cobblestone plaza a huge red Ferris Wheel stood as the centerpiece of a real amusement park. Lit with thousands of tiny red lights, each car in the rotating structure was designed in the shape of a fang; the overall effect appeared to be that of a bloody circular saw. Behind it, a wooden coaster raced along a snake-like black track streaked with orange and purple neon lighting. Cars filled with dozens of enthusiastic people screamed at every dip and turn.

On a tightrope strung some thirty feet above the plaza, an acrobat dressed as a harlequin danced with a sinuous ballerina in a froth of pink. As he watched, they bared their fangs and hissed to an appreciative crowd gathered below. *Vampires.*

The night air throbbed with the sounds of a heavy metal band, while the rich aroma of barbecued meats, kettle corn, and onion blossoms vied for his attention. His stomach growled.

He followed her through the crowd as a pair of jugglers on stilts tossed glowing balls of blue fire into the air above their heads. *This is so cool.* "I never knew this place existed. I mean, I guess I always knew it was here, but not like this. You can't see or hear anything from the road."

"There are twenty rides in the park, but until you pass through the entrance or the security tunnel, you'd never know it. It's because of the wards."

"My god, how long has this place been here?"

They waited for a rowdy crowd of people to pass by. Leggy women strutted their stuff in tattered black lace and big hair, their stiletto heels adding to the witchy, spidery look of their ensembles. Men dressed in pinstripes, bowlers, and metal-studded leather swaggered behind, admiring the view.

"The Ferris Wheel came first; it was built around the turn of the century." She pointed out the carousel; a magnificently carved folly of dragons, griffins, sphinxes, and other monsters circling a mirrored, central axis. "That's my favorite. It was added in the twenties, I think. Varrick and Santino carved the monsters themselves. Most of the rest of the rides came in the 1960s. Tryffin told me they remodeled the whole park about twenty-five years ago, and that's what you see here."

Mike shook his head in disbelief. "I grew up here. I never knew about any of this. It looks like some wild carnival from the Twilight Zone."

She laughed. "It is fun, isn't it?"

They strolled through the crowded sector, past the Tilt 'n Whirl, the spinning barrel, and a host of other mechanical carnival rides, all painted in nightmare colors, emblazoned with the Mythica logo. The theme was definitely thrills and chills of the supernatural variety, with a wry nod to the dead.

Yolanda spotted Trick skulking nearby and waved him over.

"Mike, this is Trick Adaire. He's Tryffin's head mechanic and our new Beta."

Mike cringed inwardly. The itch of her pheromones riffled across his skin when she said Trick's name. She liked the guy. *Great.* "We've already met."

Trick pushed at him with his power. "Hello pussy."

Trick never took his eyes off Yolanda, and she was giving it back as good as she got. Between him and the she-were, it was all he could do not to scratch.

The touch of Yolanda's hand on his bare skin eased the buzzing sensation. She knew exactly what she was doing. She was enjoying this.

"Mike here is joining the pack. Isn't he cute?" She ran her hand up the inside of his arm. It felt good.

He felt like an idiot standing there. He fought to keep his cool. Trick might be an asshole, but he wasn't the guy he was here to fight. "Hey, I'm only a lone wolf. Just a contractor."

Trick cut him a hard glare. "And you never thought to mention that the other night." He was leaking pheromones like a sieve. He even smelled angry. "Your Alpha is looking for you, Yolanda. You better get your sweet little ass over there."

Mike felt the cat growl silently in his head. There were some heavy vibes going on between these two. He glanced around, looking for an escape.

"Vince is not my Alpha, and neither are you. At least not yet," She smirked her disapproval at Trick. "I'm like you, Mike. I'm a lone wolf too. I haven't decided whether to join the pack or not." Her gaze settled on his mouth. "I'm still considering my options." She made a face. "Come on."

Mike allowed her to drag him away as Trick glared at them unhappily.

Ribbons of multicolored neon lit up the entire area, and a

boardwalk between the attractions followed bright avenues lit by antique streetlamps. People pressed against them on all sides, but the lines for the carnival rides were short. Costumed patrons strolled past in every kind of macabre outfit imaginable, from goth to Victorian; apocalyptic steampunk to zombies.

"You are taking me to Vince Dazak, right?"

Yolanda gave him a sideways look and smiled. "In a minute. There's something I want to show you first."

Were-women were rare as hen's teeth, Mike knew. Packs without females probably recruited aggressively. Yolanda could probably do anything within reason to the pack or any of its members without fear of reprisals. He wasn't certain of the pack protocol for dealing with a female lone wolf, but didn't want to risk offending her.

She pulled him away from the bright lights of the amusements, back toward the central plaza and the sound of heavy metal music. The pounding base and drums beat out a familiar dark melody, but the band covering it had made it their own, and he couldn't quite place the tune.

The concert hall came into view; a gloomy pseudo-gothic building with Victorian overtones. A monstrous, multi-armed, multi-jointed mechanical sea creature beckoned to passers-by from its perch on the steeply pitched copper-plated roof.

"What's that," he asked.

"This way." She jerked his arm to the right, and led him down a calmer, quieter side street, lit with red paper lanterns. Her musky perfume smelled even better than the roasting meat. "The theatre is this way"

She was tall. Probably close to six feet. Muscular, but on her it looked good. She had the kind of body that demanded close attention. This was no airy fairy princess.

The cobbled street curved past a sweet pub called the Bloody Fang and widened into a courtyard populated with colorful tent pavilions.

The aroma of food was stronger here.

They stopped in front of a yellow tent. The sign out front posted appointment times available for palmistry readings. This part of the park was relatively quiet and less well-lit.

"What are we doing here?" He wondered if she was playing with him.

"The white tents are food vendors, the striped are for souvenirs, and the yellow are for um, personal services." Yolanda's teeth gleamed like pearls in the relatively dim lighting in this part of the park. "Follow me." She led him past another yellow tent offering tantric massage to a small red pavilion, and ducked inside.

Just a quick look won't hurt. Another minute or two wouldn't matter. He slipped inside.

He caught a quick glimpse of Persian carpets and poufy pillows scattered about, and then she was pressing up against him with her lush body and full lips. It had been a long time since he'd held a woman in his arms, and even longer since one had kissed him like that. It was better than he imagined.

Her quick tongue teased, her teeth nipped at his lips. She slipped her hand down between them, and made a satisfied sound in her throat as she felt him respond.

He grabbed her wrist when she reached for his zipper. The vibe wasn't right. There was something else going on. "Wait," he protested. "I don't think this is a good idea."

"Why not?" She stepped back and pulled off her shirt. He was struck speechless when she unhooked her bra and dropped it onto the floor. She had a tattoo of a wolf howling beneath the twin full moons of her breasts. "Don't tell me you're not interested."

He rubbed his mouth.

Her eyes gleamed hard in the dim light, as she shimmied out of her tight black jeans. *Oh dear god,* she was wearing a leopard-print thong.

She held his gaze as she deliberately unzipped him and took him in hand. She chuckled, low and sexy.

"No one says no to me. Not you, not Vince. Nobody." She gave him a firm squeeze.

In spite of the warning bells going off in his head, all he could think of was getting closer to her in the most physical, intimate way possible. *What the hell.* He let her pull him down to the pillowed floor. The feel of her smooth skin beneath his fingertips was amazing. She sighed, and his focus narrowed into the now of the moment. She angled herself beneath him and bit his ear.

But before either of them had a chance to get to really get going to where they both wanted to go, the tent flap opened.

"Hello pussy. Remember me?"

Mike jumped as if he'd been burned. Standing in the doorway was Trick and what could only be Vince Dazak, the massive Alpha werewolf of Mythica.

BIG MAD WOLF

HEAT RADIATED FROM Vince like a furnace blast.

The Alpha was the most powerful-looking man he'd ever seen. He made Mr. Universe look like a minnow. Mike scrambled to his feet as Tehuantl's laughter echoed in his head.

The smirk on Yolanda and Trick's faces left him no doubt that this little stunt had been their idea. Embarrassment and fury warred within him. *Of course* she hadn't been serious. Two other were-men stood behind Vince, their faces stretched in silent laughter. *How stupid can you get?* Not inside the park for more than an hour and he'd stepped into a big stinking pile of wolf pack.

Alpha pheromones filled the tent. The huge Alpha was rigid with fury. He was older than Mike expected, his short blond hair silvered with grey.

He hurriedly tucked himself back into his pants, feeling like an idiot schoolboy. The urge to kneel before Vince was nearly overwhelming. He fumbled with his zipper, but no one was paying much attention to him. All eyes were glued to Yolanda, as she took her time getting dressed. Her eyes and fixed smile never once left Vince's face.

"Don't be mad at him," she tossed her head as she glared defiantly at the Alpha. "This is your fault Vince. Any Alpha who won't or *can't* consummate-."

"Shut up Yolanda." Stone-faced with anger, Vince's presence seemed to suck the oxygen right out of the tent.

Right beside him, Trick was busting at the seams for action. "You can't let him get away with this, Vince. Let me teach him a lesson. He's insulted the pack and violated protocol. Let me take care of this." He bounced on the balls of his feet as if he could barely contain himself, earning a demure smile from Yolanda. Trick was taller than Vince, but the other man easily outweighed him.

"When Ambrose told me he'd promised you lone wolf status, I let it pass," Vince said. "But neither Ambrose or Felix have authority over my pack. You're in my territory without explicit permission, Bane."

Mike reddened, kicking himself again mentally for his own stupidity. *What the hell was I thinking?* Felix had warned him. The best he could hope for now was to come clean. "I was stupid. I have no excuse. I apologize."

A flicker of surprise flashed across Vince's face. The oppressive tension in the tent eased, even as the other members of the pack sniggered behind him. Vince held up his hand for quiet.

Trick shouldered his way forward. "Listen to him; he's pathetic. No real wolf would ever apologize. He's weak." Agitation pheromones invaded the close space. "I say we give him a taste of pack justice." Yolanda grinned at him conspiratorially and licked her lips.

A sense of incredulity flooded through him. *She set me up.* His face burned. The two of them planned this whole charming scene.

"Knock it off, you two." The anger in Vince's voice sounded more like an irritated father now. His power washed over Mike, encouraging him to calm own. Everyone relaxed.

So this is what real Alpha dominance fells like, Mike mused. *I wonder why it affects me too.* Trick was just a piker by comparison.

With a start, he realized that Vince could decide to boot him out right now. Felix had told him that Vince was ex-army, and the guy still wore his military flat-top. No doubt Vince ran his pack the same way and would not respond to anything less than a direct appeal for discipline. He'd have to make this right; to ask Vince for his pardon without making himself look any weaker than he already had. If he could get Vince to deliver that discipline himself, he might stand a chance of being accepted into the pack. All he'd have to do would be to bare his throat to the Alpha, whereas if he went up against the entire pack, he wouldn't have a chance.

"Look, I know I am the trespasser here. What do I need to do? I'll accept whatever punishment you think I deserve, Alpha, but let's get this over with."

"He was going to fuck your bitch, boss. You can't let him get away with that."

"Shut up, Phelan. Yolanda isn't pack."

"I've made my choice, Vince. Why won't you?" Yolanda's protest sounded bitter in Mike's ears. "I refuse to beg for it. Take me as your mate or I swear I'll find someone in this pack who will and we'll have a new Alpha. One with balls." She reached for Vince's belt buckle, but he slapped her hand away,

"Knock it off," Vince cautioned. "This is not the time or the place, and you know it. I'll deal with you later, girl." He jerked his head at her. "Out."

Yolanda shot Vince a nasty look, but departed without a word.

Everyone seemed to breathe a little easier.

"You've put me in a tight spot, Bane, and I resent the hell out of you for pulling this stunt right now. Half my pack has been with me less than six months. They're inexperienced. I lost my Beta a month ago, and in spite of what you may have heard, I haven't replaced him yet." He glared pointedly at Trick.

He wants this to blow over as much as I do. Yolanda and Trick were both troublemakers. The whole pack must be in pretty bad shape.

"Yolonda is a pack prospect," Vince explained. "It's the first time we've had a female interested in joining, and as you can imagine, the tensions around here are stretched pretty thin. We're all in a 'getting to know you' stage. She has the right to choose anyone she wants, and if she decides to stay with the pack, her choice may very well decide the Alpha leadership."

Mike nodded. "I appreciate the explanation."

"This for not for your benefit." Vince turned to face the uniformed were-men gathered around the entrance. "I'm explaining this for everyone. I will dispense pack discipline tomorrow afternoon at three in the amphitheater. You guys can spread the word. Until then, I want everyone back at their assigned stations." The group of security officers drifted away, except for Trick, who was still standing next to Vince, nursing his outrage. "You too Adair. Back to your post."

Trick melted away without further protest.

Impressed, Mike wondered what was really going on here. Vince didn't appear to be anything like the guy Ambrose had described.

When Vince spoke, his voice was utterly calm "I'll see you back here tomorrow afternoon, Bane. Until then, get the hell out of my territory."

* * *

The mutt was waiting for him when he got home, and the relief Mike felt when he saw Farley coming out to greet him chased away most of the bitterness he felt for being fooled by Yolanda. The deerhound held his head low as if to apologize for his earlier cowardice. Mike knelt down and hugged the big dog to him; his pleasure sparking a teary-eyed response. He cradled the dog's shaggy face in his hands.

"You had me worried, big guy. I'm sure glad that big bad wolf didn't catch you." He checked the dog all over, but didn't find a mark on him. "If anything happened to you; well, I'm just glad you're okay."

He'd been four when his mother had died; five when his father had taken his punishment for wandering out onto the Tor. His father's best friend, Tom Jolley and his wife Florence, had taken him and the dog without hesitation. Farley wasn't really Dad anymore; there had never been any sense that the dog was sentient, or anything other than a well-loved and loyal family pet.

To people who didn't know any better, he was the black hound of the Tor or just Farley, a stray who'd been around as long as anyone could remember. Florence had passed away years ago. As far as he knew, only Tom, Uncle Taffy, and a few old-timers still remembered Farley Bane. But the thought of losing him had been almost as unbearable as relinquishing those boyhood dreams that one day he'd be able to lift his father's punishment.

He let himself into the house and fed the hungry deerhound. He checked the fridge, but it was too late for dinner, anyway. Maybe he'd go out to breakfast tomorrow. He unfurled the cat and followed the mutt toward the bedroom. Mike felt the jaguar's satisfaction echo within as he hopped onto the bed and curled himself contentedly around his friend. *Welcome home, Farley.*

THE SCENT OF BACON

EGG HEAVEN WAS an all-day breakfast café, and like the bait shops on his morning route, was running full tilt at this hour of the morning. The line of people waiting for a seat was out the door. Mike parked in the shade across the street. He left Farley in the truck and went inside hoping for a seat at the counter, but stopped when he caught sight of Sarah Powers waving to him from a booth near the window. He groaned inwardly, but it would be rude not to join her.

He slid onto the vinyl seat across from her. She smelled of bacon and coffee; mighty good. Dark crescents circled beneath her eyes, but otherwise she appeared chipper and cheerful.

"I stopped in to see Tom last night," she said. "He's going to make it. He's healing faster than they expected. They're moving him out of intensive care today. Isn't that great?"

She wore her short hair edgy and a little spikey on top. Except for the blue eyes and red lipstick, she looked like a pixie.

"Healing that fast can't be good."

"It's still too early to tell if he's been infected," she said. "It's within the boundaries of normal. Dr. Singh is optimistic."

"I thought you were the werewolf expert." He snagged a piece of bacon from her plate.

Her coffee cup paused halfway to her mouth. "I'm an ALVS therapist Mike, not a physician. I teach lycans how to control their beasts once the disease takes hold. Until it becomes evident that Tom's metabolism has mutated, or the next full moon, I am merely one of several consulting professionals to Dr. Singh."

"Sorry." She was strawberry parfait to Yolanda's smoky barbecue. "I didn't mean to offend you. I do have a question."

Her brilliant smile told him all was forgiven. "Ask me anything."

He felt Tehuantl's prurient interest stir, and shoved him back down as he cleared his throat. "I've noticed that some weres have the ability to exert influence over others. I've even felt it directed toward me. Is that wolf pheromones? It seems like the more powerful the wolf, the stronger the affect of the pheromones. Is that right?"

"To a certain extent, yes. One of the ways in which the lycanthrope virus alters human physiology is through changes in the hypothalamus and vomeronasal organ, which become hyperactive and much more efficient at emitting and receiving signals. The longer a lycan lives, the more functional and sensitive the organs become."

"So are you saying that a person who has been a werewolf for decades, say, could control everyone around him? Bend them to his will? Like mind control?"

She shook her head. "There is no evidence that humans are susceptible to werewolf pheromones, but lycans are sensitive to the effect. We do not yet fully understand the mechanics, but pressure with the tongue on the roof of the mouth stimulates the Jacobsens organ. When the stimulation is coupled with an emotional thought, intention, or phrasing, the pheromone is released. However, for whatever reason, lycans with higher status within their social structure produce higher levels of pheromones, proportionate to their standing in the pack hierarchy. Even a newly-infected werewolf can produce massive pheromone levels if he or she holds Alpha status or even Beta in the pack."

"Do you think cats would be susceptible?"

She nodded slowly. "Very likely. All felines have a well-developed Jacobson's organ and the Flehmen grimace response is well-documented in lions and all big cats. In fact, many predators share this sensory ability to transmit and recognize pheromones as a form of non-verbal communication. Cross-species comprehension has not been studied, but it would not be surprising."

That explained his reactions to Vince, and to a lesser extent, Trick. "Thanks. That helps, I guess."

He flinched when she reached across the table and took his hand. "I do want to help you, Mike."

He pulled his hand away, and the arrival of the waitress forestalled any further discussion. His stomach growled as he ordered. Coffee and a bacon cheese omelet with hash browns, and an extra side of sausage. Mike kept his hands on his coffee cup and made small talk about Tom and his recovery until his food arrived.

She drank her coffee and sat in silence as he ate. He kept his mouth full and his head down, but it didn't seem as if she was going to give up easily.

The food worked miracles. As he pushed aside his cleaned plate, he felt good enough to linger a few minutes longer. Clearheaded, but not enough to let her browbeat him into becoming her patient. Better to change the topic of conversation altogether.

"The reason I asked about the pheromones is because I've recently been around a lot of werewolves. I got a job at Mythica."

She frowned. "That's not a good place for you."

He found himself resenting her disapproval. "What would you know about it?"

She glanced out the window before meeting his gaze. "I man the community outreach booth out there for the hospital on Saturday nights. A lot of people coming into the park have questions about getting help for family members and friends with ALVS."

"And?"

She shrugged. "If you want to learn about pheromones and the dominance an Alpha exerts over his pack, there is no one more powerful than Vince Dazak. You could learn a lot from him." She covered her empty plate with her napkin. "But he can't help you with your beasts, and until you learn to control them, you're not safe to be around humans."

He reddened. "I'm not a lycan. Believe me, I'm nothing like them. Besides, it's just a short-term contract to get Tom's medical expenses covered." Damn, why didn't he keep his mouth shut when he had the chance?

She gazed up at him, her blue eyes holding his. "Tom told me what happened to you. I also feel it when I touch you. You're different. But you're still losing the fight with your beasts."

How did she do that, he wondered. How did she turn a simple statement back around to suit her purposes? He did not want to have this conversation.

"I've treated hundreds of lycanthropes, Mike. I told you, I have a gift. I can look into people and read their spirit. I teach people to communicate with their beasts. If the human and beast spirits don't converge, the beast will take over and the human spirit will succumb. But it doesn't have to be that way."

He looked around for the waitress, but didn't see her.

"I sense more than one beast in you. Your spirit has shrunk to accommodate the others. You have allowed your own spirit to become subservient to them, and locked yourself away from them. As a result, there are at least two others who are now stronger than you.' She sat back in her seat. "You know I'm right."

He stared at her. "How can you possibly know that?"

"If you don't integrate your spirit with the others that inhabit your soul, you will lose yourself. Both of your beasts are stronger than you are. I'll bet you don't even sleep in human form any more. You've *got* to let me help you."

She looked so sincere. She was smart and attractive, but her fragile humanity terrified him. But where Yolanda triggered feelings of lust, his attraction to Sarah seemed to rouse bloodier hungers in the cat and Tehuantl. They thought of her as prey. He couldn't trust himself to be alone with her. *Where the hell is that waitress?*

"I know it's hard for you to hear what I'm trying to tell you right now, but you need to listen to me. To put it simply, you must make friends with your beasts."

"I've got to get going." He pulled his wallet out and laid a twenty on the table.

"Your spirit is fading, Mike. I know you're not lycan but you *must* listen to me. Lycans resume their true human form during REM sleep. You don't. In fact, I'd be willing to be you haven't slept in human form for a very long time." She grabbed his hand again.

He jerked away from her as if burned. "Stop it. Look, I don't know how you know these things lady, but one of those spirits you're talking about is a psychotic sociopath." He lowered his voice. "The last thing I want to do into integrate anything of mine with him. He is a killer. Do you understand?" He leaned forward to make sure she heard every word. "He likes to kill people, Sarah. He's a cannibal. He rips their still-beating hearts out of their chests and he eats them." He gripped the edge of the table so she wouldn't see his hands shaking.

"This is important, Mike. You have got to integrate your spirit with your beasts."

How could he make her understand? She was way out of her depth here. She had no idea what kind of monster he'd been living with. And if he told her the truth, she'd--.

He stood to leave. "You can't possibly understand what you're asking."

"I'm trying to help you. He's the one in control right now, you just aren't aware of it. I'll bet he can communicate with your other beasts better than you can." She stood and reached for him again, her blue-green eyes blazing with intensity. "You know I'm right. Let me help you!"

"Keep your voice down." The last thing he wanted was to let Tehuantl get anywhere near her. He fought the urgent need to run like hell. "Look, I don't need your help. I'm real glad Tom is doing better, and that you'll be there to help him if he needs it. But right now I've got some things I need to take care of."

"I know what I'm talking about, Mike. I could hypnotize you; facilitate the conversation. I've helped hundreds –."

He didn't wait around to hear the end of it.

* * *

Tom had been moved into a private room. He smiled wanly as Mike pulled the chair closer to the bed. Although Tom's neck was still covered in bandages, the tracheotomy tube had been removed, and Tom could speak, albeit in a whisper.

"I know you feel guilty about this, son. I want you to know I don't blame you. Not one bit."

Mike gripped his outstretched hand. "I'll make it up to you. I swear--."

"Stop that. I was in the wrong place at the wrong time, that's all. I could have just as easily been hit by a truck. It's just bad luck."

Mike brushed his godfather's forehead. It felt a little warm. "How are you feeling?"

Tom gave him a wan smile. "You mean do I feel furry? No. I feel like I've been hit by that truck, and that's the honest truth."

"Dr. Singh says you're doing well. He's optimistic. Try not to worry."

"It's not me I'm worried about. It's you."

"I'm fine Pops. I'm not leaving. I'm going to take care of you."

"I don't want you out there at Mythica. The Fae have been battling Van Cleve and that pet Mage of his out there for centuries. Gordon was banished by the Fae for tricking some of the High Tor folk into slavery; forcing them into blood stewardships for the Van Cleves. They're sworn enemies."

"Whatever happened between the vampires and the Fae three hundred years ago doesn't affect me, Pops. I have nothing to do with any of it. And besides, it's just for a couple of months, and I'll still be able to take care of you. It's good money, and they've even agreed to cover your medical expenses if you develop lycanthropy. Not that it's for certain," he added hastily.

"I don't care. They're like ticks. Once those vampires get their claws in your business, you'll never get rid of them."

"I thought you'd be relieved." The nurse had warned him about not saying anything to upset the patient. No need to say anything about the plan to throw Vince out of the pack. "They've got a bunch of big-wigs coming in for a meeting in a few weeks and have asked me to consult on their security." It was only a little lie.

"They've already got that big Alpha wolf Dazak over there. What do they need you for?"

"They're short-staffed. Ambrose said Vince needs some experienced help." He took the glass back from Tom and put it on the table. "Although the guy seems alright to me. Bit of a hard-ass, maybe."

Tom snorted. "Vince Dazak need help? He ran that place for years all by himself. Let me tell you, he straightened out a lot of hanky-panky shenanigans going on out there before."

"What kind of shenanigans?"

Tom shrugged. "Gambling, for one. Loose women. You know they've got their own still up there. That Gordon is some kind of moonshiner."

"Oh come on, Pops. They ran a speakeasy during Prohibition." He'd never realized Tom was such a prude. "It's a private amusement park now. Kind of cool, actually."

"Van Cleve fed off his slaves right up until the emancipation. I'm not saying he was the only slave owner in the north, but he hung onto his longer than most. And your Dad used to say they kept the Fae on as hostages."

"It's nothing like that now. Just a lot of people having fun out there. Besides, that stuff is all in the past. It doesn't mean anything anymore."

"You're wrong, son." Tom grabbed his arm. His grip was as powerful as a much younger man. "The Fae of the High Tor never forgive. The feud between the Fae and the Van Cleves has been going on for centuries. How do you think the Fae would react, knowing Farley Bane's son is fraternizing with the Van Cleves? You think they'd ever be inclined to lift that Tor hound's glamour?"

He stared at Tom, shocked. "That's not fair. Don't be saying that."

Tom sighed. "To hear your Dad tell it, the Fae are quick to anger on an insult, slow to act on a promise, and they never, ever forgive. Think about it. Promise me you'll stay away from those blood stewards; they're the worst. And that Mage especially." Tom fell back against the pillow, pale and shaking, his eyes closed. "The Van Cleves are blood suckers, Mike. Why are you defending them?"

"I'm not." Mike picked a piece of lint off the blanket. "I don't know, Pops. I guess I just don't want you to worry." *I should never have told him. He's still too sick for any of this.* He tried another tack. "Guess who I had breakfast with? Dr. Powers."

"Sarah?" Tom's face smoothed out and little crinkles formed at the corners of his eyes. His eyelids fluttered and closed. "She's something else isn't she? A fine woman. I can tell she likes you. A man would have to be some kind of fool--."

He stayed until the snoring started. He kissed the older man's warm forehead. "Love you, Pop. I'll be back later."

GLADIATOR

SILAS MET HIM at the Mythica employee entrance. "Well, well. Look who's here," he grinned.

Mike could feel the heat rise in his face. "Shut up," he grumbled. "Let's get this thing over with,"

"Hold on there, Romeo." Silas handed him a case of energy drinks to carry. "What's your rush?"

Silas looked like the cat who'd just stolen the cream. "What are you so happy about," Mike asked.

The were-man shrugged and looked at his shoes, but couldn't keep the amusement off his face. "Nothin'. I'm just glad you showed up, that's all. Chaney was getting pretty good odds against it."

Mike hoisted the case under one arm and shoved his way past Silas into the park. "Glad to be of service."

Silas clapped him on the back. "Don't feel bad Mike; she's done it to most of us."

"Is that supposed to make me feel better?" He shook his head. "I can't believe she and Trick planned it."

"If it helps, Trick was her last victim."

Mike brightened. "Well yeah, maybe that does help a little." They reached the east gate on the other side of the park. "You seem entirely too cheerful about this."

Silas swiped his keycard through the reader and held the door open. "You kiddin'? With you showing up, Chaney and I stand to make a bundle. Besides, it's been weeks since we've had any whup-ass around here. Everybody's looking forward to this. Hell, Vince even got the chef over at the Bloody Fang to bring in eats afterward. It's going to be a party."

"Now isn't that just wonderful," he muttered.

He followed Silas down a winding game trail through the woods behind the park. They passed a prefab employee clubhouse, which Silas told him held a lounge, workout room, and showers for the pack. A hundred yards past the clubhouse, the trail widened, and opened onto a terraced area, where more than a dozen pack members waited.

Mike stepped down three levels into a natural arena, roughly fifty feet across. Silas, Striper Dave, and five other pack members sat in a loose cluster on the right-hand side of the arena near Vince. Each were-man in this group appeared alert, calm, and relaxed. On the opposite side of the arena, a sullen, fidgety group including Striper Dave's buddy Steve-o from the bait shop sat in a loose group around Trick Adaire. A split pack.

He took off his shirt. Yolanda, the lone female, sat all alone in a middle tier equidistant from both groups. She smiled at him, but he ignored her; hating how she'd manipulated him so easily.

Silas had assured him that this was nothing more than a ritualized dominance slam-dance. He would take a few good licks and demonstrate his respect for the Alpha. The only pain inflicted would be to his ego.

At this hour of the afternoon, the sun and humidity were intense. He slapped at the sweat files mobbing his hair. Vince raised his arms for silence as he stepped into the arena, wearing only an old pair of army green sweat pants.

"This lone shifter has crossed into our territory and violated pack protocol. Many of you," Vince nodded to the agitated group around Trick. "Have expressed your outrage and demanded a melee of retribution."

Mike shifted his feet uneasily. A melee would mean an all-out attack by the entire pack. The cat wouldn't have a chance. Tehuantl...

"Other, cooler heads have pushed for a more reasonable response, since neither of the parties directly involved is a pack member."

Mike could feel the aggression rolling off Trick and his friends from thirty feet away.

"Although I have appreciated your honesty and candor in this matter, the appropriate response is mine alone to decide." Vince glared pointedly at Yolanda, who had all her attention focused on Trick.

"The nature of the insult requires more than a simple apology by the trespasser. Therefore, the battle will be to Omega submission after blood." An instantaneous shout of exultation arose from Trick and his friends.

Wait a minute. This wasn't part of the deal. Mike looked around uncertainly. He'd come here expecting lone wolf status. He had no intention of actually joining the pack; it wasn't part of the deal. Not only that, but he would be Omega; the lowest ranking member. He was going to have to actually fight Vince. Submission after blood precluded any simple ritual submission. This was not going to be about recognizing the dominance of the Alpha wolf any longer; this was going to be a matter of face. Once blood was drawn, control of a lycan's beast might be impossible. Not only that, but the scent of blood and Vince's pheromones could affect the other wolves, too. There was simply no way the cat could fight off an entire wolf pack.

He looked to Silas, who grinned and gave him an enthusiastic, two-fisted thumbs-up. So did the guys sitting with him.

Vince slipped out of his sweats and stood nude, stretching his thick bull neck from side to side.

Mike hadn't expected to undress, much less shift into the cat. But if he was facing Vince in beast form, there was no alternative. He was no prude, but taking his clothes off in front of an audience wasn't his idea of a good time. He kept his face neutral as he took off his shorts.

Silas had warned him to keep his eyes on Vince's face. "To look away from a dominant wolf shows fear. Eye to eye is how weres sort out the strong from the weak."

But Silas hadn't said anything about where to put his hands. Standing butt-naked in front of a lone woman and a dozen guys wasn't something he'd ever done before. He took what he hoped was a casual stance, and avoided looking at anyone except Vince.

He'd never seen a were-man shift into beast form, except on TV. The time it took for someone with ALVS to shift from one form to another related to the number of years they'd lived with their beasts. No way to tell from looking at a lycan how long they'd had the disease, but Mike figured he had a couple of minutes to figure out a new strategy. If the cat wasn't on board, things could go wrong in an instant.

This is a game, big guy. A wrestling match; like we do with Farley. Inside his head, Mike felt the cat's ears perk up.

Vince's shoulders hunched and his back bowed, the crest of mane emerging first down his neck and along the line of his spine, followed by the snout, ears, and tail. As Alpha, his wolf would be bigger and heavier than his pack members, but against a three hundred pound jaguar, even an Alpha werewolf would be out-classed. Vince was shifting faster than he expected. Vince's legs began to lengthen, and hair began to cover his body. There wasn't much time.

He had no doubt at all that the cat could crush the skull of any werewolf that came within reach. But if the cat refused to submit, the entire pack would attack them and he wouldn't be able to challenge Vince for Alpha. Hell, he probably wouldn't survive.

It's just a game. Let the big dog win. He sent the cat an image of a tussle with Farley. Only Tehuantl could speak to the cat directly, but simple mental images worked. Sometimes. A little slap and tickle. The jaguar had never been aggressive toward Farley. He'd always been very gentle when they'd played. Farley would take off in a snit if the jaguar played too rough. Those were the rules here. Let the big wolf win, but make him work for it. Everyone in the pack would have a chance to get their licks in on the new Omega after he was accepted, but it would be limited to one at a time. Not what he'd wanted, but for a week or two, he was pretty certain he could get the cat to go along with it.

Seconds later, Vince completed his shift. He was big. Bigger than expected. Vince raised his head to howl his challenge and the spectators joined the chorus.

Mike unrolled the black carpet of cat.

Vince's silver and black wolf roared straight in for the throat. The jaguar slapped him to the side, raking him half-heartedly with his powerful claws, and the demand for first blood was satisfied.

The audience roared their approval, but his relief was short-lived. He hadn't counted on the cat's reaction. This wolf was a monster, and game to boot. The cat's excitement overruled his mental urgings to stop before somebody got hurt. The jaguar was loving this rough play with the big furry dog.

As far as he could tell, all of Vince's rational thoughts had left the building. The ferocious wolf was intent on going for the big cat's throat with everything he had. The cat's ear was bleeding, and Mike sensed a shoulder wound, but the cat's fierce glee was obvious. He wasn't trying very hard to hurt the wolf, but when the big beast managed to grab the jaguar by the throat, the game was over.

The jaguar growled and curled defensively, bringing his deadly back claws toward the wolf's tender underbelly. Mike's stomach lurched; he had to do something. Farley always ended their wrestling matches by pretending to savage the big cat's throat. Mike fixed his mind on a mental picture of this and *pushed* this image to the jaguar. The cat froze. The wolf worried the cat's throat from side to side as if to make a point. Mike pushed again. A moment later, the cat relaxed, and the wolf stepped back. The jaguar sprang to his feet, shook himself, and licked his chops as if to say, "That was fun, what next?"

Before Mike could celebrate, four wolves swarmed over Vince like angry hornets, each going for the soft flesh of the underbelly or throat.

What the hell? The jaguar leapt into the fray; a vortex of fang and fur. With less effort than needed to munch on a mouthful of popcorn, he grabbed one wolf by the skull and bit down. It was as if Mike's own teeth had pierced the fragile bones. The sensation of soft brain matter against the cat's tongue brought simultaneous satisfaction to the cat and revulsion to Mike. A second wolf darted in for Vince's throat, and the cat slapped it across the clearing into a tree trunk, while Vince battled the big wolf that could only be Trick.

These wolves were Trick's buddies, Mike realized. Trick must have planned to attack Vince all along, and waited until this moment to challenge Vince for pack leadership. The jaguar spit out the first wolf and grabbed a second as it tore into Vince's shoulder. With a crunch, the cat's powerful jaws clamped down on the spine of the unfortunate wolf. It began to scream and convulse back into human form. A moment later, Trick's wolf was lying belly up to Vince in a furiously submissive pose. Vince began his shift back to human form.

Mike pushed at the cat to let him out, and the cat obliged. Instinctively, he moved to stand between a still-vulnerable Vince and Trick and the rest of the wolves, several of whom were now at the midway point in their transformation between human and wolf. In the aftermath of the confusion, only four members of the pack remained in human form: Silas, Chaney, Striper Dave, and one of the younger guys, Wyatt. Silas had a taser baton, which he used to great effect to incapacitate Trick and the rest of Vince's attackers.

Chaney had a can of energy drink ready to hand to Vince as soon as he finished shifting. Vince grabbed it and drained it in a single long swallow. A lycan rarely shifted so quickly in such a short time. The fluids and electrolytes probably helped a lot, but Vince had to be feeling the pain. Vince reached for second can and handed it to Mike.

"Good job, Bane. I know what you did, and I appreciate it."

Surprised, Mike nodded. *No shit.* Apparently, weres did retain their state of mind while in beast form after all. At least Vince had. Maybe their relationship with their wolves wasn't so different from his relationship with the cat. "Any time." Already, the tension in the arena had dissipated.

"Can you believe this guy?" Vince ignored the disabled weres lying at his feet. He popped the top on another can. "When I heard he was a cat, I'm thinking mountain lion. I've never seen such a frickin' big cat in my life." Silas and Chaney laughed. One by one, the rest of the pack shifted back to human, except for Trick and the three injured wolves. The wolf with the crushed skull looked to be in the worst shape, but Mike had been told that weres were hard to kill. He hoped it was true.

Silas shot him a meaningful look. *Oh, right.* He took a deep breath and as Vince had done earlier, raised his hand for silence. He dropped to one knee and exposed his throat to Vince, keeping his hands open and at his sides. He fixed his gazed on Vince's golden eyes. Felix hadn't told him exactly what to say, so he chose his words with care. "I formally recognize and surrender to the superior authority of my Alpha. My blood is yours to shed."

Vince nodded once. "Having proven himself to me and yielding to my authority, Mike Bane, I formally recognize and accept your submission."

Vince gripped his shoulder and addressed the pack. "You all know we've been a bit short-handed lately. Although Mike's beast is obviously not like ours, he has clearly demonstrated his understanding of our ways and willingness to serve the pack. You all know how much I value personal control over blood lust, and today, Mike demonstrated his ability to remain cool in the face of chaos, and put his Alpha's safety before his own. Let it be known. Mike has passed the challenge for admission to the pack as Omega. As of this day, he is one of us."

He was tempted to ask Vince for lone wolf status, but this didn't seem like the appropriate time or place. Self-consciously, Mike gazed around the ring, nodding to each of the other pack members. Based on the nods and their expressions, it seemed as if most of the pack accepted him; those who didn't, merely offered a hard stare. He moved to stand, but the Alpha's firm grip held him. Vince wasn't finished.

"But even as we welcome him into the pack, his actions today have shown his true character. No Omega would have done what he did when his Alpha was set upon. It is their nature to always surrender in the face of dominance. Mike's beast not only drove back those who attacked me, he put himself between me and those who might have attacked me even after he'd returned to his most vulnerable human form. While the pack is served by several excellent enforcers," he nodded toward Silas and Chaney. "Trick, the declared candidate for Beta position to replace Tanner has today proven himself unworthy of consideration. Therefore, I am selecting our newest pack member, Mike Bane as our new Beta."

Mike scrambled to his feet. *What the hell is he thinking?* A Beta pack member was usually an Alpha's most trusted ally. *He barely knows me.* This had to be a mistake. He could see the confusion and hurt in Silas's face, and darker looks from some of the others.

"You can't do that Vince," Yolanda objected.

"You're not an official member of this pack yet, Yolanda. But one more word and you'll be facing the same the same punishment as Trick and his buddies."

She stiffened, fire in her eyes. "What the hell kind of game are you playing here, Vince?"

Vince ignored her, as he checked on the wounded wolves. He sentenced Trick, Bruiser, and Steve-o to the veterinarian's clinic for two days of solitary confinement. Lamarr, the wolf whose skull had been crushed by the jaguar, was dead.

The announcement hit Mike like a punch in the gut. Self-hate washed over him. He stared, uncomprehendingly, as one of the pack members picked up Lamarr's body. The rest of the pack seemed disaffected by the death of one of their own. Was it truly such an everyday occurrence, or was mourning a fellow pack member seen as a weakness?

There was no time for an inaugural hunt to forge the new pack bonds before the park opened, but Vince had planned ahead. As they showered and changed, the caterers brought over a feast of steak tartare, sashimi, deviled eggs, and plenty of barbecued meats. Mike had no appetite for celebration. It didn't seem right.

But to his surprise, one of the other pack members, Paul, spoke a few words about Lamarr. Paul seemed to voice the sentiments of the rest of the pack by saying that while dying in battle was a worthy end, attacking such a powerful wolf was the ultimate act of cowardice, and seen as a means to commit suicide. They were the actions of uncontrolled passions and desperation, not a soberly conceived, well-thought-out coup between well-matched rivals. The rest of the pack seemed to agree, and the after a single chorus of 'here here', the pack turned their attention to food.

The demand for food required a focused dedication that precluded conversation, as most of the were-men had shifted at least twice in less than an hour. Watching them eat, Mike's appetite returned and he helped himself to a plate. Gradually, the food did its job. He even felt comfortable enough to stake his claim on a worn recliner. There was a lot of horseplay and good humor as the men finished up their chow, paid their respects to Vince, and headed off to report for duty.

"Hold up, Bane, I want to talk to you," Vince said.

"Hey, I'm sorry about Yolanda. I blew it."

"Wolves never apologize, Bane. It's a sign of weakness. Now I know you didn't expect to be handed the Beta slot, but I had a lot of good reasons for doing it. With the Summit coming up in September, I need that Beta spot filled, and Trick isn't ready; no matter what Ambrose thinks. I smelled that set-up from a mile away. It's about time Trick learned a lesson the hard way. The kid has enough juice to be a Beta, or maybe even an Alpha, but not until he learns to control himself. I don't trust his judgment. I don't trust him. I need somebody who can keep his cool."

Mike hesitated, wondering if he should question Vince's decision. "I don't get it. You don't even know me. What about Silas? That Chaney seems like a good man, and I've known Dave-."

Vince waved it all away like a buzzing fly. "I've made my decision. I read your file and checked you out. The minute you stepped in to support me, you showed your true character. You backed me up today and I appreciate it. I think we can work together, so you better get used to the idea."

Calming Alpha pheromones rolled over him. He still wasn't sure about the Beta slot, but it was only for another week or two. Maybe being top cat in a wolf pack wasn't such a bad idea.

* * *

Any ideas he'd had about fitting in with a wolf pack went out the window during the celebration hunt after the park closed for the night. It was a disaster. The whole pack took off at a ground-eating lope as soon as they'd doffed their uniforms. They'd been out of sight within minutes. The cat, delighted to be out on the Tor again, had no interest in running after a pack of wolves. He tried everything he could think of to get the jaguar to at least follow their trail, but it was no use. The cat caught an unwary turtle, ate it, then spent an hour gnawing on the empty shell before finding his way back to the cottage.

Mike thought he'd go mad at the cat's stubbornness. He tried to think up excuses to tell Vince. Everyone had told him that the ritual hunt sealed the deal, but was the whole pack really expected to run together as a group?

Probably.

Maybe he could tell them the cat bruised a paw or something. Maybe they didn't notice he wasn't with them.

Not likely.

TEHUANTL IN CHARGE

MIKE PAUSED IN the main plaza, waiting for the initial surge of park visitors to swarm in through the front gates. It was bad enough that he'd blown his first hunt with the pack, but Tom had developed a high fever overnight. Mike had spent most of the day at the hospital, and had arrived late for work; even after the duty assignments had been given.

The plaza was packed with eager guests. Trams brought visitors up from the parking lot every five minutes and dropped them at the front gates. Reservations and the price of admission had been paid months in advance, so clearing the gates was a matter of checking the guests identification against the reservations. Visitors were given a badge and complete access to the park. The badge was swiped for all purchases made within the park, eliminating the need for cash. The only physical security at the gate was a metal detector for weapons. Just inside the gate, several costumed blood stewards greeted the visitors and handed out complimentary brochures containing a map of the park's attractions and a table of show times.

Vince had assigned him to work with Silas in the theatre sector at the opposite end of the park. He noticed a tuxedoed street performer near the fountain, attracting a small crowd. It was Jared, one of the blood stewards. With a series of graceful movements, he was creating art in the still air using nothing more than a bit of colored smoke. In one hand he held a white feather, in the other, a multi-colored ribbon scarf. His foot controlled the pedal of a small contraption which allowed him to control the release of smoke.

Using the feather, Jared manipulated the dense vapor, using the feather to cut it and the scarf to swirl the air and shape it into a variety of designs. Taking suggestions from the crowd, he created an assortment of shapes, animals, and monsters; each elicited an appreciative gasp from the crowd as it hung in the air for a moment before fading away. A woman offered up her name, and moment later, the magician had arranged the letters around her head like a halo. As he watched the smoke dissipate, Mike realized the whole audience had turned and was now staring directly at him.

He whirled to see a seven-foot tall figure a few feet behind him. From his silver eyes, Mike recognized him as a vampire, but he didn't appear to be wearing a costume. He was too good-looking to be anything but an actor or one of the musicians in the concert hall. Maybe this was some kind of show, he reasoned. With his long bleached-white hair, dirty black leather jeans and mud-spattered boots, he didn't seem to fit in with the rest of the 'fundead' Mythica experience. Something about this guy set off alarm bells in his head.

The vamp was armed for one thing. Weapons were expressly forbidden inside the park but he wore a bowie knife on one hip and an ammo belt of bullets draped bandolero-style across his chest. With those weapons, he should have never cleared the gate. Mike reached for his walkie-talkie.

Too late, the vamp raised his hand shot him with a stun gun.

Twin projectiles slammed into his chest like torpedoes. He fell to the ground, as 50,000 volts of electricity coursed through him. He was dimly aware of the crowd cheering, thinking this was just part of the entertainment. Vince's voice shouted at him from the walkie-talkie lying uselessly on the ground beside him. Mike reached for the cat, but in the void, found only Tehuantl, spewing forth like a volcano.

He screamed futilely, knowing there were hundreds of human victims within reach; but Tehuantl would not be denied.

The forced shift consumed him. He fought to remain conscious, but felt himself fading away beneath the mad shaman's bloodthirsty glee. Mike caught the scent of the vamp's bloody breath and felt Tehuantl's fierce rage when the vampire stabbed him, before being shoved down into the darkness.

THE DELIMMA

AMBROSE VAN CLEVE sat in stunned silence as Vince replayed the video a second time. One moment, the man they all recognized as Mike Bane was hit in the chest with a high-voltage taser; the next, a completely different man had hurled himself at his attacker.

The image quality was excellent. No one said a word during the madman's deadly rampage against the vampire. The film showed the arrival of Silas and Chaney just as the brawny killer ripped the vampire's heart out. Silas had used the bounty hunter's own knife to separate what was left of the vampire's head from the remains of the carcass while the powerful killer stomped and crowed a ritualized victory dance; no less horrifying for the lack of sound. The whole thing lasted less than five minutes.

Ambrose gazed at the men seated around the conference table, watching their faces for their reactions. His first-born, Cobb, was in a panic, his eyes as big as walnuts, while Vince's face was unreadable. Felix and Rafe looked grim. Only his blood steward Ozzie obviously enjoyed the spectacle. No surprise there. Ambrose worried that this new complication would compromise his plan to rid himself of Ozzie.

"Anybody know the vamp?" Vince asked the group.

"That's Alf Torkelson," Rafe replied. "Or, it was. He was one of the old ones."

Cobb was outraged. "That *thing* ripped Torkelson's heart right out of his chest."

Ambrose had never witnessed the death of a vampire before. Even without sound, the revulsion he'd felt as he watched the humanoid creature pull the vampire apart with his bare hands was beyond anything he'd ever imagined. He glanced over at Ozzie.

The veterinarian Ozzie was exhibiting all the classic symptoms of long-term blood steward addiction. The glassy, staring eyes, sweaty, pallid skin, and an inability to sit still were the hallmarks of the beginning of the final stage. Ozzie had always had his little obsessions, but he was very nearly out of control now. Not all blood stewards succumbed to the madness, but when they did, they were always taken care of before things got to this stage. Ozzie's craving for Ambrose's saliva was nearly daily now. Every time Ambrose forced himself to feed on Ozzie his revulsion grew. It was almost as if Ozzie was the master and he was the blood cow.

Even now, Ozzie was fidgeting like a man with his finger in a light socket, putting everyone else in the room on edge as well. Even Vince must see it. Yet Vince would not even consider allowing Ambrose to do what must be done. Any attempt made to put Ozzie out of his misery would bring Vince down on all of them like the wrath of god.

"Bane could ruin us, Ambrose. The papers got it wrong. He's no were-cat, he's a monster. You should never have brought him in." Cobb rubbed his forehead. "That sort of thing could set the whole community against us."

"None of the guests were harmed," Vince said. "No one even complained. They thought it was all part of the show. We're the scariest place on earth, remember?"

"I agree with Cobb." Felix said. "Bane is a freak of nature. Ambrose, you can't be serious. He's got no control. That beast of his is powerful enough to kill a vampire with his bare hands. He could ruin the summit. He could destroy you, and in turn all of us. Everything we've worked for."

"He's my Beta now, Felix. You have nothing to say about it," Vince said.

"You were singing a different tune when Ambrose told us he'd hired him." Cobb pointed at Vince. "You didn't want anything to do with him. Besides, this guy is no wolf. And since when do you tolerate such loss of control in your pack, Vince?"

"Seems to me he did his job," Rafe said.

"He killed him! That could have been any one of us." Cobb looked like he was about to cry.

Ambrose rubbed his temples. He'd never seen Cobb so upset. "Calm down, all of you. Mike informed me there was a contract out on him before he came to work for us. Strange indeed that the bounty hunter would be a vampire, but he did give me fair warning. Torkelson attacked him. I'm not convinced there is a problem."

"Torkelson's van was found in the guest parking lot," Vince said. "Inside, there was a receipt from a gas station in Queens. He came here for Bane, all right."

"Show it again," Ozzie demanded. "I've never seen a shape shifter in action before."

"None of us have."

The room fell silent a third time as they watched the replay. The smoothness of Bane's shift from one form to another was impressive.

"Stop it right there, Vince," Ambrose instructed. "That's where it starts, you see? Now advance it frame by frame until the transformation is complete."

Twenty-three frames later, the uniformed figure of Mike Bane had transformed into a massive, bronzed madman. He ripped Bane's shirt off like it was tissue paper. Overall, the body appeared to be that of a grotesquely-muscled human male. The killer was a good six or eight inches taller than Bane. Primitive tribal tattoos covered much of his chest and shoulders. The lower portion of his bare legs and forearms was covered in a delicate pattern of coffee-colored jaguar spots. The tips of his powerful fingers and toes ended in talons, which were used to hold and rend the vampire's flesh with devastating effect. The face was heavy-boned; with a projecting brow ridge, broad nose, and thick lips. Two completely different men.

Vince turned off the monitor. Ozzie's protests were ignored.

Felix shook his head. "Ambrose what were you thinking? Who knows how many other beasts he's got in there with him. And what about the summit? What will the Globus think when he hears you're responsible for Torkelson's unsanctioned death?"

What indeed? Ambrose stilled at the thought. The Globus was the Master of the Americas. Judge, justice, and jury for the vampire families of the New World. No telling how he'd respond. Felix was right, as usual.

Cobb scowled. "You promised me my own territory, Ambrose."

Ambrose waved Cobb's protest away. "You'll get your territory." He knew he had to make a decision. Ozzie had to be dealt with. The risk that he'd follow through with his blackmail was a very real threat to Cobb gaining his own territory. The only way to get rid of Ozzie was to get rid of his protector, Vince Dazak. And the key to getting rid of Vince was Mike Bane. "But I'm inclined to agree with Vince. I don't think this really changes anything." He steepled his fingers as he chose his words. "Torkelson was a member of the Northwestern territory which is up for grabs at the summit. Although he had no blood tie to the Master who was killed, he would have had a legitimate claim to the territory."

"Bane did you a favor, Cobb," Rafe said. "You should be thanking him. Besides, he's my bodyguard. I like the guy. I say we keep him."

Ambrose nodded. "I agree. There is no reason to believe that Vince's new pet is a danger to any of us. He was attacked and he defended himself. There is no indication that he would take any unprovoked action against us. The bigger issue, as I see it is how an armed bounty hunter got into the park in the first place."

"Yeah, Vince," Cobb sneered. "How do you explain that?"

"He pulled a small glamour or ward over the reservation hostess so she didn't see a thing." Vince played a sequence from a different camera angle. This view showed the front gate. "You can see here, he's heavily armed. Watch as he walks right by Naomi at the gate. She doesn't even see him. Neither do any of the guests around him."

"Look at all those people," Cobb fumed. "When word gets out--"

"Oh the crowd went wild for it. Gordon and Ozzie handed out complimentary Glamour shots to make sure no one would remember this as anything but a bit of street entertainment," Rafe said. "Besides, what do you care? You've never been particularly interested in our guests' safety before, Cobb."

"When it interferes with our ability to make a living, I do."

"Enough." Ambrose shut down the discussion. "No uninvited vampire has ever been able to cross the park threshold and enter the grounds of Mythica. Gordon should have felt the vampire cross the wards. I'd like to hear what he has to say about that. Even if the security cameras couldn't detect Torkelson's presence. The Mage should have reported it immediately. You protested when I brought Mike in Vince, but he spotted that bounty hunter almost immediately. I believe you were speaking to him when he was hit."

"Yeah. Somebody helped that guy get inside."

"What are you going to do about it?"

"I'll conduct my own investigation and let you know." Vince shut down the video.

"So he's staying?" Cobb sounded incredulous. "You've got to be kidding."

Ambrose surveyed the room. Rafe wanted to keep Bane for his personal bodyguard. Vince and Cobb were on opposite sides, as usual. Felix looked like he'd eaten something that disagreed with him. "What say you, Felix? What do you think of our Mr. Bane?"

"He's shown himself to be dangerous and unpredictable. He could ruin everything we've built here, Ambrose. Everything you've built."

"That's what I'm saying," agreed Cobb. "Turn Bane in for the bounty, collect the cash, and our problems are gone."

"No." Vince shook his head. "Bane stays; he's my Beta. Maybe we do have a fox in our henhouse. The vampire should never have gotten in. The smoke magician has always performed in the concert hall. Why was he doing it outside, where the slightest breeze would have made it impossible?"

Cobb stiffened. "Jared is mine. Are you saying this is my fault? That my blood steward intentionally let Torkelson inside the park? *He was doing a show!* For all I know, that bounty hunter could have been coming after me. It's no secret that I'm campaigning to take over his former master's territory."

Rafe rolled his eyes. "Don't be so paranoid, Cobb. I doubt that Torkelson would have come after you. Not when he'd have a much better chance to stake his claim at the summit."

"There's no rush to decide anything right away," Felix suggested. "Let him stay with Vince and the pack until the summit, when his contract is up." He gazed directly into Ambrose's eyes for emphasis. "*As we agreed.*"

Yes. Ambrose smiled approvingly. Felix had always been so clever. We only need him to take Vince out, out anyway. We could turn him over to the Globus at the summit. Let him deal with it. After Bane removes Vince and Ozzie is taken care of, turning Bane over to the Globus might work even better than letting him walk away. "I like that."

And Vince had made it easy for them. With Bane as Beta, Vince wouldn't be able to back down when he issues his challenge. This was working out better than he'd hoped. He would have to talk to Felix about moving up the timeline. No need in waiting any longer. *And the sooner Bane gets rid of Vince, the sooner I will be able to get rid of Ozzie.* Perhaps I could even arrange it for Bane to take the blame for Ozzie. Otherwise, turning him over for the bounty was certainly an option. A win-win either way he chose to play it.

"Where is Bane now?" asked Felix.

"I hit him with a mega dose of Ketamine. He's sleeping it off," Ozzie said. "He's nothing like the lycans. I've never seen anything like him. As soon as I hit him with the drug, he shifted again." Ozzie rubbed his eyebrow. "The cat seems to be the predominant form. It's almost like Bane and the madman are spirits within the cat. If that's the case, I don't know what the hell he is. He doesn't react to silver the same way the wolves do, either. There's nothing in the medical journals that I could find. I'll need a blood sample to narrow it down."

"Leave him alone Ozzie. He's pack now, not one of your lab rats," Vince said.

"I don't answer to you Vince," the cryptozoologist snapped. "And Bane is no wolf. He doesn't belong to you. Give the kitty to me, Ambrose. I want to figure out what he is, exactly. I'll want to run some experiments." His glassy eyes took on a dreamy look. "Don't worry, Ambrose. I'll give him back to Vince and the rest of the dogs when I'm finished," he sneered.

Vince reddened, but didn't say a word.

"I don't care what he is. I say let's kill him,"

"Oh shut it, Cobb. I heard you the first time." Ambrose sighed. "Vince's new pet Beta is here to stay. And I am confident that Vince will be able to identify our fox before the Summit begins. I expect all of you to support Vince's investigation, including the interrogation of your blood stewards. Anyone who does not comply promptly and fully with the investigation will answer to me."

"You're going soft, Ambrose," Cobb said. "If you aren't careful, a bounty hunter might be coming after you someday. Mark my words, that shifter is going to be nothing but trouble. From now on, I'm wearing body mail for protection. I'd advise you to do the same. And I'm warning you, Vince. Keep that beast away from me, or I swear I'll kill you both."

Ambrose kept his expression neutral on hearing the venom in Cobb's voice. *He's getting too impatient for his own good. There's no excuse for that kind of disrespect. I'm going to have to talk to him again*, he mused. Cobb was ambitious, but patience and tact had never been his strengths. *If I didn't know better, that almost sounded like a threat.*

BUCKET OF BLOOD

THE SMELL OF blood was all around him, bringing back the gut-wrenching memory of Tom's ghastly wounds and other, deeper memories. Mike opened his eyes to find Ozzie, the park veterinarian, cutting into the skin of his left forearm with a scalpel, just as Hector Clemente had done when he'd tried to flay the cat.

"Sonofabitch!" He jerked his arm away, and delivered a solid hook with his right to Ozzie's face. There was a satisfying crunch and blood gushed from the vet's nose.

"What the hell do you think you're doing?" From the sting of the wound on his arm, he could tell the blade used was silver. He gripped the bloody gash, applying pressure, as Ozzie wiped his face with a handful of tissues. He'd disliked the self-described 'cryptozoologist' on sight, but had chided himself for it. *I should have trusted my instincts.*

He was on a cot in the first aid station, covered in shards of bone, blood splatter, and clots of who knows what. His ribs had been taped.

The vet's nose continued to drip, but Ozzie paid no attention. He had a strange glassy expression on his face; completely devoid of emotion. "Easy, there. No harm done," he said, softly. He picked up the scalpel, which had dropped on the floor of the aid station. "I've never studied a shape-shifter before. Your reaction to silver is quite unexpected. In beast form, you seem sensitive to it, yet in this form, your reactions are nearly human. I was curious to see if you healed as fast as the wolves." He wiped the bloodied knife clean and dropped it into the metal sink. "I find your shift reflex to be quite fascinating."

"Keep the hell away from me." Mike struggled to a sitting position. There was something very wrong with this guy. He seemed to exude an unhealthy miasma, like some of the long-time crack heads he'd encountered on the street.

A wave of nausea washed over him. *Oh god, not again.* He spotted a wastebasket and grabbed it just in time. Each convulsion brought up an astonishing amount of blood and tissue, accompanied by a searing pain his side.

The door to the cramped office opened and Striper Dave was there.

"That's better. Get it all out," he urged. "We've all been there." A chorus of muted laughter came from behind him.

He panted over the plastic bin, waiting for the nausea and guilt and stomach cramps to pass. *Damn you Tehuantl.* In the hallway behind Dave, he could see Chaney, Wyatt, and the Omega, Phelan. Out of the corner of his eye, he saw Ozzie holding a surgical pad to his nose.

"How many dead," he choked.

"No humans, if that's what you're asking."

"Killing a vampire doesn't count," said Wyatt. "They're already dead."

"Although none of us had ever actually seen one torn apart before."

They crowded into the cramped room, and to his surprise, Mike felt nothing but fraternal intentions and relief in their pheromones. They'd been waiting for him to wake up, he realized. Their friendly presence seemed to suck Ozzie's fevered aura right out of the room.

Another wave of nausea washed over him, but he had nothing left in his stomach.

He wiped his face and hands with a towel Dave handed him. "You'll have to tell me what happened. I don't remember any of it."

"None of the guests were harmed," Dave said. "And Silas beheaded the vampire."

"Although by the time Silas got there, you'd already crushed his skull and gutted him." Wyatt clapped him on the shoulder. "All I can say is I'm glad you're on our team."

"Who was he?"

"Bounty hunter from Queens."

"That's enough for now," Ozzie interrupted. "You're off for the rest of the night. Make sure you get enough protein." Ozzie handed him a small packet of pain medication. Now that Dave and the others were here, the greasy look he'd noticed on Ozzie's face was gone. Except for the red nose, where he'd hit him, he looked almost normal. "Silver retards the healing mechanisms in lycanthropes, but I need more data before I can determine precisely how it affects you. I'd like to run some tests."

Like hell you would. "I'll pass." No way he would let Ozzie get anywhere near him again. When Dave offered him a ride over to the clubhouse he accepted immediately. A shower and some clothes were definitely in order. He wrapped a bloody towel around his waist, eager to escape. "Let's go."

They hopped into one of the park's electric carts parked outside, and Dave drove. "Hey Mikey, that leopard man of yours could be a headliner in Atlantic City. Scared the bejeezus out of me, if you want to know the truth of it."

"It's called a Nagual. They're an ancient race of shamanistic jaguar people. They protected the Olmec people from evil spirits."

"Well your Nagual guy beat the shit out of that vampire guy. Drained him dry and ate his heart."

Mike's face flamed. *Oh god, everybody knows now.* How could he face Vince or the rest of the pack again? He glanced at Dave, glad for the darkness. Oddly enough, Dave didn't seem too disgusted. In fact, based on the other guys' attitude when they came into the aid station, it was almost as if they'd been worried about him.

He was still feeling a bit thick-headed. Ozzie had told him he'd given him a mild sedative, but based on how he felt, Mike knew from experience that the so-called sedative was Ketamine; a powerful animal tranquilizer. The drug always made him sick to his stomach. He was glad he'd puked up all that blood through. He wondered if drinking vampire blood would affect him. *Isn't that how vampires are made?* He also wondered what else Ozzie had done to him while he'd been sedated.

"The victory dance was the best part." Dave was grinning like an idiot. "That guy was bustin' moves all over the place. The crowd went wild for him. Phelan told me people were using his moves on the dance floor tonight. You're a sensation."

"Can it, jerkbait," he said, without heat. "I feel like a damn freak."

Dave turned serious. "Well join the club, Mikey. Welcome to my world."

Mike sighed and rubbed his jaw. It was the first time Dave had talked about his lycanthropy. "Sorry, man. That was uncalled for."

"Don't be weak. If you think like that you'll drive yourself nuts. Somebody invited that guy to the party tonight. No strange vampire has ever been able to cross the threshold at Mythica. It shouldn't be possible. I've never seen anything like the show your beast put on tonight. No one has. Even Vince was impressed. He didn't punish you for shifting on duty. That's a first, as far as I know."

"What are you saying?"

"I'm saying you did your job. I'm saying you saved lives tonight. I'm saying our new Beta kicked ass and killed a vampire with his bare hands. That's huge. Weres don't get much respect, Mikey, and that kind of thing makes our whole pack stronger. When we're strong, it pulls us together and we're safe. Everyone has been on edge about the summit. We've been losing members right and left. There've been a lot of squabbles and fights. It's almost like we have two factions now. With you here, all of a sudden Ambrose's nest is in a much more solid position to expand into new territory. We're united again. You're a hero."

Mike grunted. "Well I sure as hell don't feel like it. The way you say it, I almost wish I could remember."

"It's all on tape, just ask Vince."

He choked back a gag reflex. He'd never actually seen what Tehuantl looked like; only the bloody aftermath of his attacks. "No thanks. The nightmares are bad enough. I don't know that I could stand to see him in action."

Unhappy as he was to have his worst secret laid bare, Mike felt a curious lightness of spirit; an easing of the worry he'd carried around for more than half his life. People had seen Tehuantl. Seen what he was. Letting go of that secret was almost like saying goodbye to an old friend. The pack had accepted him as one of their own, even after they'd seen him at his very worst. Surprisingly enough, it felt good. He glanced at Dave. It wasn't just Vince who'd changed his mind about werewolves. Dave was one, too.

From somewhere deep inside his mind, he heard echoes of Tehuantl's manic laughter.

THE ODDITORIUM

MIKE STOOD QUIETLY in the back of the dim control room of the Mythica operations building. He'd spent the last three hours observing the action of the park on the monitors, praying that his fourth night on the job would be incident-free. Seated at the console, three figures hunched over the bank of video displays tracking the action for each sector in the park from multiple angles. Cobb Van Cleve spoke into his headset; redirecting a security officer from sector three to support a drunk and disorderly incident in the sector two beer gardens behind the park restaurant, The Bloody Fang.

It was close to ten o'clock when Vince arrived, and assigned Chaney to escort him over to the theatre sector. "I'm partnering you up with Silas, Mike. He can show you the setup. He and our old Beta, Tanner, worked the shows together. You ever see a vamp act before?"

"No."

From his seat at the console, Phelan snickered.

"Can it, Omega," Vince said. "I'll tell you what I tell all the new guys. The fire codes restrict the number of people we can seat inside the theatre, and those are the only laws we're bound to enforce. I expect you to keep your mouth shut and the guests happy, not stop the action. You got any issues, or see anything you don't like, you can talk to Rafe or come see me after the show."

"Yes sir."

He and Chaney left the building and slowly wove their way through the central plaza, past a crowd of fifty or sixty people watching a pair of dancers doing a sexy tango near the fountain. An accordion and guitar were their only accompaniment.

The redhead wore a backless number that clung to her lean figure and was slit on one side clean up to her hip. She kept herself pressed up against her partner as they danced.

"Who is *that*?"

"Santino and Lyrissa. You'll see them later at the theatre, too."

Lyrissa slid a long coltish leg up and down her partner's side as he bent her backward, nearly touching her hair to the ground. Their eyes locked into each other, as if they were the only two people in the world. Every step and movement was perfectly choreographed with the fiery music. The audience clapped along with the beat.

Santino pulled his partner around so that she had her back to him. Slowly, he ran his hand all the way up her inner thigh.

She wasn't wearing any underwear.

"Don't even think about it." Chaney shoved him. "She's one of those Fae vampires; very scary."

After a final look, he followed Chaney away from the performers. The music faded behind them as they made their way down the street of red lanterns. "What is a Fae vampire?"

"Just what you think. A Fae made into a vampire," Chaney said.

"So what's the big deal? A vamp is a vamp, right?"

"Not for Fae vamps. Human blood doesn't quench their thirst. They can survive on it, but it doesn't satisfy," Chaney explained. "The Fae consider them to be an abomination. Evil. They drink Fae blood to satisfy their thirst, but they feed off humans by draining their sexual energy as well. So that's why I warned you about Lyrissa. Even us weres know better than to tangle with her."

"If she's so dangerous, why would Ambrose make her? "

"He didn't. The way I heard it, Gordon was in love with her, but she died. He persuaded Cobb to turn her, but when she rose as a vamp, she wasn't the same. She despised Gordon for what he'd done. Rejected him completely. She made a big stink about how he'd been forsworn by the High Tor Fae for conspiring with the Van Cleves. She can't stand him. If I were you, I wouldn't mention Gordon's name around her."

"Sounds complicated. Thanks for the warning."

"Besides, she's Cobb's woman, anyway. You ever work with vampires before?"

"Everybody keeps asking me that."

"When I heard you used to be a cop, I just figured you worked Fang Patrol."

He shook his head. "I worked narcotics. Undercover mostly." Geeze, his place spread rumors faster than the precinct. NYPD had its own bloodsucker division for hunting down and aggressively staking any vampire which fed on any human without a signed release form. A bite mark was all the evidence needed for a warrant of execution. Queens didn't have many lycans, but it hosted a robust population of vampires.

"How many vampires actually ah, live here?"

"Nobody's supposed to know, but if you work here, you get to know all of them. Ambrose has six offspring. Cobb, of course. Then there's Orcas, who is a seamstress. She makes all the costumes for the street performers and actors. Gawl is the music promoter and his sister Roosa is the event planner. Tryffin is the mechanical genius that keeps all the equipment running. Varrick is a blacksmith. You rarely see him away from the forge or the theatre. He's done a lot of the decorative ironwork for the park. Cobb created Willem, the acrobat, and Lyrissa. Rafe and Santino are independents."

"Vince told me I'm to be assigned to Rafe."

Chaney nodded. "Ambrose and Rafe are the only vamps assigned personal protection. Cobb wants his own guy too, but we don't have enough guys in the pack who work security to give him his own body guard." Chaney paused in front of two low buildings at the end of the street.

"The building on the left is the Odditorium. The one on the right is the theatre, but I want to show you the Odditorium first, since it's my post and you and Silas are my backup. Come on."

They stepped out of the cacophony of the park into the hushed and softly lit atmosphere of the Odditorium. A sign just inside the door said, 'Welcome to the land of Strange', and as Mike looked around, he appreciated the warning. The place was set up like a modern art gallery, with white plaster walls, strategic lighting, and glass-fronted cabinets displaying fossils, bizarre artifacts, unusual objects, and peculiar relics. Jars of conjoined embryos and larval monsters decorated the shelves. A myriad of two-headed snakes, and four-legged chickens posed in life-like taxidermied splendor.

"It's a freak show."

Chaney laughed. "This is Gordon's personal collection."

The exhibits each followed a theme; each new display attempting to shock the audience more than the previous.

"Oh crap, these are alive." A pair of birds slept on a branch inside one of the exhibits with their heads tightly tucked beneath their wings. He moved closer for a better look in the dim light.

"Those are blood doves."

"Seriously?"

"They drink only blood. According to Gordon, they're the only blood doves in captivity. The legends say their eggs can remove curses and enchantments. I don't know if it's true or not, but they lay eggs twice a year. Gordon and Ozzie always fight over them. Gordon insists that he needs them to power the blood wards. Ozzie says they're the key to his research." Chaney shrugged. "Who knows?"

The next glass-walled enclosure housed a large brown, feathered creature with a set of pronged antlers and a long tail like a pheasant. Mike read the sign, but didn't understand.

"What in heck is a Piasa Bird?" Unlike the doves, the creature regarded the intruders with hostile red eyes, but remained fluffed up in a corner of its cage. "It doesn't look like a bird."

"It's another Fae creature. An eagle, actually. The early Europeans called it the North American dragon, but it's the thunderbird of the native American myth. They say it rules the coming of storms. I don't know about that, but it's got a nasty temper. Come on, I want to show you the Attorcroppes."

Mike followed Chaney to the next exhibit.

Chaney tapped on the glass and the creatures swarmed up against it. "These little guys are my favorites."

Basically, they were lizard people or snakes with hands and legs. Their eight-inch-long bodies were striped yellow and iridescent green. They stood upright on their hind legs, trailing half their body length in a tail behind them. Thin yellow arms with split fingers like a parrot's claw enabled them to scamper up the twigs placed in their cage with remarkable agility. Several of them stood up against the glass; their wedge-shaped heads staring at him with great intensity; almost as if they were pleading with him. Mike couldn't resist putting his hand up to the glass. They scrambled over to him; like they wanted to touch him, too. The sign said they were venomous.

"These guys are just babies. They're Gordon's pets, too. They get much bigger. Come on, I'll show you the layout."

"They don't look very happy."

"This way." In addition to the museum hall, Chaney showed him the research library, the media room, and a large conference room. "That door there leads to Gordon's private living quarters. The other leads to the warming room and vault, where the vampires sleep in the daytime. Access is controlled through the keypads. Vince is the only person authorized to enter the vault, but since you're now Rafe's guy, he'll probably assign you a passcode."

They headed back to the public area of the museum. "As you can see, this part of the park doesn't get a lot of visitors, but if there's a disruption over here, it usually has to do with the vamps, so if you get a call to the Odditorium, it's got priority, unless you're working a guest problem."

"Got it."

A PAIN IN THE ASS

THEY STEPPED OUTSIDE the Odditorium and Mike paused to read the sign outside the whitewashed wooden building next door:

MAUSOLEUM THEATER
AND
BLOOD DONATION CENTER

He frowned. "Is this a joke?"

"Not at all." Chaney pulled the door open for him. "See for yourself."

Inside, the large foyer seemed to take up the entire front half of the building. Art deco murals covered the walls and the deep brown and maroon paisley carpeting muted the acoustics of the room. On the far side of the room, three dozen patrons reclined on individual upholstered fainting sofas as attendants in crisp white uniforms monitored the ongoing donations of blood. The far left side of the room was set up with café tables, benches and chairs as a lounge area. A large group of people chatted quietly amongst themselves; a sense of quiet eagerness pervaded the atmosphere.

"Hey, Mike." Rafe came toward them, wearing a charcoal brocade suit that probably cost five grand. A frilly-front white shirt frothed out from behind a black suede vest fastened with silver buttons. The slim walking cane in his hand was obviously an affectation.

"Look at you," Mike grinned. "You're all duded up like a rock star." Charcoal eye-shadow around Rafe's blue contacts and the natural sneer of his mouth deepened Rafe's resemblance to Elvis. They could have been cousins.

"Thanks, Chaney. I'll take over from here. Come on, Mike, the show will be starting soon, and I want to show you around." He spread his arms expansively. "Welcome to my domain. This is the one place where I am able to indulge myself completely."

"Pretty fancy, if you ask me."

"Ambrose, and his kin are driven by responsibility and a need to succeed; to expand their territory, their family, and their span of control. I, on the other hand, have no such ambitions. I don't want the responsibility. This theatre is my little corner of the world, and I am perfectly satisfied to indulge my passions within these walls. I prefer to stay out of Ambrose's business entirely. We like to have fun too, you know."

Mike thought about the Mythica motto. No kidding. "I thought you and Ambrose were partners."

"I suppose you could say that, although I confess I have very little interest in the running of the estate. I have my little corner, and he has the rest. When Ambrose came to America, he intended to start a vineyard. He was looking for a business partner, but I wasn't interested in farming. I introduced him to Felix, who found him the land. Ambrose got it cheap because of proximity to the High Tor Fae." Rafe lowered his voice to a confidential tone. "I'll tell you a little something about Ambrose. His people were frugal. He is very careful with his pennies. I, on the other hand, have always depended on my wits for survival. I believe that you have to spend money to make money."

As he looked around the lobby, Mike could see that Rafe was telling the truth. While the park couldn't be called neglected, the inside of the theatre was posh in a very old-world way. The carpet beneath his feet was thickly padded; the walls were adorned with tasteful, hand-painted murals depicting art deco motifs. The overhead lighting was an artful blend of Baroque chandeliers and modern spotlights.

"You two don't seem to have much in common."

"Ambrose and I have always had very different priorities. When I first met him, his entire focus was his family. Cobb and Orcas were still newly minted, so to speak. He was obsessed with the need to secure a permanent source of sustenance. In those days, Ambrose's only ambition was driven to provide his family with a stable blood supply. I am much more the catch and release type, if you get my meaning."

"Except for Taffy." The words slipped out unintended.

"He told you?"

"No, I was stupid and he set me straight. I thought blood stewards weren't much more than spit junkies. I was wrong. I appreciate what you've done for Taff."

Rafe brushed a fleck of imaginary dust off his sleeve. "I count Taffy Bane as one of my closest friends, Mike. As long as he will allow me to help him, I will. I would appreciate it if you would keep the matter quiet. In the old days, blood stewards were slaves, and they didn't have a choice."

He tensed. "Ambrose was a slave-owner."

"It was a different time. Slave ownership was not uncommon, even in the north. And in the south, even poor whites sold their children into slavery. I was of those."

Deep emotion flashed in the vampire's eyes. "I was four when my parents sold me to an evil man who abused me in every way imaginable. I ran away dozens of times before I finally escaped him. It was the best day of my life. That was the day my maker killed him as I lay dying of an infected knife wound. Needless to say, I cannot tolerate the idea of slavery in any form. Fortunately, my maker felt the same. After he lost interest in me, we parted ways. Ambrose, on the other hand, has a very different view, and always dreamed of fathering a legacy. He was determined to have his own nest, which required a permanent supply of donors. It wasn't until well after the civil war that he released his slaves. Of course by that time, his blood stewards were just as bound to him as if they were still chained."

"Why partner with him at all?"

Rafe shrugged. "The past is the past. Times change. Ambrose changed, too. When the original homestead burned, Ambrose was in a tight spot, financially. I told him I would consider partnering with him in a private gaming club. Eventually, he built this theatre for me. This lobby was the original grand salon and gaming room. After seeing a Ferris Wheel at the Chicago World's Fair, Tryffin wanted to build his own, and bit by bit, the park expanded. At the end of the second World War, we started a blood drive, and after that, everything took off. It's the land and vineyards that Ambrose loves the most, but it's the theatre, the blood bank, and the amusement park which have enabled Ambrose and I to fulfill our dreams and live the way we do. Our partnership works because Ambrose does all the hard work. He provides me with the stage and my little troupe of performers and I repay him in blood."

"I doubt it's as simple as that."

"Watch and learn, fledgling." Rafe steered him toward the entrance of the theatre proper. The doorways were heavily draped in black velvet. He paused, motioning to the group of blood donors. "Admission to the live show is by lottery. Only ten percent of our nightly visitors win a chance to see the show. The cost of admission is a simple blood donation. Every donor receives a complimentary Glamour cocktail." One of the uniformed attendants handed a yellow ticket to one of the donors and helped her to her feet. The woman joined the other donors in the café, and received a tiny glassful of golden liquid.

"Is this legit?"

"Of course," Rafe smiled. "They even get to keep the glass as a souvenir. It's got the park logo on it and everything. You'd have a riot on your hands if you were to ask any of them to leave. Gold ticket donors give their donations before the show, red tickets get to experience the real thing. The amusement park and concert hall are recent additions, and they do attract many more customers than the theatre could ever hold, but this is the heart and soul of Mythica. Follow me."

They stepped through the velvet curtains and entered the theatre. Mike followed the vampire down the aisle toward the stage, his curiosity keeping pace with his uneasiness. Silas and a half-dozen vampires gathered casually around the stage, each dressed in extraordinary costumes. Silas offered him a friendly nod, the others glared at him with an intense, unreadable expression. For all his phoniness, Mike felt more comfortable around Rafe. *Maybe it's the silver eyes that makes them look so intense.*

Rafe stepped onto the low stage and made the introductions. "This is the new pack Beta, Mike Bane. Mike, don't feel slighted if no one offers to shake your hand. They're preparing themselves for the upcoming performance, and you don't smell like wolf. In fact, I daresay you do smell good enough to eat, but Vince has warned us all that you're not on the menu."

Mike nodded to the group. *So that's what a hungry vampire looks like. Good to know.* Six sets of handsome faces stared at him; four men and two women. Beneath the scent of dust and bleach and Rafe's aftershave, the cat picked up the scent of old blood. In his head, he felt the cat regard them as he would a cold-blooded creature like a lizard or a snake. Like Rafe, they all wore make-up. Mascara, rouge, eye shadow, the works.

One of the vamps smiled and showed off his snicked-down fangs. "So you're the Jag-were." With his accent, it came out 'yag-weeer'. It was the tango dancer he'd seen earlier. With those knee-length suede boots and skin-tight purple jeans, he looked more like a pimp than a vampire. He held an ice pick loosely in one hand.

"Easy, Mike," Silas murmured. "This is Santino."

Santino leaned in to sniff his neck. "You smell nothing like wolf." This brought a chorus of meows from the troupe. When Santino leaned in again, Mike backed away angrily, rather than allow the vampire to lick his cheek.

Rafe put a cautionary hand on his arm. "You'll have to excuse Santino here. He's an artist and a bit of a diva at times, but he means you no harm."

"Don't make excuses for me, Rafe. I'm just having a little fun." Santino held out the ice pick, handle first. "I've brought you a gift. It's from all of us."

Bewildered, Mike accepted the pick, noticing as he did that several of the grinning vampires had dropped their fangs. He cleared his throat. "Um, thanks."

"Use it if you find yourself overcome with the magic of our performance." This from a goth vamp in artfully shredded black leather, a ton of silver piercings, and pointy-toed cowboy boots. "It will keep you out of Ozzie's hands."

He slipped the pick into his back pocket. There was general laughter from all the vampires at this; even Silas grinned.

The careless expression on Rafe's face disappeared as he addressed the troupe. "Now listen up. Mike is the new pack Beta. He's pack. That means teeth off; no matter how he smells." He thumped Santino in the chest. "Hands and tongues off too, unless you have permission. He's mine."

"Are you saying you've finally taken a blood steward, Rafe?" This from the hot redhead, Lyrissa. "That doesn't sound like you."

"He's Beta. Beta belongs to me, so fangs off. Any questions?"

Santino examined his fingernails. "Watch out, Beta. Lyrissa has a way with that tongue of hers. She can be *very* persuasive." The other vamps thought this was hilarious. Even Lyrissa laughed. Mike frowned as the group followed Rafe backstage.

"Ignore them," Silas said.

"I hate them already. What's the ice pick for?"

"You won't need it. Just be glad you're assigned to Rafe. I saw the look Lyrissa gave you, and believe me, you do not want that woman to notice you."

"I'm a big boy, Silas. I can take care of myself."

"Who are you kidding? You do remember Yolanda, don't you? How did that work out for ya?"

He smirked. "I'm a little out of practice, that's all."

"I'm serious. She's crazy. You may have bit off more than you could chew with Yolanda, but I'm tellin' you that Lyrissa *will kill you*."

Mike grinned and shook his head.

"What's so funny?"

"You know, it's weird, but I think I'm starting to like this place."

"Addicting, ain't it? Let's go. Show's about to start."

Silas explained the set-up to him briefly before the crowd began to arrive. Guests with red tickets were seated in the front row, just steps from the horseshoe-shaped stage. Gold tickets went to the recent donors, who filled the rest of the theatre seats. The atmosphere was intimate; every seat in the house was a good one. The crowd seemed predominantly composed of women, although nearly third of the audience was male. Silas instructed him to only to step in if a guest became unruly.

"Remember, these people are club members," Silas cautioned him as the ushers helped the audience find their assigned seats. "They've paid to come here, and they signed up for this chance to feed the guys who pay our salary. Each of them has a signed waiver on file.

You can think whatever you want, but there is nothing illegal going on here."

"I'm fine with it," Mike protested. "I'm not a cop any more."

"Yeah, but this is your first time. Keep a tight grip on your beast, and don't let the sight or smell of the blood get to you. You're here to keep order. It helps to keep your attention on the audience, not the vamps."

"I'll be fine." Mike took up his assigned position near the top of one of the two aisles leading down to the stage, while Silas moved into position on the other aisle. The audience was strung tight as a drawn bow with anticipation. The house lights went down, and Mike felt nervous. He sensed both the cat and Tehuantl peering out from behind his eyes, eager to see the show.

The blue-lit empty stage drew the eyes of everyone in the theatre. A hazy fog seeped up from the floor, and the haunting sounds of a pan flute floated an eerie melody across the audience. The fog rose into a thick mist, swirling aimlessly around the eddy of the music. The mist gained in substance and form until a figure appeared.

The piper was the red-headed vampire, Lyrissa, garbed in a hooded cloak, her hands pallid and bony as she played the wooden flute; her face veiled to the audience by dark lashes of focused concentration. The music grew as a second flute joined in with a harmonizing tone and a male figure appeared at her shoulder. His eyes glared out over the audience, and demanded attention. Mike inched forward, feeling the dramatic pull of the scene along with everyone else in the house.

The smoke began to pulse around the pair, as their canticle began to weave a spell, which crawled across his skin with an itchy sensation. He glanced over at Silas, but the were-man's attention was focused entirely on the stage. The beat of a drum joined the pulsing of the mist, and a bodhrán player appeared seated next to Lyrissa. The music swelled hypnotically with the addition of two more drummers and a fiddler. As the volume swelled, the tempo and beat of the drums reverberated off the walls and seemed to thrum up from the depths of the floors. A driving rhythm built up. Mike realized the sound mimicked a throbbing heartbeat. A heartbeat later, the vampire performers suddenly materialized onto the stage.

Their appearance had been completely masked by the mist. Rafe stood at the center of the lineup, flanked on each side by four vampires. Of the nine, three were women. The women were dressed provocatively; garbed in tightly corseted bodices coupled with short frilly skirts showing a lot of leg. More cocktail waitress than French maid. The men wore black; each dressed as a different fetish character. Santino was dressed as a pimp-musketeer-pirate guy, while another vampire wore only a tightly-fitted leather mask and straps covering his bloodless groin. On the other side of Rafe stood a guy decked out like a Viking standing next to a three-piece business suit with pointy Italian shoes.

The music softened in volume, but the relentless beat continued without a pause. Rafe stepped off the stage and slowly, deliberately, gazed directly into the eyes of every person in the first row. A wave of wordless sighs rolled across the audience. With a casualness that seemed to project both disinterest and extreme desire, Rafe pointed to a twenty-something man in front of him, and invited him to rise.

The young man's face glowed as if he'd just won a new sports car, and he eagerly bounced forward, his arms flung wide to greet his about-to-be dining companion. He lifted his chin in offering, and Rafe smiled widely at the audience, allowing them a good look at his now snicked-down fangs.

In spite of Silas's warning, Mike couldn't tear his eyes away from the moment when Rafe embraced his volunteer victim like a lover and bit deeply into his neck. As the music reached a crescendo, the man in Rafe's arms spasmed; his back arched and his legs dragged limply toward the floor. As Rafe dug in and the blood began to flow, the audience sighed as one, then howled their approval.

Unexpectedly, Tehuantl roared himself awake in a surge of power. Mike fought to maintain control and made a mute appeal to the cat, but got no response. The taste of blood filled his mouth as he watched a drop of blood escape Rafe's lips and roll down the neck of his victim. *Oh god no!* The theatre was full of people, but it was Rafe that Tehuantl was lusting after. It didn't matter. Nothing with a heartbeat was safe when Tuhuantl came out to play. He had to stop it.

He fought the onslaught, his arms and legs cramping from the stress of the forced change. *Not this time, asshole.*

Suddenly Silas was standing right beside him. "Fight it, man," he whispered, he grabbed his arm. "You can't shift here."

"Help me," he grunted.

Silas fished the ice pick out of his back pocket. "It's silver. If I stab you with this, it's going to hurt like hell. Are you sure?"

Rafe shifted his angle on the stage. *He's watching us.* The pace of the music increased as the two vampires on either side of Rafe stepped forward to select their victims from the front row. The scent of blood and Tehuantl's irresistible hunger filled him.

He nodded. "Do it."

Silas stabbed him in the ass with the pick.

He grunted; the acid sting of silver raced through him like venom. Tehuantl and the cat instantly vanished. He yanked the pick out of the fleshy part of his ass, rubbing his butt cheek furiously where he'd been punctured. "Son of a bitch."

Silas grinned. "Sorry, it's the best spot for missing anything important."

Every inch of his ass felt as if it was being stung by electric wasps. "I can't believe that worked."

"Burns like hell, though don't it? Ozzie invented it. They're pretty handy in emergency situations. Better a pain in the ass than two days in Ozzie's clinic. You okay now, or do you want me to hit you again?"

He shoved Silas away from him. "Hell no," he whispered.

Neither the cat nor the psychotic priest had left the slightest trace of themselves behind. His butt felt like a queen bee was doing a bump and grind act, but it was better than the alternative, and the emergency hadn't disrupted the show. The music continued to rise and fall as the vampires continued to select and feed on the volunteers.

Still shaking, Mike watched as the last two vampires fed. Rafe released his dazed victim into the arms of an usher, who reseated the donor, and handed him his complimentary cocktail. The vampire then selected a second donor from the audience.

By the time the feeding was finished, each vampire had fed from two volunteers, and the audience was chanting in time with the throbbing of the music. The donors in the first row appeared glassy-eyed and smiling in their seats. The vampires were bright-eyed, rosy-cheeked and fairly vibrating with energy. The mist reasserted itself across the stage, and the music began to fade. One by one, the vampires and musicians began to disappear into the fog. Eventually, only the caped figure of Lyrissa remained, until in a final wisp of smoke, she too vanished.

With the last echo of the flute, the house lights came up, and the audience stirred. The now-subdued crowd rose to leave as if they were exiting a Sunday movie matinee. Mike checked the faces of the volunteers, but although one or two seemed a bit unsteady on their feet, they all appeared thoroughly satisfied by the experience. *Son of a gun.* He'd never seen anything like it.

After everyone had gone, Silas showed him how to secure the premises for the night. Even as the ache in his butt receded, his body still thrummed with the music and power of the performance.

"Is it always like that?" His butt still burned where Silas had stabbed him.

"If you're asking about the performance, yeah. That's how most of the nest feeds, except for Ambrose and Cobb. They've always preferred their own blood stewards. And Lyrissa lost her public dining privileges decades ago because she's well, crazy. She likes to play with her food. The estate stores the excess blood donations for research and to cover the slack on nights when the park is closed."

"What kind of research?"

"Ozzie's supposed to be working on finding a cure for the lycanthropy virus, but don't believe it. Ambrose even built Ozzie his own clinic for processing and typing the blood donations. He does a little lab work for the local vets, but that's it."

"What's his deal, anyway? When I woke up the other night, he was slicing me up with a scalpel."

Silas seemed uneasy. "Now you know why nobody wants to lose control on duty. The guy gives everybody the creeps, but Vince won't listen if you complain. I try to stay away from him."

"Well, you were sure right about that ice pick."

"Yeah. Tanner, our old Beta had to do the same thing to me on my first night. The very next day he hooked me up with this therapist, Sarah Powers. She helped me take my control to a whole new level. I never lose control any more."

Mike nodded. "She's working with Tom. Just in case."

"Oh she's the best. I don't know much about shifters, but Dr. Sarah has helped every single wolf in Vince's pack. The company even pays for it."

"What happened to Tanner?"

Silas shook his head. "Nobody knows. When Tanner disappeared, everybody was certain that something bad had happened to him. It was too much of a coincidence that we'd lose so many guys in such a short time. And he had amazing control of his beast; almost as good as Vince. But the fact is, he wasn't an easy guy to like."

"Ambrose told me Vince was the one people didn't like."

Silas snorted, as if the idea was preposterous. "No way. Vince is the best Alpha around. Other packs send their new wolves here to train. That's how we got Yolanda and Wyatt. You're still new, but give him time. Vince is a very good Alpha. You'll see."

"He's going to bust a gut when he hears what happened here tonight." He'd been blindsided by Tehuantl's interest in the vampires. He wasn't safe to be around, he realized. Nothing was going as he'd expected. He was going to have to talk to Vince about being reassigned to another area of the park.

"Nothing happened here tonight, Mike. Nothing. Vince and Rafe both like you. And as for the rest of the pack, the only person who would rather have Trick as Beta is Trick. We need you, Mike; everybody feels it. Lycans don't have a lot of options when it comes to jobs these days, but generally, Mythica is a good place to work. This is a good pack to be in, Mike. You'll see."

WOLF'S LAIR

VINCE DAZAK LIVED just outside of Rushville, about two miles from Mythica. When Mike knocked on the front door, he was surprised to see that Merlene Zimowski-Dazak was human. She possessed the blue eyes, silver hair, and gentle figure of a healthy woman in her mid-seventies. She greeted him warmly and asked him to wait in the living room while she checked to see if Vince was awake. His esteem for Vince went up as he recalled Yolanda's earlier frustration with the Alpha. He wondered if Vince's wife knew about Yolanda.

The room was cozy and homey; comfortable-looking furniture covered in a brown floral fabric. A small photo gallery on the fireplace mantle held a number of faded family photos arranged around a sixties-era wedding photo. Even through the bushy-hair and groovy tie-dye tee shirt, Mike could see the tell-tale golden eyes of Vince's wolf. Beautiful Merlene wore a peace sign necklace over her simple white shift and a wreath of white flowers in her long dark hair. A freckle-faced boy wearing a flowered garland around his neck stood frowning between the happy couple, his resemblance to his mother obvious. Mike recognized Ozzie immediately. Mike squinted at the photo to be sure. Yup, Ozzie hadn't changed much.

A collection of faded photographs documented Ozzie's growing up years; elementary school sports pictures, high school, and college graduation. Nothing recent. No grandchildren.

"This way, Mike." Merlene beckoned to him from the kitchen. He followed her through the family room; noticing his and hers matching recliners flanking a shared end table before a second fireplace. Through floor-to-ceiling windows, he glimpsed a meticulously-groomed back garden framed by dense woods before he was ushered down a short hall into Vince's home office.

Vince sat enthroned behind a massive desk which easily filled half the room. Floor-to-ceiling bookshelves, crammed to overflow with books both old and new lined the walls. Vince's taste in books appeared to lean heavily toward non-fiction; military strategy, civil war history, politics and the like.

"Does my library surprise you?" Vince's voice still held the deep timbre of early morning. It was barely afternoon; still early for Mythica standards.

"I think I'm more surprised by the picket fence and signs of domestic bliss. The garden gnome out front is a nice touch."

Vince showed no sign of embarrassment. "My wife makes all the decorating decisions. I bought the place for its location and privacy. What's on your mind, Mike?"

He paused to gather his thoughts. He'd have to choose his words carefully. He wanted to ask Vince for reassignment, but didn't want to explain why. Vince was such a stickler for control; if he found out what had nearly happened in the theatre last night, he might be out of a job before he got the chance to fulfill his contract for Ambrose. And rightly so.

"I've never been part of a wolf pack before," he began.

"That's a bit of an understatement, wouldn't you say?" Vince's tone was light, but the power of his presence filled the room. "That jaguar of yours won't even hunt with the pack."

He didn't appreciate Vince putting him on the defensive. "There's nothing I can do about that. I never planned on joining the pack. I came here on a lone-wolf contract. If you have second thoughts about having me as your Beta, that's fine with me. Give it to somebody else. Stick me in the control center or on the perimeter somewhere. The contract runs out after the summit anyway." *That was easy. I didn't even have to ask.* _

"I've made my decision, Bane. You'll find a way to fit in to our little family here, I expect."

"What exactly are your expectations? What does a Beta do?"

Vince leaned back in his chair. "Why don't we lay our cards on the table, Bane. When you came to us, you neglected to mention that you have more than one beast. You also neglected to mention that you could destroy a vampire with your bare hands. Is there anything else I should know?"

A nervous tic started at his eyelid. "No sir, you're right. I didn't get a chance to tell you before." He rubbed his eye to stop it. "If you want to reassign me away from the vamps, I'm good with that."

The lines around Vince's eyes crinkled. "You sure did put Ambrose and his boys into a tizzy when that Mayan warrior of yours ripped Torkleson apart like an overcooked turkey."

"My point exactly, sir. I don't want to upset the vamps."

"That's Rafe's problem. I don't care what the vamps think; you work for me. On the other hand, some of the wolves think maybe I made a mistake in bringing you on board. They think you're too dangerous. What do you say to that?"

They were right, of course. Mike had to admit this had been a terrible idea. Tehuantl could not be trusted around vampires. Or humans. And probably not werewolves, either. Stabbing himself in the ass every day was not going to work for long. He sighed. "They're probably right. When that vampire hit me with that taser, I lost control." The admission stung more than he expected.

"No wolf can withstand a stun gun, Bane. That's why I didn't punish you for shifting on duty. Torkelson came prepared; he knew what he was doing."

"It's not just that. Running with the pack is impossible. I didn't realize the hunting thing was going to be such a big deal." The place had grown on him, he realized, but who was he kidding? Mike shook his head. "A cat doesn't belong in a wolf pack."

The Alpha's massive jaw twitched. "You came forward to protect me when you didn't have to. I value loyalty in my men, and reward it wherever I find it." He waved his hand dismissively. "The hunting thing will work itself out."

He's arguing with me to stay? Mike rubbed the tension out of his neck. "My contract ends after the summit. Give the Beta spot to someone else, and put me someplace less critical."

"Forget it. Let me tell you something. There are times when as a leader, you have to make a decision that's not the popular one. You make the hard call. You did the right thing by stepping up to defend me. You also defended the park from Torkelson. You didn't have to do either of those things. Maybe you didn't have much control over what happened, but in that situation, the end justified the means. You protected the flock. Hear what I'm saying? I value that."

"It could happen again, Vince. I can't-." A soothing wave of calm washed over him, stopping him midsentence. *Pheremones.* Trick was a pansy next to this guy.

"I've lost seven pack members over the last year. Good men. The replacements we've gotten have been less than satisfactory. Decent enough raw material, but inexperienced. It takes time to mold them into the soldiers we need. Trick has the juice, but I won't have him until he shows some maturity. I tell you, I'd rather have a dangerous guy like you at my back than facing me. I want you on my team. Now, if you're done pussyfooting around, why don't you tell me why you're really here. Why did you come to Mythica?" Vince's eyes drilled into him.

Mike kept the tension out of his voice, but his hands were sweating. "Ambrose asked me to come in as a consultant. Nothing specific. He mentioned that the pack was short-handed and thought maybe a fresh set of eyes on the security setup before the summit might be useful." He hoped Vince couldn't smell the lie.

"That's a load of crock. Let me tell you something, Bane. Ambrose can be as bad as an old woman. He worries too much. He always wants to fiddle with things; not because there's anything wrong, but just for the sake of change. He won't leave well enough alone. That's what Ambrose does. He pokes at things. Other than being a little lean on security personnel, the pack is fine. I thought I'd finally convinced him we'd be better off waiting until after the summit to bring in anyone new when he heard about you."

"He was very persuasive."

"I'll bet." Vince rubbed his unshaved chin. "Losing our Beta so close to the summit shook everybody. But now that we have you, there's nothing to worry about. The pack is solid. The vampires and the guests are safe, in spite of what Cobb thinks. I've got a feeling about you, Bane. You might be just what we need around here. You might think about staying on after your contract is up. I'm making you a real offer here, if you're interested."

Mike couldn't believe Ambrose really wanted to get rid of Vince. *If I do my job, Vince will be out and Trick will be Alpha.* Vince was right. Trick as an Alpha would ruin the pack. *What if I don't roll over to Trick after I defeat Vince? What if I stayed?* The idea had real appeal.

"Everyone keeps talking about the missing wolves. If you don't mind my asking, what happened to them?"

Vince stood and faced the window. "Living with lycanthropy isn't easy. Some guys thrive in a pack, some do better as lone wolves. Some heed the call of the silver bullet."

"Not you."

The Alpha turned to face him. "No."

"You really think all those guys offed themselves?"

Vince shrugged, but wouldn't meet his gaze. "Like I said, this life isn't for everyone."

He's lying. "A vampire is strong enough to take on a full-grown werewolf."

"So is anyone with silver-tipped ammo." Vince was emphatic. "I hear what you're saying, Bane, but there's no reason for the Van Cleves to take out one of their own wolves. They can't trust humans to guard them while they sleep. Humans are food. A bonded wolf pack is all that stands between the Van Cleves or any other nest and true death at the hands of an angry mob. Besides, none of missing weres were on duty when they disappeared. They'd all clocked out."

"Could one of Ambrose's competitors had someone waiting in ambush? Cobb says they're all fighting over that new territory. Phelan told me that Cobb thinks Torkleson was coming after him."

Vince smirked. "You and I both know he was here for you, Bane. Cobb has always been a bit paranoid, and the territory thing has put him in a real state. Even if it were true, there's nothing we could do about it. We have no proof that anything sinister happened to the missing weres. And this close to the summit, there is no reason why any of Ambrose's enemies would risk poaching on this territory."

"Could someone inside the park be working against Ambrose? How did Torkelson get past the gates, anyway?"

"You're not the only one wondering about that." The Alpha's jaw clenched rhythmically. "I'm planning to get the pack together to do a thorough review a of the security policies for the summit. Brainstorm scenarios and see if we've missed anything else. What do you think, Beta?"

Getting the pack together would be the perfect time to issue the challenge. Mike hesitated, torn by indecision. After Vince had just praised him and offered him a permanent position, he'd felt a real obligation to accept. But maybe Vince was using pheromones on him to make him want to stay. On the other hand, no matter what Vince said, the hunting thing was deal-breaker for the rest of the pack. *Not if I was Alpha. If I was Alpha I could decide about the hunting thing, I'm sure. What if I don't take the dive? Would the rest of the pack accept me?*

He counted Silas and Dave as friends, and maybe Chaney and Wyatt, but who knew how they'd react? They'd never accept me, he realized. Tom's face flashed before him. Hell, Tom was probably going to end up as one of them. Better to just do what Ambrose wanted and get out.

"Yeah, sure. Count me in."

SOMETHING'S HAPPENING HERE

LATER THAT DAY, at the hospital, he ran into Sarah. "Look, I'm sorry I walked out on you the other day. That was rude."

She blushed and shook her head. "No, it was me. I was pushing too hard. I forget sometimes, that people have to be ready to receive help. You're going to have to want to make peace with your beast before you learn to control it. I accept that. But I'm still worried about you, Mike."

Yeah, me too. His butt still ached from the ice pick. "No, I owe you an explanation. I don't know how you know, but I do have two beasts. One is the jaguar that was mentioned in the newspaper. The other is this Olmec Indian priest guy. The legends say that the shamans shared the blessings of the jaguar god in exchange for the blood of his followers. I don't know if that's true or not, but this shaman *likes* to kill. Every time he gets out, people die. So there's no way I can make peace with him. Two nights ago, he killed a vampire with his bare hands. Last night, he nearly got out inside a roomful of people. Can't you see? I'm totally screwed."

She froze, her shocked expression pale. "Actually, I wasn't talking about that."

"Oh." *Shit. Silas was right. I don't know anything about women.*

What an idiot. "Never mind, then." He turned to leave.

She grabbed his arm, pulling him to face her. "What I meant was that when you told me you'd started working at Mythica, I neglected to warn you." She frowned. "Although that other thing sounds pretty bad too."

"Warn me about what?"

"A lot of the lycanthropes who work there have disappeared."

"A few," he shrugged.

"More than a few." She chewed her fingernail, as if debating whether or not to tell him. "Kevin Taylor, one of my patients, was one of them. Kevin was the first to go missing."

A sense of unease came over him. "The Sheriff and Vince seem to think they're suicides."

"It was just before the end of the season last year." She explained that Kevin had come back from the gulf war infected with ALVS and had been unable to control his beast or get a job. He'd applied for a job at Mythica, and been rejected, but Vince had recommended Sarah as a therapist. Several months later Kevin had passed the Mythica interview with flying colors and gotten the job. "Everything was fine for over a year until he disappeared. He never left the estate."

"You must be mistaken. The whole park is under camera surveillance. Vince told me none of the missing guys disappeared while on duty. He must have left the park without you realizing it."

"It was a Saturday night. I was on duty in the ALVS information tent. My car was in the shop and Kevin gave me a ride. After I closed up for the night, I waited for him in the parking lot, but he never came out. I went back inside to look for him, but he wasn't there. He wouldn't have left without me, and his car was still in the lot. We only lived a few blocks from each other. I walked the four miles home from the park in the dark. The next morning, I saw his car parked in his driveway. It was early when I knocked on the door, but he didn't answer."

"Why didn't you tell the sheriff?"

"I did. On Monday, when he didn't return my calls." She sighed. "Vince had already reported him missing. But I know he never left. You have to believe me."

"What makes you so certain?"

She looked uncomfortable. "The same way I know about your beasts. Kevin and I had a connection."

"What kind of connection?"

"When we met, there was an instant connection between us. Like you, he was struggling to control his beast." Her eyes filled with the memory. "I helped him to make peace with it. Once he achieved that inner balance, he was able to gain enough control to persuade Vince to give him a job and join the pack."

"Did you talk to Gordon?"

She shook her head. "I don't understand."

"The Mage. He maintains the wards surrounding the estate. He told me he's sensitive to anyone who crosses the wards. Maybe he could tell you if Kevin is still on the property."

The color drained from her face. "Oh my gosh. You're right. It's the wards. Mike, how much have you seen of the grounds?"

"Most of it, I guess. The house and vault are off limits, of course. But I've seen everything else."

"So where's the distillery? Where's Ozzie's clinic? I tell you, there's something going on out there."

Mike tried to remember if he'd really seen the whole estate. "I don't think so. I'm sure they're there. I'll ask one of the guys."

"Don't you think I've already done that? Every time one of the pack shifts on duty, they are sent to me for a counseling session as soon as they're released from the clinic. Don't you think it's odd that none of them can remember where the clinic is?"

* * *

He ran into Lieutenant Dixon in the parking lot as he was leaving the hospital. Dixon told him he was there to interview Tom about the attack, and asked about his condition.

"His fever is gone. The doc told me they're planning to send him home tomorrow." In a way, the fever had made him feel better about the possibility that Tom might not have contracted the virus, but it didn't matter now.

Dixon gave him a grim smile. "That's too fast."

"Yeah."

"I'm sorry. I know you probably don't appreciate me telling you this right now, but it's not the end of the world. These days, lycans can live reasonably normal lives."

Mike sighed. "The people that say that aren't infected."

"This isn't the dark ages any more. Especially in this part of the country. We've got a world-class set-up here, and there are new diet and therapy programs that can help ease the transition. I'm not saying that it's a good thing, but it's not a mandatory death sentence either. They do lose their rights and citizenship, but at least they're not hunted any more. Fifty years from now, I expect things will be even better. Look at the civil rights movement."

"That is a rather enlightened point of view for someone in law enforcement."

"I've got family with ALVS. My aunt is married to the Alpha werewolf out at Mythica."

No shit. "You're Merlene's nephew?"

Dixon nodded. "You know her?"

"I was just at their house. I've got a contract with the estate."

Dixon's face hardened. "I thought you were leaving town."

"Tom Jolley is my godfather. I'm not leaving, surely you can understand that. That's *my* family infected with ALVS now. Tom only has me to take care of him. He doesn't have a son like Vince does."

Dixon gave him a quizzical look. "What makes you think Vince has a son?"

"I was just at their house. I saw pictures of them with Ozzie."

"Merlene's first husband died in a car accident. Vince adopted Ozzie after they were married, but don't ever make the mistake of calling him Vince's son. At least not in front of Merlene and Vince. Ozzie has always hated Vince. He belongs to Ambrose, now. He's one of Ambrose's damn blood stewards."

"No shit."

"He was a lot older than me. A smart kid, but nobody liked him. Liked to play 'doctor' with the local road kill. A couple arrests for animal abuse that were covered up. Got into vet school, but nobody around here believed he liked animals any better than he liked Vince. He did well, though; finished near the top of his class. The whole family attended his graduation. I remember Merlene and Vince were so proud. At the celebration dinner, Ozzie told us all that he'd already accepted a job offer. Then he dropped the bomb. He said Ambrose Van Cleve had offered him the veterinarian job for the Mythica wolf pack. I'll never forget the shocked look on Vince and Merlene's faces when he showed off the bite marks on his neck."

THE TIME HAS COME

MIKE PAUSED TO read the bronze plaque posted in front of the brick and stone Queen Anne. The inscription stated that the residence had been completed in 1792 as a hunting lodge for the Van Cleve family. The brick and wood-shingled home was painted in a dark forest green with fox red accents and trim. Separated from the amusement park by a high hedge and service road leading to outbuildings behind the residence, the front of the house looked out over a formal rose garden and the estate's vineyards.

Felix had summoned him to the house an hour before his shift was due to start, saying that he wanted to speak to Mike privately. He stepped up to the wide veranda, where Adirondack furniture sprawled haphazardly in clusters around homespun rag rugs. Vince had told him that the residence served as housing for many of the vampires' blood stewards. The place had a homey bed-and-breakfast type of appeal.

Felix answered the door, dressed casually in chinos and chambray button-down, and they rode an antique elevator to the third floor.

The elevator opened directly onto a large, open living room. The spaciousness of the nearly-circular room was dictated by the architecture; banks of large windows gave the place an excellent view of both the amusement portion of the park and a large field of sunflowers directly behind the house, flanked by the deciduous woods beyond. In the distance, a craggy peak rose above the trees.

"What a view. You can see the Tor from here."

"The site for the house was carefully selected. Ambrose wanted to be able to keep an eye on the neighbors."

A rustic stone fireplace dominated the white, high-ceilinged room, decorated with crystal chandeliers, plush Aubusson carpets and classical art. A zebra skin draped over the cream-colored sofa, which was flanked on each end by ornately carved chairs with swanshead armrests. A glass coffee table doubled as a display case for more antique Japanese swords. The rest of the furniture in the room was a blend of pale leather and steel. While none of the elements of the room appeared to match, the overall effect was pleasing and masculine.

"Interesting décor."

"Ambrose and I designed this room as our special place."

Mike wandered over to the fireplace to inspect a life-sized portrait of Felix, Ambrose, Cobb, and Gordon standing in front of the great fanged Ferris Wheel. Fireworks lit up the night sky above them. Each man held up a glass of wine, as if in a toast. A posed scene; vampires didn't drink wine. "You said you wanted to talk to me."

"When are you planning to challenge to Vince?"

"He's planning a meeting with the pack tomorrow afternoon to review security procedures. I figured I'd do it then."

"Excellent. Ambrose is eager to get this issue resolved."

Now that he'd gotten to know Silas and the pack, he no longer believed Ambrose's reason for getting rid of his Alpha. In spite of what Ambrose had told him, the entire pack respected Vince. He was tough, but more than fair, and on a personal level, he'd come to value Vince's approval of him. In a weird way, the whole park was a hoot. Rafe was nothing like he'd expected to be. He really was a good guy. *I could see myself working here*. It didn't feel right to throw it all away.

"The Globus has been asking for the duty roster for the summit. Ambrose does not want to have to change the names at the last minute. Especially of his Alpha. I'm sure you understand. It would send the wrong impression."

"What kind of impression is Ambrose worried about?"

"That he is not in control of his family. That the nest is in a state of flux. That he is promoting his heir at the risk of destabilizing his own nest, and in turn, the region. That he is risking his own safety to ensure Cobb gets his own territory."

"What if something did happen to Ambrose? What would happen to the nest and blood stewards?"

Felix glared at him over his little half-moon glasses. "Anything happens to Ambrose affects all his direct offspring and blood stewards. A steward's addiction is unique to his host vampire. The older blood stewards like myself would certainly die, although some of the younger ones might survive. Unless the steward is able to serve another master in the same bloodline, the death of his master will kill him."

Felix started to say something, then shook his head. "I assure you that Ambrose is in no danger. At any rate, the all-hands meeting sounds like the perfect time for you to confront Vince. With the entire pack present, he will have no alternative but to accept your challenge."

* * *

Mike left the residence and re-entered the park through the south entrance. He crossed the silent amusement park deep in thought. Now that the time had come, he didn't want to do it. He respected Vince too much to challenge him.

How had that happened? He'd been here less than a week, and he'd already put himself squarely on Vince's side. Pheremones or no, he liked the guy. Respected him. Staying loyal to his wife when Yolanda--."

"Hey wimp." Trick's burly form loomed over him; too close and too hot for comfort.

"Out of solitary so soon? Gee, Trick, I never even missed you."

A flash of uncertainty crossed the big man's face. "What were you doing up at the house, pussy? That part of the estate is off limits."

"Felix wanted to give me a medal for whipping your ass."

Trick's face reddened. "Answer me." The air around them began to thicken and roil with Trick's change pheromones.

With a start, he realized that Trick's pheromones no longer affected him. He felt no compulsion to do anything. Mike grinned up at the bigger man. "That's it puppy, go ahead and shift. I dare you. I'm sure Ozzie would love to have you back." He remembered what Sarah had told him about pheromones, and tried pushing back like he tried to push the cat, by focusing his thoughts and pressing on the roof of his mouth with his tongue.

Trick paled, his anger dissipating as quickly as it had come on. He stepped back so quickly, he nearly tripped.

Surprised at his own success, Mike grinned at his would-be aggressor's immediate change in attitude. *Well, that's a neat trick. I guess I've got a little juice of my own.*

Trick backed away, seemingly baffled. "Don't think this is over, Bane. I'm watching you. You and I have unfinished business."

But Trick's words lacked conviction. "Looking forward to it, wolf-pup." He shook his head as the were-man stumbled back to his post. What the hell was Ambrose thinking? Trick as Alpha would be a disaster.

HIDE AND SEEK

AFTER HIS SHIFT ended that night, Mike hung out with Rafe, practicing the coin rolling trick across his knuckles, shooting the breeze with the vampire until Rafe retired, just before dawn. After making sure that the rest of the wolves had gone home for the night, he headed over to the empty clubhouse. The view from Felix's quarters had given him an idea, and he wanted to check it out. There were no security cameras out in the fields; he could approach the private areas of the estate through the woods at the rear of the property. No one had gone out on the Tor hunting tonight, so this was the perfect time to poke around.

Three game trails led away from the clubhouse. One led back to the park, one led to the amphitheater where he'd fought with Vince, and the third led toward the house and private grounds of the estate. He followed the path on a circuitous route through the dense woods and emerged at the edge of the sunflower field behind the house. Most of the windows facing the field were closed and shuttered. Even the blood stewards were asleep at this time of night. On the third floor, where Felix lived, the lights were on, but he saw no movement. A half-moon hovered just above the treeline to the west.

In the field before him, heavy-headed sunflowers drooped;

their weighty blossoms towering six to eight feet above the ground. He skirted the field, searching for a branch off the path, not exactly certain what he was looking for.

He opened himself to the cat's senses and searched for scents or sounds that might have been masked by a ward. He didn't find anything, but persisted. There was something about this field that didn't seem right. While it was possible that the distillery and clinic were hidden somewhere in the woods, he had a feeling that the buildings had to be close to both the house and the park. Two-thirds of the land closest to the house was surrounded by immaculately groomed formal gardens. This field was screened on one side by the tall hedge that encircled the park, on two sides by the woods, and in the front by the house itself. It had to be here.

He closed his eyes and unfurled just enough of the cat to pick up on Gordon's scent, and after a few minutes quiet searching, he found a spot where the scent entered the field of sunflowers. He followed the scent spores down a row between the sunflowers for about thirty yards until the scent disappeared.

Blindly, he reached out with his hands, feeling for anything that didn't feel like sunflowers. Sure enough, he came up against a solid panel which felt like wood. He slid his hands across the surface, searching for a latch. As soon as he felt the metal bolt, he opened his eyes, and the barn-like building appeared before him. As soon as he took his hands away, the structure wavered out of sight. Pretty damn clever. Reaching out again, he slid the latch to the left, and the door slid open on a silent track. He stepped into the distillery and slid the door shut behind him.

It was a warm summer night, but stifling in the distillery. Casement windows circled the room just below the twelve-foot ceilings, letting in the glitter of starlight, just enough to see by. The room contained three huge vats, copper tubing, assorted racks, and bottling equipment. A bank of refrigerators and a stainless steel sink were set up along one wall. The place was spotless and smelled faintly of bleach. A long work table in the center of the room held a computer and printer. He was tempted to power up the computer and check its contents, but decided to keep looking until he found the clinic, which had to be nearby. Now that he was here, he wasn't leaving until he'd had a chance to look around.

Two doors on the wall opposite the vats appeared likely. The first opened onto a flight of stairs leading down into utter blackness. The scent of harsh chemicals and the stink of a roadside zoo assaulted his sinuses. He fumbled for a light switch and followed the stairs into what could only be Ozzie's clinic.

The room was approximately twenty feet square; crowded floor to ceiling with Ozzie's cluttered desk, overflowing bookshelves, cupboards, a sink, a centrifuge, a small freezer unit and two immense refrigerators. An examination table stood in the middle of the room, and there was barely enough room to walk around it without bumping into something. Opposite the entry, a large, solid, sliding door was flanked on either side by a pair of steel cages, built into the floor. The cages were no more than four feet square. This had to be where the werewolves were held in solitary confinement when they were being punished. His blood boiled at the thought of spending two days locked up in one of those cages, like animals. The putrid stench of feces, urine, blood, and filth was strong, but the cages appeared spotlessly clean and disinfected. *So where was the stink coming from?*

It seemed to come from the other side of the door. It was padlocked; but there was a key hanging from a wire on nearby hook. He unlocked the door and it slid aside on a well-oiled track, opening onto another darkened room.

The overpowering reek of death and rotting meat hit him like a blow. He felt around for the light switch, and stood stunned at the sight of a huge cavern stretching out before him.

Thick planks atop garbage cans on one side of the room served as a makeshift counter for bottles of bleach, medical instruments, and an odd assortment of tools. On the left wall, metal lockers provided storage. He stepped cautiously into the room, illuminated only be the glow of two bare bulbs suspended over a beat-up work table made from rough-hewn oak. He reached out to touch the heavy woven straps attached to the table and choked a swallow of bile when he realized that they were stained with dried blood. Beneath the table, a pair of heavy-duty truck batteries caught his attention. He recoiled as he realized their purpose. The goose-bumps that raced up his arms had nothing to do with the chilly basement.

This was a very bad place.

The dim light wasn't enough to fully illuminate the extent of the hall-like cavern. Beyond the massive table, a long row of stables stretched into darkness. This must have been the old slave quarters, he realized. As he approached the gloomy center aisle, he noted each self-contained wooden stall was gated across the front with sturdy wire mesh. His heart skipped a beat as he looked into the first stall.

Inside, a filthy, emaciated wolf lay collared and chained to the floor. He opened the cage, but the creature didn't move. As he squatted to check for a pulse, a thready heartbeat confirmed that the werewolf was still alive. The shape of its skull showed starkly through the thinning pelt covered in long-dried feces. The wolf's fur felt like dead grass. The poor thing was starving to death. It was too far gone even to open its eyes. Cold anger rolled through Mike. *What kind of sick fuck would do something like this?*

He remembered the curiously detached look he'd seen on Ozzie's face when Mike had woken up and caught him slicing into his flesh. *Damn you, Ozzie.* These were the missing werewolves. His outrage grew as he raced from stall to stall. There were far more than seven wolves here. Not one wolf stirred. He shouted and banged on the doors. All were too sick or drugged to even respond. *This is Ozzie's work.* It had to be. As far as he could tell, about half the cells were occupied. He'd need help to get them all out.

When he reached the end of the aisle, he stopped and groaned with dismay. Another black cavern branched off to the left where the dim, distant lighting could not penetrate. This was where the scent of rotting corpses was coming from.

There had to be another light switch somewhere. He felt around for a switch, but when his hand brushed the grill across the front of the nearest stall, something hissed and slammed against the mesh. He stumbled back. Strange, unfamiliar scents blended with the rank air. No doubt these things thrived in darkness. He remembered the Fae creatures he'd seen at the Odditorium. Oh my god. These are Fae creatures from the Tor. Gordon's hostages. How long had they been here? Scavengers for Ozzie's handiwork, he guessed. *Disgusting.*

He had to see. There had to be a flashlight around here somewhere. But as he turned to go look, a strange scent came to him. A familiar scent. Female. Not Yolanda or anyone he knew, but familiar. Behind his eyes, Tehuantl pushed, nudging to let him out. No way.

Cold anger coursed through him as he ran back toward the work room. He searched the lockers for a flashlight. Disgust and fury coursed through him as he found catchpoles, stun batons, and long, stout sticks with metal collars and pinchers on the ends; probably used for moving the prisoners from their dungeons to the table for torture. This was no workroom. The collars had sharp silver-tipped spikes *on the inside.* This was a hall of torture.

Finally he found a working flashlight. His footsteps echoed across the cavern as he ran back to the Fae section. He *had* to see what was in those cages. He kept a tight grip on his emotions as he checked each stall with the flashlight. Occasionally, the light caught the gleam of an open eye, but no movement. Once he turned the corner, however, the Fae skittered away from the light and the half-eaten wolf corpses they'd been feeding on. One stall held a pale white scorpion the size of a washing machine, with twin curling stingers curved over its back, and eight clear blue eyes glaring balefully at him over a tiny screaming mouth full of needle-like fangs. Its two front legs looked more like tiny hands than pincers. It whistled its hatred of the strong light. Other stalls held larger versions of the tiny lizard people he'd seen in the Odditorium. *Oh my god, they're breeding in here.* Other cells held dark, clumsy things that flopped and flapped away from the light. He couldn't tell what they were.

Not until he finally reached the solid stone wall at the end did he find the cage he was looking for; the one that smelled so familiar. It was déjà vu all over again. In the farthest corner, as far away from the door as possible, lay the still form of a female Nagual. He couldn't even tell what species it was. Her fur was caked with dirt and clumps of dried filth. He looked for signs of life in the beam of the flashlight, but she was still as death. The door squeaked loudly when he opened it, but she showed no sign of life.

"Hey there," he murmured. "I'm not going to hurt you." He sweated profusely in the chill damp air. There was no rotting wolf corpse here; the smell of decay inside this stall was old. He crouched beside her. It was a bear, he realized. Tehuantl pushed at him to touch the matted fur; to make contact. He kept his hands to himself, even as he longed to touch her. Now was not the time. Hot tears streaked down his cheeks.

"I'm going to get you out of here," he choked. But even as he said the words, the enormity of the problem hit him. He'd need help getting everyone out. He'd need to bring the pack in on this. And Rafe. *Now.*

He headed back to the workroom, determined to put an end to the torture and make Ozzie pay for this. No sooner had he turned the corner than he realized someone else was in the cavern. Two men stood talking at the worktable in the torture room. He turned off the flashlight and stepped back into the darkness.

"I tell you Cobb, that door didn't unlock itself. And the lights were on. There's someone down here."

"What is that stink?"

"Oh come on, it's not that bad," Ozzie answered. "It's the Bestiary. What do you think?"

They're coming this way. He retreated back toward the Nagual's cage.

"What do you want me to do, Ozzie? It's nearly dawn."

"Come on, this'll only take a few minutes. Down this way"

The bright beam of flashlights penetrated the gloom as the men closed in. Mike slipped into the still open door of the Nagual's cage.

"What the hell is that?"

"Oh don't be such a prude, Cobb. The wolves aren't as hardy as you'd think, and these Fae monsters will eat anything."

Mike heard a snorting, gagging sound from Cobb, followed by a string of oaths.

"Forget it. I can hardly breathe. I'm out of here, Oz. You probably forgot to lock up. If you really think there's somebody down here, then lock 'em in. There's no way out. The smell alone should kill 'em."

"No wait," the sounds of Ozzie's protests followed the heavier step of Cobb's footfalls until their voices receded and the light in the main cavern went out. After a minute, Mike flicked on the flashlight and ran back to the work room to check the sliding door, but it was closed and wouldn't budge. He tried his cell phone, but there was no signal.

Great. Caught like a rat in a trap. Cobb and the rest of the vamps were down for the day, but he had no doubt that Ozzie would be back with reinforcements. Adrenaline flooded through him; his mind raced as he tried to figure a way out. *I've got to get help. I've got to get out of here!*

In the tomb-like silence, he heard the scratch of claws on stone as a creature approached in the darkness. His heart skittered as he fumbled for the flashlight.

A cold wet nose nudged his arm.

He jumped, and the flashlight clattered to the floor. In the dim reflection of the flashlight, Farley panted and wagged his tail, as if delighted to find him here.

"Dammit, dog. You about gave me a heart attack. Where the hell did you come from?"

The dog trotted back toward the Fae section of the cavern, and paused as if waiting for him to follow.

What the-? He followed the dog until they reached the back wall next to the Nagual's cage. The dog woofed at him softly, then passed directly through the wall. *Well I'll be. It's another ward.*

Feeling for the edges with his hand, he squeezed his way through the hidden crack. The roof of the tunnel was too low to stand up in so he followed Farley on hands and knees. It was awkward to hold the flashlight, but he couldn't see where they were going without it. He considered shifting into cat form, but decided against it. The estate was miles from the Sheriff's office. He'd have a better chance of being believed if he arrived wearing clothes.

The tunnel climbed upward and opened into a shallow cave as they reached the top of the ascent. More of a den, really. Too low to stand up in, it was ten feet across, with the entrance screened by a thick copse of willow. The humid night air smelled as sweet as perfume after the putridity of the cavern. The sky above the horizon was light. The sun would be up soon. They were on a rocky outcropping on the Tor.

He heaved a sigh of relief. He couldn't see the road, but knew it couldn't be far. He followed Farley down a narrow game trail to a stream, where the mutt turned south, heading toward the cottage.

"No boy, the road is this way." He turned west, keeping to the tree line, not wanting to risk being spotted. "We've got to get to the road."

The deerhound ignored him and continued to trot south, without looking back. *Stupid dog.* No matter. It would be easier to hitch a ride without the mutt, anyway. It was rough going, but the trees could provide cover all the way to the road. Gordon had probably felt him cross the wards. He'd probably report the trespass to Vince. Would the Mage know that it was him?

The thought stopped him cold. *Does Vince know about the bestiary?* Pack punishment for disobedience was being solitary confinement in Ozzie's lab. But the lab was nothing like the bestiary. Vince might not know about it. Besides, Vince would never let anyone do something like that to a member of his pack. And Dixon had told him that Ozzie and Vince weren't close. Mike shook his head. No way. Vince couldn't know. And Vince's house was a lot closer than the Sheriff's office.

He turned northwest, finding the going even tougher, until he stumbled across a game trail. But the moment he stepped onto the trail, he realized his mistake. Thirty feet in front of him stood a man armed with a hunting bow. Tethered to him by a thin cord tied around his waist, Farley wagged his tail, as if to say, 'Look who I found!'

Before Mike could react, he was grabbed from behind; his arm twisted up his back, and a very sharp knife held to his throat. "If you fight me you will die," a woman's voice cooed.

AMBROSE

"WHAT DO YOU mean, *he got away*," Ambrose snarled. The heat of Gordon's blood called to him, but he kept the Mage at arm's length. Gordon's need for him was at least as strong as his own, but Gordon deserved to feel his anger.

"Bane isn't one of your pet wolves," Gordon protested. "I tried to tell you that when you first brought him in. He feels different. And when he crossed the *inner* wards, I tell you, he felt like full-blooded Fae."

"You told me no one could pass through the inner wards," Ambrose answered. He squared off against Gordon in the center of the warming room, while Cobb lounged carelessly on the sofa, watching them argue with a knowing smirk.

Gordon shook his head. "I never said that. The wards cannot prevent anyone from passing through them. Like all the other inner wards, the tunnel exit from the bestiary was heavily warded. I said it should have been impossible for him to find."

"Yet somehow he did." Silently, Ambrose fumed. *How could this have happened?* "What was he doing wandering around the estate in the first place? Are you sure it was Bane?"

"He's the only one who didn't show up for his shift tonight," Cobb answered. "Nobody's seen him since last night. He's not answering his phone."

The blood fever brought on by his hunger and Gordon's bad news was getting worse. Even his teeth hurt. Ambrose couldn't put the Mage off much longer or they'd both be hurting. But if Bane had found the bestiary, he wasn't likely to ignore it. He was an ex-cop; he'd probably make a stink to the local authorities. Unfortunate. It wasn't the end of the world, but the timing was inconvenient. He would need to do something.

The ache at his temples throbbed unbearably. He'd be useless for the rest of the night if he didn't feed, and from the sheen of sweat on Gordon's face, he could see the Mage was also in need. He sighed and held his arms out to Gordon.

The Mage moved into his embrace and Ambrose sank his fangs dug deep into his blood steward's neck. Hot blood filled his mouth. The feel and taste of Gordon always affected him strongly. Fae blood was truly a wondrous nectar. A pity the Mage was his only full-blooded Fae steward. He drank deeply, keeping the other man from pressing too closely and damaging himself in his eagerness. Something about the combination of Fae blood and vampire saliva created a powerfully heady experience for both predator and prey. His steward's intoxicating heat spread through his limbs like a flame.

As his hunger subsided, Ambrose retracted his fangs, and carefully cleansed Gordon's already healing wounds with his tongue. He settled his swooning donor into a recliner. Gordon recovered quickly from his rapture; his cheeks flushed, his eyes bright. Even after all this time, Ambrose marveled that Gordon's blood could still satisfy him as no other. His fever, fury, and frustration had disappeared along with his headache.

"Alright, Gordon. Carry on. I expect to be informed immediately if you detect any other unusual disruptions in the wards. You may go."

As soon as Gordon left, Cobb started in again. "I tried to tell you he was dangerous, but you wouldn't listen. What are we going to do now? Bane could ruin everything. We should have killed him when he had the chance."

Cobb was always so quick to panic. Ambrose remembered the moment when, as a mortal, Cobb had discovered that his employer of two years was a vampire. He'd fled in terror; using the knowledge as an excuse to go off on a bender of drinking and brawling. When Ambrose finally found him, he was broken and bloodied, left for dead in the alley behind a slaughterhouse. A broken rib had punctured his lung, and pink bubbles frothed from between his mashed lips. Once he recognized that the body belonged to his missing foreman, he almost passed by, but paused to reconsider.

The man had been invaluable to him when he'd first arrived in Baton Rouge. Cobb was well-known, albeit on the seamier side of the city, and had steered several profitable opportunities in his direction. He wasn't just smart, he was *clever*. He would not be easily replaced. So Ambrose tossed his foreman's dying body over his shoulder and took him to his lair beneath the St. Martin's Hotel and made Cobb his first-born son. In spite of Cobb's shortcomings, Ambrose had never regretted it.

"Calm down. It's not the end of the world." Ambrose took a seat at the puzzle table and put on his glasses. "And after seeing what he's capable of, I'm not inclined to go up against him."

"What are you talking about? He wouldn't stand a chance against all of us. Or if you're too squeamish, send the wolves after him."

"As usual, you're missing the big picture, Cobb." The only areas of the puzzle remaining un-pieced were either the brownish-grey pattern of the windmills, or the sky. "We need Bane to get rid of Vince for us. We need to think this through." He tried placing a sky-blue puzzle piece, but it didn't fit. "It doesn't matter if he discovered the bestiary. There are no laws against keeping pets or having a menagerie. It might be awkward if some of the others got wind of it, but it isn't the end of the world. All we need is a bit of leverage."

Cobb began to pace the room. "I don't understand you. You're willing to risk our future, my future, because you don't have the guts to handle this. Vince wanted to leave years ago. Why didn't you just let him go while you had the chance?"

"I cannot tell you how many times I've asked myself the same question. Vince Dazak is the finest, most loyal wolf I've ever known. He is a credit to his species. When he married Merlene, her political connections were a boon to us. When I made Ozzie my blood steward, my only thought was to keep Vince with us always. As a bonus, we got a veterinarian for the pack. A win-win for everyone."

"Ozzie's a frickin' nut job."

Ambrose peered over his glasses at his first-born. "Obviously. I made a mistake."

The admission stung, but it was the truth. He'd never considered how deeply Ozzie hated Vince. Or how badly Ozzie wanted to hurt him. Ozzie's cruel obsession with the wolves had only grown worse as the years passed and his addiction to his master's saliva had deepened. It happened that way with some of them. Psychological predilections sometimes bloomed into full-scale psychoses.

The Vampire Minority Political Action Committee, VMPAC, had spent years and millions of dollars to dispel the unreasonable human fear of being fed upon by a vampire. By the Globus' own secret decree, all blood stewards who exhibited the advanced symptoms of blood steward's dementia had to be terminated in a manner that could not be traced back to a vampire or result in an autopsy. If humans ever found out that there was a chance of physical impairment or decline from addiction to vampire saliva, the eternally-feared Armageddon of the undead would begin.

For a long time, Ozzie had been satisfied with just one pet. But as the years passed, Ozzie's demands for more fresh 'lab rats', as he called them, had gotten out of control. He'd taken the last two wolves without permission. The physical symptoms of his madness were becoming obvious to all the vampires. Ozzie's recent decline and corresponding sociopathic moral decay left Ambrose with no other options. He had to go. This wasn't just a matter of keeping Ozzie out of sight until the end of the summit. One word to the wrong vampire, and the future of the entire nest was at stake.

"I cannot eliminate Ozzie while Vince is Alpha."

"You're letting your feelings for your pet wolf get in the way of what needs to be done here. Ozzie's symptoms are becoming obvious to just about everyone. Even your pet wolves are starting to notice. And Bane knows all about Ozzie's little playroom now. I say kill them both."

He rubbed his forehead. "Damn it, Cobb. That's not the answer. If anything happens to Ozzie, Vince has unrestricted access to every corner of the estate. He and that pack of his will come down to the vault in broad daylight and kill us all."

Frustration flashed across Cobb's face. "If Bane goes to the Sheriff, not even Merlene's connections will keep us safe from an executioner's stake."

"Not true," Ambrose corrected. "We have broken no laws here. There are no humans in the bestiary."

"Have you been down there recently? It's disgusting. To be honest, until Gordon confirmed it, I thought that Ozzie made the whole thing up. Why didn't you tell me there was another exit?"

"It's been so long, I'd forgotten. Besides, it opens on the Tor. It's unusable to us."

"When are you going to listen to me?" Cobb slapped the arm of the couch for emphasis. "You're going to have to do something. Ozzie and Bane could ruin the summit; and Vince could bring this whole park down around our ears. The idea that you need to depend on a wolf pack for protection is archaic, at best. Vince has always been far too particular about hand-picking his weres for the pack. Don't you see? With all those weres behind him, it's no wonder he's gotten so powerful. I've been telling you for years that we should be hiring professional lone wolves to handle our security. I know you don't like the idea of hiring mercenaries, but it's the fastest way of getting the personnel we need to support both our territories. I will *not* be denied my own territory, Ambrose."

"That is exactly why we need Bane to get rid of Vince for us. Once Vince is out, Felix will arrange for Ozzie to die in a tragic car accident and our hands will be clean. Trick will take over the wolf pack, and the summit will go just as we planned. Once the Puerto Rican bitch accepts him and joins the pack, filling the other empty slots will be easy. The Globus is a traditionalist; he'll be more impressed by the size of our wolf pack than by hired help. It's a win-win for everybody."

"Are you mad? Bane is gone. That were-cat is not going to get rid of Vince for us. We're running out of time," Cobb said. "It's time to call in the mercs."

"Of course he will. Bane's godfather, Tom Jolley, is in the hospital recovering from major surgery. All we need to do is pick him up and hold him until Bane fulfills the terms of his contract with us."

Cobb scowled at him. "Taking wolves is one thing. Kidnapping humans will get us all staked."

"My dear boy, kidnapping is a term reserved for humans. One way or another, Tom Jolley is going to develop full-blown lycanthropy at the next full moon. Our timing is perfect. A little Glamour cocktail will keep him from retaining any memory of his stay with us, and in two days, we'll be able to put this all behind us."

"What about Bane?"

"There's a bounty out on him," Ambrose said. "We will give him to Ivey and that Clemente fellow and collect the reward." He positioned a piece of pale blue sky into place. It fit perfectly.

"Good thinking." Cobb grinned. "Now you're talking. I'll pick up

Jolley myself."

"No, I want Felix to handle it. He understands the situation and delicacy required."

"Let Felix handle the negotiations with Bane. That's what he's good at, anyway. I'll take care of Jolley. This is more my line of work than Felix's and you know it. This is my future we're talking about. I will not allow you or Felix to screw this up for me. If I lose that territory, I swear I'll take Mythica from you."

"Watch your mouth, son. Your future depends on me, not the other way around. I could have you chained in your crypt for such insolence, so don't threaten me."

"It's not a threat, Ambrose. It's a promise."

THE HIGH TOR FAE

THE WOMAN BEHIND Mike held him in a grip like iron. Several more hunters approached from either side, dressed in a muted, patterned fabric that changed to mimic whatever color it touched—perfect camouflage. They held their bows casually, but each had arrows knocked.

Oh great; High Tor Fae. All the warnings he'd ever heard came back to him. *The Fae are territorial; stay off the Tor. No humans allowed on the Tor. Beasts only allowed on the Tor.* He tried to unfurl the cat, but for the first time in his life, the jaguar wouldn't come.

"I greet you Xentochi," said the leader, as he approached Mike. "I see you Tehuantl. We welcome you and are honored by your presence as guests on our land. Our business is with your host."

A dozen questions flooded through him as Mike struggled to remain calm. "Who are you? What are you doing with my dog?"

"I know you too, cousin," the leader answered. "This is not the first time we've met, Mike Bane. I am Nixese."

He had a slender build, skin the color of polished oak, and pale eyes. Not blue, but not brown, either. Grey, maybe.

"This is the second time you have broken our laws. There is no one to take your punishment this time." He patted the deerhound and Farley panted happily.

Mike bit back a groan. *How could I have been so stupid?* He tried reaching for Tehuantl, but came up empty. It was as if neither had ever existed. "There are people in trouble back there. Some of them are your people. They need help; they're being held prisoner."

"We are not interested in the problems of men," the woman with the knife snarled. She shoved him forward and he stumbled. "You have no honor." She horked loudly and spat.

"Enough Daneah," Nixese said.

Nixese was their leader. "I told you, there are Fae prisoners back there. Help me get them out."

Nixese remained impassive. "Three hundred years ago, one of our clan agreed to become the blood steward of Ambrose Van Cleve. This traitorous act was bad enough, but he took the daughter of one of our elders with him. Lyra did not go willingly. He then tricked us into signing a blood treaty with the Van Cleve vampires, using her and others of our tribe as hostages. As sometimes happens, once removed from the land of her clan, Lyra lost her will to live and began to weaken and die. Rather than risk losing her beauty and magic, the vampires made her one of them. It is an abomination. The traitor Gordon used our own blood and magic against us when he invoked his dark wards. We cannot cross them without breaking the treaty. If the treaty is broken, the hostages will die."

"All the more reason to let me get them out of there," he protested. Why wouldn't they listen? "They're being kept in horrible conditions. They're dying."

Nixese seemed unperturbed. "Our clan is immortal unless we choose otherwise, cousin. In a war between vampire and Fae, many human lives will be lost. The Van Cleves have surrounded themselves with blood stewards and use them as human shields. We are also bound by a treaty with your American Government to stop taking human life in exchange for our sovereign reservation. If war erupts between the undead and the Fae, your government will destroy us."

"What about the others? What about the wolves? Surely you can't allow them to suffer." Mike sensed that Nixese was conflicted; that he might actually let him go, if only he could convince him.

"They are not our concern," Deneah hissed.

Nixese nodded in agreement. "In the eyes of your own government, lycans are neither human nor clan."

"This is crazy," Mike said. "Listen to me. I can bring out both your kinsmen and the wolves."

"No!" Daneah was vehement. "This is none of his affair. He is not one of us. He works for the vampires! Choose your punishment, cousin," she spat. "Imprisoned beneath the Tor or allowed to roam in a form of our choosing. Deliver the punishment and be done with it, Nix."

"She's right," one of the others agreed. "We are not here to negotiate terms."

"Florian, would it hurt to let the elders decide?" Nix asked. "You see he hosts the spirits of Xenotchi and Tehuantl within him. With magic of the First Jaguar behind him, perhaps there is a way to free our loved ones."

Somewhat reluctantly, the others agreed.

Hope rose within him, and he prayed is wouldn't take long. Every minute in that dungeon brought the wolves closer to death.

"Very well," Nix said. He lowered his weapon. "We will present you to the court of elders to answer for your trespass. I warn you that they may not accept your offer. They could decide to inflict a harsher punishment." Two of the warriors bound Mike's arms behind his back, and looped a thread-like leash around his neck. He tried again to call the cat, again with no luck. He had no choice but to follow his captors.

They walked for hours. With each passing minute, Mike's anxiety grew as he worried about the prisoners left behind in that cavern of horrors. The idea of leaving them to Ozzie's abuse and neglect tore at him with every step.

As they travelled, the character of the woods gradually changed from native beech, alder, and maple to darker, older trees of hemlock, oak, and cedar. Beneath their feet, the lush green summer grasses thinned and dried beneath the forest canopy. The drone of cicadas faded, as did the quality of light and intensity of the sun. They were no longer in the High Tor Wilderness Management Area anymore, he realized. He doubted they were even in New York. He remembered the stories that his father and Taffy had told him about the Fae lands. The lands *inside* the Tor, they'd told him. This must be the place, he mused. Repeatedly, he reached for the cat, but the cat was nowhere to be found.

The hazy sun was past its zenith when they crossed onto a wider track. His captors picked up their pace and he was forced into a jog. After a couple of miles, they left the thickest part of the forest behind and the character of the terrain changed again. The land here consisted of low, rolling hills interspersed with dense copses of trees and woodlands.

Eventually, they reached a settlement clustered within a grassy clearing among the hills. The village consisted of hide-covered pavilions and low buildings built of log and stone. Pheasants and bronze turkeys wandered the unpaved streets with the same air as domesticated chickens. The air was cooler here, even in the hazy light of the mid-day sun. Lush vegetable and flower gardens flourished around each structure. Indian corn hung from simple wooden drying racks; apple trees, heavy with ripe fruit indicated that the seasons inside the Tor did not match up with the calendar year.

They left him in a storage barn, with the fierce woman, Daneah, to watch over him. He fidgeted uncomfortably, but the woman refused to release him. She seemed to enjoy his discomfort.

* * *

After what seemed like hours, Nix finally returned and brought him before the elders. They were seated at a low table located inside one of the long houses that seemed to serve as a general gathering place. Two women and four men; each brown-skinned, slim, and clad in the same soft patterned leathers that the hunters wore. Each also wore a length of woven fabric draped across their shoulders and held in place with a carved wooden clasp.

They were a handsome group, although none of them looked pleased to see him. Men and women alike wore heavy cuffs of polished silver around their upper arms. Mike knew their actual age was beyond reckoning. Time passed differently in the Tor, he knew. The elders appeared older than Nix and his companions. They looked to be anywhere between forty to sixty years in human years, but true Fae were immortal. They could change their appearance on a whim.

As a boy, he'd believed the stories and taunts he'd heard from the other kids at school. He and Striper Dave both carried the darker complexion of their Tor clansmen. People said that the Fae of the High Tor had lost the ability to have children of their own and so stole the children of humans from their beds at night. They hypnotized them with the magic of their music and honeymeade wine so that they would forget their parents and where they came from. None of the children kidnapped by the Fae were ever seen again.

"This is the son of Farley Bane." Nixese announced. "He has knowingly trespassed a second time onto the Tor. We would have carried out his punishment, but he claims that the Van Cleves have been mistreating our people. He has offered to destroy the Earth Mage and return our missing clansmen."

Instead of answering Nix, one of the women spoke to him directly. "I see you, Xenotchi. I see you, Tehuantl." She bowed her head respectfully. "Why is the First Jaguar here? Why does he concern himself in matters between the High Tor clan and the undead?"

"Who is Xenotchi?" Mike asked.

The answer came from a man on the far left. The lower half of his face was covered with a stylistic blue tattoo. "Xenotchi is First Jaguar. Not of our clan, but legend. Always an honored guest in our lands. Tehuantl is his high priest."

Xenotchi. Immediately, he felt the cat's presence beneath the surface of his skin. Tehuantl's too.

"Why have you agreed to destroy the earth mage, Gordon?" A woman wearing a silver toque around her neck asked.

"I didn't say that I would kill him, but with your help, I will release the wolves and Fae imprisoned behind the Mythica wards."

"You broke our laws. You trespassed on our land in human form," the tattooed man said. "It is our right to punish you."

"I was trying to get help, There are lycans and Fae being held captive in a cave beneath the Van Cleve estate. They're being tortured. It's been going on for a very long time."

"Only mortals count the passage of time; it has no meaning for us," said the woman with the silver toque.

"If you knew what was going on in there you wouldn't say that. They're starving. There is no water. They are forced to feed on corpses. Maybe your people can't die, but they're living in misery."

"Don't let him distract you, Torgh," protested Daneah. "He works for the vampires. He came onto our land in human form."

Torgh, the heavily tattooed elder pointed at angrily at Mike. "By crossing the wards, he has also broken our treaty with the vampires. No Fae may cross the wards."

Mike struggled to maintain his composure. "You can't have it both ways. If I'm Fae, I broke no law by entering the Tor in human form. If I'm not Fae, I didn't break your treaty with the Van Cleves by crossing the wards. Don't punish me for what I am or am not. Help me get those people out of there."

"We cannot cross the wards," the woman shook her head sadly.

"And the passing of time means little here. Perhaps the magic of First Jaguar is greater than that of the blood wards. But we cannot allow the son of Farley Bane to thwart our laws a second time. You will remain within the Tor as our permanent guest. Are we agreed?" She looked at the others, each of whom nodded.

He fought to control his rising panic. "Wait a minute. What about Xenotchi and Tehuantl? Where I go, they go. They've broken no laws. You said they were honored guests. How can you keep them here against their will?"

"We are different clans of the same ancient tribe. Xenotchi and his priest will be happy here."

What is wrong with these people? Couldn't they see he was trying to help them? It was almost as if they'd rather see him punished than rescue their clansmen. Talking to them was about like talking to Internal Affairs. Their arguments didn't go anywhere, they merely circled the drain. It didn't make sense. Wasn't it enough that they'd already taken Farley? He had to find a way to get through to them.

"Give me two days. I swear I'll get your people out of there. What have you got to lose?"

The elders at the table all turned to the woman with the silver toque. "What say you, Altheah," asked Torgh.

They made him wait in the barn while they discussed it. He paced; alternatively cursing his captors and praying they'd accept his proposal. Nix did not return until the next morning. In spite of Daneah's angry protest, he was untied and released with a two-day deadline: "Release our people and we will reconsider your punishment."

PRIORITIES

DANEAH AND NIX escorted him through a portal which emerged directly into his back yard; the very tree which the jaguar Xenotchi used as a scratching post. Tom was right. The cottage was on Fae land. He realized with a start that Tom was being released today.

Or was he? The clock in the kitchen said 6:30am, but he was certain he'd lost at least a day out on the Tor. What day was it? He called the hospital and they told him Tom had been released the previous day. Dr. Sarah Powers had made the arrangements.

He called Tom but there was no answer. His uneasiness grew as he checked his messages. Vince, Silas, and Rafe had all called looking him. *There.* Tom had called less than an hour ago. As he replayed the message, his pulse pounded with every word.

"Hello Mike, Felix Tolland here. Tom is unavailable at the moment. Your stepfather and your girlfriend are currently enjoying our hospitality. Based on our previous conversation, I believe you are aware of our timetable and the overdue need for action on your part. As soon as the party in question is relieved of his duties, your loved ones will return from their little stay-cation. Should you delay further, or jeopardize our agreement in any way, I'm afraid we will

have no other choice but to terminate your contract."

He swore and threw the phone across the kitchen. He dragged his hand through his hair as he frantically tried to figure out what to do.

"Do you sleep in the cage or on the bed?"

He jumped. Behind him, Yolanda stood in the doorway, wearing nothing more than a smile and one of his old tee-shirts. "What the hell are you doing here?"

"I was waiting for you." She came toward, him, her eyes smoldering, sleep lines on her cheek. "Where have you been? Everybody's looking for you."

He moved past her, down the hall to his bedroom. "I don't have time for this."

"Don't you walk away from me. What was Felix talking about? Why didn't you tell me you had a girlfriend?"

"I don't." He changed into jeans and a tee-shirt while she sat on the bed and watched. He ignored her as he reached into the closet and pulled a box down from the upper shelf. "You've got to get out of here. And don't go back to Mythica, either. Leave town. Go back to wherever you came from."

"Did you know Vince is married? Tell me."

"What?" *Oh geeze.* "Yes. But that's not important." He set the box on the bed and went into the guest room to get the key out of the desk." She followed him from the bedroom to the guestroom and back again, her agitation growing with every step.

"Vince brought me out here on false pretenses. He told me I could be his. He's been lying to me the whole time." She tugged at his arm, her expression intense. "I would never have come here if I'd known he was married. He has no intention of leaving his wife. You have to do something."

He twisted out of her grip. "I've found the missing wolves. They're locked up in the old slave quarters, I think." He unlocked the box and pulled out his service revolver. Automatically, he checked the chamber. Empty. Good.

"Vince needs to go. Trick is weak. I know that now. But you're not. You've got plenty of juice; Beta pheromones don't lie. I like you, Mike. We could be good together." She moved closer and rubbed against his arm. Still warm from sleep, she smelled like heaven.

"Shut up." He shook her. "Did you hear me? Ozzie's got the missing pack members caged beneath the estate. He's torturing them. They're starving to death."

Her expression changed to one of uncertainty. "Trick told me there's something wrong with Ozzie. He overheard Ozzie and Cobb arguing about Ambrose. Cobb offered Ozzie a lot of money to leave the estate, but Ozzie told him he's got something called 'blood steward's dementia'. He's addicted to Ambrose's saliva, but it's eating his brain cells. If he leaves, he'll die. Cobb told him that Ambrose already knew about it, and was planning to kill him. He said the only thing stopping him was his fear of retaliation from Vince."

He shook her. "Is Trick absolutely sure about that?"

She hid behind her dark mane. "No. It happened when Trick was in solitary. Ozzie kept him doped up on ketamine most of the time. He wasn't sure whether it was a memory or just a dream."

"Does Vince know? Does he know that Ozzie is keeping the wolves locked up beneath the estate?" He selected the small box of silver ammunition from the bottom of the box and began to load his weapon.

She shrugged. "I don't know. I haven't been here long enough to know for sure. I didn't even know he was married," she added, bitterly. She looked so unhappy.

"Forget this place," he told her. "Find another pack. Anyone would love to have you."

Her face softened. "Thank you for that." She seemed to notice the gun in his hand for the first time. "What are you going to do?"

"I'm still working on it. I've got to find Tom and Sarah." If they were really gone, they hadn't been missing long enough to file a missing persons report. Dixon wouldn't lift a finger without a warrant. "And I've got to get everybody out of there."

"Let me help you."

"No. Look, I don't know what's going on. Once I find out, I'll talk to Vince."

"Take me with you."

He slipped on his shoulder holster. "Ambrose hired me to challenge Vince for Alpha so they could replace him with Trick. You heard Felix. They're holding my godfather and his therapist. They must think she's my girlfriend. I don't know if Vince knows what's going on, but I've got to make sure Tom and Sarah are safe. And I've got to get the wolves and Fae out of the bestiary. That's all I care about."

"Well I'm not just going to sit around waiting."

"I'm not asking you to. Go on, get out of here. This place isn't safe for you, and neither is Mythica." He slipped a light cotton windbreaker over his shoulder rig. "Get as far away from here as you possibly can until this whole thing blows over. I can't risk something happening to you if things go badly. This is not your fight."

THE SEARCH FOR TOM

YOLANDA AGREED TO let him borrow her Camaro. He dropped her off a mile from the estate with the keys to his truck. He had to make sure that Felix hadn't been lying to him about Tom and Sarah.

Pedal to the metal, he raced over to Jolley's Outdoor Outfitters. A white Toyota hatchback sat parked next to Tom's SUV. He used his key to let himself into the back of the store, and checked the ground floor. Other than the new plate glass window in the front, there was no sign that anyone had been there. He crept up the stairs, his ears straining for the slightest sound.

The door to Tom's apartment upstairs was ajar. With his heart pounding in his throat, he pushed the door open. A toppled-over lamp, a woman's pocketbook, and two bags of groceries lay strewn across the floor. Whoever it was, they'd been waiting in the apartment for Tom. Sarah had probably been a surprise.

No doubt Felix was holding both of them at the estate. With a sinking feeling, he realized they'd probably be held in the Bestiary. The only other alternative would be the house, but he doubted that Felix would allow it. Not when the underground cavern was such a perfect hiding place.

He made a quick search of the apartment, then scooped up the keys to the Toyota and headed downstairs. Sarah's car would be less recognizable than Yolanda's. He left Yolanda's key under the passenger's seat of the Camaro, and called her cell phone. She didn't answer, so he left a message telling her where she could pick up her car.

Ten minutes later, he was back at Mythica, where he parked the little white hatchback in the 'Guests Only' parking lot. Using the rows of planted vines as cover, he angled his way through the fields up toward the main house. He skirted the woods around the back and slipped into the sunflower field. As he'd done previously, he opened his senses to the cat and let the First Jaguar's nose lead him directly to the warded entrance. Piece of cake.

He slipped inside and slid the door shut behind him. Early morning sunlight streamed through the windows. The place was as bright and spotless as a shiny new penny. But before he could make his way to the door leading to Ozzie's clinic, he heard the distillery door slide open behind him. He debated whether to make a run for the clinic, but Gordon had already seen him. He'd have to play this one by ear.

"There you are." He hurried forward to greet the Mage. "I've been looking for you."

Gordon gave him an appraising look. "This building is off limits. How'd you get in?"

Mike pretended to be surprised. "Oh really? Nobody told me. Ambrose hired me as a security consultant. After that vampire got into the park the other day, Vince gave me carte blanche to search the entire estate. I was actually hoping you could tell me a little more about the wards." He looked around the spotless room, as if for the first time. "Very impressive setup you've got here. I've never been in a distillery before."

He held his breath as uncertainty twitched across Gordon's features. "I guess it couldn't hurt to show you around."

Relieved, he grinned, reassured that for the moment, at least, he was above suspicion. It was bad luck that the Mage had found him, but that didn't mean he couldn't move forward with his plan. All he needed now was a little distraction. "Are the wards around this building the same as the ones for the grounds? It's hard to believe you can make something this big invisible."

"It's not invisible. The ward merely deflects the senses away from the subject. To the casual eye, the distractions of nearby un-warded objects such as trees and shrubs become the focal point. How did you find it?"

Mike tapped his nose. "I figured it had to be near the house, and that meant either the sunflower field or the woods. I followed your scent. I knew I was getting close when it disappeared. Then I closed my eyes and felt around for anything that didn't feel like sunflower. Once I touched the door, the building became obvious."

Gordon didn't look very happy. "The sense of smell is difficult to fool. The wards told me someone had crossed the threshold, but I couldn't tell who."

Keep him talking. "So why hide it? And why go to the effort to brew wine for a bunch of vampires who can't even drink it?"

"It's not like that," Gordon said. "Ambrose loves this land more than anything. Just because he doesn't partake of the harvest doesn't mean he doesn't take pride in it. And I don't do all the hard work myself. Most of the grunt work is done at night; Ambrose himself oversees the hand picking of the crop."

"Hard to picture vampires working those fields."

Gordon shrugged. "This is a farm. Everyone in the nest works the fields except Rafe and Santino. The only real difference is that the fields are tended at night."

Mike looked around the distillery. "So where is this intoxicating brew I've heard so much about, anyway?"

"In the wine cellars of course. Care to take a look?"

"That's why I'm here."

Gordon grinned slyly. "Think you can locate the entrance?"

Mike jerked his head toward the door to Ozzie's clinic. "That would be my first choice."

"And you'd be wrong. Come with me." Gordon grabbed a couple of liqueur glasses from a cabinet and motioned to Mike to follow him. He tapped an area of bare cement floor with his foot, and a wooden trap door appeared. Gordon reached down and lifted the door up, revealing a well-lit stone stairway leading down. "Watch your head," he cautioned.

The shallow steps curved along a wall toward the right. Overhead, recessed lighting turned on automatically as they descended into the cellar. The chilly basement was filled to the very brim with racks and racks of bottled wine alternating with rows of wooden casks. "My god, what do you do with all of this?"

Gordon set the glasses on top of a nearby table made of barrel staves and lifted a bottle off one of the nearest racks. The label was solid black, except for the word, 'Glamour' and the year 1965 scripted diagonally across the label in lavender script.

"Nice."

Gordon slipped a corkscrew out of his pocket and proceeded to open the bottle and pour a half-glassful of pale golden liquid into each of the cordial glasses. "Just a taste. So you'll know what we're doing here." He handed Mike the glass and waited expectantly. Too expectantly.

A feeling of unease crept over him. Gordon had seemed a little too willing to show him around. "I'm not much of a wine drinker."

Gordon's jaw twitched; the thin curve of his smile didn't quite make it to his eyes. He raised his glass in a mock toast, then drained the glass in one gulp. "Go on, Mike. It's not poison."

He took a tiny sip. A little sweet, but not bad. He downed the hatch. An unexpected glow of well-being flooded through his body.

"Wow."

Gordon was quick to fill the two tiny glasses again. "This time, roll it around on your tongue a little. Get the taste of it."

Yeah, Mike thought. There's a little peachy, pineapple-y, champagne thing going on there. "It's got little bubbles."

Gordon laughed. After that, everything went dark.

TRAPPED

THE HEAVY CHAIN was only a few inches long. The big cat had been collared and chained to an iron bolt in the floor with very little slack. Silver-tipped prongs on the inside of the collar penetrated the fur of the cat's neck, digging into his tender skin. The burning sensation was inescapable unless he remained perfectly still. The cat could lay on his side or his belly with his chin on the stone floor. The walls of the stall were blocks of stone and mortar. No more than six feet high, but they might have gone on forever. He couldn't stand. He couldn't move around. All he could do was wait.

There was no sense of time passing in the bestiary. The dim light came from two bare bulbs suspended over the table in the work area. The alternative was total blackness that not even the cat's superior vision could penetrate. The world had closed down into two dimensions: pain and darkness. In the darkness, there was safety and fear; when the lights came on, there was only Ozzie and pain. Ozzie always started with the cat.

The veterinarian was afraid of the jaguar, and unlike his careless attitude with the wolves, he would not come into the stall. He had jury-rugged some sort of cattle prod that allowed him to reach through the bars of their stall-like prison and deliver massive electric shocks anywhere and everywhere. As his captives screamed and writhed in pain, Ozzie timed their agony with a stopwatch and made notes. Sometimes, he even videotaped them.

But the cat didn't react the way Ozzie expected; he seemed to derive some perverse pleasure from the shrill screams of the wolves, and wanted to evoke a similar response from the jaguar. Every time the lights went on, Ozzie had a new tool to try on the cat. Something worse. Ozzie didn't stop until the cat lost consciousness. Mike suspected that Ozzie was trying to get Tehuantl to come out.

Mike's cold fury grew every time the lights came on. He didn't experience the cat's pain directly, but the electric shocks jolted him just as they did the cat. He felt the cat's physical suffering as phantom pain, no less real to him than the torture inflicted upon the cat. The smell of scorched hair and flesh and the pitiful cries of the wolves tore into his very soul.

All the while, the silver spikes inside the collar ate into the jaguar's neck like a slow, agonizing acid. Unable to shift, the cat's wounds festered. Eventually, as dehydration and starvation set in, the cat shut down. Not even Ozzie's worst attention could trigger a response any longer.

With the light on, his range of vision was limited to the three stalls across the aisle. The wolf on the right was breathing, but never moved. He smelled very bad. Directly across from him, a big grey with plenty of fight left in him suffered horribly from Ozzie's attentions. Based on size alone, Mike guessed it was Tanner, Vince's former Beta wolf.

In the stall to his left, they'd shackled Tom. Unlike the wolves, Tom's wrists and ankles were manacled with enough length of chain so that he could walk back and forth across the back of the stall. He paced for hours on end; shuffling like an old man who'd lost his mind. Tom's condition deteriorated quickly. Ozzie seemed particularly delighted with the onset of Tom's lycanthropy. He took a lot of photos of Tom's face and hands and feet, and came frequently to take blood samples and gouge hunks of flesh from Tom's back. After a time, Tom began to blubber and sob every time the lights came on.

Tom's suffering nearly unmanned him. *I've done this to him. Everything I touch goes to shit. He gave me everything, and I've repaid him by taking his humanity and putting him in Ozzie's hands.*

But as bad as it was for Tom, it was worse for Sarah. She was in the stall next to him. He couldn't see her, but he could hear her grunts of pain. The look of hatred and frustrated rage on Tom's face when Ozzie was in the cell with her told him more than he ever wanted to know.

Sarah was a fighter. She screamed bloody murder and fought when Ozzie dragged her out by her hair. The cat continued to play dead, but the big wolf across the aisle went crazy. He snarled and frothed at the mouth in his frustration. Tom cursed Ozzie, promising to kill him; his wrists and ankles stained and crusted with dried blood. Mike fought with everything he had to push the jaguar aside, but the cat refused to yield, and didn't move a muscle.

Come on, he urged. *You've got to do something*; but the cat remained still as a stone. They were all forced to listen to the sounds of fists pounding flesh, as Sarah's threats and cursing gave way to begging and pleading as she promised Ozzie anything if only he would stop.

"Just lay still. That's not so much to ask." Ozzie's voice was a low monotone. "Yes, that's right. Up on the table with you. Lay back. That's it." The sounds of buckles being fastened. "I know you've been looking forward to this as much as I have."

There were sounds of a cardboard box being opened. Packing being removed. "What a beauty. Now where did I put those batteries?"

Sarah was silent. Tom was the only one who could see what was happening. "Don't you dare," he sobbed. "You fucking animal, I will kill you. I swear it."

An electric hum filled the air. Ozzie moved to stand in front of Tom's stall, his back toward the cat. A long black baton hissed and crackled in his hand; sparks flashed from its tip.

"I see we have a volunteer. Just to let you know, dog-boy, this is the Dominator Tru-Jolt Baton. Twenty inches of fabulous fun delivering five hundred thousand volts of stopping power at my fingertips. Check out the rubber handle and nifty wrist strap."

Ozzie opened the door to Tom's stall and the manacled man threw himself toward Ozzie, heedless of the weapon. Ozzie never flinched as he raised the baton and touched it to Tom's chest.

Tom's reaction was immediate. He fell to the ground and cowered. Ozzie moved into the stall, delivering repeated shocks until Tom lay unconscious in a fetal position on the floor. Mike caught the scent of fresh urine and feces.

Ozzie shut off the stun baton. "Interesting. That wasn't the reaction I expected." He prodded Tom with his foot, but there was no resistance.

The room had gone silent. Across the aisle, even the big wolf Tanner crouched; silenced, licking his lips nervously.

"I guess you're just too fragile to be much fun yet. I guess I'll have to wait until the full moon before I can really play with you, dog-boy."

Ozzie came out of Tom's stall and closed the door behind him. He stood in front of the big wolf's stall this time. The wolf growled a warning that echoed through the entire cavern.

"Now I see here we have a second volunteer. You probably feel neglected, don't you? And I'll just bet that you'd love to bite me. Let's see you try." He turned the baton back on and opened the iron door to the stall.

The wolf lunged, but the short chain prevented him from reaching his tormentor. Ozzie began tapping each of the wolf's feet and legs, sending the wolf scrabbling to get away. Yelps turned to screams, each time Ozzie moved the baton. With his back to the jaguar, Mike didn't need to see Ozzie's face to know he was enjoying what he was doing.

"Now I get it. A little goes a long way, doesn't it?" The wolf screamed hysterically; eventually collapsing into a catatonic huddle on the floor as the scent of his burning flesh added another chorus to the stink in the air. Finally, Ozzie turned to face the jaguar.

"I have you to thank for my new toy, kitty cat. After your little dance with Tokelson, Ambrose let me order this. You know, they're illegal in New York. I tell you it took a bit of doing to get my hands on this beauty."

Ozzie squatted down in front of the stall. "I'll just bet you'd like me to open your cage, wouldn't you? I don't believe you're sleeping for a minute. But it doesn't matter. With a twenty-inch reach, I don't have to. Check this out."

Ozzie inserted the baton through the bars and touched the big cat's nose with the baton. A white light exploded in his brain and the jaguar bellowed in pain and anger. He fought the baton as the spikes inside his collar dug deeper into his neck. Ozzie laughed. Another and then another and another surge of electricity surged through them. The memories of Hector Clemente returned, and Mike prayed desperately that the cat would finally release Tehuantl. The battery gave out before Ozzie was satisfied; he took the remainder of his impotent lust out on Sarah.

Despair filled Mike as he tried everything he could think of to get the cat to let him out. With thumbs, he could get that wretched collar off their neck and get them out; away from Ozzie and his sick games. His neck felt as if it were on fire. But the cat wouldn't budge. Time and again, he appealed to Tehuantl, but the shaman told him that the cat was implacable. *He is waiting. Sooner or later, someone will open the door and come close enough to see if he's alive. It always works this way.*

When the lights went out and they were left alone in their misery,

Tom and Sarah talked. Tom would tell Sarah to be strong. "Don't let him win. It doesn't change who you are inside. He can't touch you where it really matters."

Sometimes, he spoke to Mike and the wolves as well, telling them not to give up. Mike felt his heart break with every word of encouragement Tom spoke, but in time the lycanthropy virus began to take its toll. As Tom's sanity ebbed, his vocabulary dwindled until the only word that remained was Sarah's name. For hours in the darkness, Tom moaned and cried her name like a prayer, over and over. Only her soothing voice could calm him.

"Don't fight it Tom," she told him. "You have to go with it. You are becoming at one with your inner self. You are evolving. The beast is one small part of the greater universe that is you. Everyone fears change. Don't fight it, embrace it. Go to your peaceful place. Picture yourself in a canoe floating with the current beneath azure skies. Your wolf is always with you. Feel the warm sun on your faces. Feel the gentle current take you. You are together on this journey. You are growing and expanding in new and unfamiliar ways. Allow the current to take you to the new life that awaits you."

"Acceptance is the key, Tom. The key to happiness lies in acceptance, not in anticipation of outcomes. That which you fear most can only harm you when you resist. Release your emotional attachment to the past. Move forward into a stronger and better self. He is you and you are *him*. There is no one else. There is only you. Follow the call."

She spoke softly, but her words carried. When she spoke, it was as if she spoke to all of them. Mike could feel the silent alertness of the others in the cavern.

"Don't fight the beast, reach out to him. Embrace him. Give him a name. He is your partner; accept him. Learn his ways. Seek to understand him and he will always have your back. Let your spirit drift within the current, not against it."

Sarah told him the key to surviving and thriving with ALVS was to retrain the unconscious mind to accept the physical changes and the conscious mind to open itself to the new mass consciousness which came to all lycanthropes. Over and over, her words to Tom spoke of acceptance, of allowing, of curious inquiry, and seeking to understand. She often wept after Ozzie finished with her, but she never faltered when she spoke to Tom. "You are going to survive this. We're going to get out of here. We will. You have to believe that. Answer me if you understand," she pleaded.

And Tom would moan her name and all who could answered her with a series of whines and grunts which echoed Tom's acknowledgement. Even the cat chuffed a reply. Eventually, Tom lost his power of speech completely, and sounded no different from the rest of the pack.

Mike nurtured a slim hope that Rafe or Silas or one of the other wolves might come looking for them. Sarah's absence should have been noticed by now; by the hospital and her patients, certainly. And if her family realized she was missing, they would of course report it. She worked the ALVS information booth at Mythica on Saturday nights. He had no idea how long they'd been down here, but somebody must have noticed that Sarah and he were both missing. Maybe they'd call Tom and discover he was gone too. Yolanda might have said something to Vince before she left. *If she left.*

They all grew weaker. Ozzie provided Tom and Sarah with water and a little food, but it wasn't enough. The rest of them got nothing. A lethargy overtook him. He began to drift; to follow the current of Sarah's sweet voice down the river.

Tehuantl?

The priest had been surprisingly quiet since they'd been captured by the Fae.

Tehuantl, how is it that the Fae knew you? How did they recognize you?

He didn't expect an answer, but he could feel the shaman's presence.

We are different tribes of the same clan.

The voice in his head sounded as real as if he were standing right in the cell beside him.

Long ago, when the Great Creator made the first predators, each was given a clan to tend. The soul of a spirit priest from each clan resides within each of the First Predators. All First Predators and spirit guardians recognize each other. Many of the elder Fae tribes also have this gift.

Tehuantl. We have to get out of here. If you and I work together, we can overpower the cat.

Of the three of us, you are the weakest. Of the three of us, you are not a predator. Of the three of us, you are the only mortal. When your spirit dies, there will no longer be three of us. The First Jaguar and I will be one again. Tehuantl vanished and refused to return.

Damn him; he's waiting for me to die.

After Sarah's voice faded and all was quiet, Farley would come. His toenails clicked against the stone floors, announcing his arrival through the warded exit at the back of the cavern. The cat's ears would flick forward, but the jaguar never stirred. The dog always scratched at the floor in front of the stall for a few moments before settling himself down with a sigh. They'd all sleep then; but when the lights came on, the dog was already gone.

THE VISIT

MIKE KNEW SOMETHING was up when Gordon and Cobb came into the bestiary. Gordon led the vampire past his stall to the very back of the cave to show him the warded exit.

"As long as they come in beast form, they'll be able to cross the Tor," Gordon said. "They can carry whatever equipment they need on packs strapped to their backs. Vince doesn't have any surveillance equipment in this part of the estate, so one will see them arrive."

"How can I get a signal to them? Cell phones won't work down here or out on the Tor.

I want to make sure they're here *before* I make my move. I have to be sure these guys will be here when I need them."

They stopped in front of the jaguar's stall. Cobb slapped the heavy wire mesh with his hand. "You stink Bane. You hear me?"

"Don't bother," Gordon said. "That's not Bane anymore. He's just like the wolves now. Just another dumb beast."

Cobb wrinkled his nose and gave the cat a dismissive glance. "He's just one of the reasons why Ambrose is no longer fit to run this place. If we'd brought in mercenaries in the first place, like I wanted, Vince and that sicko sonofabitch Ozzie would both be gone. We'd have a solid pack of seasoned wolves to present to the Globus at the summit.

But Ambrose won't see reason." Cobb leaned closer to inspect the cat. "He looks dead."

"Don't you believe it. That cat is Fae. It won't starve like the wolves. You can't kill it. Ozzie says that the jaguar is in control; Bane is just a parasite. Speaking of which, have you told him yet?"

"Ozzie?" Cobb smirked. "You should have seen him. I thought he was going to have a heart attack. He couldn't believe that Ambrose was planning to kill him. He's on board."

"How can you be sure?"

"I told him Ambrose was planning to feed him to that bad-ass scorpion thing back there. Blood almighty. Is that Sarah Powers? What the hell is she doing down here? What's happened to her?"

Gordon sighed. "I don't know. There's another one too." He motioned to where Tom lay curled up on the floor of his stall.

Cobb swore. "What was Felix thinking? Ambrose is getting soft in the head, putting humans down here."

"Now, now. It's not that bad. With enough Glamour, we can pretty much eliminate their memories."

"Don't give me that that same line of crap you use on Ambrose. Look at them. They're a mess. What's Ozzie been doing to her? No, don't tell me. It's pretty obvious."

Sarah began to cry. Neither man moved to help her.

"Let's go," Cobb said. "I can't stand to look at her. Things are going to change around here. I don't like this place and I don't want anyone else using that warded back entrance again. I'll make sure my guys bring plenty of C4 plastique. As far as I'm concerned, the sooner we shut down this little corner of hell, the better. Come on. We've still got a lot to do, and there isn't much time left. As soon as I'm in control of the estate, we'll seal off this cavern permanently."

XENOTCHI SPEAKS

MIKE KEPT TRYING to send mental pictures to the cat, trying to show him that they would be sealed up inside unless the cat let go of control. The big cat's impassive patience overruled his hunger, his thirst, and his frustration. *He's an ambush hunter. That's all he knows. He's lived for centuries with the knowledge that sooner or later, someone will come and open the cage.*

Sarah's voice was only a whisper now. "Go with the current. Embrace the change. Be at one with your beast. Love your wolf."

He could hear her even in his sleep. He was sick of it.

Tom was nearly mute now. They could all feel the moon coming full, even below ground. Only Ozzie's visits broke the blackness. The cat had found a way to bury its feelings so deep that it did not react to the stun baton any more, although Mike jumped and writhed invisibly with the phantom shock of each tap of the baton.

Awake or asleep, he drifted numbly. Awake was pain and light; sleep was hunger, thirst, and Sarah's soothing voice in the darkness.

We are going to die here, Tehuantl. I've got thumbs. I could get us out of here.

I cannot die, mortal. I have no physical body. Xenotchi cannot die. He is First Jaguar. Time means nothing to us. We are. We always will be. We do not need you in order to exist. You are but one of many who have shared this space.

I don't buy that any more. You're the one inside of me, not the other way around. You must need me.

He felt the shaman's amusement. *Who is inside who? Your physical form is but a temporary reality which will fade over time. We are eternal.*

The shaman's arrogance infuriated him. The cat, on the other hand, had always seemed to regard him with an amused benevolence; affection even.

Tell me, Tehuantl, is Xenotchi really the First Jaguar?

Yes.

And you've been with him from the beginning?

I alone was chosen to be sacrificed to the god as his priest.

Could you talk to him? Please? Tell him I can get us out of here. Silver doesn't bother me and I've got thumbs. All I need is a few minutes and we could all be out of here!

You are not of the people. I serve only the people of the First Jaguar.

A headache began to form at the base of his skull. He wondered if the cat or Tehuantl felt it. *Probably not.*

I saw the Olmec statues when I was in Central America before. They're your people, right? I read where the priests ate the village children. Is that true?

Don't be stupid. The people of the Jaguar brought their children to the priests to be blessed. We took their heads into our mouths and breathed the breath of the god into them. Cradled within the maw of the Nagual, the children of the fang become at one with First Jaguar. We are warriors. It is our way.

Did the people of the First Jaguar pray to you or Xenotchi?

First Jaguar is a God. Of course the people prayed to their God. But only those who know his name may appeal to the First Jaguar directly. All others brought their requests to me at the temple.

Didn't everyone know Xenotchi's name?

At first, Tehuantl didn't answer. *Only the enlightened ones who opened their hearts and accepted the First Jaguar as their god received his name directly. The rest made their prayers through the priests at the temple.*

Can I talk to Xenotchi?

Tehuantl refused to answer. Mike could still feel his presence, but the shaman remained unresponsive. He waited until Farley showed up again. Once the dog had settled into his usual spot in front of the cage, Mike called on the jaguar by name, using the formal greeting he'd remembered from the Fae.

I see you, Xenotchi. I see you First Jaguar.

I see you, Mikebane. I see you, cub of the High Tor Fae.

The voice of the First Jaguar reverberated though every bone in his body. It was a rich, resonant sound, with a whiskied edge like an old bluesman. It was a voice that carried a certain wry humor.

He kicked himself, realizing his mistake in thinking that Tehuantl was in charge. *I could have spoken to him years ago.* He fumbled for the right words.

I would speak with you, First Jaguar. Is it permitted?

You may address me as Xenotchi. The cat slapped its tail against the floor, but Mike could feel the calming affect Farley had on the Jaguar.

If you would let me out, I could free us easily. We could get out of this cage. I know you hate cages. I could release everyone else, too.

With patience, opportunity always present itself.

We're running out of time. They are going to blow up this cavern and seal is inside permanently. We will never escape.

Perhaps your clansmen of the High Tor tribe will send someone after you. They seemed quite intent on punishing you.

His heart leapt at the idea, but it wouldn't work. *They can't cross the wards. They won't be coming after us.*

The cat coughed in agreement. *It does not matter. Your physical form has been without food and water for too long. If I were to release you now, you would perish.*

Oh crap. What about Tehuantl?

My priest shares my intolerance for the silver metal and does not possess the hardy constitution of those with Fae blood in their veins, such as yourself. Tehuantl takes in no nourishment other than blood sacrifice. He too, would perish if I were to relinquish myself to him. Only my form is eternal. It is far better that I wait for the opportunity to come to me. The cat kneaded the stone floor, extending and contracting his claws. *Be patient.*

Xenotchi would not be moved. The cat's stubborn reasoning convinced him more than anything Tehuantl had told him. Mike gathered his will and tried to force the cat out, but all he got for his trouble was a splitting headache that seemed to have no affect on either Xenotchi or Tehuantl. *All I need is a frickin' thumb and we'd all be out of here.*

MERCS RISING

MIKE'S LAST HOPE of rescue turned to ashes when Vince and Cobb brought Silas down to the bestiary in handcuffs. He listened mutely was they held him down and Ozzie strapped him to the worktable. Vince demanded that Silas tell him what else he'd seen and who he'd told. Silas refused to talk, but it was clear to Mike that his friend had come looking for them.

The stunning revelation of Vince's betrayal burned like acid in Mike's gut. He stormed in impotent fury at how badly he'd been duped by the Alpha. Hell, Vince had fooled the entire pack.

How could Vince have stood by and done nothing, knowing where the missing wolves had been all along? And unlike Cobb's disgust of the place, Vince seemed well-acquainted with it, going so far as to instruct Cobb to retrieve a spiked collar from one of the storage cupboards.

Mike searched his memory for earlier signs of Vince's treachery and found nothing. Everyone agreed Ozzie was strange, but no one thought it had anything to do with the missing wolves. He remembered Dixon telling him the family had known of Ozzie's abuse of animals as a kid. Vince must have known about Ozzie even then.

Even the lowest dealers on the street wouldn't treat one of their own this way. Sarah had told him the pack oath was sacred to the weres; a physical acceptance into a greater social consciousness and belief system. Only blood went deeper than that. And Ozzie wasn't blood kin to Vince. How could he allow this to happen to the members of his pack?

Werewolves could not reproduce with human partners. Unlike Silas's father, Vince's self-control had kept Ozzie from being infected with ALVS as a child. Mike remembered Dixon telling him how much Vince and Merlene had doted on Ozzie. Was Vince really so willing to overlook Ozzie's problems?

He didn't have to look any further than his own father. Farley Bane had given up his own humanity for his son. Mike glanced at Tom, huddled miserably in the corner of his cell. As difficult as it had been to believe, he had no doubt that Tom had been sincere when he said he didn't blame him for the werewolf attack. His father had made the ultimate sacrifice for him out of love. He'd never doubted Tom's love for him, either. Could it be that Vince's love for his stepson was just as blind? Yeah. Maybe.

Vince left without a word when Ozzie started in with the electrodes. Mike raged; the cat was a wall of indifference against him. *How could Vince just walk away? How could he pretend not to see what going on?* The answers eluded him. Some day Vince would answer for this, he swore. Someday, Vince would answer to all of them.

Ozzie and Cobb spent an hour questioning Silas. Up and down the row, the wolves began to struggle and howl. Even Xenotchi slapped his tail against the pavement in agitation. Eventually, Silas lost his control and began to shift.

As wolf pheromones flooded the cavern, Tom went into convulsions.

"What the hell is wrong with him," Cobb demanded.

"It's his first change," Ozzie answered. "With the moon so close to full, Silas's change pheromones affect him."

Another wolf began to howl.

"They all feel it."

"Blood almighty. Get me out of here."

"Oh it's no big deal. I've got enough ketamine in him now to knock out an elephant. I'll put the collar on him in a minute. As long as he's got silver against his skin, he won't be able to shift back into human form. I can keep him like this as long as you want, but if you want him back on the job, I'll have to start dosing him with Glamour. The wine works better than Ketamine for ensuring short-term memory loss."

"We don't need him," Cobb said. "We can't afford to have him walking around topside. This guy's too nosy for his own good."

"No problem. I'll be glad to have him."

After Cobb left, Ozzie dragged Silas's limp white wolf down the aisle. As they passed the jaguar's stall, Mike could see Silas's silver-white pelt and muzzle bloodied and singed. He listened as Ozzie chained the wolf to the bracket in the floor of a stall two doors down. The lights went out a few minutes later.

The rage inside him burned futilely. Whatever was coming, it would have to come soon. They were running out of time.

* * *

The day arrived. Gordon brought several loads of boxes and crates into the bestiary. On his final trip, he walked to the back of the cavern and returned with a group of eight big wolves, each carrying heavy packs on their backs. They shifted quickly and dressed in the park uniforms Gordon provided. As they unpacked their equipment, Mike could tell by their practiced movements and silent efficiency that these guys weren't just hired hands; they were a trained team of professionals. Hard men; mercenaries, probably. They'd come prepared for a fight. There were stun batons, tear gas canisters, blocks of C4 plastic explosives, blasting caps and plenty of guns and ammunition.

"No guns," Gordon told them. "We can't risk attracting the

attention of the locals. The wards aren't going to be able to muffle gunshots effectively. This has to be a silent operation."

"No problem," one of the big mercs said. He was every bit as big as Trick or even Vince. He handed a pistol to Gordon. "Take a look at this. I made 'em myself. You won't even have to worry about muzzle flash with these babies. I didn't have enough time to make one for everybody, but I've got five of these lugers. Ammo is hollow-point lead."

Gordon sniffed dismissively. "That caliber is too small to bring down anything here at Mythica."

"It doesn't have to. A body shot will hurt like hell, and anything in the head or legs will take 'em down long enough for one the boys here to get silver on 'em. More importantly, if you accidentally hit one of us, it won't kill us."

"Not to worry," Gordon told them. "We've got enough Kevlar here for all of you."

The big merc, who Gordon called Hale, leaned in to inspect the cage of the big wolf across from Mike. "What's with the captives," he asked.

Mike's heart skipped a beat. *Maybe...*

"They went up against the same Alpha wolf we brought you in to take down. They failed. I trust you and your team will not."

Hale gave a curt nod. "You've got two humans down here," he said. "I was told there would be no humans to worry about."

"Let's not argue technicalities." said Gordon. "We're paying you extremely well to follow orders, not ask questions. I want to go over the plan again. We can't afford to make any mistakes. What do you need from me?"

Hale pressed his lips together as if pondering a response, but shook it off. "Have it your way. Just stay out of the way when the fighting starts. We'll be the only ones on the estate with weapons."

"No problem. I've got to move those crates of chains from the restaurant down to the vault. Watch out for Felix. He's been snooping around. I don't think he believed me when I told him that the chains were for the farm. He'll have some sort of backup plan to protect Ambrose."

"Let me worry about Felix. We'll send a guy down to help you with those coffins just as soon as we finish topside. Listen up guys," Hale addressed the room. "The park was open last night, so the blood stewards will all be in the main house, sleeping late. Vince is the only one we're looking for. We take him out and the pack will be easier to deal with. He thinks he's having lunch with Felix today at the Bloody Fang. As soon as I see him go inside, I'll unlock the gate between the estate and the park. My inside guys will be monitoring security, so don't worry about the cameras. As soon as I neutralize the Alpha, you'll get the signal to go."

"Those of you with assigned targets, keep your focus on neutralizing them first. Once they're contained, move on through your assigned sector and make sure you search thoroughly for any civilians or anyone else we might have missed. The park is closed for the next three nights, so there shouldn't be more than a few delivery people to worry about. Take it easy with the blood stewards or any other stray humans you find. Keep them in the main house. If somebody gets hurt, I want to know about it immediately. Even if it's only a hangnail. Any questions?"

"Will you and your men be able to maintain your control through the next three days?" Gordon asked. "It's the full moon."

"Let me worry about that. Every warrior here has proven mastery over his beast. The moon beckons to us as much as it does any wolf. The difference is that we've trained under these conditions and learned how to work within our limits. Any other questions?"

Nobody said anything. Hale and the rest of the mercs completed their preparations in silence, then followed Gordon upstairs.

* * *

I see you Xenotchi.

I see you Mikebane.

We are out of time. When those men finish their business, they will seal this cavern. We will be buried alive. I have an idea I would like to try.

I am listening.

When I shift into your form, and you shift into mine, there is a period when we are both present. Couldn't we hold that form? I would have your strength and you would have my thumbs.

Ah. It is a good suggestion. However, Tehuantl and I are already able to merge our forms.

At this point, even letting Tehuantl out would be better than staying trapped inside the cave forever. *Well, then why don't you and Tehuantl merge? Tehuantl could get us out of here.*

Silver is an anathema to both of us. This collar prevents either of us from shifting form.

What about when we were caged that other time? In Queens?

Xenotchi hissed angrily with the memory. *You were lost to us. We believed you to be dying. Tehuantl used his magic to infuse your life force with our combined spirits and you did not resist him. Our bodies blended into a new form. Something completely different. Your immunity to silver allowed Tehuantl to overpower and destroy our captor. The energy from our combined spirits as a triad revived you. We very nearly became trapped in the triad form.*

It hadn't been a dream after all. Mike's stomach churned with the memory. He'd really been there; seen everything that happened to Hector Clemente. Not because of what had been in the papers, or what his partner had told him, but because for the first time since becoming the Nagual, he'd actually been present while Tehuantl was present. That had been his own fierce, savage joy he'd experienced when he'd torn their tormentor apart limb from limb, not the shaman's. Oh god, he thought; I really am a beast.

Why couldn't we do that again, Xenotchi?

You were near death, Mikebane. You offered no resistance when we invaded your spirit. Without that, a triad is impossible.

Hey, I give my permission. Let's do it. Lets call Tehuantl and get out of here.

He felt the First Jaguar's amusement. *You are so very young, Mikebane. Until this very moment you have despised and feared my priest, and yet you are now so very willing to give up your mind, body, and soul to him?*

He paused.

You fear that you will become a heartless killer, no? Tehuantl's methods of devotion are alien to you, but he only acts to save his God and clan.

He eats their hearts and brains.

He has dedicated his entire essence to the First Jaguar for eternity. And so he remains. His people are warriors. The eating of an enemy's heart has always been an acceptable tribute. As for the brains, well, I find them quite tasty.

That practice is abhorrent to humans and punishable by true death. What will happen to me if I became part of this triad? Will I end up craving hearts and brains too?"

Xenotchi was silent for a while, as he considered his answer. *I do not know for certain. Your spirit is not the first to have joined us, but Tehuantl never managed to forge a triad until we were in that basement in Queens. We were of one mind and body then, or nearly so.*

If he could do it again, would I still be me?

A triad is formed only rarely. Always a Fae has been the third party. You are not pure Fae, and not immortal in your own skin, so I do not know whether it would even work. Your current form could weaken and die. Make no mistake. A triad is a being that is not priest, not human, and not Fae. But the new form, and the new consciousness would survive.

You didn't mention First Jaguar.

First Jaguar is eternal. I am always here.

BREAKING HELL

THE LIGHTS CAME on and Ozzie banged his way into the Bestiary, reeling like a drunken sailor. He appeared highly agitated. He rattled around in the cupboards, as he appeared to search for something, then rifled through the packs for weapons. He found none. From the corner of his eye, Mike could see him standing in front of Sarah's stall for a long time, as if trying to make up his mind before he went inside. Mike heard the sound of her shackles being unlocked.

"Come on, get up. We're getting out of here." He grabbed her and she stood dirty and naked, in the aisle in front of the jaguar's prison.

Mike's heart winced at the sight of her. *Good lord, she's nothing but bones.* Her face was slack; her expression dull. The lump in his throat trembled until it became a silent growl. The cat laid back his ears.

"Felix is dead. Cobb has taken over the park and the estate. He's in charge now. You're my new bargaining chip. Here." He handed her a white lab coat. "Put it on."

It was far too big for her. She attempted to button it, but he slapped her hands down.

"Forget that." He helped her into a Kevlar vest. "Now keep your mouth shut and follow me."

It hit her then; Mike could see she finally understood. She turned to Tom's cage and fumbled with the latch. Tom grunted and gnashed his teeth, and even the cat chuffed a low word of encouragement, but Ozzie had different ideas. He grabbed her by the vest and jerked her nearly off her feet. "I said, let's go."

"What about Tom? And the others. We have to take them with us."

"Are you nuts? They're animals. You open those cages and they'll kill us all. You and I are the only humans here, sister. Let's go."

Sarah began to struggle but she had nothing left to fight with. Ozzie had her by a hundred pounds or more. "We can't leave them," she cried.

He slapped her so hard her teeth clacked together. "Listen, they're planning to seal this place as soon as they finish up in the tombs. How long do you think we'd last down here? I'm putting my life on the line for you. Are you coming or not?"

Ozzie didn't wait for her answer. He grabbed her by the straps of her Kevlar jacket and dragged the hysterical woman up the stairs. A moment later, they were gone.

With a gut-wrenching howl, Tom's beast arrived. He began to shift.

A NEW MAN

TOM'S BONES CRACKED as he fought the change. He bellowed in agony as his face lengthened and his spine bowed. Mike watched helplessly as Tom's hands clenched, his fingers melding together. Change pheromones flooded the cavern and grew to stifling proportion as the stress pheromones of the other wolves joined in. The cat began to pant. Across the aisle, the big wolf Tanner lay on his side, keening softly.

Farley trotted in, whining. He paced up and down the aisle, scratching and barking at each occupied stall, as if to say, *'We've got to get out now!'*

He had to make the First Jaguar understand what was happening. *I see you, Xenotchi. The next person who comes down here is going to use explosives and seal this cavern. There is a time to be patient like the cat and wait for the right moment, but that time is past.*

The First Jaguar didn't answer, but Mike could feel his uncertainty. The First Jaguar had picked up on Farley and the wolves' anxiety.

We are no longer the predator, Xenotchi. We are the prey.

You are only a frightened rabbit, Mikebane. You are afraid. Afraid of death. Afraid of Tehuantl. Afraid of what you might become.

253

Tell me what to do. How do we come together as one?

The cat refused to answer.

If Felix was dead, that meant Ambrose was out of the picture. He was either chained in his coffin or truly dead. What about Rafe? He didn't think Rafe would stick around if Cobb was in charge, but what if something had happened to Rafe as well?

Taffy would die.

His uncle wouldn't last long without Rafe. He had to do something.

Farley's panic and Tom's agony was affecting all of them. Unlike the shifting of the other werewolves Mike had seen, Tom's shift was agonizingly slow. The sound of Tom's bones breaking was far worse than anything Ozzie had done to him. They were all squirming in sympathy.

I see you Tehuantl. We are together in this. I know Xenotchi is God spirit of the First Jaguar; he possesses the strength of the predator. I know you are the spirit of the shaman; you've got the magic and the knowing of the ancients. I'm the third piece, aren't I? I possess the spirit of the Fae; I am the cunning warrior. I am immune to silver. I know the ways of men. You need me. That's it, isn't it? The triad is three, but it's an equal three. Each of us brings our strengths to the one.

Xenotchi chuffed his amusement. *Perhaps you are more clever than you seem.*

Believe me, you're not the first to tell me that. Now tell me what to do. Tell me how to come together.

It is not a thing for you to do. It is a thing for you to stop doing. You have clenched yourself against the flow of us. When you sleep, you release yourself naturally, and we are, to a lesser degree, united. What you must do is to release your grip on yourself intentionally. Only then will we flow together as one.

Mike remembered what Sarah had told him about retraining the unconscious mind to accept and embrace the change. Hell, he'd been listening to her coach Tom for the whole time they'd been down here. *What will happen to me?*

I cannot answer that; it is a leap of faith, Tehuantl answered. *I was human once; more human than you. I left that life; I left that world behind. Once you take that path, you will never be able to go back. We will be the triad. We will be one.*

Yeah, but which one of us will we be?

Tom's howl reverberated off the walls of their prison. Mike's throat thickened with guilt and grief for Tom's misery; for all their misery. *We can't be left to rot down here.* Win or lose, his own future didn't matter anymore.

Promise me, Tehuantl. Promise me we'll get every single living creature out of here, and destroy those responsible.

Tehuantl's laughter echoed in his mind. *We are more alike than you imagined, no?*

So be it. He took a deep breath and *let go.*

The familiar melting sensation washed over him, and with it, pain. He grunted as he fought to regain consciousness; maintain control.

This will not work if you fight us, Mikebane. You must allow. Pressure built up inside him like a kettle about to boil. *You must open yourself to all of us.*

What do you mean, all of us?

The only answer was laugher. *Allow the flow to come into you, my friend. As Sarah has said so many times, embrace your beasts. All of them. Flow with the current. That is the only way we will be one.*

He opened himself to the pain. The force tore into him like water from a fire hose. He threw his hands up against the torrent. It felt as if his skin was being flayed from his bones. He screamed. He fought the onslaught with every fiber of his being.

It will not work, Mikebane. You fight us before it even begins.

You lied to me, he panted. *How many spirits are in there? You said we would be a triad, but I could feel the presence of thousands and more thousands. I'll drown. I'll be lost.*

Tehuantl is the guardian of souls for all who worship the First Jaguar. He is the warrior protector. His spirit is the vessel for all who worship the First Jaguar. Your spirit is strong, but you are one alone. One spirit is no match for Tehuantl. Your sacrifice will give him the physical form we require to gain our freedom.

Something Xenotchi said clicked into place. He reached out mentally to the First Jaguar with an open mind and curious inquiry, as Sarah had so often suggested. What he found astounded him.

The First Jaguar seemed to also be linked to the First Wolf. And the First Bear. And many others. As Mike reached out to the First Wolf, he found a spark of light that led him to Vince. And Dave. And Silas; the whole pack was there, right in the back of his head. And then, like a shiny new milk tooth, he found Tom.

The dam broke.

He was the pebble at the bottom of a great waterfall as the universe poured into him. He gasped for breath as every thought, emotion, and cell was ripped apart and blasted away.

He swirled in a vortex; a maelstrom of chaos, light, sound, and all the colors of darkness. He drifted, alone in the universe, moving slowly toward a cluster of tiny lights, glowing like a constellation in the vastness of a black hole. After a time, other patterns began to coalesce and he began to discern a sense of reassembled self. A self remembered, yet foreign. Something new. Something greater, broader, and deeper than anything he'd felt before. His muscles moved in novel configurations; his mind filled with memories and knowledge that hadn't been there before.

He was one.

He was many.

As the tide ebbed, a coolness flooded through him. The pain

dwindled, then disappeared; replaced by a new self-awareness. A rightness. A new equilibrium.

And it was done.

LAST ONE OUT IS NOT A WEREWOLF

THE SOUND OF Farley's whining woke me.

I'm still here. A surge of raw emotion flooded through me. I trembled like a newborn, overcome with relief and gratitude. Hot tears poured down my cheeks as I fumbled for the collar at my neck. Inch-long talons had replaced my fingernails, but I found I could retract them somewhat. I finally got the clasp and the hated collar fell harmlessly to the ground. I scrambled unsteadily to my feet in total darkness.

I gritted my teeth against the thirst; a craving for blood so strong, it was like gasping for air. As I panted in the silence, the realization that I was still me shook me too my core.

A quick check confirmed I still had all the rest of my basic equipment, and that I hadn't grown a tail; a huge relief. My unshaved cheeks were as smooth as a boy's, but my nose was broader, more flattened; but still human, from what I could tell. My old ears were gone; replaced by jaguar ears able to swivel back and forth toward sound. I stretched where I stood; the muscles of my new body cramped and protested. I felt as if I were an inch taller. Maybe two.

I ran my hands through my hair. My skull felt the same, but my mind was not. I knew things. New things. I had memories that didn't belong to me, but it was okay; I knew what they were for. I was smarter now, and I knew what I had to do.

Farley woofed gently. I opened the door and heard him retreat a respectful distance. My new feet were thickly padded; my nails clicked against the stone floors with almost the same sound as the dog.

"It's me, Farley." My words were clumsy. Talking around canine teeth would take some getting used to. I was nearly mad with thirst. Blindly, I checked the pile of equipment left behind by the mercs and found a couple of flashlights and a box of matches, but they'd left no water or food. I found a pair gym shorts that fit and put them on. Everything else I useful I stuffed into one of the packs.

I grabbed one of the mag-lights and headed down the corridor toward the back of the cavern; sensing the life spirit in each wolf and Fae creature I passed. That was new. I searched my mind for Tehuantl, and stumbled, as I realized he was gone. Not as in hiding, but as in no longer present as a separate entity. He was me, but I had prevailed. The revelation gave me pause. Somehow, I had absorbed *him*. His memories and talents were mine now. I was me.

When I reached the back of the cavern, my new vision immediately detected Gordon's ward. The portal wavered and shimmered, clear as day. When I touched it, it dissolved completely, leaving the exit in plain view. I gasped when I inhaled the sweet scent of the Tor. I hesitated as I considered what the Fae would think of my new form. Would they still consider me human? I flexed my fingers and my new claws popped out. *Not likely.*

I would never pass for human again. *Or Fae either, for that matter. Too late to think about that now.* There was work to be done here, and I was the only one for the job.

Somewhere, nearby, was the unmistakable scent of water. I scrambled forward and upward, through the tunnel, up to the light and the entrance. Blinded by the late afternoon sun, I followed the scent trail left by the mercenaries down through the rocks to a shaded clearing by a stream and threw myself face first into the cool water. I drank and drank until my belly hurt, then puked my guts out and drank some more.

I woke up nose to nose with a curious yearling buck who'd come down for a drink and decided to check me out. I sprang without thinking, and rode the deer to the ground. I broke his neck with a quick wrench, and bit deeply into the creature's throat with a fierce joy I'd never experienced before. The blood held no revulsion to me. At that moment, it tasted better than a vanilla milkshake. Only the buck's still-warm heart tasted better.

I flexed my bloody fingers experimentally. New talons emerged from where my fingernails used to be. It felt natural; like they'd always been there. With my fingers relaxed, the claws slid back into place and looked like thick, oddly pointed nails. It looked freaky. Not X-Men freaky, but definitely not human anymore. As long as I kept my fingers relaxed, the claws didn't seem to affect my dexterity. Striking a match or flicking a leaf was no problem. I wondered if my fingerprints had changed.

In the light of day, my skin was a few shades darker than I'd ever been; like a deep tan. A darker, coffee-colored pattern of jaguar spots marked my forearms and calves. My face felt unfamiliar. It didn't belong to me anymore. My nose was broader than I remembered; my cheekbones heavier. I couldn't tell what I looked like, but I hoped it wasn't too bad. I'd never considered myself vain about my appearance, but hell, I'd been pretty used to the face in the mirror. I wasn't looking forward to seeing the new me, but thinking about it didn't make it any better. It was too late now, anyway.

The one thing I did appreciate was how clear my mind felt. It was as if I'd been living in a fog for ages, and now it was gone. My senses were sharper. On the inside, at least, I was all me again. Right down to the slow burning need for payback.

I didn't have time to think about revenge just yet; there was more to be done. After cleaning the stink off me in the creek, I climbed back to the cave. I brought out the female Nagual first. She weighed next to nothing; her aura was so pale, there was no telling how long she'd been there. I took her snout into my mouth and breathed the healing breath of the First Jaguar into her lungs. Her eyelids fluttered, but she made no other response. There was nothing more to do for her; either she'd survive, or she wouldn't. I lay her down next to the creek, near the carcass.

The snakelizard things went next; I shooed a dozen of them as far as the tunnel to the surface, then let them find their own way out. Next came the other creatures, most of which ignored me in their eagerness to escape, although a couple of the more grotesque forms made small flopping lunges at me on a false pretext of aggression. A couple of bright flashes with the flashlight had them turning tail and out the portal as fast as they could scurry.

The last one to go was the huge white double-tailed scorpion thing with blue eyes. A drop of poison gleamed at the tip of each of her twin stingers as she regarded me with intelligent blue eyes. She held her front hand-pinchers across her carnivorous maw like a professional boxer.

"I'm not the one that put you in here, so don't attack me. You're free to go. Don't dick around and come after me; there are more who still need my help getting out. Go."

I opened the stall and stood back, waiting for her make a run for it, ready with the flashlight if she decided to turn on me.

She was surprisingly graceful for a creature with so many legs. She sidled through the gate and backed toward the portal, her eyes never once letting go if mine. She hissed and kept her tails raised in strike position the whole time. Once she was gone, I raced back to get the wolves.

Tom was in the most urgent need of attention. He'd shifted

completely into wolf form without any water to ease the shock to his body. In beast form, he'd slipped out of the manacles they'd used to restrain him. He smelled terrible; like raw meat left in the sun too long. He threw himself at the bars like a rabid dog. I tried talking to him like Sarah had done, but he wasn't Tom any more. They called it 'mad wolf syndrome', but other than getting him to water and letting him run free in the wilderness, I didn't know what else to do for him. No one but Silas was in any shape to shift without getting rehydrated and fed first. If I let Tom out last, they would be helpless against his madness.

I found a catchpole from one of the cupboards and used it to maneuver Tom's wolf toward the tunnel and outside. Once he scented the creek, he paid me no attention and I cut him loose. I followed him out to check on the Nagual, but she was already gone.

Silas was next. He was in pretty bad shape. Too weak to shift, but able to move on his own. I showed him the tunnel. "Once you're outside, you'll be on the Tor. You'll be safe there."

Silas' golden eyes gleamed with intelligence. It was weird, but I could feel his presence in the back of my head, and I was pretty sure he felt it too.

"There's plenty of water and a deer down by the creek at the bottom of the trail. As soon as I get everybody out, we'll see what else we can find. The moon will be full for the next three or four nights. Everyone is going to need a lot of protein before they can shift. Some of these guys have been locked up for months."

But Silas proved too weak to scramble up the tunnel. I half-pushed, half-carried the white wolf to the surface cave. The white scorpion cowered there, trying to hide herself in the rocks, using her front claws like hands to cover her eyes. The wolf growled.

"Don't worry about her. She's one of the Fae. It's too bright out here. The sun will be down soon. I don't think she'll bother us." I carried him down to the creek and went back inside for the rest of the weres.

None of the other wolves were strong enough to stand on their own. I gave each of them the breath of Xenotchi and carried them up to the surface and down the rocky cleft to the creek. They were too dehydrated to drink. I lay them down beside the creek and rinsed their mouths with handfuls of water until they were able to manage on their own. The sight of them gasping limply beside the water was a grim reminder of what Ozzie and Vince and the others had done. My anger grew each time I opened an occupied cell.

Of the fourteen captive wolves chained inside the bestiary, only seven still had a heartbeat. As each regained consciousness, their names became known to me. There was Tanner, the old Beta; Sarah's client, Kevin, twin brothers Corbin and Conrad, Lenny, Wynn, and the little black wolf, Rizzo. Silas made it eight. Tom's tan and black wolf had taken off at a dead run. I didn't know if I would ever see him again. I could only hope that he'd be able to find us when he regained his senses.

We lingered at the creek until sunset. I helped them to drink and eat until they were able to manage on their own. Tanner's wolf was the first to rise to his feet and feed. He tore at the carcass for several minutes, choking down huge bites, then moved away to lay exhausted in the grass. Once he was resting comfortably, I unfurled Xenotchi and Silas and I went hunting.

We got lucky and caught a beaver that had strayed too far from the water. After taking a few bites to take the edge off our hunger, we returned to the pack. All the wolves were on their feet, and seemed willing to follow us back to where we'd left the beaver. The additional sixty pounds of sweet fatty meat, in addition to the remains of the buck, was enough for everyone to get their feet back under them again.

The beaver kill was in a good location. Close to water, with the woods nearby and on a slight rise of land so we had good visibility if anyone were to approach. As long as the moon was full, none of the wolves would be able to shift back into human form. That meant three days at least, maybe more. Right now, the Tor was the best place for us, but I'd need to do something to hide us from the mercs who would no doubt come looking for us. Time enough to hunt and rebuild the wolves' strength, but I needed a plan; I couldn't chance someone shifting into human form on the Tor. I wasn't worried about myself; I'd never pass for human again.

I gave serious thought to leaving the wolves while I went after Sarah. My desire to tear Ozzie to pieces burned like acid in my gut. Every time I closed my eyes, I pictured the look of terror on his face when he saw me coming for him. He would pay for this, if it were my last act on earth.

But I couldn't do it. I couldn't go after them on my own. I had no idea where Ozzie had taken her. Tom's wolf was still running wild out there, somewhere on the Tor. I couldn't leave the wolves unprotected. They were my wolves, now. My responsibility. I felt connected to each of them. Leaving them was not an option.

Tehuantl's memories and knowledge were mine now. His contempt for Gordon's amateurish blood wards was mine too. I knew that Tehuantl's magic would hide us better than the Mage had hidden Mythica, and rejoiced in the certainty that I had the skills and know-how to make it work. We needed a sanctuary. A base camp where we would be protected from the hunters who would come after us, and a place where we could shift into human form without alerting the Fae.

I paced out an area roughly fifty feet square around the carcass of the dead beaver. I closed my eyes and breathed deeply, allowing the shaman's magic to fill me. It welled up from the earth at my feet, filling me completely, like liquid metal into a mold. A shimmery heat of power rippled across my skin. A mild tremor rumbled beneath me as I lifted the ward from deep within the earth. A moment later, the glamour was in place, and I was once again in the grip of a blood thirst.

I gritted my teeth and turned my back to the wolves while I shook off my compulsion. I would never go there. Wolf blood would never be food for me; any more than the flesh of humans or the sap of opium poppies. The call of warm blood was strong, but not irresistible. I recognized my need for nourishment, but any protein would do, and beaver meat would be good enough.

When I stepped outside the ward to check my work, the pack disappeared. Unlike Gordon's clumsy blood ward, my glamour shimmered with a faint silvery outline that only I, with my newly improved vision, could see. I tested the air by opening my senses to Xenotchi, but neither the scent of wolf, blood, or beaver was detectable. *Pretty cool.*

As I stepped back inside the ward, I grinned as the itch of magic slid across my bare skin. Farley and all the wolves were watching me, ears pricked forward, their heads all cocked in the same direction. As I came closer, the wolves shied warily. I stopped and crouched down to their level. They seemed to understand that I wasn't going to hurt them, but there was no trust there; they were just too weak to run away. I didn't know if they'd understand me, but I gave it my best shot.

"Okay, here's the deal. For now, we're safe. If anyone comes after us, they won't be able to see us, hear us, or smell us. They'll come to a dead end on the scent trail. For the next three or four nights, this is our home base. So remember where we're parked."

The effort of setting up the wards made me ravenous. Farley stayed right beside me while I gathered up enough dead wood to start a fire, then settled against my side as I heated chunks of meat on a ring of stones which encircled the flames. After I ate, I stretched out near the fire, with Silas and Farley close by. Eventually the wolves settled down as well.

Hang on, Sara, I prayed to the First Jaguar to keep her safe until I could get to her.

Patience, priest. You would serve none by acting out of passion.

Give your brothers time to heal. You cannot succeed without them.

Is that how it is now, Xenotchi? Do I serve you as Tehuantl once did?

I could feel Xenotchi's confusion as he considered his answer.

That is not a question which can be easily answered. The jaguar clans are children of the earth no longer.

Does that mean you're not a god any more?

I am First Jaguar. I am Xenotchi. I am eternal.

What do you want from me?

Xenotchi didn't answer. I could feel him working on it, though. In the distance, a howl floated across the Tor, followed by another and another. The wolves snarled and snapped themselves awake. I sent out soothing pheromones and almost immediately, they settled back into their restless dreaming.

BROTHERS OF THE FANG

IN SPITE OF the full moon, I kept a small campfire going all night. The wolves were nervous; unable to relax, and the light seemed to offer them some comfort. To my immense relief, Tom's wild wolf stayed nearby, and the rest of the pack backed off to let him feed on the leftovers. He ate enough to fill his belly and took off, but didn't go far. He'd lost his rage and bad smell, but didn't quite have the scent of healthy wolf yet, nor the golden gleam of understanding behind his amber eyes like the rest of the wolves.

Silas trusted me, but none of the other wolves did. They didn't run out of the camp, but they couldn't seem to settle down. They wouldn't even eat until I backed away. They huddled together the first night, keeping the fire between us. Every time I moved, all seven heads came up and they crouched, as if on the verge of running off. I didn't blame them for being wary of me. After what Ozzie had done to them, I understood. And I was certain they'd never seen or smelled anyone like me.

The only time they appeared to lose their anxiety was when I sat quietly and spoke softly to them. They liked that, I could tell. They wouldn't look at me, but they settled a bit and their ears twitched in my direction.

So I talked to them. I told them about growing up on the lake and about all the stuff that Striper Dave and I had done as kids, and how we spent most of our time hiding from Ray Tarwater and his gang who were two years older than we were and had better, faster, bikes. I told them about Tom and how he'd taught me to fish and tie flies. I told them about worm farming, and showed them how to call worms out of the ground; something the little black wolf, Rizzo, seemed to find amusing until I reached out to try and pet him. I described the different species of fish that lived in the lake, where to find them, and what kind of tackle to use. I told them everything I could remember about the habits of the snapping turtle and the smaller, more common painted turtle. I even told them the real story about Hector Clemente and what really happened in his basement. And how his brother Diego had set Randall and his werewolves on me and how Tom had gotten bitten. After that, I had to stop when my emotions got the best of me. Gradually, their heads lowered onto their front paws and their eyes closed. Serenaded by the small sounds of the Tor wilderness and the snapping of embers on the fire, I kept watch while the wolves slept.

* * *

For the first time in years, I woke up in my own, albeit new skin. I felt like a new man; literally. I was no longer held hostage by the threat of Tehuantl. He was well and truly gone. Through his memories, I remembered giving the breath of life to countless chubby, brown-skinned infants. I recognized weeds and plants by their Olmec names and knew how to use them to heal the sick. The knowledge was as deeply ingrained within me as muscle memory. I shared Tehuantl's craving for warm blood, but realized it was connected to his use of magic. Every time I used his magic, the blood thirst rose. Raw meat took the edge off, but only the blood of a fresh kill quenched it. My worries that Tehuantl had been like the vampires proved unfounded.

The First Jaguar was still there, but except for being able to maintain my form when asleep, our relationship remained pretty much as it had been. I now realized that Xenotchi was connected to a shared consciousness that was too vast for me to grasp. The wolves were there, but it was more than just wolves and jaguars. I sensed coyote, foxes, bears, and other cats. Sarah had been right about embracing the beast. I didn't know if the wolves could see beyond the First Wolf like I could see beyond the first Jaguar, but it seemed as if all the predators were somehow connected.

I worried about Sarah. Several times, I considered leaving the wolves and crossing the Tor to find a phone. There was no way I could report her abduction in person. One look at me and even Dixon would have me locked up with no questions asked. I had to believe that the hospital had reported her missing, and that there was already an official investigation underway. The thought of her in Ozzie's hands nearly drove me mad, but I didn't know where Ozzie had taken her. Going after them alone was not an option. My plan wouldn't work without the wolves. She was tough; she was a fighter. I had to trust that she would stay alive until we were strong enough to come and get her. I tried to imagine that she'd fought her way free or been rescued, but couldn't convince myself that it was true.

Waiting for the wolves to recover was the hardest. I had to keep reminding myself to be patient. I'd made a rookie mistake on my first big bust by pushing for the warrant and take-down too soon. We'd ended up with nothing more than a couple low-level couriers and missed the big game. Except for hunting, waiting for the wolves to gain back their strength was a lot like working undercover: hanging out with a bunch of guys who didn't trust you, waiting for them to get used to you and finally accept you.

Silas's wolf, Farley, and I brought in smaller game several times a day. Raccoons, mostly; there was plenty to eat. Gradually, the wolves lost their fear of me and edged closer. On the second day, their ears and tails began to perk up. Their coats began to thicken and take on a bit of sheen.

On the third night, the big wolf, Tanner, scented a deer, and the pack took off in hot pursuit. There was no way I could keep pace with a wolf pack on the scent. Eventually, however, Farley turned the deer back toward me, and this time, the pack circled for the kill just a few hundred yards from camp. It was the first time the cat had been with the pack at the kill.

After everyone had eaten their fill, they followed me back to camp, where I built up the fire and waited for them to shift. Screened behind the safety of the wards, not even the Fae would be able to sense them in human form.

Silas shifted easily enough, followed by the little black wolf, Rizzo, Tanner, and the rest. In human form, they appeared gaunt, but clear-eyed and alert.

Wynn Lambert had been Ambrose's lone wolf lawyer for more than a century. He'd never actually been a member of the Mythica pack. He bore an uncanny resemblance to a young Gregory Peck. Cobb had managed to persuade Ambrose to put Wynn aside, saying he would do a better job managing the nest's legal interests.

Wynn had been imprisoned inside the bestiary the longest. "There were other wolves already down there when I first arrived. When they died, Ozzie fed them to the Fae creatures. He told me he'd do the same to me when I died. I don't think I could have lasted much longer. I managed to get at a little moisture seeping up through the floor of my cell. I think that's the only thing that kept me alive." He shivered. "I kept thinking someone would come looking for me. Gordon and I had been friends, or at least I'd thought so." Like me, Wynn had been drugged with a shot of Glamour.

Sarah's former client, Kevin, never knew why he ended up in the bestiary, but suspected that the pack's Omega, Phelan had set him up. He had no memory of who'd hit him with the ketamine dart.

Tanner was the oldest-looking were-man I had ever seen. His hair was completely gray; he and Vince had served together in Korea. When he retired from the military, Vince had convinced him to join the Mythica pack. He had been Vince's Beta for decades. One day, Tanner suggested to Vince that Ozzie needed psychiatric help. The next day Ozzie drugged him with ketamine when he went for his distemper immunization.

The twins, Corbin and Conrad, had been hired as landscape developers for the estate. They'd also been drugged with Glamour shots by Gordon on their very first day of work. Ozzie told them he'd never heard of twin lycans before; and decided he wanted to 'experiment' with them.

Lenny had been caught trying to break into The Bloody Fang one night after the park had closed. He had a string of misdemeanor offenses as a juvenile, but had kept his nose clean after contracting the ALVS virus on his second tour of duty in the Middle East. Vince had him cold on the park's surveillance camera.

"Vince gave me a choice. Thirty days in lockup in the clinic, or he'd turn me and the tape over to the sheriff. I took the thirty days, figuring I'd get free squares and a cot while I was in. As far as I can tell, it's been more like three months of hell."

The little man, Rizzo Torino, turned out to be a hit man hired by Felix to make Ozzie's death look like an accident. Unfortunately, Vince had caught him tinkering with the brakes on Ozzie's car. Vince brought him down to the bestiary to give Ozzie a crack at finding out who'd hired him. Of all of us, Rizzo was in the worst shape. Hollow-cheeked and sallow, he looked like a concentration camp refugee. But his grip was firm and his eyes fierce when he thanked me for rescuing him.

"My family is from Calabria," he explained. "Omerta is a way of life for us. Ozzie and Vince will be repaid for their actions tenfold. I will not rest until that debt is paid."

With the introductions complete, Silas filled us in on the latest. "When Mike disappeared, everything started to fall apart. There was a huge argument between Ambrose and Cobb. Rafe broke it up, but it wasn't over. Ambrose shut down the park, saying it would remain closed until Cobb apologized. It was pretty tense."

"What was the fight about," asked Tanner.

"Vince wouldn't say. We were all tippy-toeing around each other, and Cobb and Ambrose were trying to get Vince to choose sides. With the park closed, there wasn't much to do. Everybody was pretty shook up. I thought about leaving, and I wasn't the only one. Even Rafe talked about it.

"One afternoon I noticed Gordon taking deliveries over at the Bloody Fang. But he's the farm manager, right? I couldn't figure out what he was doing at the restaurant. I kept an eye on him and after he left, I snooped around. The shipping cartons were full of chains and padlocks. Thick, heavy chains. I got to thinking that the only reason anyone would need that many big chains would be to lock the vampires into their crypts. When I told Vince about it, he came after me with that damn stun baton of his. Next thing I knew, Ozzie was lighting me up with couple of live wires and a battery."

From the outer edge of the firelight, Tom gave a warning growl. Two wolves stood just outside the wards, sniffing curiously. It was Striper Dave and Chaney. I sent Silas out in wolf form to greet them, and after a bit of hesitation, the two of them joined us inside the warded camp.

They panicked a little when they saw me, but we all sent out reassuring pheromones. I think they recognized my voice when I told them it was safe for them to shift inside the camp.

Dave was talking almost before he finished his transformation. "What the hell happened to you, Mikey?" he demanded.

I gave him a grim smile. This was only the beginning. I'd never look human again, so I'd better get used to it. On the plus side, I'd never have to hide again. My biggest, baddest secret was out in the open now. The monkey was off my back.

As I explained, I flexed my guns to show off my new markings and showed them how I could extend and retract my claws. "I've still got the jaguar, but the priest is gone. I'm pretty sure this is permanent."

Dave looked doubtful, then cracked a wide smile. "Guess you won't have to worry about fending off Yolanda Rivas any more. I think I've got a real shot now."

"Shut up," I said. "What are you guys doing out here, anyway?"

"Who's Yolanda," asked Wynn.

"Quiet," Tanner said. "I want to hear about what what's going on at the park."

"Ambrose is out, Cobb is in." Chaney explained. "He brought in a pack of mercenaries."

"Yeah, we saw them come through the bestiary," I said, and explained about Ozzie and the dungeon and what had happened to us.

Both men looked stunned.

"Vince told us Ambrose was planning to get rid of him, and that Cobb made him an offer he couldn't refuse. Then he put us to work in the vault, chaining coffins."

"Whose coffins," Wynn asked. "And how many?"

Dave shrugged. "They just pointed us at the ones they wanted chained. Eight, I think. Cobb is in charge now."

There was general muttering as we chewed on the news. I'd never been close to Cobb, but it sure seemed to me that Ambrose had given him every advantage. It didn't seem right.

"The nest is split. If Cobb's in charge, that means he must have Willem, Lyrissa, and Tryffin in his court," Wynn said. "Who is the fifth? Rafe?"

I shook my head. "No way. Rafe would never align himself with Cobb. And it's probably not Santino either."

"I agree," Wynn said. "And it's not Orcas. If they took out Ambrose, they'd take out his woman too. And Gawl and Roosa are loyal to Ambrose; they won't be split up, they're brother and sister. So that leaves Tryffin."

"Makes sense," Tanner nodded. "He's a frickin' mechanical genius. He runs the rides; maintains the equipment. He's always been neutral, and Cobb can't run Mythica without him."

My stomach churned. In a sick way, it did make sense. If Cobb had power of attorney for Ambrose; the transfer of the estate into his hands would be easy.

"But why take over Mythica at all," Silas asked. "Ambrose was setting him up with his own territory. It doesn't make sense."

"Yeah it does," Wynn answered. "Cobb has always been ambitious, and he's always been jealous of Ambrose. When Cobb finally decided to leave and start his own nest, Ambrose kept making promises to get him to stay, but never delivered. There was always something else that was more important. Ambrose made a big mistake when he put Cobb in charge of his legal affairs. If you ask me, I think Cobb got tired of waiting."

"Maybe he made a deal with Phelan too," Dave said. "He acted like he knew what was going on all along. I'm not sure about Steve-oh or Yolanda."

"Yolanda wasn't in on it," I said.

"Well, we didn't stick around to find out," Dave said. "As soon as we finished chaining the coffins, Chaney and I told Vince we were going over to the clubhouse to shower. Instead, we shifted and ran like hell out onto the Tor. We ran across Silas's trail, and followed it here. What's the plan?"

Tanner immediately took charge. "We take out Vince; that's the plan. We go in hard and fast. Once Vince is dead, we take back the park and negotiate for the best deal between Cobb and Ambrose."

Tanner was right. Vince had to go; but getting Sarah and the rest of the Fae hostages out of there was more important.

"No can do, Tanner," I said. "Ozzie's got Sarah. If she's still at Mythica, I'm going after her and the other Fae hostages. We can't go against Vince or the vamps until they're safely out of there. If she's not there, I'm going to find her, wherever she is."

Tanner rose, his pheromones rolling off him like waves. "Back off, kitty-cat. I'm in charge here. We're going to play this thing my way." He gave each of us a measured look. "We do this right, we could all end up rich."

"Ease off, Tanner. You guys want to go after Vince, fine. You and I aren't pack." I turned to Dave and Chaney. "Ozzie took Sarah with him when they left. Have either of you seen them?"

Chaney shook his head.

"I didn't see her, but I saw Ozzie," Dave said.

My hopes soared. "If Ozzie's there, so is Sarah." I clenched my fists. "We all know what he's doing to her. We've got to get her out of there."

I heard a sound behind me and turned to see a lone figure cross the wards and step up into the firelight beside me. "I'm with Mike on this," Tom clasped my shoulder.

I grabbed him into a bear hug. Neither of us spoke. His were-man form was broader, heavier, and more muscular than before.

Tom looked good; lucid and alert, if a little tired around his now-golden eyes. "I'd follow you to hell and back, Mike, as long as we go after Sarah first." His voice was hoarse as he addressed the group, his faced hardened into an expression I'd never seen before. "I may be new to this wolf-man business, but Mike and Sarah saved our lives. Mine, at any rate. Now we're out of that hell-hole and that ass-wipe Ozzie has still got his hands on her. We've got to bring the sheriff in on this."

"You're still just a pup, so you don't know what you're saying," Lenny said. "Let me tell you how lycan execution warrants are carried out. First they force the lycan to shift into beast form, usually by using a taser on him. Once the victim is no longer recognizable as human, they fire a silver bullet into his skull at a point-blank range."

Tanner nodded. "He's right. One of the first things a lycan has to learn is to avoid the scrutiny of law enforcement. If Sarah is reported missing, they'll go after her. If we get involved, it will only go badly for us."

Tom paled and took a step back.

"Easy Pops." I put my hand on Tom's shoulder. "We're going after Sarah, don't worry. The Van Cleves are respected members of the community. We know what we're up against, but when it comes to going against the Van Cleves, Dixon's hands are tied. We don't have the same constraint. I'm sorry I got you into this, but there are no second chances for lycans. If we're going to get her back, we'll have to do it without the sheriff."

Tom made a face, but nodded. "I never thought I'd hear you say that."

Lenny reached out and shook my hand. "I appreciate what you did to get me out of there, but I'm not sticking around." With that, he hunched himself over and shifted into wolf. A few minutes later, he slipped away from the camp and disappeared into the darkness.

"So what's the plan, Mike?" Rizzo asked.

"It's not going to be easy," I began.

"Wait a minute," Tanner interrupted. "I'm not saying anything against going after the woman, I'm just saying that we need to take back the park first. Of course we'll force them to release the hostages as part of our negotiations with the vamps."

"I've got a better idea," I said. "I can set up a couple of warded areas where we can observe the activity on the estate and park without being seen. There are a couple of places just outside the park that will give us a good vantage point. If they've got her, we'll know where they're holding her in a day or two at most. Then Tanner can go in there and challenge Vince as a distraction while Tom and I get her out of there."

"I can't let you do that, Bane. By my count Vince has more than a dozen wolves on the Mythica payroll, at least half of which are hired professionals. Counting you and Tom, we've only got eleven. We'll need every man here to bring Vince to heel." He nodded at Farley.

"Even that damn mutt of yours."

No way. I didn't like Tanner much, and I liked him less every time he opened his mouth. I told myself it wasn't personal, but I just couldn't bring myself to agree with anything he said. I fact, I wanted nothing to do with him. I was probably going to regret this, but I couldn't bring myself to go along with him. "You guys go ahead without us. We're not part of the pack anyway."

"Like hell you aren't," Silas stepped forward. "I swore an oath to you, Mike. I'm not part of the Mythica pack anymore, but I'll follow you. You're my Alpha now."

My heart warmed with Silas' vote of confidence. Forget Tanner. I trusted Silas.

"Wait a second," Tanner stepped forward, his cheeks flushed. "I'm the only Alpha here. Get back over here Silas. Nobody is going anywhere without my permission." A heavy blanket of pheromones spread over us. "Everyone, to me. *Now.*" The twins, Corbin and Conrad, obediently stepped up behind the big man. "You don't want to play, *fine.* You're free to go, kitty-cat."

"Watch your mouth," Rizzo warned. "Bane breathed life into you, same as me. You owe him your loyalty, not the other way around." Rizzo came over to stand beside me. "I don't know any of you guys. All I know is that Mike got me out of there. We've hunted together." He tapped his chest. "He's part of me now. In here. I owe him."

"He's right," Chaney agreed. "Mike's our guy. Whatever you decide, I'm with you, Mike."

Silas and Chaney joined Tom and Rizzo beside me. If we were going to be choosing up sides like some damn game of baseball, I was glad to have them with me.

"Get your ass over here, Chaney," Tanner ordered. "You too, Silas. Bane here is no wolf. I'm the only Alpha here. It's not that I'm ungrateful, Bane. I appreciate everything you did for me and all, but I will never follow a kitty cat."

I shrugged. "You're not the first lycan to say that."

"Listen to him, men. He knows he's not fit to command. I'm going in there and teach Vince and those mercs a lesson. Then I'm going to personally put Ozzie into a bath of acid and watch him die. This is what you want. This is what we all want. So who's with me?"

No one moved, except the lone wolf Wynn. "If Mike is good enough for Silas and Chaney, he's good enough for me. You always were an asshole, Tanner."

All eyes turned toward Kevin and Striper Dave. The tension in the air thickened.

Dave grinned. "Don't look at me, I'm with worm-breath." He punched me playfully in the chest.

"Thanks, man," I said.

Kevin moved toward Tanner. "Tanner gave me job and made a place for me in the pack. I won't desert him."

As badly as I needed them behind me, I wouldn't make any false promises. "Kevin is right, guys. If you want your jobs back, you would be a darn sight better off with Tanner. I'm going in to get Sarah and the rest of the Fae out. If they've chained up Rafe, I'll get him too, but I don't plan on hanging around afterward." Maybe Tom and I would have better chance of sneaking onto the grounds if it was just the two of us.

Tanner went rigid with fury. "You just don't get it, Bane. This is not some fifth-grade pee-wee league where we choose up sides. You have provoked the anger of your Alpha. Submit to me now or feel my rage." His beast was already there. Quicker than anyone could react, Tanner's wolf came for my throat.

Just as quickly, I was waiting for him. I side-swiped him with a solid cuff to the side of the head and sent him sprawling. He was on his feet in an instant, hackles raised, darting quickly for my legs. He struck, snapping for my belly with lightning speed.

I whipped around and felt the whisper of his teeth against my bare skin. I grabbed him by the scruff of his neck and dug my claws into him so the he could not squirm loose. I shook him like a rag doll. If he hadn't been so weak and thin, I probably wouldn't have managed it, but I heard his teeth clack together as I threw him to the ground.

Before he could recover, I pounced and grabbed the wolf by the throat. As he writhed and squirmed, desperate to protect himself, I felt a moment of panic as my blood thirst rose. I would *not* drink wolf blood. I shifted; calling on the cat's greater weight to pin the wolf, but the fight was over before it ever really started.

He cried and whined as he scrabbled with his claws, scratching ineffectually at the cat's thick fur for a moment before he submitted. When I growled, Tanner's wolf went utterly limp. With his neck and belly exposed, he urinated on himself. I couldn't bring myself to accept his apology. He wasn't worth the effort.

I released him and rolled the cat up; more easily than I'd ever done before.

"Get up, Tanner," I told him. "And get out." Behind me, I felt the excitement and blood lust pheromones welling in the guys. I countered it with a blanket of my own, and stayed near Tanner as the humbled wolf panted at my feet. "Nobody touches him. Anyone who wants to leave is welcome to go now. No one will come after you. You have my word."

Only Kevin and the twins shifted to join Tanner's wolf. Then all four of them trotted out of the camp and onto the Tor.

Rizzo spoke first. "Good riddance."

"So what do you say, Mike," asked Chaney. "Will you be our Alpha?"

"That's right," Dave agreed. "We don't need those guys."

"It's not a pack until you say the words," Wynn said.

I considered the question. I hadn't asked for this. The wolves' yearning for the bond was undeniable; it was a need I felt as well. I wanted it.

"Don't expect me to hunt with you," I warned.

"What does that mean?" Wynn asked.

"Oh that jaguar of his is a total waste of space," Silas explained. "Unless you herd the prey right to him."

"Yeah, and don't even think about trying to share that cat's kill. Especially if it's turtle," Chaney grinned. "He'll try to rip your head off."

"None of that matters." Dave tapped his temple. "What really matters is in here. I can feel him in my head, even from the other side of the Tor. I know he's got my back. Not even Vince could do that."

Silas raised his voice in a victorious howl. The rest of the guys added to the chorus until even Tom and I joined in. When Wynn gave me the words, I was ready.

"*I stake my claim as the sole and legitimate Alpha of the High Tor Pack. I will protect my bothers as I would my own life. Any who dare to oppose us will feel my teeth their throat.*"

A cold blue flame rolled off my naked skin, sending a tsunami of Alpha pheromones over our new pack. To say it felt weird was an understatement. One by one, each of the men shifted into wolf form, rolled at my feet, and bared their neck to me. I bit into the vulnerable skin of each of their throats and gave each a vigorous shake. With each shake, I pushed my new Alpha will into them, and each wolf responded by scrabbling closer and trying to thrust their neck further into my mouth. Their thoughts came to me as if they'd been spoken aloud; each identical and fervent:

I submit to you, for you are my Alpha.

I will follow you and run beside you and help you defend my brothers for as long as you will have me; as long as we are pack we are invincible.

By the First Wolf, my life is yours, for we are brothers of the fang.

INTO THE TOR

THE NEW PACK bond came with a new sense purpose. It wasn't just me; the seven of us had become a unit with a single purpose: to rescue Sarah and the others; be they human, Fae, or vampire. The sense of connectedness that I felt to the wolves was like nothing I'd never experienced. It was like actually *being* bigger, stronger, and more knowing. We couldn't speak to each other telepathically, but we could sense each other's presence, and the sum of our strengths was magnified to a greater whole.

The rescue wouldn't be without risk; we'd be going into an armed camp where our common enemy was a multi-headed monster. Slaking our thirst for revenge on Ozzie wouldn't be enough. Taking down Vince wouldn't change anything. Ambrose and Cobb were cut from the same cloth. At its core, Mythica was rotten as road kill.

They had to be holding Sarah either in the vault beneath the Odditorium or in the main house where the blood stewards lived. If she was in the vault, there was no way to tell without actually going down there. But getting her out of the house might be even more difficult. We'd be going against Felix and the rest of the blood stewards. In spite of what we'd all heard Ozzie say, no one really believed that Felix was dead.

"I got to know Felix pretty well," Rizzo said. "Did quite a few jobs for him over the years. We got to talking one day and he told me the place is riddled with escape routes. He'd be able to get out and no one would ever know. I wouldn't count him out."

"I agree," Wynn said. "And we need to consider the allegiances of the other blood stewards. Figure eight to ten stewards per vampire, and we could be talking about forty or fifty people, in addition to Vince and the hired wolves."

"I don't like those odds, boss," Dave said.

"Neither do I." Spit junkies or no, blood stewards were still classified as US citizens, and any lycan-caused injury, large or small, would incur serious consequences. For all their human frailty, they had the law on their side. Even the lowest crack head on the street had more rights than lycans. Regardless of their reasons for becoming blood stewards, we couldn't lift a finger against them without running the risk of legal execution. They, on the other hand, could shoot, stab, electrocute, torture, or even blow us up with impunity. Whatever plan we devised, we would need to figure out a way to safely contain Mythica's blood stewards.

I sketched out a diagram of the estate in the dust. "The rest of the Fae hostages are here in the Odditorium. If we can't sneak them out, we'll need some sort of distraction. But before we make our move, I want to know where Sarah is."

I drew a couple of circles in the dirt, just outside the outline I'd already drawn of the park. "These are a couple of areas that are close enough for us to see and hear what's going on, without actually crossing the inner wards. We can approach from the east and use the woods for cover; the vineyard will screen our approach from the surveillance cameras. We'll need to split up. Silas and Dave will set up here, in those big trees near the concert hall. You'll be able to see the comings and goings into the operations center and the front gate. Count heads and keep an eye out for any food deliveries. If Sarah is still alive, she'll need to be fed."

"What if Ozzie has taken her out of the park?" asked Tom.

I shook my head. Ozzie had lived on the grounds since the night he graduated from vet school. "Ozzie is addicted to Ambrose's saliva. If Cobb has taken over the park, Ozzie will need to find himself a vampire of Ambrose's line. If Ozzie is still around, he must have worked out a deal with Cobb. And I'll bet that's why Vince is still here. He won't leave Ozzie."

The men nodded in silent agreement, but all we really had was guesswork. I pointed to the second stake-out position. "Chaney and Wynn can set up here, between the Odditorium and the Theatre. The main vault lies beneath the Odditorium, and there's an underground passageway leading from the warming room to the dressing rooms behind the back stage of the theatre. You'll have a direct line of sight to the road leading to the entrance of either building. You'll be able to see anyone coming or going."

"Rizzo and I will be here." I pointed to a third spot near the house. "Ozzie lives in the house with the rest of the blood stewards. It's where I would stash Sarah, if I were him. We'll try to figure out how many people are inside, and who they are. We'll go in after sunrise. The vamps will be down for the day, and the watch should be lightest then. The numbers should favor us."

With the plan set, we settled in to catch some sleep until sunrise. The mood was relaxed but determined. Farley curled up beside me, but I couldn't sleep, knowing that after all this waiting, we were finally going to see some action.

* * *

Before we could set out the next morning, Trick's huge wolf came out of the woods, nose down onto a scent trail. We left the warded camp to meet him, but he was so focused on the scent, he didn't see us until he was less than fifty feet away. Once he spotted us, he didn't hesitate. He lowered his head and tail and made a bee-line to me, and rolled over to expose his belly and throat.

As soon as I acknowledged him, the whole pack was swarmed over him, and he submitted to each of them in turn. We led him into camp to hear what he had to say.

"I'm done with Mythica. The whole place has gone crazy," he began. "Vince has got the mercenaries in charge now, and more keep arriving every day. He made one of them, a big guy named Hale, his Beta, but Hale is really the guy making the decisions. Vince defers everything to him. It's like he doesn't even care anymore." Trick was nearly beside himself.

I sent out soothing pheromones, and the rest of the pack joined in. "Take it easy," I said. "Did anybody follow you?"

"No," Trick said, with real bitterness. "I don't think they even know I'm gone. Not yet, at any rate. They were too busy dealing with Yolanda. She went after Vince. Challenged him in a fight for Alpha."

Tension spread through us like wildfire, as we clamored for the explanation. Silas had told me were-women sometimes took over pack leadership if their Alpha partner died or became incapacitated. It was always a bloodless coup; no decent wolf would fight back against an Alpha bitch. Basically, if she wanted the job, it was hers.

"Yeah. Ripped him up pretty good, too." Trick gave me an appraising look. "She blamed him for your disappearance, Mike. Hale took her down with a stun baton."

A murmur went through the group.

Trick frowned. "I couldn't believe it. Vince never said a word against it. He even helped Hale cage her. Ozzie put a silver collar on her so she couldn't shift. They took her into the Odditorium; no one has seen her since." He shook his head. "But that's not the end of it."

Trick looked around nervously. "They know you guys are out here. Tanner came in last night. Walked right through the front gate and challenged Vince for leadership of the pack. Vince refused, saying that Tanner wasn't pack anymore. Told him he'd have to defeat Hale before he'd allow him to issue a challenge."

"That's not right," Silas said. "Vince always did his own fighting. Why is he hiding behind a hired gun?"

Trick turned thoughtful, all his previous swagger gone. "You know, I don't think he really wanted to fight Tanner. The guy was wound up, but he looked pretty bad. As bad as all you guys. Skinny. Weak. It was kind of embarrassing, really."

"We don't look that bad," Wynn said.

Trick made a face. "Uh, yeah. There's not enough meat on you to flesh out a chicken. And Bane here looks like frickin' freak show. What the hell happened to you?"

It would be stupid to get mad a Trick for asking what they all wanted to know. I hadn't figured out a way to say it without sounding like I'd lost my marbles. "It's a shifter thing," I shrugged. "Kind of a long story. Tell us what happened with Tanner."

"Tanner's dead. He never had a chance. Hale creamed him, and Phelan chopped off his head. Vince said he needed to make an example of him. I tell you, Vince has totally lost it. Hale won't let anyone leave until after the summit; the place is an armed camp. Everyone is working like crazy to get the park back into operation. I guess Cobb needs to prove that he's in control and everything is running smoothly."

"They're going to re-open the park?"

"They have to. Cobb wants to show the Globus how much better a Pomp he is than Ambrose was. He's planning to have enough blood on hand to feed all the vampires at the summit. Besides, they're running low."

"How many blood stewards are left?" I asked.

Trick looked nauseated. "It makes me sick. And this was the last straw. Cobb had Ozzie infect some of the blood stewards with ALVS-infected blood taken from the pack. He claimed it was legal because there's no bite involved."

I felt revulsion flow through every member of the pack. ALVS research had been developed in the Middle East by extremists and introduced as a combat weapon against US soldiers and POWs during the Gulf Wars. A single soldier hit by infected shrapnel could spread the virus undetected through an entire platoon or hospital ward within weeks. The intentional use of the ALVS virus on humans was considered a war crime. Although blood stewards weren't viewed as much more than spit heads, technically speaking, they were still human.

"By the first wolf, no," Chaney swore softly.

"That's right. He made it sound as if infecting them was the only way to save their lives. Last night, Vince introduced us to the near-weres. These guys used to steward for Ambrose and Orcas. They're were going through some pretty heavy withdrawal symptoms without their regular feeding, but the vamps won't touch them now that they've got the virus. I don't know if they'll live or what Cobb promised them, but they agreed to take Ozzie's injections. I don't think they realize yet what going to happen to them at the next full moon."

"That's sick," Rizzo said.

"That's what I'm saying. Hale and the rest of them are all lone wolves. Even though Vince made Hale his Beta, neither Hale or any of the other hired guns took the oath. They're not pack. We don't have enough members now to absorb that many first-moon wolves." Trick was practically in tears. "Ozzie told the near-weres that Sarah is going to help them transition. Tanner told Vince that she'd worked some sort of miracle with one of you guys."

"You've seen Sarah?" I asked.

Tom made an anguished sound. "Where is she?"

Trick shook his head. "I don't know. I didn't stick around. All I know is that the pack is broken." He gave Tom a thoughtful look. "You the one Tanner was talking about? The superwolf?"

Tom and I exchanged confused glances.

"Yeah, that's our Tom." Silas said, proudly. "I've never seen anyone come into their wolf so well. Look at him. He shifted for the first time four days ago. He's already shifting like one of us."

"That first moon is a bitch," Dave explained. "It usually takes a first-timer at least a month to recover."

A look of wonder came over Trick as he took a good look at Tom. "I was a total mad dog for three weeks. It took another ten days more before I was able to shift back. Anyway, after Tanner spilled the beans about you guys, Vince set a posse of mercs out to patrol the Tor. They came back with Kevin and two other guys I didn't know. He's got them stashed somewhere too. I was all alone in there. I came out here hoping to find you."

"We're just on our way over there. We're going to do a little house cleaning," I told him. The others nodded in silent agreement.

Trick went to one knee before me. "I don't apologize, Bane. You know that. But if you'll have me, I'll make it up to you; I swear."

I nodded. The need to belong was strong in Trick; I could feel it. His desire to be part of a pack was greater than his desire to lead. His presence would make us all stronger.

"Get up, Trick. If you're serious, you're welcome to join us, but Silas is my Beta. There's no chance for you."

A small tic pulled at the corner of his eye, but Trick's face remained passive. "I don't care about that right now. Let me come with you. They've caged Yolanda and three other wolves. Everyone else is in lockdown. The place is no better than a concentration camp. If you'll have me, I am willing to submit to you."

Fifteen minutes later, we headed out onto the Tor. The pack made allowances for me and kept their pace slow enough that in my new form, I could keep up. I jogged at the rear, with Tom, Rizzo, and Farley off my left hip. As we neared the estate, I noticed several warded portals into the Fae lands. Good to know that the Fae hostages wouldn't have far to go to reach safety inside the Tor.

We were less than a mile from the estate when the wolf posse found us. They'd obviously been laying in ambush for us in the trees. As soon as we crossed onto open ground, they attacked. The wolves were coming hard, and we were outnumbered.

Facing a dozen charging wolves while wearing only a pair of gym shorts is a terrifying experience. My first instinct was to run like hell, but the savage roar of my pack all around me was like riding into battle with a battalion of buzz saws. I thought about shifting, but decided against it. The cat wouldn't have a prayer against these guys, and I was faster and stronger than I'd ever been. Taking a cue from my new brothers, I took heart and faced them head on. We spread out to meet our attackers, and the battle was on.

They zeroed in on me as the weakest. The first wolf lunged for me as my right fist connected with a solid hit to his eye socket. I felt the satisfying crunch of bones and the wolf staggered, shaking his head and licking his chops. A second wolf leapt for my throat, and I ducked beneath him; twisting as I reached out with my claws extended to gouge deeply into the tender skin of his belly.

I grunted as a third went for my knee and held on. I went down; wincing as he pulverized the joint cartilage of my knee against bone. I tried to scrape him off me, but he had my knee in a vise. I drove my shoulder forward and rolled; the claws on one hand still gripping the underbelly of my second attacker. With a wrenching movement, I flung that wolf away from me, and used my thumbs to gouge at the eyes of the wolf at my knee. He released his grip and backed off. I was free.

A fourth wolf slashed at my face but I got my arm up in time. I threw myself toward him, using my arm and the weight of my body behind it to force him to the ground. Chaney and Silas tore into him from either side. He yelped and let go, then scrambled to his feet and lit out like his tail was on fire.

I crouched, waiting for the next attacker, but the fight was over. Any and all of our attackers that could still run were making their escape, leaving three of their dead colleagues behind. Trick's wolf made a half-hearted move to go after them, but I called him back.

We were punch drunk on victory, adrenaline, and the smell of blood. None of our guys was badly injured; only Wynn would need to shift in order to heal a nasty bite and torn tendons on his leg. I marveled at the advantages my new form brought me. While I wasn't nearly as strong as the cat, I'd held my own. My reflexes were as good as the wolves. The big disadvantage to my new form was that my skin was still as tender as tissue paper, but the bites and cuts were healing quickly. Already, the gashes in my flesh had stopped bleeding, and after a quick shift into cat and back again, my knee was sound. It still hurt like hell, but I could feel the tendons in my knee knitting back together. I flexed my knee experimentally. Painful, but still functional, and getting stronger by the minute.

Silas and the little black wolf, Rizzo, were scraping their back feet contemptuously, sending a shower of dirt and grass over the bodies of the dead wolves. The rest of us panted and walked in circles, loosening our tight muscles. We all needed water.

Tom's warning growl brought us up short.

Nixese stepped through a portal not far from us. The Nagual Bear I'd rescued from the bestiary was with him.

"Easy guys," I spoke quietly to the growling wolves beside me. Tom and Rizzo were stiff-legged with alarm.

I greeted the Fae warrior formally. "I see you Nixese." The wolves gathered around me like, well, a pack. I could feel each and every one of them in my head. Their pheromones rolled over me; wordlessly offering their staunch support and comfort. "We have broken none of your laws," I said.

"Greetings, Xenotchi. Greetings, cousin." He looked at me quizzically. "Where is Tehuantl?"

"It's a long story. Let's just say he's no longer with us. Why are you here?"

Nixese frowned. "I have come on my own. The elders are angry. Not all of the hostages have been returned. Although the First Bear vouched for you, they will not move against the vampires until all the hostages are freed."

"We're still working on it," I said, absently. I only had eyes for the Nagual. Hesitantly, I moved forward to greet the bear. She sat up on her haunches, her eyes nearly at eye level to me. I'd never given much thought to the beauty of bears, but this one was beautiful. Nothing like the bag of bones I'd carried out of the Bestiary. Her coat was deep black with reddish tips where the sun had touched her. I felt her intelligence gazing back at me.

"I see you." Her name came to me as if he'd always known it. "Kiyayo. First Bear. I see you, Nekeyah. Nagual priestess of the First Bear." Instantly, an image of the priestess Nekeyah came into my mind. She was a tall woman with strong, bronzed limbs, and silver streaks in her waist-length, dark brown hair. Her name suited her. Nekeyah. Her name had a feel as well as a sound. She was a healer, I could tell.

I see you, Xenotchi. I see you too, MikeBane. I thank you for releasing me from the bad place. I knew you would come.

I looked at Nixese. "Are you here to help us?"

He shifted uncomfortably. "She convinced me to bring her. We cannot cross the wards while the Mage lives. But Kiyayo-Nekeyah is not bound by the terms of the treaty. She can cross the wards as freely as you do. Will you accept her help?"

I grinned. "We'll take all the help we can get. Does that mean we can count on you and the rest of the Fae once the wards are down?"

"There are some who disagree with the actions of the elders. The Earth Mage, Gordon, was an elder of the tribunal before he was foresworn. We will come."

"He betrayed his own people?"

Nixese nodded, his eyes sad. "Humans are not alone in their passions."

I eyed the bow and quiver slung across his back. "Tell me you've got more in your arsenal than bows and arrows."

He bared his teeth. "There is no weapon better suited for hunting vampires than arrows, cousin." He cocked an eyebrow at the pack gathered around me. "Ours are silver-tipped, so they work against wolves as well."

Kiyayo grunted, as if to express her agreement.

"Bring down the wards and free my kin. We will come."

THE MAGE

THE GROWLING ESCALATED immediately. The wolves didn't care much for the bear, and she was uncomfortable around the pack. I sent out soothing pheromones and gradually the wolves calmed.

"She's a shifter, like me," I told them. She's here to help us." I kept the bear close and explained that she was one of the other Fae prisoners from the bestiary. I went on to explain about the blood wards and how Gordon could feel us whenever we crossed them.

"There's been a change of plans. We'll have to take down the wards first. We'll need a couple of wolves to draw off the patrol while Kiyayo and I go in there and take out the Mage. Once the wards are down, we should be able to get Sarah and the rest of the Fae out of there before vamprise."

I sent Dave and Chaney to keep an eye out for the patrol, and keep them off us. Trick and Rizzo would cover the house, and Tom and Wynn would position themselves just outside the park near the Odditorium. Silas and I would meet up at the front gate as soon as the wards came down. While Silas and I confronted Vince, Tom and Wynn would search for Sarah and the others.

I gave Dave and Chaney a few minutes head start, then set off with Kiyayo. But in spite of our precautions, two wolves caught us by surprise as we approached the vineyards at the outskirts of the estate. This time, the odds were better, and the wolves were no match for us. I unfurled the cat.

The jaguar snagged the lead wolf by the cheek, dragged him into bite range, and crushed his skull. The second wolf ripped into the bear's shoulder. Kiyayo slapped him away, and the cat slipped between them. Xenotchi hunkered low as the wolf circled, darting in to bite at anything it could; missing each time as the cat flinched away. Distracted by the jaguar, the wolf didn't see Kiyayo's attack until too late.

The bear grabbed the wolf by the rear leg, and I heard the bones snap. The wolf screamed and wheeled away, then took off running back to the estate on three legs. We had to let him go; even on three legs, he was faster than we were. The wolf would be back with reinforcements. Getting onto the estate was going to be more difficult than I'd planned, but failure wasn't an option. If we couldn't go in like I'd planned, we'd go the other way.

I rolled up the cat and we turned west, crossing back onto the Tor until we reached the creek where we'd rested after escaping from the bestiary. We followed the game trail up to the rocky outcrop and though the shallow cave into tunnel leading down into the putrid blackness of the bestiary. The bear whined unhappily at the warded portal, but there was no turning back. Too late, I realized that I hadn't brought a flashlight, but there was only one direction to go.

I was betting that Gordon would feel us cross the ward and come and see who the intruder was before calling security, but we would need to move quickly. We slipped through the warded portal and moved silently between the row of silent, empty stalls. The only sound was the clicking of our claws on the stone floors.

When we reached the workroom, I found the light switch and in the dim glare of the bare bulbs, we could see the place had been cleaned out. Every shred of equipment, including the gear and weapons the mercenaries had brought with them had been removed. *Crap.*

The door to the clinic was locked. With my new strength, I managed to lift the door completely off the track. Unlike the Bestiary, the clinic had been left undisturbed. I tore drawers and cabinets open, looking for something to use as a weapon. I found a box containing a dart pistol and a hypodermic needle with six darts, and several boxes of ketamine. Not what I'd had in mind, but maybe they'd come in handy. I put everything into a big black garbage bag and took them with us.

At the top of the stairs, I eased open the door to the distillery, listening for sounds that would indicate someone was inside. The lights were on, but the hum of the refrigerators masked any other noises. Motioning to the bear to wait, I crept into the room. Gordon's computer was sitting on his workbench, next to a still-warm cup of coffee. *Bingo.* The Mage wasn't far.

I made a cursory search of the barn, and satisfied myself that he must have gone down into the cellar. I motioned to Kiyayo to follow, and we moved to the portal warding the cellar entrance. With my improved vision, the wards did seem rather obvious now. I tapped the ward on the floor with my foot.

We surprised Gordon as he was coming up the stairs. He froze, and I threw myself at him. We tumbled down the staircase, my claws extended and groping for his neck with every ounce of fury I had in me. I felt the Mage drawing on some kind of energy, but before it could build into anything, the she-bear was all over him. She batted me aside like an irritating fly, and tore at him with her teeth and three-inch-long claws.

Gordon screamed. He cried. He begged me to stop her. I wasn't certain that the wards would drop if he was dead, and to be honest, death was too good for him. I grabbed her from behind and pushed my will into her. She stilled; her jaws at Gordon's bloody neck. She wasn't big, but she was heavy enough to hold him down just by sitting on him. Blood flowed freely from deep gashes she'd inflicted all over his neck and chest and shoulders. His upper torso looked like so much Swiss steak.

Cold fury coursed though me. "Lower the wards, Gordon."

He sobbed hysterically, but I wasn't fooled. I could feel the power continuing to well up within him. I stepped back and the Nagual bear bounced on his chest, making it difficult for him to draw a breath.

"Last chance, Mage. You've made enemies of two shamans and the entire clan of the High Tor Fae. I daresay that Kiyayo here would love to spend some real quality time with you. You remember Kiyayo, don't you?"

Kiyayo gave a resounding growl.

"No, it's not my fault."

"Dissolve the wards."

He shook his head. "The Fae lied to me. They double-crossed me," he gasped. Tears of frustration rolled down his face. "I'm trapped here. You don't understand. I can't leave. That was never part of the agreement," he hissed. "I'm the prisoner here."

I backhanded him. "I don't care. Lower the wards."

"They tricked me. Nobody told me not to use blood. If I take them down I'll die."

"I don't give a shit about you, asshole, you're going to die anyway. You are at the root of everything rotten that's going on here. Drop the wards or I swear I'll tear you apart myself." I unsheathed my claws.

He was crying now; blubbering, pathetic sobs. "Okay, okay. Give me a minute. Um. I need to concentrate." Gordon wiped the blood off his face and closed his eyes. He took a deep breath.

I tensed, not trusting that he wouldn't try something. I felt the power build within him as he strained with the effort. Then suddenly, it was gone.

His face paled and sagged. "I'm sorry, I can't do it."

With a roar, the bear lunged for him, shoving me aside like I was nothing. I tried to pull her off him, but she turned on me in a fury and I backed off. I stood back and steeled myself as Kiyayo took her retribution. Gordon never stood a chance; he barely lifted a hand against her. It was an ugly death. Kiyayo clawed furiously at his body, but when she was done he was nothing but a limp and bloody corpse. She looked at me as if to ask where he'd gone.

"You did it, girl. He's gone, but we're not done yet. Come on."

She moaned as she shifted; a long low sound. I watched in amazement as she transformed from the bulky bear into the beautiful, panting, and very naked Nekeyah. Above her high, sculpted cheek bones, fire still burned in her dark eyes. The word magnificent didn't do her justice.

I tried to keep my eyes on her face.

She tossed her head like the wild, magnificent creature she was. "The Fae of the High Tor will never thank you for this, but I will." She panted with the effort. "I owe you my life. Today I destroyed the man who betrayed me and many of my clansmen. Name your reward and if it is within my power I will grant it."

My hopes soared as my thoughts went to Farley. Would she be able to lift his glamour after all these years? It was almost too much to think about. It would have to wait; now was not the time. I jerked my head in the direction of the stairs. "I appreciate the offer, priestess, but let's get through this first, okay? We've still got to meet Silas and get Sarah and the others out. Let's go."

"As you say." She smiled, and a moment later, the bear was back.

THE BATTLE FOR ALPHA

WHEN WE STEPPED out of the distillery, the world was not the same.

Without the wards, the silver-grey pallor of the weathered distillery stood in plain view amidst the forest of sunflowers. The main residence too, was sorely in need of paint, shingles, and fretwork. The lawns were brown from lack of water; the rosebushes drooped in the summer sun. The twelve-foot-tall thorny hedges, seen without the glamour of the wards revealed a line of scruffy, dying shrubs ringing the edge of the park. There were gaps in the perimeter fencing wide enough to walk through.

Silas was waiting for us at the edge of the field. We approached the front gates together, using the scanty hedges surrounding the park as cover. The bear, Kiyayo, shambled well behind us. We spotted armed sentries with walkie-talkies on the roof of the concert hall and on top of the theatre at the other end of the park. We ducked behind the thickest shrubbery.

"Looks like they're expecting us," Silas observed.

As I armed the tranquilizer darts with ketamine, I kept my voice low. "Good. Let's hope we can keep their attention long enough for the rest of the pack to move into position. Now that the wards are gone, the Fae should be here soon."

In the central plaza, Vince leaned against the fountain where Tehuantl had killed the vampire bounty hunter. To his left stood the big mercenary Hale, his new Beta. Both men were shirtless, and Hale held a katana sword at his side. A half-dozen mercenaries in camo-gear came out of the security building and formed themselves into a half circle, along with a dozen or so blood stewards. They couldn't see us, but they knew we were there.

They were waiting for us.

I handed the dart pistol to Silas. "Follow my lead. I need to give Tom and Wynn time to locate Sarah. The ketamine won't stop them right away, but it might make them think twice about rushing us."

"Got it."

We stepped out of our hiding place and came to a halt just inside the park entrance; Silas at my left shoulder.

Vince did a double take. "Is that you, Bane?" The mercs all snapped their heads up, and the blood stewards pulled closer together. Their hands went to their sidearms.

"It's over, Vince," I said. "This stops now."

"This is private property." Vince's pheromones rolled out over the group, but there was a fragile, skittery feel to them. He was uncertain, and I could tell that none of the mercs were bonded to him. He wouldn't be able to depend on them and he knew it. "You've got two seconds to bare your throat to me, Bane, before I rip it out. Same goes for you, Silas."

I rolled out a few pheromones of my own, noting the momentary confusion in the faces of the lycans. "You've got balls, Vince, I'll give you that. But you're not my Alpha. Not any more. You always knew what Ozzie was doing. You let us rot in that hell hole. I'm calling you out Vince. You've had your run, but I'm shutting you down."

"I don't know what the hell happened to you, Bane, but you're no wolf. Take my advice and get out now, while you're still standing."

The air around me thickened with Vince's shift pheromones. In my head, I could feel Dave and Chaney off to my left; and Trick and Rizzo to my right, near the house. Behind the crowd, Tom and Wynn were moving in. Surrounded by my brother wolves, I felt invincible. We were as solid as Fort Knox. This was what Sarah had tried to explain in scientific terms. But she was wrong. It felt like a part of my brain had been awakened for the first time, and discovered a dimension that was only accessible through the sworn oaths of brotherhood. This feeling of shared strength and power went far beyond anything that could be explained by science. This was pack magic.

The jagged shreds of Vince's pheromones told me beyond a doubt that his pack was in shambles. I could sense erosion in the bonds of the few remaining Mythica members and his Beta, Hale, but the rest of the mercs were not bonded to anyone. They were all hired guns. As lone wolves, Vince had no access to their power base.

"You're right, Vince, I'm no wolf, but it doesn't matter. I'm the Alpha of the High Tor pack. We've come for Ozzie and the prisoners. No bullshit, Vince. We're taking over. Yield or die."

The mercs stiffened, and pressed closer, but Vince motioned them back. "You have no authority here," he sneered. "You're out classed and outmanned. I will not give you my son."

Phelan unholstered a stun gun in an overt threat. Phelan was the lowest ranking member of what remained of the Mythica pack. His usual job was selling corn dogs. Vince must have given him a promotion.

With an economical flick of his weapon, Silas nailed Phelan with a ketamine dart right in the neck. The Omega screamed like a girl and dropped like a rock.

I grinned. "Helluva shot."

"There's more, if anybody wants it," Silas said.

"Ozzie's sick, Vince. For years you've protected him while your own people suffered at his hands. You're no better than he is. It ends now." I pointed at Hale. "What did Vince tell you when you asked about all the wolves locked up in the bestiary? And Sarah. What did he tell you about the naked, bloody, woman?"

"Shut up," Vince roared. Pheromones rolled off him like hot lava. "Just shut the fuck up, Bane. You've got no room to talk. Your father gave up everything for you. This is no different. Any father would do the same." His voice cracked. "Any father who loves his son."

"Who the hell is this guy?" Hale demanded.

My face flamed. "We're the ones you planned to seal up in that dungeon. "Payback's a bitch, asshole." I raised my voice so that even the guys on the roof could hear. "We were starved, beaten, violated and abused by Vince's stepson, Ozzie. Those who didn't survive were left to rot or used for animal feed. You knew it, Vince, and you did nothing to stop it."

Vince stiffened, but didn't deny it. I needed to keep the crowd's attention. I needed to give Tom and Wynn time to find Sarah.

"You must have been proud when he did well at vet school. Of course, you'd mention it to Ambrose." The crowd was silent, listening. "Ambrose always chooses his blood stewards for their skills, and you practically served him Ozzie on a dinner plate."

Vince clenched his fists. "I never imagined that son of a bitch would decide to *take my son*." He spat the last words out, the color in his face high. He was losing control of his beast.

"I'll bet your wife couldn't stand the thought of Ozzie as a blood meal for a vampire. Her perverted, sociopathic son. Ozzie turned his back on you and your family, and you just couldn't let him go. You knew all about blood dementia, and when you saw the symptoms in Ozzie, you knew what Ambrose would do to him."

A rumbled murmur stalked the crowd.

Vince motioned for silence. "Knock it off. Look folks, the truth is that Mike here has gotten himself hooked on that Glamour hooch that Gordon brews. You know what I'm talking about." He looked around at the crowd and smiled broadly. "I caught him drinking on duty a few weeks ago and fired him."

"Gordon's dead."

Vince waved at the crowd. "Don't believe a word he says. Come here, Mike; let me smell your breath."

"I challenge you, Vince. Alpha to Alpha. Here and now. This is a legitimate beef."

Vince's face reddened. His back bowed. "You're not pack, Bane. You never really were. I've got a new Beta now. You'll have to go through him first."

"Coward."

Dark rage mottled Vince's face as he tore his pants off and leapt, changing into beast in midair. He scored a deep gash across my right shoulder before Xenotchi unfurled and slapped him back, raking deep grooves across the wolf's face. One of his ears dangled by a shred of tissue, and blood dripped into his eyes, but he'd done plenty of damage to Xenotchi's shoulder. The cat was on three legs.

Unchecked fury glowed in his yellow eyes, but it paled to the heat of my rage. Vince came in low and fast as he feinted for the jaguar's other front leg.

The jaguar scrambled back and landed a blow that sent the Alpha sprawling. He landed ungracefully and fought for his footing. Caution crept into his eyes. He began to circle, hackles raised, head held low, favoring his left side.

I noted with satisfaction that he was nursing at least a broken rib or two.

The blood stewards moved back, but the air was growing thick with change pheromones; other weres were beginning to shift. Silas was already half-way there. I heard one of the mercs say that Tanner hadn't lasted a minute, and one of the near-weres started taking bets.

Xenotchi faced the wolf as he circled, letting him do all the work. The shoulder wound would not allow us to any weight on the paw yet, but it was healing fast and I shared the cat's fierce confidence. The jaguar knew we were playing for keeps this time. This would be a fight to the death. An injured front leg meant there would be no killing blow, but Xenotchi's hind legs were equally deadly. Exposing the cat's belly was dangerous, but would draw Vince in. The First Jaguar was a master of patience. We would wait for him to come to us.

We didn't have long to wait. The Alpha wolf feinted at the good leg again, and the cat crouched to protect it, offering his rear to Vince's swift attack. I felt the crunch of cartilage and screamed in shared pain as Vince's wolf shook and worried the cat's flesh. Xenotchi withdrew, and rolled himself up, but I was ready. I grabbed the huge wolf by the scruff of the neck and hurled him into the fountain with all my strength. The force of the wolf's impact cracked the stone basin. Water poured onto the plaza.

Vince lay half in, half out of the water, stunned by the force of the impact. I leapt directly onto the wolf's injured ribs using my weight to force his head below the surface of the water. The wolf struggled mightily to raise his head out of the water, but I wasn't about to let him drown. The smell of his blood awoke my own craving. I shoved my hand beneath his ribcage and clawed my way through his torso while he screamed and twisted in agony. Vince thrashed and gave a final roar as I dug my claws into his frantically beating heart and ripped it from his body.

I tore bite after bite from the bloody pulp until there was nothing left, then staggered away from the body. I collapsed into a bloody heap, repulsed by what I'd done; hissing and panting as the flesh in my torn shoulder and leg mended itself.

I'd killed a man with my bare hands. This wasn't Tehuantl's doing, it was mine alone. Every eye in the plaza was watching me. I grunted as I lumbered to my feet. The words I spoke weren't mine; they came from someplace deep inside.

"By rite of battle, I stake my claim as the sole and legitimate

Alpha of the Mythica Pack," I panted. I held my bloody fist to my chest and willed my dominance out over the crowd. "Any who dare to oppose me and mine will feel my teeth at your throat. I swear I will eat the heart of anyone who refuses to recognize my rightful place as sovereign leader of this pack."

I stalked stiff-legged across the plaza. "Those who surrender peacefully and lay down their weapons will receive safe passage off the grounds. Those who resist will feel my wrath."

A surge of alpha pheromones roiled out from my skin and rippled over the crowd. Half the mercs took off running, the others glanced around uncertainly, and handed their weapons to Silas without complaint. When I took the katana sword from Hale, the near-weres fell to their knees. I could feel the spirits of Wyatt, the near-weres, and one of the mercs connect with the collective pack in my head. The others, I could tell, weren't having any of it.

Tom, Striper Dave, Wynn, and Chaney all came racing up.

"Where's Sarah," I demanded. The blood thirst was still on me, but I refused to give into it again.

The look on their faces said it all. "The Odditorium and Theatre are locked." Chaney answered.

"Is it true," Steve-o asked Dave. "Did Vince really know?"

"I wouldn't be here with Mike if it wasn't," he answered. "Vince had the wool pulled over our eyes for a long time."

"They've got Sarah and Yolanda down in the vault," Wyatt said. "You'll never get in there without the access codes. Vince was the only one who knew them."

"What about the others?"

"Kevin and the twins are locked inside the Odditorium," Hale volunteered. "I've got the keys and the code to the vault. Let me go, and I'll give them to you."

I took a quick head count. Nixese and his warriors hadn't shown up yet, but I knew they would as soon as I released the Fae. I'd take

Tom, Silas, Wynn, Chaney, and Dave with me into the tombs.

"Make it quick. We're running out of daylight."

We locked the mercs and near-weres inside walk-in refrigerator at the Bloody Fang for temporary safe-keeping. I sent Rizzo and Trick to round up any stray blood stewards and keep them confined inside the house until we finished up in the vault. That left Wyatt and Steve-O in charge of the park, and keeping anyone from coming down behind us. The rest of us followed Hale to the Odditorium.

Sure enough, we found Kevin and the brothers chained together in silver handcuffs on the floor of the Piasa bird's glass enclosure, covered with guano. After using Hale's keys to release them, I instructed Dave to prop open the front doors of the Odditorium and we released the last of the Fae hostages. The eagle scrambled and half-hopped toward the late afternoon light streaming through the entrance. It paused in the doorway for a few moments, before launching itself skyward. The Blood Doves caromed off the glass-fronted exhibits as they frantically fluttered toward freedom; the young Attocroppes half-slithered, half-ran right behind them.

No sooner had last of the Fae disappeared into the sunlight, than a barrage of gunfire broke the silence of the afternoon.

"That's got to be the Fae," Tom said. "They're here."

"No way." I raced for the front door. "The Fae don't use guns." A bullet whizzed by my left temple and struck the open doorway. "Where's the vault?"

"You want to go into the crypt this time of day?" Kevin rubbed his wrists where the silver handcuffs had eaten into the skin. "Are you mad?"

"Sarah and Yolanda are down there, and we don't have a lot of time. Nobody here is going to stop you from leaving, but we could use your help." I turned to Hale. "Get us into the vault and you're free to make you own way out of here. If you decide to stay, I'll do everything I can to keep you safe."

"I'm out of here," Kevin said. "I do not want one of those vampires coming after me."

Tom grabbed Kevin by the front of his shirt. "How can you say that? Sarah told me you two were close."

"I'm not going down there for nobody."

Tom shoved Kevin toward the open entrance. "Shut up and get out then. We don't want you." With a howl of rage, began to shift.

Kevin wiped his bloody nose on his shirt, and made his way toward the front, where the twins were already waiting. As the hail of bullets paused, the three of them ran outside.

"What about me," Hale asked.

"How many mercs are still running around out there?" I said.

"Hard to tell. I had six armed lycans stationed on the roofs; another four patrolling the perimeter. From the sound of gunfire, I'd say maybe two or three are left."

"We took two of them out when we came in," Chaney said.

Silas paused to listen. "Those shots sound like they're coming from the house and the roof of the operations building."

I wondered what was taking the Fae so long. We were losing more men than we could afford, but I wasn't going to force Hale into the vaults.

"Get us into the Tombs and you're on your own."

INTO THE TOMBS

WITH THE WARDS gone, finding the entrance to the tombs was easy. A door from the conference room in the Odditorium led down three flights of stairs to a tunnel, which led to what the Hale called the Warming Room. The stone-walled room was decorated in modern chrome and leather with a couple of sofas, recliners, and a big screen television mounted on one wall, over a built-in media storage console. A jigsaw puzzle was set up on a table in the corner. Downright cozy. Everything a civilized vampire needed to spend a quiet evening at home.

Tom's wolf nosed his way through a swinging door and we followed him into a small kitchen. Beside a bank of stainless steel refrigerators and a utility area, lay the unconscious and bruised body of Yolanda. I kneeled beside her and checked her throat to make sure she was still alive. Like the others, she had been handcuffed in silver to prevent her from shifting into wolf form. Tom's wolf licked her face while I unlocked her, using Hale's keys.

I glared at the big merc. "What the hell is wrong with you??"

The merc reddened, his mouth an angry line. "That one's nothing but trouble." He rubbed his jaw. "Vince had me put her down here for safe keeping until she cooled off a little. She'll be okay."

I didn't have time to argue. We'd take her with us on our way out.

As much as I hated to admit it, Hale was right, and we were running out of time. "Alright asshole, get us into the Tombs."

Hale crossed the room to a metal door next to the sink and jabbed several numbers onto a recessed keypad. The door slid to one side on a silent track. "This is it. This is the coffin room," he said.

The smell of dry earth greeted us from the chilly cavern. Unlike the smooth concrete floors inside the Bestiary, the floors here were roughly chiseled from bedrock. The stone crypts were an eclectic mix of traditional and old-world gothic coffers, crammed together in tight quarters. Oddly enough, the vault had the same surreal, quirky quality as the amusement park topside. Pink and orange neon lights pin-wheeled across the ceiling; the walls were plastered with posters of old monster movies: *Vegas Vampires*, *The Thing*, and a really hot *Resident Evil*, to name a few. Rafe's idea, I'm sure.

I shoved Hale up against the wall. "Where the hell is Sarah?"

He shook his head. "She's got to be here. I saw Vince and Ozzie bring her down." His eyes swept the room. "Maybe they made her a blood steward."

I wanted to punch him, just for saying it. The thought of Sarah becoming a blood steward chilled me. Rationally, I knew it hadn't been the end of the world for Taffy, but the thought of Sarah-- it was too much. And there was the other, darker thought right behind it that was too awful to consider. What if they'd made her one of them?

I opened my senses to Xenotchi. Her scent was everywhere, but so intermingled with the blood smells of the stewards, I couldn't trace it to a source. It obliterated the much fainter scent of vampire.

"See if you can find her," I told Tom's wolf.

Oh god, I hoped we weren't too late.

Half the crypts were wrapped in chains, but there was no way to identify which vampire was in which stone coffin.

I slapped the top of the nearest crypt. "We know she's here. She's got to be in one of these. Help me get the lid off."

"You've got to be kidding." Hale's face had lost it's color.

"She could be in any one of these," Silas said.

"I don't care. We've got to find her. Give me a hand." It took four of us to slide the heavy stone top off the stone casket. Willem was inside, along with one of his blood stewards, a petite blonde. I swallowed my disappointment. It wasn't Sarah. We all recognized her as Willem's partner from the high wire act. Silas swore, and even the other pack members appeared shocked.

"What's wrong?" I asked.

"That's Francine. Willem has turned her," Wynn said. "They're enlarging the nest."

I didn't want to believe it. "No, it can't be. I don't think she's dead." I checked her for a pulse. "She's not cold. Feel."

Silas felt for a pulse and shook his head. "Wynn's right. This is a new vampire. When the sun sets, either today or tomorrow, she'll rise as a new vamp. Very thirsty, very powerful, and very determined to feed."

"But she's still warm. How can you be sure?"

Hale slapped her face. "If she was human, she'd be awake by now. She's newly dead. Or close to it."

"Use the sword," Hale nodded to the blade Dave was holding. "Kill them both."

Dave hefted the sword, uncertainly.

The idea of killing Willem and the new vamp in cold blood didn't sit well. The rest of the pack looked uncomfortable, too. Willem was well-liked, and he and Francine were very much a couple. The idea of decapitating them seemed like cold-blooded murder.

"Or stake 'em," Hale said. "If you stake Cobb, Willem and the woman both die. Or better yet, stake Ambrose."

An unhappy look crossed Chaney's face. "Yeah, and most of the nest. Looks like Cobb chained half the vampires in the nest. My guess is he's eliminating his competition. That would mean Ambrose, Gawl, Roosa, and Orcas for sure. They didn't ask for any of this."

I counted seven chained crypts. If every stone coffin held two vamps, we wouldn't have a chance. We were badly outnumbered, but no one but Hale had an appetite for murder.

"All we need to do is find Cobb and chain him," I said. "He's the one we want. This is a rescue mission, not an execution."

"You willing to bet your lives on that? I'd be looking for something to use as stakes, just in case." Hale shuddered. "Look, I got you in here, my job is done."

"Coward," Silas muttered, as Hale took off.

"It's not a bad idea." I sent Striper Dave to find something we could use for stakes and pointed to a pile of chains lying next to a box of padlocks on the floor in a gloomy corner of the cavern. "For now we chain them. We can sort it all out later, but we're running out of daylight. Let's get this one chained first." I pointed to the crypt where Tom's wolf was sniffing with interest. "We'll try that one next." I sent out a silent prayer that Nixese and the Fae would show up pretty soon. Hell, I'd even be happy to see Daneah.

The chains looked like those used to anchor big ships. Each required two men to lift and each of the stone coffins had been wrapped with three chains. It took us the better part of an hour to wrestle the chains around the heavy crypt. We had to tip the thing to one side to get the chains underneath it, and couldn't do that unless we all lifted together. In spite of the chill of the cavern, we were all sweating by the time we finished locking the third chain into place. There was no time to waste. At this rate, the sun would be long set before we finished chaining the vamps.

"We've only got enough chains for three coffins," Dave observed.

"Then we'll just have to unchain some of the others," I said. "Anyone but Ambrose."

"That's not a good idea," Silas answered. "Whoever wakes up is going to be very cranky. Friend or foe isn't going to matter. A desiccated vamp is going to drain everyone in the vicinity. If we uncork two of the bound vamps, they could kill us all."

I sent Chaney to check the refrigerators. He returned a short time later, carrying an armful of plastic blood bags.

"There wasn't much in there. Is this enough?"

"I hope there's more than that," Silas answered. "Whoever we unchain is going to need at least ten pints of blood."

Wynn patted one of the crypts. "One of these must be Tryffin's. He's a mechanical genius; he doesn't care who runs Mythica. He had nothing to do with Cobb's takeover. Cobb needs him to keep the park rides operational. Why not leave his crypt unchained? He'll listen to reason and won't need more than a pint or two of blood when he wakes up."

"Good thinking," I answered. It was the only gamble that made sense. Between what's left in the blood bank and the blood stewards upstairs. I hoped we'd have enough. We couldn't risk the lives of the humans outside the park to a bunch of starving, desiccated vampires.

"That works for me," Wynn said.

We opened the crypt that Tom had been scratching at. The good news was that the coffin we opened belonged to Tryffin. The bad news was that he wasn't alone. Next to him lay another new vampire. New vampires required more blood than the old ones. They had to be chained. There was no other option.

"The Fae should have been here by now." I grunted as we lifted the stone box for Wynn and Silas to slip the chains underneath it. This time, we knew what we were doing, but we were conscious of the time slipping by with every minute. "We need more manpower. And where the hell is Dave with those damn stakes?" Every moment that passed made me more frantic to find Sarah.

The plan was falling apart. We needed to find Rafe's coffin. The weight of the stone lids on each crypt effectively sealed the inhabitants' scent inside, making it difficult to determine who was where. I took a closer look at the chained crypts. There was only one that was carved to resemble a familiar-looking building.

"It's this one."

"How do you know?" asked Silas.

I ran my hand across the replica of the historic monument. "It's Graceland."

We cut the chains and shoved the lid aside just far enough to slip a dozen plastic bags of blood inside. My blood thirst rose as I punctured one of the blood bags and dripped a bit of blood onto Rafe's lips before laying it along with the rest of the bags atop Rafe's chest. I resisted the temptation to drain the blood bag myself. As much as I craved it, my own will was stronger. I was no vampire.

Time was running out, and we still hadn't found Sarah. Maybe she wasn't down here after all. The next coffin we opened belonged to the Fae-vamp, Lyrissa, and she wasn't alone, either. Three coffins left, and Cobb was in one of them. We'd just finished putting the first chain around Lyrissa's coffin when Striper Dave finally returned with a hammer and the box of wood blanks he used for custom fishing pole grips.

"I couldn't find much in the way of wooden stakes lying around, but these should work."

"What the hell are you talking about? There's enough trees around the clubhouse to build a stinking fort," complained Wynn.

"For your information, willow isn't strong enough to pierce the sternum or rib cage of a vamp." He picked up the katana sword and with a few whacks, fashioned a crude but effective point on one end of the two-by-two.

He held it up to admire his handiwork. "Curly maple." He grinned fiercely, and tossed the stake at Wynn. He began to sharpen another stake.

"Trick and Rizzo have the blood stewards trapped inside the house. They can't get out, but they're using silver ammo, and firing from the windows. Rizzo took a bad hit. Trick says they've got enough to hold them for a while longer, but no promises. There's gunfire coming from the roof of operations building. Steve-o and Wyatt have the mercs locked out up there, but they're armed, and shooting at everything that moves. It isn't easy getting around out there. Steve-o told me the phones are out. Sun's going down in about fifteen minutes. Vamprise won't be long after."

"We've got no time." Wynn looked like he was ready to bolt.

I couldn't ask anyone to stay, but I couldn't leave. Not now. "Whoever needs to go, go now. But I'm not leaving without Sarah."

"Mike, it's too late. They've all been turned. We haven't found a single blood steward. There's not enough time to chain the rest of these coffins. If Sarah's in there, she's one of them. We can come back tomorrow."

I shook my head. "I don't believe that. She joined our pack the day she was dragged down into that hell hole with the rest of us," I said. "We don't have time to quibble about this. We'll stake whoever we have to until we find Sarah. Now shut up and help me open this."

It took three of us to shove the heavy lid aside. We heard Sarah's panicked shouting before we even got it open. She lay tightly wrapped in the dead, stiff arms of the newly-created vampire, Ozzie.

"I'm here, I'm here! Help me!" Sarah sobbed hysterically. When we pulled her out, she was wearing only a bloody Mythica tee-shirt. She was pale, filthy and covered with bites and dried blood.

She took one look at me and screamed. Her eyes rolled back in her head and she collapsed.

"It's okay, Sarah," Chaney patted her cheek to revive her, as Tom and the rest of us crowded in. Her eyes fluttered and she shook her head, moaning. A moment later, the sound of stone scraping against stone caught our attention.

The lids of the other coffins began to slide open. Ozzie opened his eyes.

RAISING THE DEAD

"GET HER OUT of here," I shouted. Cobb was already taking aim with a pistol. I leapt for him and he fired at me from less than two feet away. The bullet slammed into my shoulder and I grunted with the impact. I crashed into him and the gun went flying across the cavern.

I caught a glimpse of Tom's wolf and the Nagual bear attacking Ozzie as Cobb seized me by the neck. Tryffin was rising too, but I had my hands full.

Cobb pulled me toward him, his fangs fully descended. His strength was unbelievable. Cobb wasn't alone, either. A brand-new vampire was also rising right beside him. It was Cobb's number one blood steward, Jared. I got a glimpse of Jared's fangs as Dave attacked him with the katana sword in one hand, and a crudely sharpened stake in the other. I hauled the Cobb away from the coffin, each of us straining for advantage in the tight space.

I wrapped my taloned hands around Cobb's neck. I struggled to snap it, but he bore down on me with a relentless force, his fangs fully extended, aiming for my throat. I smashed him in the nose with my forehead and felt the satisfying crunch of bone. He cursed and threw me across the cavern with enough force to knock the air out of me.

I crouched on my hands and knees, struggling for air. Silas and

Chaney were busy with Tryffin. Rafe looked like an animated skeleton, as he drained the blood bags as fast as he could swallow.

Cobb came at me faster than I could have imagined possible. He tore at my wounded shoulder, tearing at me with his teeth, again going for my throat. I tried to hold him off, but he was relentless. I scored his abdomen with my clawed feet, shredding his burgundy velvet shirt but doing little damage. The sonofabitch was wearing chain mail underneath his shirt.

I rolled to the side, using one hand to keep him off me, the other to get under his protective armor, but he jerked away and delivered an uppercut to my jaw that had me fighting not to lose consciousness.

He bit deep into my neck and held on. I heard the unmistakable sound of the single chain around Lyrissa's coffin breaking and realized that two more angry vampires were about to join the party. We were all going to die.

A feeling of lassitude washed over me as Cobb's jaws worked, sucking my life's blood out of me. His skin grew warmer, and I felt the heartbeat at his temple throb against my cheek. The smell of blood came to me, bringing with it Tehuantl's tremendous craving for blood. I pulled Cobb closer, and he relaxed.

As his thirst lessened, my own grew until it became unbearable. I reached out to the earth beneath me, and used Tehuantl's magic to feed my resistance. Instinctively, I knew that feeding off a vampire was not a good idea, but the smell of blood and my own need overwhelmed me. I waited until Cobb had descended into his own thrall of feeding, then rolled into him, using the weight of my body to force him to loosen his grip.

Cobb screamed and bucked as my own fangs bit down into his exposed neck. I reveled in the taste and sensation of his blood pulsing against my tongue. I'd nicked an artery, and the blood poured into me as he tore at my mangled shoulder. With his throat locked between my canines, I slipped my hand under his mail shirt. I forced my hand beneath his ribcage and clawed my way toward the throbbing shrunken muscle that animated his corpse.

Cobb panicked. He twisted violently, trying to wrench me off him, but I held on, my lower incisors hooked around his collarbone. With agonizing slowness, my hand inched upward through his chest cavity until I felt the throbbing of his gristly heart muscle. He grabbed at my arm, but it was too late. I had him. With a wrenching twist, I tore his heart from his body. Cobb collapsed, and the flesh of his inanimate corpse began to tighten and dry.

An instant later, Lyrissa and another vampire hit me from behind. Lyrissa bit deeply into my upper back, while the other vamp sprawled across my lower body, her teeth embedded in my hip. It hurt like hell. I couldn't get them off me. Striper Dave lay face down on the floor, with the katana sword still in his hand. I yelled at him, but he didn't respond. I fought and scrambled uselessly, trying to reach it. Lyrissa let go of me just long enough to wrap her hands around my throat.

Neither vamp was nearly as strong as Cobb. I got my knees under me and bucked, but Lyrissa clung to my back like a limpet. I managed to kick the other vamp off my hip, and lunged for the sword, but the other vamp seized it first. She screamed and raised the weapon, shrieking at Lyrissa to get out of the way.

Lyrissa released her grip on my neck, I threw myself backward, and heard a satisfying thunk as she whacked her skull against the stone floor. The other vamp tried to slash at my throat with the blade, but she didn't know what she was doing, and I wrested the blade out of her hand. I caught her on the side of the head in a furious blow, which took most of the fight out of her, along with the upper half of her skull. Lyrissa charged me from the floor, and launched herself straight at me. I dropped the weapon and grabbed her face between my hands. I gave her head a sharp twist and heard her neck snap.

I dropped her and grabbed the katana to finish decapitating the other vamp, then delivered a killing blow to Lyrissa, severing her head from her body. I stumbled and wiped their blood from my face.

I looked around, trying to make sense of the chaos. Silas and Chaney were holding Varrick up against the wall. He wasn't really fighting them, but they weren't letting him go. Rafe and Wynn held onto a convulsing Jared who had one of Dave's stakes sticking out of his chest. Tom's wolf and the bear were fighting a losing battle against Ozzie, who had the bear Kiyayo in a choke hold, and was draining her of blood.

I threw myself at Ozzie and bore the three of them to the ground. I caught a glimpse of Sarah coming at us with kitchen knife in hand, her expression a grimace of rage.

Ozzie fought like a madman, but with Cobb's death, his strength wasn't nearly as strong as his makers'. And his strength was fading; just as it had for the women. I held him down, but he wouldn't release the bear. Sarah rushed in with the knife. I yelled for someone to bring me a stake, and Ozzie released his grip on the bear. In the confusion, Kiyayo turned on Sarah.

The bear grabbed her, raking her savagely with her deadly claws. I shouted at Kiyayo to stop, but she wasn't listening. Tom's wolf attacked the bear to protect Sarah and Ozzie turned his attentions to me.

He laughed. I grabbed the katana and hacked at him, using the blade like a machete. With every blow, he laughed harder and harder. I kept going until there was nothing left of him but a bloody pulp. I couldn't stop; I kept hitting him even after he began to parch and wither beneath my blows. It was Rafe's shout that brought me back.

Kiyayo had Sarah down beneath her killing claws. Already weakened by starvation and blood loss, she was no match for the enraged bear. I didn't want to kill Kiyayo, but I couldn't let the First Bear kill Sarah, either.

I grabbed the bear by the scruff of the neck and dragged her off Sarah. She turned on me and clouted me a good one. We rolled and tore at each other until Xenotchi emerged, his fury now rivaling the bear's. Xenotchi grabbed the bear by the skull and rolled as the bear scratched and fought the increasing pressure on his thick skull. I heard shouts as we fought for our footing on top of the bloody shreds of Sarah's inert form. I felt the First Bear's skull crack beneath the jaguar's teeth and she collapsed, silent as the dead. With the last of my strength, I rolled up the jaguar.

I staggered to where Sarah's inert form lay. Dimly, I heard Rafe's voice issuing orders. Silently, I begged Tehuantl to do something. But Tehuantl wasn't there anymore. I was Tehuantl. He was part of me.

"Her pulse is thready," Silas said. "She's lost too much blood. She's not going to make it." I folded Sarah's mangled hand within my own. My tears dripped onto Sarah's bloodied, mutilated body. No. It couldn't be. This can't be happening. Something in me would not accept it. I checked Kiyayo's pulse. It was steady. The bear was unconscious, but still breathing.

Rafe tenderly wiped the blood off Sarah's face. "I could make her one of us."

My gorge rose in my throat. I felt sick. "No."

She'd saved Tom's life. She'd gotten him safely through the first onset of lycanthropy. If not for her, I would never have defeated Tehuantl. We would still be trapped inside the bestiary. She'd given everything she had to help us. And maybe countless others. She'd fought so hard to survive the horrors of this place. *How could this have all ended so badly?*

An idea came to me, and I truly didn't know if it was mine or Tehuantl's. It didn't matter. What if I could bring Sarah's spirit into Kiyayo-Nekeyah's? What if I could make her like me?

She was so badly injured; I wasn't certain it would work. But the same had been true of me when Xenotchi first attacked me. There was no reason that Sarah couldn't share Nekeyah's spirit like I had shared Tehuantl's. I had to try.

FORESWORN

THE GUNFIRE HAD stopped by the time we carried Sarah out of the Odditorium. Steve-o, Wyatt, Trick and a badly limping Rizzo were there. They told us that the resistance had disappeared when most of the blood stewards keeled over and died. Yolanda was awake, but neither she nor Rizzo wanted a veterinarian. My best friend from childhood, Dave Stripe, had died of a broken neck, but I had no time to mourn him. Not yet.

Silas and Rafe carried the unconscious bear between them as I led the way to the beer gardens behind the Bloody Fang. I needed a quiet place where I could draw power directly from the earth.

We lay Sarah on the grass next to Kiyayo. I kneeled beside them, and reached with Tehuantl's power deep below the surface of the soil, into the original lands of the Fae. The old Fae. The energy field was there, pulsing deep within the earth. I didn't need any divining rod to feel it. With one hand, I cupped my hand to the bear's semi-conscious head and called out to Nekeyah. I told her what I wanted, and asked for the favor she'd promised me. After a small hesitation, she agreed.

She took a deep breath and exhaled the essence of her life force into my mouth; I opened my pure being to her and allowed her to fill my soul with her spirit.

I lowered my teeth to Sarah's neck. She wasn't breathing. The pulse at her throat gave a beat and stopped. I bit deeply, drawing her blood into my mouth. The essence of Nekeyah surfaced hungrily and consumed the blood and spirit of Sarah Powers. For a moment, I felt some confusion and discomfort as the two women elbowed at each other within me, then their embrace as Sarah's physical form died in my arms. I waivered, wondering if Sarah would ever forgive me for this. But after all she'd been through, she had demonstrated her strength and determination to survive. Maybe this wouldn't work, but she deserved the chance. Turning back to Kiyayo-Nekeyah, I exhaled their combined essence within the breath of the First Jaguar Xenotchi back into First Black Bear. I felt their amusement as they departed, leaving behind an empty spot in my psyche.

It was done.

The bear Kiyayo took a deep shuddered breath and faded away, leaving behind a dark-haired, sleeping woman.

"Did it work," Tom asked, as he covered her with a blanket.

I couldn't answer. I had no clue.

"We've got company," Rafe murmured.

Nixese and Dineah approached, with a dozen Fae warriors spread out behind them. Unlike the color-shifting leathers they'd worn inside the Tor, they were all dressed in regular military-style camouflage, complete with heavy boots and plenty of good 'ol American firepower to supplement their bows and quivers full of arrows.

I stood to greet them.

"Now they show," Wynn muttered. "It's about time."

To my surprise, Nix and his people were rigid with barely suppressed anger. The realization hit me then. I understood why they hadn't arrived sooner. Bitter acid burned the back of my throat.

"Let me handle this," I said. If I didn't make this right, we'd have another war on our hands.

I met Nix's accusing glare without blinking. "I understand your grief, Cousin, but you must accept that Lyra died a long time ago."

"She was my wife," Nix choked.

"No. She was the vampire Lyrissa. She hadn't been your wife, or even Fae for a very long time."

"Time has no meaning for immortals." His voice cracked as his emotions betrayed him. "You swore to release all the hostages. I convinced the elders that you would honor your oath. Instead, you destroyed her."

I had nothing to offer him. At that moment, I could not conjure up the slightest bit of remorse for killing Lyrissa, or Cobb or Ozzie or any of them. I was sick of death. "We destroyed her maker. She was already dying."

"You don't know that."

"She attacked us and we fought for our lives. She killed Dave, and she would have killed me. I derived no satisfaction from her death."

"You lie," Dineah hissed. "You stink with the blood of your victims, Bane. You are one of them now." With a swift motion, she drew an arrow and knocked it against her bow.

"I loved her, and you took her from me," Nix said.

The simple statement tore at me. "I do understand your grief. After all, you took my father from me."

Nix nodded, grimly, his face set. "So be it, blood drinker. The wards are destroyed, but the treaty between the Fae and the Blood Drinkers will not be broken by me this night. But hear me, oath breaker; as of this moment, you are foresworn of the Fae, Mike Bane. You are no longer cousin to me or my clan."

"I never really was," I answered.

Silas stepped beside me and a wave of aggression grew around us, each wolf in turn adding their pheromones of solidarity until I felt surrounded by a wall of will, as strong as any Fae glamour. "Bane is our Alpha. When you threaten him, you threaten all of us."

Out of the corner of my eye, I saw Chaney heft the katana in his hand. This could all go to pieces in a hurry.

"Easy, brother." Tiredly, I put my hand on Silas' shoulder and rolled my power out over the pack. The tension backed down a notch, but all it would take was a spark to set it off.

"By your own words, you have sworn to abide by the treaty," I said. "There has been too much bloodshed here today already. Go home, Nix. Accept that Lyra is well and truly gone, and mourn her properly. I sympathize with your loss, but I will not apologize. Now go in peace."

"On the life you owe me, Bane, I will not hold my fire when next we meet."

"Nor will any of us, blood drinker," added Dineah.

"So be it." I nodded and the pack surged forward. The Fae edged their way back through a gaping hole in the park fence near the Odditorium. I watched as they trotted out onto the Tor and disappeared into the tree line. Farley nosed my hand, as if to reassure me.

I patted his head with as much comfort as I could offer. Not much chance of getting the Fae to lift his punishment any time soon. I rubbed his ear. "Sorry boy," I whispered.

I straightened and turned to address the pack. "Come on, guys. Let's get this place cleaned up. I want everyone who wants to leave out of here by morning."

DIGGING IN

A WEEK LATER, Rafe and I stood in the main plaza, watching the fireworks and a surge of happy visitors as they swarmed through the front gates. This was the first time the park had been open to visitors in weeks, and based on the number of reservations, we were expecting the park to be packed to the gills tonight.

"Don't worry," I told him. "So what if we're a little light on the street performers? Santino thinks we can hire some actors away from the Sterling Renaissance Festival. Lucky for us their season ends next weekend." Santino had already hired new musicians, street performers, vendors, grounds people, and servers for the Bloody Fang.

"We've got eighteen days until the Summit," Rafe said.

I was a little worried about him. He'd never wanted to run Mythica, and now the whole stinking mess had been dropped in his lap. He had only Tryffin, Varrick, and Santino to help him run the park, because none of them were of Ambrose's line. He'd decided to wait for the summit and let the Globus determine Ambrose's fate.

The jugglers on stilts moved through the crowd, to scattered applause. "New costumes," Rafe said. "I keep forgetting to remind Santino we need new costumes." He shook his head. "How are we going to get new costumes without Orcas?"

"Lexie is already working on it," I answered. In addition to being Ambrose's lover, Orcas had been the park's costumer. Santino's blood steward, Lexie had been her assistant. "Santino asked her to design a whole new look for the park performers and employees."

For a guy who never wanted the responsibility, Rafe was doing a remarkable job of getting the park back in order. Mythica was heavily dependent on blood stewards to run the rides, staff the concessions and restaurant, and perform general park maintenance. With their vampire masters either dead or chained in their coffins, most of the park's blood stewards were either dead or incapacitated by withdrawal symptoms. Rafe had sent the survivors off to rehab. Only Varrick's, Tryffin's, and Santino's blood stewards were able to work. He'd hired local craftspeople to remodel, repaint, replant and generally spruce up the overall appearance of the estate. New handicap-accessible ramps were being installed, along with new signage for the amusements. Rafe had pushed hard, but was equally insistent that we didn't cut corners where quality and safety was concerned.

"When are you leaving?" He asked me.

"Tomorrow. I want to make sure everything runs smooth tonight. Silas will be in charge until I get back."

Trick had agreed to stick around until after the Summit, on the condition that I would write a letter of recommendation for him to the pack of his choice. Phelan and Steve-o were out of the pack, and Yolanda had also left after accepting an invitation to join a pack in New Mexico. Rizzo was driving back to his home in Detroit. Only one of the mercs, an ex-Marine named Jim Garrity, had asked to join the pack, and he had been a great addition. Tom was helping out when he could, but he had a business to run. That left the pack only five lycans strong. We needed at least six or eight solid guys with good control, and we needed them before the Summit. I was pretty sure I knew where to get the lycans we needed. "I'll be back in a couple days. You won't even miss me."

"Excuse me, are you a vampire?" Asked a woman dressed in a tattered lace mini-dress with torn fishnet stocking and thigh-high boots. Blonde hair cascaded in curls around her pretty face.

I grinned and showed her my canines. "I'll be anything you want, princess. How can I help you?" From the corner of my eye, I could see Rafe staring at me in amazement. I'd been practicing.

A flush bloomed in the blonde's fair skin. She waved a red ticket in the air. "I'm looking for the theatre. I've got a seat in the front row."

It was Rafe's turn to smile. He gave me a wink and then slid his arm around her slim waist. "I'd be delighted to escort you, beautiful. I think I can promise you the best seat in the house."

She giggled, and I watched them disappear together into the crowd.

I shouldn't have worried. Rafe would be just fine. *Blood almighty, I love my job.*

BROTHER OWL

JUSTIN OWSLEY'S BOOTS echoed loudly as he paced through the empty storefront that had once housed the Brothers of the Fang Community center. The hollow sound was yet another reminder of the emptiness in his own life.

He'd loved this place. In less than four years, they'd gone from meeting in bus stations and under railroad bridges to a real brick and mortar building, with the donation shop in the front and the meeting room in the back. They'd educated the neighborhood and managed to help several ALVS clients attain a new level of control over their illness. Queens didn't have a big population of lycans, but he loved feeling that he could make a difference in their lives.

Three weeks ago, when the borough president put pressure on their landlord, they'd lost their lease. Donations dried up. Their membership dwindled. Most of the members decided Queens was no longer safe. Many, like Torres, had left the city altogether.

Justin checked the back door to make sure it was locked, and turned out the lights. He gave a last look to the old meeting room and headed out the front door.

A lone figure stood just inside the door in a military stance, feet at shoulder height, his hands clasped behind him.

Justin began to sweat. He was alone here. He reached his hand into his pocket for his cell phone.

"Keep your hands where I can see them, please."

Justin quickly put both his hands in the air, in a gesture of surrender. "I don't have any money. I was just leaving, honest. I've got to drop these keys off." Justin froze as a wave of Alpha pheromones washed over him.

"Justin Owsley, right?"

Something about the guy's voice sounded familiar. "What do you want?"

"I'm Mike Bane. You gave me some good advice and I'm here to return the favor."

The were-cat cannibal cop. Justin's mouth went dry. "I remember you."

The tension eased in Bane's shoulders.

Justin realized that they were both nervous. "Sorry, but we're closed. I mean, we're out of business."

"Yeah, I know. I'm here to offer you a job."

Me? "What kind of job?"

"Ever hear of a place called Mythica?"

Jason shook his head.

"It's just outside of the town of Canandaigua."

Jason's heart skipped a beat. "That's werewolf country."

"That's the place." Bane rolled up his sleeves and showed him the faint pattern of brown markings against his tan skin. He flexed his fingers and Justin was shocked to see claws emerge from the man's fingertips. "I'm the Alpha of the pack down there. I'd like to talk to you and maybe a couple of your buddies. We've got a few openings in the pack, and I'm looking to fill those spots with experienced brothers like yourself."

"What do you mean, like me?"

Bane smiled, and Justin recognized the man he remembered.

Bane's hard look had softened a bit, and the hunted expression on his face was gone. "Sarah Powers says you were one of her first successes. She says you've been doing good work up here. How would you like to do that down in the Finger Lakes? We've got a lot of brothers and their families down there with no one to serve them." He paused. "You'll be safe."

Behind him, the door opened, and a beautiful woman with long dark hair shot through with silver stepped up beneath Bane's outstretched arm. She wore faded denim jeans, a white velcro-seamed blouse, and a lot of native American silver and turquoise jewelry, which brought out the color in her startling aquamarine eyes. She gave Bane an intimate kiss on the neck, then grinned at Justin like he was an old friend.

"What did he say?" she asked.

"The jury is still out, I think." Bane rested his arm casually across her shoulder. "I think he's waiting for you to sweeten the deal."

"Well, what's your answer, Brother Owl? Will you set up a Brothers of the Fang outreach program for us?"

Only Dr. Sarah had ever called him Brother Owl.

Justin didn't hesitate.

END

ACKNOWLEGEMENTS

The idea for Mythica as a private amusement club is based in part on long-standing private clubs such as the Huron Mountain Club, Seattle's Ranier Club, and John Aspinall's legendary private gambling club, The Clermont Club.

Many thanks to the folks at the Academy of Magical Arts: The Magic Castle, Kings Island Haunt, Six Flags Fright Fest, Disneyland Park and Disneyland California Adventure Park for their assistance in bringing Mythica to life. Also the folks at HauntCon, The Midwest Haunters Convention, Monsterpalooza, and the International Association of Amusement Parks and Attractions, which were invaluable in helping me get a feel for Mythica's business model.

ABOUT THE AUTHOR

Award-winning author Sharon Joss writes science fiction, fantasy and horror. She is the author of six novels, including the Aurum, Brothers of the Fang, and the supernatural alternate history thriller, Steam Dogs. In 2015, she won the Writers of the Future Golden Pen award for speculative fiction with her novella, Stars That Make Dark Heaven Light. She lives amid a thicket of blackberry vines in Oregon and writes full-time. Find out more about her and her books by going to www.sharonjoss.com

AUTHOR'S NOTE

Thank you for giving this book a read. If you enjoyed it, please tell your friends and consider leaving a review on Amazon or Goodreads, even if it's only a line or two; it would make all the difference and would be very much appreciated.

If you'd like a quick note when I have a new release, please sign up for my new release mailing list at:
http://bit.ly/1MhS3lb

Your email will never be shared and you can unsubscribe at any time. I'll send you a free e-book right away and occasionally send out information about contests or opportunities to snag review copies).

MORE GREAT FICTION FROM SHARON JOSS

STARS THAT MAKE DARK HEAVEN LIGHT

Winner of the
2015 GOLDEN PEN AWARD

Worlds and species collide on the planet Hesperidee in this classic winning tale of love, duty, and the future of humanity.

"STARS THAT MAKE DARK HEAVEN LIGHT is an amazing story, as powerful as it is beautiful. Award-winning author Sharon Joss manages to prove herself to be one of the best writers of our time."
--*New York Times bestselling author David Farland*

DESTINY BLUES

Some people attract stray cats.
With Mattie Blackman, it's demons.
At work, in her car, even at the foot of her bed. And with the FBI on the hunt for a rogue demon master, she's desperate to get rid of them. Thwarted at every turn to solve her problem through legitimate channels, she turns to Shore Haven's sexy mage for the answer: a fate she refuses to accept.
But as the serial killer's victims pile up, Mattie realizes there's only one way to stop a demon master. To save her friends and the people she loves, Mattie must choose between her life and her destiny.

"...amusingly off-beat...fun...romp."

- Locus

AJA PUBLISHING
WWW.AJAPUBLISHING.WORDPRESS.COM

MORE GREAT FICTION FROM SHARON JOSS

LEGACY SOUL
ZOMBIES, WIZARDS & DRAGONS (*oh my!*)

Mattie Blackman is the last living descendent of the Goddess Morta. As the new Hand of Fate, she discovers her powers over the undead can't help solve her problems with the living. When Shore Haven's supernatural community is threatened and one of her friends murdered, Mattie is accused and must solve the mystery on her own. This time, she and her demon Blix face a vodoun sorcerer with powers more dangerous than death itself--and he wants nothing less than her immortal soul.

CHAOS KARMA
LET THE SPIRITS REIGN

As Grand Marshal of the 50th annual International Spirit Festival & Gala, Mattie Blackman soon discovers that fame isn't all it's cracked up to be. Some days, even the Hand of Fate can't get much respect. The week-long bacchanal has brought every sort of spirit, demon, shape-shifter, and vampire to town, and one of them is preying on the supernatural citizens of Shore Haven. With the authorities trying to keep the story quiet, Mattie will need more than Morta's magic to stop the killer.

AJA PUBLISHING
WWW.AJAPUBLISHING.WORDPRESS.COM

www.ingramcontent.com/pod-product-compliance
Lightning Source LLC
Chambersburg PA
CBHW020358260626
47156CB00007B/2174